Bound

OBSESSION

THE SHADOWED SOULS
SERIES BOOK TWO

To the souls who find beauty in shadows, strength in vulnerability, and thrill in forbidden paths.

Thank you for trusting me to guide you into worlds where darkness has its own light, where love is fierce, flawed, and dangerously unforgettable. This journey wouldn't be the same without you.

TRIGGER WARNINGS

Please check the Trigger Warnings below before diving in. If you're a dark romance lover, you can skip through. You belong here.

Eyes on me Sex
Domination/Control
Exhibitionism
Somnophilia
Asphyxiation
1:1 Bullying
Stalking

Panic attacks
Possessive behaviour
Body dysmorphia
Mental health decline
Hallucinations/delusions
Suicidal thoughts/near attempts
Memories of child abuse
Drug/alcohol use
Flashbacks/Nightmares of sexual trauma

Contents

AVERY

"Oh, Little Swan. It means you always were a Shadowed Soul after all."

Those words flutter on the edge of my consciousness as I rouse from yet another fitful sleep. Huxley is flush to my back, his deep even breathing fanning my ear. Each morning, I wake naturally before the sun, allowing me a fleeting moment of reflection before the confusion and worry sets back in.

Within my mind, there is a constant, slow ticking. How long will I be safe here before Fredrick comes for me? What am I going to do when he does? Fight with those who have proven their loyalty to me, or go quietly to save them from any more pain? The answer isn't clear, but the ticking remains, my soul reminding me I'm on borrowed time.

The days have been slipping by, each one becoming lost since Wyatt...well, since he became lost too. I haven't brought him up. No doubt, the others know where he is. What he's up to. I don't want to know. The way he looked at me when he left. So filled with hatred, regret and revulsion. I couldn't comprehend the feelings at that time.

My twin. My own flesh and blood. The other half to my soul, apparently. I had finally been gifted with something in life that was real. A person irrevocably connected to me since birth. But the reality of what we did, what *I* did, came crashing down like a ton of bricks.

Lying still in the dark and maintaining the pretense of sleep, I slowly build up the layers around my heart, burying it far beneath the surface. Huxley shifts and rolls over, his movement giving me the green light to launch myself from the bed without him noticing. Dropping from the mattress into a crouch on the floor, I peek to check he's still asleep. The cover rises and falls smoothly over his new position on his left side. Picking up my phone from the bedside table, I tiptoe on silent feet around the bed. I make it all the way to the bathroom door before his voice echoes throughout the room.

"Where are you going?"

"I need a shower." My tone is too sharp, escaping before I can clamp my teeth down onto my lower lip. For so many nights, Huxley's room was an oasis. It's quickly becoming a steel-barred cage. I need to excuse myself before I say something I'll regret. None of this is Huxley's fault, he was just the messenger. The bearer of bad news. He's the one who told me I didn't really know who I am. He turned my world on its axis. My brain just needs a little more convincing to separate those facts.

"I'm sorry. I just...I'm going to shower. You should go back to sleep, it's early."

"Do you want me to sit in with you?" Hux asks hopefully, pushing himself upright. His blond hair tumbles over his shoulders as he blinks the sleep from his eyes. The pink, puckered scar on his broad chest is barely visible as the early rays of sun begin to spill through the curtains. I know Huxley means well, and the puppy dog look in his eyes almost makes me say yes but I need some space. His protectiveness is suffocating me.

"It's fine. I'll be back soon." I disappear through the door and sag against the counter on a sigh. Checking my phone, the screen illuminates with a selfie of Meg and I at last year's New Year's party. Her eyes are glimmering to the purest shade of aquamarine in the flash, her red painted lips curved into a huge smile as I'm running the pad of my tongue up her cheek.

My heart twists painfully. The festive season is fast approaching. I'd hoped that, whatever my life looked like at this point, I could rely on being back at the manor with Meg at my side. Pushing back the tears, I open the contacts and tap on Meg's name. Holding the phone to my ear, I try to steady my breathing. The entire weight of the world is resting on my shoulders, threatening to crush me flat.

With each drone, I silently beg her to pick up and my hopefulness slowly ebbs into dread. I know it's nearing the end of semester and she will be busy trying to wrap everything up, ready to return home. I vaguely remember Meg's lacrosse team had a big match last weekend, and I suddenly feel even worse. Shit, I've been a terrible friend. I'll apologize as soon as she-

'Sorry, we are unable to connect your call at this time. Please try again later.' As I listen to Meg's automated message play, I slump to the floor. The backs of my eyes sting as I try to keep my voice as level as possible.

"Hey Meg, I don't want to bother you. I know you're super busy and I hope the game went well. I just needed to say that I really miss you. We've never gone this long without talking. There's so much I need to tell you and *really* need your opinion on. It's not the same being here with only the boys to talk to. So, give me a call if you get a chance. I love- "

A beep cuts me off and I toss the cell, hugging my knees and leaning my forehead against them. Those blasted tears I've been fighting begin to fall onto my bare thighs, running a trail down to my pajama shorts. The floodgates are open now and I don't know how to close them. My body shakes violently with loud sobs I can't conceal. Distantly, the sound of the door opening reaches my ears and causes me to glance through the watered glaze in my eyes to see Dax approaching.

Bending low to collect me from the floor, I slide my arms around his neck as he straightens with ease. I bury my face in his black T-shirt. The firmness of his chest beneath the fabric presses against my cheek, a solid support for my limp body.

Carrying me to my own room, Dax sits on the edge of my bed and cradles me tightly while I use his warmth and scent to reign myself back in. His sea mineral scent, filling my senses with each deep exhale I force myself to take. He doesn't say a word, just holds me and rests his cheek on top of my head. His growing afro tickles my ear. Despite myself, I find a small smile behind the sorrow. Shifting my head so I can glance over his darkly tanned shoulder, I see ominous dark clouds filling the sky through the glass.

"Did he come home last night?" I ask quietly. Dax shakes his head and strokes my arm gently, causing goosebumps to rise beneath his touch. Sleeping next to Huxley is like having a radiator in the bed, but now I'm sitting in a flimsy top and shorts combo in an approaching winter. Dax's shoulder bunches as he reaches over to my pillow, pulling the orange hoodie out from beneath it. The burn of a flush ignites in my cheeks, embarrassment flooding me as I accept Wyatt's hoodie with an awkward thanks. I know it's wrong to keep a piece of your step-brother's clothing hidden beneath your pillow so his scent is nearby. Or my...whatever-he-is.

Slipping the hoodie over my head, I remain huddled into Dax until I hear the splatter of rain against the glass behind us. It looks like I'm going to spend another day stuck in the frat house with four brooding guys. They are missing Wyatt, and the void is too obvious to ignore. Their self-appointed leader of their group has gone AWOL and their dynamic has shifted massively. Huxley is back to hiding away, Axel and

Garrett have coupled up again and Dax has taken it upon himself to be my comfort blanket.

"I'll fix breakfast. Come down when you're ready." Dax kisses my head and places me aside. I watch him leave, a heart wrenching pull almost tugging me straight after him.

That's the difference. Huxley says he can't sleep without me, asks to sit in while I shower, and wants me to eat in his room with him. Dax gives me space and is prepared to wait for when I'm ready, yet can perfectly gauge when I need picking up off the ground. Literally. It's not that I'm questioning my feelings for Huxley, but that our relationship is going at a different pace. I need to slam my foot on the break and remind him there are boundaries.

Yanking on a pair of soft gray tracksuit bottoms, I twist my hair up and secure it with a claw clip. Spraying myself with antiperspirant, deciding to have my shower later, I step into the hallway to see Axel and Garrett heading down the stairs. Thankfully, their attention is on each other, allowing me to hang back in my doorway unseen. I don't know what's bothering me more, the way we're all ignoring the obvious or the long looks I keep receiving. Are they waiting for me to crack, scream and lash out? Maybe they've forgotten I've spent my childhood alone in a cupboard. Internalizing is my specialty.

I sigh. Let's get this over with. Ignoring the stacks of paperwork littering the dining table, confirming that Cathy did in fact give birth to twins, I head directly for the kitchen island. There's a steaming mug of tea waiting for me, and Dax flashes a wide smile as I appear. Always so happy to see me. His pearly whites are perfectly straight and his blue eyes shimmer, giving me a wink as I perch on a stool in front of the steaming mug. He's magnetic. The way he moves, smoothly gliding from one pan to the next, his hips swaying to the music his phone is playing in the background.

Garrett appears as soon as the scent of eggs and bacon fill the air, Axel's fingers intertwined with his. The three of us are swept up with the show, especially when Dax splashes oil on his T-shirt and whips it off, tucking it into his waistband. Tanned muscle tenses reaching across the kitchen for a spatula. Holy mother of Brazilians. Misjudging the mug, boiling liquid spills over the edge. I shoot up with a hiss, large hands ushering me to the basin. Axel forces my palm under an icy spray of water while I struggle against him.

"Axe, it's fine. Just leave it." His grip on my wrist doesn't budge, his hazel eyes stern.

"It's not fine. Twenty minutes of cold water will stabilize the blood vessels and prevent blistering." When it comes to first aid, Axel doesn't leave any room for argument. Unfortunately, I'm not in the mood for a lecture.

"So what? A blister isn't the height of my problems right now." That bitchy tone has returned in full force, clearly having no filter on who receives it today. Groaning, I drop my head against Axel's shoulder and relent my struggles. I need to get a handle on myself. "I just mean, what's the point of trying to protect me anymore? The world seems set on screwing me over."

Axel's free hand skates to my chin, tilting my head up to look at him. The sternness in his gaze ebbs away, relieving the raw emotion I'm used to in him.

"I told you, I would always protect you. Nothing has changed there." I melt into his touch, my eyes closing briefly. Those strong fingers remain on my chin, basically holding me up as another shifts in behind.

"I get what this really is about." I twist to raise a brow at Garrett's solemn appearance, his brows furrowed beneath a mess of dark hair.

"You do?"

He leans against the counter, nodding to himself. "You don't want to heal the hand you jerked off your twin brother with."

"Dude?!" Dax yells, smacking the back of Garrett's head at the same time as Axel shouts, "What the fuck is wrong with you?!" Despite all of this, Garrett can't hide his grin. Oh how he loves stirring shit up first thing in the morning. He reaches for some paper towels, crossing the kitchen to clean the island. When the mug has been wiped down, Garrett gently places the remaining tea into my uninjured hand.

"He's not, by the way." Garrett's tongue rolls across his teeth, barely containing whatever bait he's dangling for me, his eyes gleaming with a dare. With nothing else to do while Axel is continuing to hold my hand hostage under the water, I bite.

"Who's not what?"

His answering grin is too smug not to want to punch him. "Wyatt. He's not your twin brother." I feel myself harden at the same time Axel does. Dax has given up on cooking, all the stoves off and a hand towel thrown over his shoulder. Everyone is still, except Garrett who's starting to vibrate with smugness.

"If this is a prank," I say carefully, "it's not funny." Garrett rolls his eyes, as if such a notion is ridiculous. Whipping a piece of crumpled, folded paper out of his shorts pocket, he waves it around for all to see. Even Huxley, who has appeared at the kitchen island since I last looked.

"I raided Wyatt's room for some hair samples, and you shed all over the house. It's like having a cat," Garrett picks a hair from his T-shirt and flicks it away. It was most definitely one of his own. "And then there was the old brush in the box under your bed labeled 'Mom's stuff'. I sent all three samples off to a lab for DNA testing."

I reckon a gut punch would have had less effect.

"And you're only just telling me now?!" I gasp, simultaneously throwing the mug into the basin and jerking my hand free. Reaching for the paper, Garrett holds it high out of my reach.

"I mean, even on express, these things take time. It's not magic, you know." Garrett is rolling his eyes and tutting while I prepare to climb him like a tree.

"Give it to me!" I shriek. Garrett's laugh echoes through his chest.

"Oh, I've missed hearing those words." After a few more failed attempts, I grow frustrated and shove at his chest with one wet and one dry hand.

"Tell me what it says," I almost plead, encasing my desperation within anger. It's naive to think these guys don't know exactly how eager I am to hear the slither of truth Garrett is feeding me. If Wyatt isn't my twin, everything can be okay in the world again. I can shed this shit-ton of guilt consuming me. Wyatt always worried I would drive a wedge between him and his Shadowed Souls. He was right.

"Take a seat," Garrett nudges me towards Huxley. I don't immediately respond. "Trust me. You're going to need it." As soon as my butt touches the stool, Garrett lays out the page. He takes the time to smooth out the creases, his hand pausing over a paragraph at the bottom of the page. The others crowd in around me, three muscled men holding their breath as Garrett talks us through the results. "See here, there are no genetic markers between you and Wyatt. You're not related."

My heart is unraveling. The relief is too much to comprehend, and I'm not even thinking about how long Garrett has had this piece of paper. Instead, I poke at his fingers still shielding the bottom section.

"And this?" I look into Garrett's dark gaze. He's a sucker for my large eyes and the slight frown I put on for him. Chewing on his inner cheek, he looks the most nervous I've seen him all morning as he removes his hand.

"There's always a catch, Peach. Turns out Wyatt doesn't match the markers to Cathy either. But you do." The silence in the room is thick enough to choke. No one wants to speak first and I finally understand. This is what Garrett had been hiding. Not for my sake, but for Wyatt's. Once this truth is out in the world, everyone will know. Wyatt will be devastated. Garrett folds the paper and tucks it back in his pocket, then takes both of my hands tenderly in his. I've accepted that I'll be getting that blister after all.

"You're her daughter. Wyatt is not her son."

I shake my head. Lifting the neckline of the orange hoodie, I dip the lower half of my face into it. The expensive cologne still clinging to the fabric grounds me, an anchor to a world turning on its axis once again. Why can't I just be a normal girl, going to a normal school where nothing that isn't normal happens to her?

Of course, there's been so many times I would pretend Cathy was my real mom. She loved me without limits, gave me all of her attention and affection. Since the diary pages surfaced, this was the one part I hadn't dare let myself wish for. I couldn't handle that glimmer of hope being snuffed out. But there's no use denying the black and white text on the page. I'm Cathy Hughes' biological daughter. I have a real mom. Well, *had*.

"We can't tell anyone this." I breathe harshly. Huxley's firm bicep shifts against me, his voice of reason ringing out.

"We can't lie to him, Little Swan. He deserves to know." It's true. I know that as much as I can detect the twinge of regret in Huxley's tone. He doesn't want to be the one who keeps disagreeing with me, but he is right. I can't hold that against him any longer. Shaking off the men caging me in, I round Huxley's stool and tug on his arm.

"I'm ready for that shower now."

"Really?" Huxley asks, too full of hope to deny. My smile is small as I give him another tug. He stands, towering over me yet pausing until I walk first. These men are used to a leader, someone to bind them together. I suppose I can step up temporarily.

"Everyone get ready and pack an overnight bag. Meet back here in an hour."

"Where are we going?" Dax asks, glancing over at the unfinished breakfast. He doesn't need to worry, Garrett is looking in the same direction and visibly salivating.

I squeeze Huxley's arm for reassurance. "We're bringing Wyatt home." Like a snap of a rubber band, the energy in the room suddenly becomes charged. The men are beaming, nudging each other playfully. The stress of the past week fizzles away just like that and before he heads out, Axel places a kiss on my forehead.

"I hope you're ready to drag him back kicking and screaming," he chuckles. Oh, I'm not ready at all, but for the men in this room, I'm quickly coming to realize I'd do anything.

WYATT

This is the life. This is the way I should be living.

High energy music seeps under the booth's curtain, pounding from the club in full swing beyond, the sound of stomping feet accompanying the bass. Vibrant colors burst in rhythmic patterns behind my closed eyelids, like an internal never-ending kaleidoscope. My mind feels light and empty as I roll my head across the back of the velvet sofa, enjoying the high of whatever drug I swallowed a little while ago. I have no idea what it was, just that the hot waitress promised me a good time. With her head now bobbing between my thighs, she wasn't lying.

Sighing contentedly, I stretch my legs wider and slouch down a little further to accommodate her open mouth. A tray of drinks she was supposed to be delivering sit on the low table behind her, the ice melting and diluting the alcohol with every passing second. I watch the droplets roll down each glass, the rest of the world falling away. For all the expert deep-throating she's giving, there's really no need. I barely feel anything anymore.

The scent of weed travels across from the next booth next door, also shrouded in curtains. I chuckle to myself quietly with a stupidly large grin across my face. We're all looking for an escape tonight. For a pocket of the world where we no longer have to exist.

I'm not sure what day it is. Between gate crashing celebrity-exclusive parties, placing high bets at casinos and taking girls back to the penthouse suite upstairs each night, I've successfully avoided all things real. My phone died some time ago and I didn't bother to charge it. I avoid the papers and news channels at all costs - just in case Avery decided to go public with her *Lynch Wyatt* campaign. I bet she's having the time of her life, cackling 'I win' from the rooftops.

Fuck, I'm thinking about her again. I know the rules.

"Hey," I rasp my knuckles on the waitress' head. "You got another pill for me?" Her look of annoyance doesn't faze me. Producing a small packet from her back pocket, she watches me take it with a gulp of whiskey. I don't like the pinch in her eyebrows. In fact, I find it damn rude. "Did I say you could stop sucking my cock?" She gives a small smile then, awarding herself some miniscule victory. Whatever it was, I just needed her to stop staring at me.

Small tremors take a hold of my body, the blissfully numb feeling dancing across my skin. It continues to tingle faintly as the music pounds heavily, my thoughts drifting away on a tumbleweed. A couple of weeks ago, I was getting straight A's and was in peak physical health. I was worshiped by the basketball subs as much as the cheerleaders, and my men still held respect for me. How easily it all came crashing down. How quickly Avery took it all from me. Fuck, not again.

"I'll overdose at this rate," I mumble to myself. The waitress either doesn't hear or ignores me, seeming to be getting herself off more than me. I'm barely hard anymore. The drink worked at first. Then the drugs. Now, a blonde figure in a ballet skirt pirouettes through my mind. The harder I push her away, the easier she springs back. She dominated me in the dressing room, had me against the wall and panting. A feat no one has managed before or since. And just like that, I'm fully erect again and I can see the waitress' eyes brighten. Sure babe, it's all you. I pat her head like a dog.

Flashes penetrate the thin curtain. Shadows pass, laughter echoes. I find myself smiling again, the emotions passing through me like water meandering down a stream. Lifting my glass of whiskey from the flattened arm of the sofa, I hold it up to salute my men. But there's no one there. No one to clink my glass, no one to watch the waitress choke herself on me. I've become so used to not having personal space, now I don't know what to do with it. I can't think of a time in my adult life that I've been alone like this.

Yet I can't call them. They would be here within the hour, trying to 'fix' me. The truth is - I don't want to be fixed. I want to ride this storm and feel every ounce of self-loathing because I deserve it. I'm twisted in ways I didn't even realize; I need time to be reckless and banish the darkness within before I hurt someone I care about. Eventually, I'll be able to return home without looking twice at *her.*

Clutching the back of the waitress' hair, I encourage her to go deeper, harder. To use her teeth and make me *feel.* Anything to banish the blonde mirage now appearing in front of me. She moves faster, her black hair covering my thighs like an ink spill as she takes me all the way in the back of her throat, but any ounce of pleasure I might have felt through this high has gone. Her thick lashes flash up to me, a trick of my mind seeing them as blue in the strobe light that passes over the curtain. My dick weeps excitedly at the notion and I hate myself even more.

She would look so beautiful. Golden hair, lean athletic body. My hallucination goes as far as to put her in that pink tutu and slippers, the leotard dipped low to tug at her taut nipples. Then there's her beautiful blue eyes. They are all I can see, no matter how many times I blink. So wide and innocent, hiding so much truth. There's nothing innocent about Avery. She's just as sick and twisted as I am, and she wants me. No matter what she says or does, it's always been painfully obvious that she wants me in whatever form I'll give her. The bully, the asshole. But now. Fuck, now...

Her *fucking* twin.

Bile rises in my throat. I grip the sides of my head as my mind begins to spin with all the thoughts I've been suppressing. I can't think about her. Suddenly, I'm sweating.

Inside my designer shirt, I writhe, boiling alive in my own skin. My thoughts spin, considering just how many packets of pink pills this waitress has on her.

But no. I may be temporarily unstable, but I'm not stupid enough to get addicted. Once I've worked this episode out of my system, and I've somehow dragged the pieces of my broken soul back together, I need to return to Waversea and finish my degree. My last saving grace. I've known for a long time now, the only way I'm going to succeed in this life is through my own perseverance.

Instead, I reach for a folded stash of money from my own pocket, secured with a clip and drop it onto the puddled drinks tray. Pushing the waitress off me, I stand and fasten my slacks, needing to spend too much focus on remaining upright.

"That's enough," I growl, although my tongue is thick in my mouth.

"Wait, don't you want me to finish you off?" Nails claw at my thighs desperately. Stepping over her, I successfully make it to the curtain and pause to roll my eyes in her direction. At least I hope it's just my eyes, because my head feels ready to roll right off my shoulders.

"Nah, I'm bored." And isn't that the truth.

AVERY

My head tilts back, craning my neck to see the top of the skyscraper hotel while Axel's fingers toy with mine, stopping me from swaying. It's times like this I realize how small my world is, like an ant beneath a magnifying glass of windows and scaffolding.

On the street outside the grand hotel entrance, the city's nightlife is in full swing. A group of women pass, displaying a host of lipstick colors and varying heel heights, all of their dresses hitched high up their thighs. To fight the bitterness of winter but not to deter their party-going, they've donned huge fluffy jackets. Worlds away from the sweat-ridden and crumpled lounge wear I'm standing in, complete with the body odor to match.

The drive was much longer than I'd prepared for, and Huxley insisted on stopping as little as possible. I was just happy he came with us so I didn't argue. Currently, he is searching for a parking space somewhere in the vicinity, whilst Garrett is hunting down some food for everyone. He also hadn't prepared properly for the journey, quickly running out of snacks he refused to share with the rest of us.

"This is the place," Dax retraces his steps from where he took his cousin's phone call. Some top-hacker who seemingly traced Wyatt's excessive credit card usage to this hotel. "The card has been registered to the penthouse suite since the night he left us."

Dax probably didn't intend to include me in his statement. *'Us'* as in the Shadowed Souls. I'm just a tag along, the very reason he stormed out the door and didn't look back. Yet I'm hurting too. I probably have no right to feel anything after discovering Wyatt and I are practically strangers who unknowingly assumed each other's lives, but still. The pain is raw. Since Garrett showed me the DNA results yesterday, I've built a connection in my head, a bond of parental betrayal Wyatt and I both share. If only we can lock him down long enough to see if I'm right.

Tugging my arm, Axel guides me into the foyer and towards the bar. Since Dax has all the inside information, we've agreed to let him take the lead with the receptionist. Fine by me. Rather than twiddling my thumbs and trying not to look nervous, I get some one-on-one time with Axel. He shifts a heightened stool for me to take a seat before settling into the next one along. Twisting his body, Axel's thighs press against mine, his hazel focus solely on me as if we're not the only ones in this entire bar dressed like we can't afford to be here. I'm fairly certain some of Garrett's drool is still in my hair from where he fell asleep against my head.

"One day, I'm going to bring you to a place like this on purpose," Axel's mouth tilts. A dimple deepens on the side of his smile and I grip onto the stool's edge so I don't swoon straight off the side.

"You want to date me, Axel?" I manage to keep my voice level.

"I want to do a great many things to you, Sweetheart." I suck in a breath, feeling the heat coat my cheeks. Axel chuckles, prying my hands from the metal. His long fingers envelope mine easily, stroking and teasing. "I wish I'd had the chance to meet you properly. To catch your eye from across the room and have that burning need to speak to you. To get to know you without any of the other bullshit hanging over us."

I nod in agreement. Only Dax had that opportunity, and when it came crashing down, it was as if we'd both been robbed. I didn't consider that's how everyone else felt too. A sigh escapes me.

"Without your boyfriend climbing through my bedroom window and my fake brother forcing you to read my therapy transcripts, you mean?" It's Axel's turn to blush. I hadn't meant to say it so bluntly. Blinking rapidly, I wonder what other thoughts I'm suppressing for the worst possible moment to say them.

"Wyatt's an asshole," he groans after a short pause. My brow raises.

"But...?"

"No but's. Regardless of what Wyatt has done for me and what I owe him, when it comes to you, he's always acted like an asshole. There's no excuse for his actions." If I thought I couldn't melt for Axel anymore, he's just proved me wrong. I was so prepared for him to come to Wyatt's defense that I'd already started hardening my heart against it. Now, there's a crack in the armor and Axel is swiftly prying his way inside.

"Yet here we are, looking for him anyway," I find a smirk, ignoring the rumble of my stomach.

The irony isn't lost on me. I've spent months silently wishing Wyatt would fuck off and leave me alone. Now he's done exactly that, and I'm chasing him down. Just to deliver the DNA results, that's all. Nothing else, like the fact I miss his moody face and irritating existence watching on from the sidelines. I definitely haven't come to depend on him always being there as a fall guy for my anger. My personal punching bag who bites back, who reminds me what's real amongst the pretty words his friends offer me. They mean well, but I should know better than to become comfortable. Huxley's gunshot wound is evidence enough.

"Here we are," Axel reiterates. His thumb brushes against mine. A gentle reassurance which draws our focus to our joined hands. The noise of the bar falls away, the music and excited chatter becoming muffled. I lose myself to Axel's simple touch, hunting for that same grounding presence.

The warmth of his skin radiates through me, a steady pulse anchoring me in the chaos of my mind.

I glance up, meeting his stunning hazel eyes filled with understanding. We're in our own bubble, separate from the world around us. His lips curl into a soft smile, and I can't help but return it. In this moment, there's nothing but us. None of the bullshit, only the hope that we could wade through and find something beautiful waiting at the other end.

"Bad news," Dax appears and slumps on the stool on my other side. The trance is broken and the volume of the bar slams back into me. Using the tilted angle of my body facing Axel, Dax rests his head on my shoulder, arms wrapping around my middle. We attract a few curious gazes then. "They won't even let me up to knock on the door and speak to him."

"So what are we going to do? Sit in the foyer and hope he happens to pass by?" Suddenly defeated, I lean into Dax's weight now. Everyone else back at Waversea will be finishing their classes this week, preparing to head home for the holidays. And then there's the five of us, stuck in limbo and unsure of where to go. Should we give up on Wyatt and find somewhere to hide away, wait for Fredrick to be caught? His silence has been both comforting and unbearable. Has he grown bored of me, or is he building up to something worse?

Collectively, as if sharing the same thought, the three of us sigh. The waiter hovers on the edge of our three-way entanglement to ask if we'd like anything. Axel places an order of three white wines, the house best. At my questioning glance, he shrugs.

"It's Wyatt's card on file, right?"

"Garrett is having a bad effect on you," I roll my eyes. I don't bother getting into how we now know Wyatt's card is, in fact, loaded with the money I should have always had access to. I'm the rightful Hughes' child, yet I was raised to beg for scraps and live in fear. Fuck, I've got so many questions. If only Nixon would respond to my messages.

As our drinks are served, Huxley quietly enters and sits on Axel's far side. He doesn't speak, his eyes hooded and tired. I long for the charmingly protective man I knew him to be, and instantly chastise myself for being selfish. Huxley shouldn't bounce back from what he's been through just because I wish it. While he's been healing, all he's asked for is me. He's still protective, just in other ways now, and it's me who's been pulling away, scared of the trap closing in on all sides. None of it is fair on him. With my mind distracted, I sit and sip, watching the ticking of the clock above the bar.

"Great news!" Garrett barges in like a wrecking ball. I choke on my drink. Axel reaches up to scrape his thumb over the corner of Garrett's mouth, removing a smudge of sauce left there. "I found Wyatt!" My heart jolts and we're all out of our seats, fatigue forgotten in an instant.

"Where is he?" Dax cuts in first, voice laced with concern. Garrett's grin spreads wider.

"At the club across the road. There's a group of paparazzi outside. Said they got a tip-off so they're waiting for him to appear."

"They told you all of this?" I ask skeptically. Garrett rolls his eyes, his body practically vibrating with the urge to get going.

"Well, not to my face. I was leaning against the wall, eating my burger and eavesdropping. They didn't even notice me." I blink up into Garrett's dark eyes. They're gleaming with this new information and I reckon if I were to pet him on the head and call him a good boy, his tongue would lull out of his mouth. I reach up slowly, and the moment my fingers touch his floppy brown locks, my fist tightens around them tightly. "Ahh!" Garrett shouts, but allows his head to be yanked down to my height anyway.

"And where are our burgers, Garrett?" I narrow my eyes. Garrett looks around, suddenly realizing he's returned empty-handed to a group of people who also haven't eaten for most of the day. Lord knows he hogged all the car snacks to himself.

"Oh...you guys? Um, but...I found Wyatt." His puppy dog expression is too much. I release him and pat his cheek.

"Well done, Gare Bear." I concede, giving him the praise he's waiting for. His tongue does indeed flop out of his mouth. Twisting my head to Axel, I nod resolutely. "Let's get a room and our bags. I need a shower and some room service."

"And Wyatt?" Huxley speaks for the first time, watching the exchange from the outside. I smile warmly at him whilst placing a hand on Garrett's chest.

"We know where he is and we know where he's staying. Somewhere between the two, Garrett should be able to intercept him."

"Me?" Garrett whines. "But you said, *'a room'*, as in singular. I'll be missing out on all the fun." I nod up at him, slowly drumming my fingers on his collar bone.

"And hopefully you'll remember this night the next time you only think about your own stomach." Downing my wine, I wrestle my way out of the bodies surrounding me. We've attracted the attention of almost every person in the bar now.

Taking Huxley's hand, we pass through the foyer. A security guard has appeared, eyeing us as if we're the riffraff he's been tasked with discarding. I catch Huxley's small smile. If only they knew who he was beneath his top knot and baggy sweats. A constricted ball in my chest I hadn't realized was sitting there, unfurls slightly. Huxley and I haven't spoken as much lately, between his pledge to always tell me the truth, whether I want to hear it or not, and my guilt of putting him in that position. No one else wants to give me bad news. It's all on his shoulders and he has to face my resentment for it.

Back in the street, the air is a welcome balm over my frayed nerves. I was happy to let the others think my hunger has taken over, not the sudden fact Wyatt is so close. Until now, finding Wyatt was an idea. Something I could play over and over in my mind, creating the fantasy outcomes I prefer. But knowing he's just across the street in a club, probably dressed in his finest with women hanging on his every word, sends me into overdrive. Would he even hear me out? Or will he shove me away and step over me in the street? One camera flash and the image of me sprawled across the sidewalk and possibly crying would be splashed across the tabloids tomorrow morning. No thank you.

Either way, I don't get a choice. Two steps down the street, I hear the uproar. A rush of voices and bodies, jerking to life. Those telltale flashes consume the other side of the street, and amongst them, a repetitive flash of red and blue. Huxley's hand tightens around mine and in a flurry, Axel is at my back, ushering me across the road. We become lost to a crowd screaming Wyatt's name. Between bopping heads, I catch sight of his dark hair and my heart sinks.

He looks drawn, ill even. Deep crevices hang beneath his eyes, his cheeks looking hollow and pasty. His hair is an overgrown mess, sticking out in all directions from tugging his hands through it. The open buttons of his shirt reveal hickeys lining his neck and the glimpse of a scratch across his chest. He looks like shit. Like some STD-riddled sleaze who's crawled out of the gutter in search of his next victim or a hit of something stronger.

All of these thoughts rush through my head so fast, I barely have time to step aside as he passes. Our shoulders connect, and his dazed green eyes swing back with a glare. A singular glance that halts the entire world, my ears filled with the roar of my blood rushing. My lips part, a choked breath withholding everything I want to say. What he *needs* to know.

This is my moment. The chance I've been waiting for, until it's suddenly not. Wyatt is shoved along by the uniformed officer at his back. His hands are bound by cuffs, blood dripping from his knuckles and leaving a trail on the concrete. He's gone as quickly as he appeared, shoved into the back of the police car and sped away. The paparazzi take chase, not even noticing me standing there. I can't look away from the blood splatters. Some have been smudged during the panic and by morning, no one will even notice them at all.

"Fucks sake!" Huxley hisses, dragging his hands over his face. "Nixon's going to lose his shit about this. Wyatt has never even had a detention, let alone been arrested. The media is going to have a field day." I swallow hard, vaguely wondering how I'm even going to get a hold of Nixon to tell him. Putting genetics and recent discoveries aside, he is still Wyatt's father. He's the man who raised him, and ultimately the one who disciplines him.

"Hey, Aves. You okay?" Dax tentatively rubs my arm, drawing my attention away from the blood splatter once more. I must be white as a sheet, and the cold has settled into my chest cavity. I try a nod, but I don't know if the numbness taking over has permitted it.

"Are we going after him?" Axel asks no one in particular, looking in the direction that the cop car sped away. No one answers and it's with a little jolt, everyone else has their eyes on me. Waiting for my instruction, as if I'm their stand-in leader. I suppose coming this far was my decision. I inhale deeply, closing my eyes in search of composure.

"Let him sweat. He was high as a kite. A night in a cell will do him good." A beat of silence follows until Garrett steps out into the road.

"Peach is right. We'll head down to the station first thing, once Wyatt's worked this bullshit out of his system." A horn blares as Garrett wanders in front of cars without a care in the world. We hastily trail behind, apologizing to the vehicles who have skidded to a stop. Huxley's face is still strained but he doesn't comment further. We split apart, Garrett's arm around my shoulders while the others begin their trek to the SUV for our bags. I get the impression they wanted to speak privately, maybe to talk Huxley around. If Garrett senses the tension radiating from me, he doesn't show it.

"Looks like I'm out of a job. Does this mean I can join in the singular bedroom fun?" He grins. All of the fight has escaped me.

"Unless you and Axel feel like putting on a show, there won't be any fun. I'm eating and going to bed. To sleep," I quickly add. Garrett smirks away and drags his tongue up my cheek. The security guard at the hotel entrance tries to hide his disgust. I don't even bother wiping the saliva away. I'm used to Garrett's ways by now.

"I'll hand feed you, Peach, and then tuck you in for the night. How does that sound?" Despite being almost certain that was a euphemism for being *hand-fed* Garrett's cock, I grunt in response, allowing myself to be led back into the foyer. Maybe a distraction is needed, now that I have twelve more hours to worry about Wyatt's reaction to what I have to say. Dammit, Garrett's going to get his own way again.

WYATT

A loud bang jolts me from my sleep. Fluorescent overhead lights are disorientating as my head tenses. I easily could have taken a hammer to the temple, given the throbbing radiating there. My back aches from the twisted position I'm lying in on a solid wooden bench. Where the hell am I and what happened to me?

Suddenly, hands grab my ruined shirt, dragging me upright. I groan at the assault on my protesting body. Attempting to shove the overweight brute away, I discover my wrists are bound painfully in tight metal cuffs. No, not a brute - a cop. He shoves me out of a cell and then continuously prods my back with a blunt object to shuffle along a dimly lit hallway. In terms of small mercies, my eyes have a chance to adjust to the vice-like grip on my head. All self-inflicted, evidently.

A guard dressed in black pushes the door open at the end of the hallway, glaring at me in disgust as I walk past. Squinting, I find myself being prodded through a busy police station. Stacks of paperwork rival towers of empty donut boxes on dozens of desks. Officers either scowl or completely ignore me as a strong hand grips my shoulder and pushes me through another set of metal doors. After removing the cuffs, he barks at me to sit down before leaving the interrogation room. I just about hide my wince until he's slammed the door closed.

Catching sight of myself in the two-way mirror, I can see why so many people were snarling. Even I'm appalled by my own reflection. My once-white shirt is covered in filth and blood, which I'm going to guess is mine judging from the line of disposable stitches running across my temple and into my right eyebrow. Many of the shirt's buttons have been ripped off, my belt is missing and now I realize I'm not wearing shoes. My hair resembles a bird's nest while my eyes are more bloodshot than green.

I round the table in the center, rolling my wrists and twisting my back. The door reopens to reveal a short Latina woman, her rigid posture and grimace not looking good for my immediate future. The navy uniform hugs her frame tightly and a shiny badge sways from her thick black belt. A similarly dressed male cop, who I vaguely recognize from somewhere, trails in behind her and shuts the three of us inside.

"Mister Hughes, is it? Take a seat." The woman points to one of the collapsible chairs around this side of the table. I drop into it, despite the pain shooting through my back. My head is spinning but I keep a calm expression on my face. Sitting opposite, she opens the brown folder she carried in and places it on the table. A mugshot I don't remember having taken is clipped to the inside cover, apparently before I was cleaned up since a blood smear covers my right cheek.

"Hughes as in Nixon Hughes? He owns the mansion up in Brookhaven?" The male cop asks. I nod slowly, trying my best to place his thinning hair and rounded belly. Where do I know him from? He makes a low whistle and smirks at me. "I wonder what your father would make of your overnight stay with us. Hardly up to par with your penthouse suite."

"If you manage to contact him, feel free to ask." I reply bitterly. Little Latino, as I've decided to call her, clears her throat to regain control of my apparent interrogation.

"Master Hughes, you've been arrested for damage to private property, possession of drugs and assaulting a police officer. These are very serious charges." Staring at the picture on her file, I search my brain for the events that led me here. There was that waitress and her drugs, and the rest is fuzzy. Something about too much self-loathing and a mirror? I'm not sure. Something is triggered, because when I look back to the male cop, a smile pulls at my lips. I remember him now.

"How fortunate you were so close by," I drawl, an image of him on the dancefloor with his shirt wide open and cuffs swinging around his fat finger springing to mind. "But I must ask, as a man of the law - what were you doing partying in uniform, Officer-" I lean forward to read his nametag, "Phallus?"

"It's Phillis, you little shit, and I was undercover hunting for scum like you." He sneers, something resembling pink icing stuck in his overbite. Crossing my arms over the disgustingly soiled shirt I'm still wearing, I lean back and ignore the rest of their practiced spiel.

Little Latino plays good cop and tries to reach my conscience as I laugh internally. I couldn't give less of a shit if they locked me up and threw away the key. In fact, it may be preferable since my life is rapidly swirling out of control. I used to be someone to the Shadowed Souls. I used to think that to them, I was finally irreplaceable. I was wrong. I'm utterly alone and no one is coming to save me.

The door bursts open with a loud clang. *Hold that thought.* "Don't say another word," a dark haired man in a pinstripe navy suit strides in with a black briefcase in hand. Chunky gold rings adorn his meaty fingers, a shiny gold watch poking out from his cuff. He casually takes a seat beside me, not seeming fazed by the glowers he's receiving from across the table.

"Sorry, who the fuck are you?" I break the silence. I place him around mid-thirties as his blue eyes slide to me.

"Jeremy Charlton, your lawyer." He extends his hand which I hesitantly shake, still confused as to why he's here.

"Did my father send you?" The easy smile on his face doesn't falter, but he doesn't answer my question. Opening the leather briefcase, he pulls out large images of Officer

Phallus raving it up in the club and slides them across the metallic surface.

"My client was detained while the arresting officer was intoxicated, which makes his statement inadmissible in court. For all we know, you could have planted the drugs on him in a bid to boost your career," he glares accusingly at the sweating man across from him. Officer Phallus blubbers and grunts incoherently in anger, his face turning a beetroot red. Charlton continues.

"As the son of a billionaire, I'm certain you wouldn't want your boss to find out about this, so why don't we agree that my client walks out of here with his record intact and he, in return, will not press charges?" My attorney cocks his eyebrows at me for back-up, so I shrug and nod. Following his lead, we both stand and exit the room without another word.

With more assurance than before, I stroll through the building, spotting my phone in a clear evidence bag on the edge of an empty desk. Swiping it, I push through the double doors leading onto the main street and inhale deeply. The crisp air of late afternoon fills my lungs, the dying sun peeking around tall buildings. Charlton clears his throat as I begin to walk away, gesturing for me to slide into the black limousine parked against the sidewalk. His driver, dressed in a suit and flat cap, flicks his half-finished cigarette to the floor and squashes it beneath his shiny loafer.

"Since when do attorneys drive their clients home in limos?" I ask. He pulls the door open with an easy smile, waiting for me to duck inside before following and slamming the door shut. That pounding headache is still ever present in the front of my skull. The driver takes his seat up front and rolls up the dividing window separating us.

"I'm not your attorney and you're not going home." Charlton chuckles as the limousine lurches forward and speeds away from the precinct.

From then on, the man with beasty rings becomes the annoyingly silent type, not answering a single one of my questions. The drive is long, easily over an hour but I do drift into a light sleep somewhere along the way. I try to wake several times but my head is heavy on my shoulders, my eyelids refusing to obey the screaming inside my ears. I don't know these men and I can't trust them, but I clearly don't care enough about what happens to me either. Another mile between me and my new sibling is nothing but a blessing in my eyes.

I finally manage to rouse as we pull into a curved driveway. The limo circles a fountain beside a huge mansion. Twice the size of the one I grew up in, judging from this angle. A curved doorway is surrounded by exposed, gray brick and framed by potted plants. The rest of the building is a rich wood color with darker gray tiles forming the roof, as visible on the garage we stop next to.

Following Charlton out, I stop on the concrete and stretch my neck. As soon as I close the door, the limo pulls into the garage. Two muscled men, dressed all in black, exit the mansion and storm directly towards me. Charlton steps aside while I'm roughly patted down, although where or what they think I'm hiding, I don't know. I removed my tattered shirt in the limo, so Mr. Handsy only has my trousers to grope, my phone hanging loosely in the side pocket. Grunting, he slowly rises to his full height and stares me down. His brown eyes narrow, then he gestures to follow as he turns away.

Either side of the main door, small lanterns flicker to life in the fading light of day as I pass. A vast staircase fills the center of the foyer, gold banisters complimenting the sparkling chandelier high above. Open archways either side lead further into the lower level, the same cream glossy wood flooring throughout. The guards guide us down a hallway to the right, Charlton's shoes clicking loudly beside me as we stroll behind.

Meandering through a seemingly unused living room, Mr. Handsy knocks upon a mahogany door and waits to be permitted entry. Once a crackled voice sounds from within, he pushes the door open but nobody moves. All sets of eyes turn to face me, Charlton giving me a nudge with his shoulder so I enter the dimly-lit room.

I'm plunged into darkness as a click signals the door closing behind me. The beeping of a machine penetrates the strain of my eyes, guiding me forward. At the edges of the room, I notice the outlines of a sideboard and desk hinting that I'm in an office. Or what should be an office. I shuffle towards an armchair I noticed while I still had the light of the hallway to aid me. Finding the velvet material with my outstretched fingers, I round the chair and sit down to focus on the shadowed figure opposite. Only the occasional orange glow from a cigar and his heavy breathing alerted me to his presence, as well as the air of danger he's shrouded in.

The silence stretches between us, my impatience starting to flare up but I bite my tongue. My instincts are yelling at me that despite the cloak and dagger routine, I shouldn't be in a rush to piss him off. The routine beeping continues with each passing second, a rhythm I start to twitch my toes along with. Shifting forward, the man flicks on a lamp that burns my eyes.

Blinking to clear the spots from my vision, I spot the wires first, the figure before me hooked up to the heart monitor. A face mask hangs around his neck, linked to an oxygen tank that rests beside his high back wheelchair. His thinning slicked-back hair is a pale shade of gray, his skin scarred with years of drug and alcohol abuse. Also topless, blurred and faded tattoos litter his sagging frame that must have once held muscles to rival all of the guards outside put together. A horizontal scar lies across his upper left side, judging by his age probably from a pacemaker being inserted. Fear freezes my blood flow like liquid nitrogen as I consider that this man could be a future glimpse of who I'm going to become.

"I've been looking forward to meeting you, Wyatt. I must admit, I almost lost hope." His croaky voice fills the air, shaking me from my internal panic.

"How do you know my name? Why am I here?" The answering chuckle I receive is anything but reassuring. Lifting the lid on a cigar box balanced on his thigh, he weakly attempts to hand it to me. I shake my head slightly, more focused on what he has to say.

"I know everything there is to know about you, my boy. Despite how desperately Nixon has tried to keep me away all these years." Creasing my eyebrows, I wonder which one of those sentences to focus on first. Has this man had his goons following me, and if so for how long? And how does he know my father?

"Forgive me, you seem to know a lot about me but I'm unsure who I'm speaking with." I tread carefully, not wanting to become one of his guard's punching bags today. I didn't mind coming here, but I'm starting to think I may be in over my head and don't have a way to get back home. Hell, I don't even know where I am.

"Where are my manners? Ray Perelli." He announces, as if the name should mean something to me. My blank expression causes him to frown. "He really didn't tell you anything, did he?"

"Who?" I ask, utterly lost now. Fatigue is starting to seep into my bones, the headache I'd managed to shake taking hold again. A bath and bed would do me wonders right about now. Leaning forward into the light, his faded green eyes contain a surprising amount of venom for his age.

"The man who stole you from me."

AVERY

"Well, that was a bust," Huxley slams the precinct doors open. He's down the stone steps, his movements jerky and fists balled. I can hear what his mind is thinking as if he were screaming it in my face. *I told you we should have come last night. We should have been here.*

As if I was supposed to know Wyatt would be let out before eight in the morning and whisked away. The officers wouldn't give us any information on what exactly happened, just that a lawyer had posted his bail and taken him 'home'. I can't imagine Nixon would send a lawyer with the instructions to take Wyatt to the one place he's been telling us to avoid, but I've given up questioning these things.

I'm just being pushed from pillar to post these days, along for the ride if nothing else.

Despite sleeping like the dead last night, exhaustion is heavy in my body. I'm lethargic, struggling to voice to those around me that I've had enough. I'm done. In the space of half a year, I've lost all of those I relied upon. I can't even get in contact with Meg, her end of year responsibilities at college most likely keeping her busy.

And although the Shadowed Souls are doing their best to keep my spirits high, they've never known me like this. The girl who needs to take a step back and wallow in bed, to read and escape from reality until she's resolute enough to resurface. It happens sometimes; a coping mechanism is what Keren would call it. I just know it as a young child who spent hours, sometimes days, locked away and needing to rely on her own imagination to keep going. Faced with the uncertainty I'm currently living in, I just need time.

"Well," Garrett stretches his lower back by sticking his crotch too far forward, "I don't know about you guys but I need to burn off some steam."

"Where are you going now?" Axel groans as Dax mutters, "Someone get this guy a leash." Now there's a suggestion. Garrett has already started walking away, turning mid-step to face us still standing by the police station.

"There's a gym nearby. What do you say, you sexy beasts? Fancy working up a sweat with me?" Garrett wags his eyebrows at us all. I bite down a smile, hating how easily he does this to me every time. One minute I'm contemplating falling into literary limbo, and now I'm biting my inner cheek and acting as if I wouldn't follow Garrett to the ends of the earth. Wherever he goes, whatever he's doing, it's sure to be one hell of a ride.

I take a few steps in his direction, much to his delight, when Huxley's sharp tone stops me. "You can't seriously be going to work out at a time like this? Wyatt is fuck knows where and we need to be on high alert for..." I glance back at Hux. He does his very best not to look at me and fails, the unspoken words hanging heavily in the air. For my apparent stalker to stop hiding and make his next move. The ball is in his court.

"Relax, big guy," Garrett doesn't seem to notice any tension between the rest of us. "The second those photos hit the morning papers, Nixon would have dragged Wyatt out of his cell so fast, he'll need a chiropractor to fix his whiplash. I have no doubt Wyatt is getting an ear-full and drinking whiskey for breakfast. He'll come back to us soon enough."

Huxley doesn't seem convinced but doesn't argue any further. His gaze returns to mine, as if to say, *you should be on my side*. I cross my arms, my hip popping to the side.

"Have you got any better ideas?" I ask, preparing for this fight. It's been a while coming, and as much as I'd hoped we could avoid it altogether, it's becoming apparent we'll need to hash it out soon. Garrett closes the distance between us, dragging me into his side.

"If it helps, this particular gym has a basketball court which I happened to reserve this morning. I thought there would be five of us to play, but it looks like you'll have to substitute for us, Peach. I guess an unskilled Hughes is better than none."

"Rude," I purse my lips. Garrett's smile grows wider. "I have a very particular set of skills which makes me a nightmare for people like you." His laughter echoes around the street, a full bellied sound which dislodges the birds from the sidewalk's planted trees. Turning, we're then walking in time with each other's steps.

"And what kind of person am I, Peach?" Garrett murmurs into my ear. His raw voice spirals through me, my core clenching on instinct.

"A self-centered jackass with more confidence than sense," I manage to deliver evenly. I expected him to reel back and deny it, but instead, he presses even closer, the crease of his smile against my neck.

"God, you make me so hard."

***

Exiting the female changing rooms, I can already hear the repetitive sound of a basketball bouncing. I wrestle the tags out of my workout shirt and shorts, having just purchased them in the upstairs sports store. Tossing them into a trash can and tackling my hair into a high ponytail, I emerge onto the court in time to see Dax dunk the ball into the hoop. Regaining control of the ball, he dribbles up and down the court while I enjoy the view far too much.

Wearing loose shorts, white sneakers and nothing else, I drool over the rippling muscles of his abdomen. With each twist of his tanned body, his chest flexes and pulls taut. Even the hardness of his calves are affecting me as he runs across the wooden surface. His icy blue eyes latch onto mine, halting his solo game as he catches the ball and walks towards me.

"Have you been staring at me?" He cocks a brow, coming close enough to force my head back. I copy his playful smile, pushing the butterflies aside. Dax never ceases to affect me this way. In the rare moments we get to be alone, it feels like the whole world fades away, leaving just the two of us. His full lips are a few inches away, reachable if I were to tiptoe, but I've never been one to play easy-to-get.

"Of course not. I was just wondering how you don't have any game, considering you play for a team." Throwing his head back on a laugh, his Adam's apple bobs. I clamp my mouth shut in fear my tongue will get ideas of tracing over his smooth skin. Stroking his fingers along the length of mine, Dax beckons me onto the court.

"Well, well, Little Swan. You have the talk, but let's see if you can back it up, shall we?" Bouncing the ball towards me, I catch it easily and dribble it in a circle around him. I stop when we are face to face again and smirk.

"What?" I cock my head at his raised brows. "Did you really think I lived in a manor with its own personal court, and never practiced shooting a ball?" I mock, turning to throw the ball towards the hoop. Bouncing off the backboard, it slips into the net with a satisfying 'swoosh'.

Grinning to myself that I managed to pull that off with an audience, I don't hear Dax move until his whisper breathes into my ear.

"No using the backboard in my rules." His hands smooth around the front of my T-shirt, holding my waist as he presses his body against my back. Suddenly hot for a very different reason than excursion, I focus on keeping still. Dax places small kisses behind my ear.

"Dax," I breathe heavily.

"Yes, Avery?"

"Is this you finally pushing to the front of the line?" I lean back into his chest, savoring the warmth that seeps into me. I haven't forgotten what Dax said at the roller disco, how he'd be content holding himself back and letting the others take center stage. He's given me space to explore and settle into their dynamic, but I want more. I want to see his selfish side. "I've been waiting." Dax's chuckle vibrates through my back.

Shifting his hands, one trails up the inside of my arm before coming to rest lightly across my collar-bone while the other winds around my body to hold me in place. "If I catch you using that backboard again, traveling with or carrying the ball, there will be punishments." He mutters seductively, grinding his crotch against my ass.

"Are we expecting Garrett, or did you drug and stuff him in a locker?" I push back and roll my hips. Two can play at this game. Dax groans quietly.

"I don't need Garrett to enforce punishments. I'm capable enough all by myself." Proving his point, Dax's hand at my collar bone dips south, into my sports bra. He rolls my nipple tightly, tugging until I whimper. My head drops back, exposing my neck to his mouth. "And to answer your other question; the last time I saw them, the guys were arguing in the shop about which shade of green goes best with Axel's eyes." I smile at this.

"Even Huxley?" I ask, managing to keep the quiver from my voice. Dax moves onto my other breast, grabbing me roughly. I gasp. *Finally*. This is the Dax I've been needing, one who takes what he wants instead of waiting for me to ask. Taking his hand, I dip his fingers into my short's waistband.

"I think he needed an outlet for his frustrations. He was strictly Team Olive." Those long fingers find my clit as if they've memorized the way, shifting in small circles. I push up onto my tiptoes then, wanting every inch of my body connected with Dax's.

"And what about you?" I turn my head into his neck. His fingers enter me slowly.

"I don't necessarily care for the color green." He shrugs, too invested in following the cues of my body. I turn, momentarily dislodging his hands. Those devilish fingers are straight back where I want them, Dax's other hand now cradling my ass.

"No. Do you need an outlet?" I blink up, my eyes growing hazy with need. Dax's mouth remains an inch from mine, his fingers skating over my pussy. The heel of his palm applies delicious pressure to my clit and unashamedly, I bear down into him.

"Are you offering me one?" Dax wets his lips. He watches me intently, absorbing my every expression. He has me a writhing mess of need already and he's barely done anything.

"Always," I vow. A small smile passes over Dax's features, making him all the more handsome. How did I get so lucky? The hand on my ass jerks me impossibly forward, closing every gap between us. The movement jostles his hand over my cunt, which is already soaking wet. Crashing our lips together, Dax's kiss is short, leaving me chasing for more.

"I wish I could give you what you're yearning for," Dax says into my ear, our cheeks pressed firmly together. "But unfortunately, I was recently told I don't have any game." In the next second, he's halfway across the court retrieving the ball while I'm left stumbling for stability, clenching my thighs and panting. Oh, that bastard played me like a freaking fiddle.

"Go get him, Peach!" Garrett suddenly calls out. He, Axel and Huxley are sitting in the middle of the bleachers, varying expressions of lust and curiosity settling on their faces. I blush furiously. Not only did they watch what just happened, including my rejection, without my knowledge, but now they want to watch me play a sport I'm no good at. Gritting my teeth, I huff through my nose.

Never one to back down from a challenge, like the one shining in Dax's eyes, I step between his asshole-ish smirk and the hoop. I'm getting all sides of Dax today. Keeping my eyes focused on his body language, I notice a slight tremble in his right knee. Ballet training sure comes in useful for noticing weak ligaments. Following my instincts, I lunge right while he fakes left and steal the ball from right beneath his huge hand. The shock on his face makes me laugh as I step out of his grasp and shoot the ball straight over his head. The orange sphere circles the hoop twice before dropping through the middle. The guys in the bleachers roar with cheers and laughter, Garrett reclining on the bench before he falls off it.

Collecting the ball, I round the court while bouncing it beneath my palm and resuming the position Dax was just in. He swiftly changes tactics, which somehow isn't against his own rules. Pretending to yawn, he stretches one arm behind his head while the other hand trails down his washboard abs to the waistband of his shorts. Pushing the material down slightly to reveal a hint of curls nested underneath, my mouth goes dry at the display. Holy mother of heavy balls, he looks hot. He almost succeeds in unhinging my focus, using every tool in his arsenal and my libido is his target. Biting my lip hard, I do what any logical, rational person in this situation would.

Throwing the ball into his gut, Dax grunts as I retrieve the ball from the ground and continue to make my way to the hoop. Lifting the ball above my head with one hand to aim, Dax plucks it from my grip and chuckles as I attempt to get it back. Lowering it back into my reach, I try to swipe it but he's too fast for me, twisting around to shoot the ball straight into the net.

"Nice recovery," I praise. Dax is the image of self-assurance. On the court, he's the boss. The king even. I deflate my shoulders. "Too bad you just scored in my net." Dax's face falls and again, those howls of laughter echo around the arena. I'm fairly certain Garrett is close to laughing out a lung.

I run towards the ball, until Dax grabs my waist and tosses me aside so he can get there first. "No fair!" I shout, not that I'm surprised. Everything about this mini one-on-one has included foul play. But if that's the way he wants it, I'm only too happy to deliver. I grip the hem of my T-shirt and pull it over my head. A black sports bra that enhances my cleavage distracts Dax long enough for me to lunge at him, after a different type of ball this time. I grab his crotch, resulting in a high-pitched yelp.

The 'thump, thump, thump' as Dax drops the basketball is music to my ears, having the intended effect. Feigning innocence, I pretend not to feel his cock beginning to harden. Did I just unleash a new kink?

"We have something in common, you and I," I grin menacingly. Genuine fear crosses Dax's face and I almost take pity on him. "When you break my rules, you also get punished." Before I can carry out any further squeezing, tattooed arms band around me from behind. Garrett holds me tight whilst Axel carefully extracts my hand from Dax's testicles.

"I love watching you dominate all of the balls on the court, Peach," Garrett chuckles into my ear. "If I'm a good boy, do I get my turn to be manhandled too?" Twisting myself free, I look him over and cock a single brow.

"Nah, you'd enjoy it way too much," I grin, brushing our arms as I pass by. Huxley hands over my discarded T-shirt, an unspoken truce between us. At least, I hope it is. My smile grows wicked, the power I'm gifted by their lingering stares bordering dangerous. "I'd prefer to watch you all sweat for me."

Like Garrett, their eyes track me the entire way to the bleachers, hungry like predators. Despite reclining into the seat, I sit proud and gesture for their game to begin. Watching them fumble over each other, a mess of horniness and testosterone, is comical but I manage to keep a straight face. Just about.

DAX

Focusing on any type of physical release was pointless after Avery took her perch into the stands. A queen overseeing her men. The game started out like most, lighthearted and fun, but it soon shifted. Garrett is on a mission to prove himself the best of us all, to keep her attention centered on himself. With that came Huxley's need to vent some frustration and Axel's competitive nature. Me, however, I do what I always do and fade into the background. A prop to their show, and Avery doesn't seem happy about that.

She's propped back, elbows on the bench behind and her chest pushed up to the ceiling. My pulse beats in time with the tapping of her foot, her pout doing something weird to my chest. It's in my nature to please, to smooth everything out. Whatever was happening between my cock and her commanding grip before Garrett rudely interrupted has rocked me to my core. Lust flooded my system, giving me a brief glimpse into why the others seem to enjoy exhibiting her so much. I'm not that kind of guy, but for Avery, I'd be whoever she wants me to be.

The basketball hits me in the back of the head and I stumble. Glancing back, Garrett shrugs with the boyish smile that tells me he hit me on purpose. I can't deny I've been letting down my side of our paired team. Last time I took any notice, Huxley and Axel had us five to one. Opening my mouth to apologize, a flash of blonde whips past.

"The fuck was that?!" Avery slams her hands into Garrett's chest. His smile spreads wider. Holding his hands up in defeat, Garrett takes a few steps back.

"Sorry, Peach. Just trying to get Dax's head in the game. Although I might have given him a small concussion. Why don't you take him into the locker room and check him over?" Grunting, Avery takes my hand and leads me away. I look over my shoulder in confusion. Garrett somehow has Axel on his knees and is pretending to fuck his face as he mouths *you're welcome* at me. Now there's an image I can never unsee.

"Are you okay?" Avery asks, her eyes filled with concern. I walk on numb feet, not too sure if I nod or just blink too much. Maybe I really am concussed. Settling on a bench in the locker room, I vaguely notice a woman walking by in a towel. Another is drying her hair in a mirror which spans the far wall, reflecting a row of shower stalls around the corner. Shit, this is the women's locker room. Averting my eyes, I stare at a spec on the Lino flooring while Avery crouches between my knees.

"Can I get you a drink or something? I'm sure there's a med kit here somewhere, they might have ice packs." Looking in all directions, her hair falls free of its tie. She gives my thighs a reassuring squeeze and moves to leave. I quickly grip her wrists, holding her in place.

"I think...Um, no I need..."

"What is it? Anything," Avery says in earnest. Her face is so close, those wide eyes swallowing me whole. I don't even care about the women milling around in the background anymore. Reaching out to gently tuck a loose strand of hair behind her ear, my voice is thick and husky.

"I need to finish what I started." Those eyes darken instantly, a quick inhale parting Avery's plump lips. I'd think myself as too bold and totally out of line if it wasn't for the visceral response I watch take over Avery's face. Pulling her lip into her teeth, she quickly glances over my right shoulder. Then we're moving, her gentle tug firm and her gaze avoiding those watching on. Opening a door beside the one marked for the main gym, I'm promptly shoved inside.

A light flickers to life, illuminating shelves of equipment. Pink dumbbells and medicine balls, half steps and foam rollers. A standing rack juts out at the far end with hanging yoga mats. The door clicks. I watch Avery's hand retract from the lock, her cheeks deepening with crimson as she passes me and takes a yoga mat. Tossing it on the floor, she suddenly looks at me and I forget how to breathe.

"Strip and lie down. We won't have long."

"I feel like you pre-planned this," I mutter, quickly doing exactly what she said. Avery does the same. Sneakers are kicked in all directions, my shorts tossed and catching on a shelf. My boxers are chucked aside and I'm on my back in the next breath, my cock jumping to attention. Not my first choice of venue but I can't deny the desire anymore. Avery, now gloriously naked, settles over my hips.

"Habit I suppose," she shrugs. My hands are too busy trailing the indents in her waist. "With someone like Garrett, it's a good idea to have all of the private spots picked out ahead of time."

Like a bucket of ice cold water dousing my excitement, my hands go still on her hips. Avery realizes her mistake a moment too late, gasping and leaning forward to stroke my chest.

"Oh shit, I'm sorry! I didn't mean-" I shift us both in a flurry. Avery yelps, forced to hold onto my shoulders as I stand and take her with me. If Garrett was in my place, he sure as shit wouldn't be laying on his back waiting for instruction. Pushing her back into the shelves, my eyes are hooded.

"Is this better?" I ask. There was no venom in my tone but Avery winces anyway.

"Dax, I didn't mean it like I was expecting to be here with him. I'm glad it's you. I want it to be you." Avery's naturally-thick eyelashes fan closed. She's mentally berating herself, and even though my dick is a throbbing pest between us, I stop to smooth the crease from her eyebrows with my thumb.

I know the saying - nice guys finish last - but I can't help it. It's not in me to be controlling. I won't be the one to dominate Avery and draw out every ounce of pleasure she didn't know she had. And that's okay. She has that already. I bring something different to the table.

Not having the words to explain the unfurling in my chest, I press my mouth down onto Avery's. She responds instantly. Tentative at first, our lips soon grow more confident, matching the urgency we felt on the court. I pour everything I'm unable to say through the connection, forcing the world out. It's just us now.

Soft touches soon turn heated, forcefully crashing against each other in a bid to get closer. Avery's nails scrape gently across the upper half of my back while her other hand skates over my hair. Holding my head firmly in place, she eagerly pushes her tongue into my mouth. A low moan escapes me as our tongues fight for control.

Unable to hold back any longer, I grip the back of her thighs and push her further into the shelves. The metal is probably pressing into her back but she urges me on, rolling her hips and drawing me further into the drawing whirlpool of her eyes. My dick is sliding over her slick entrance, toying with her clit. I've forced myself to hold back, allowing Garrett to hound her like a dog in heat every day, but there was no need. Being the fallback guy doesn't mean I'm incompetent. It doesn't mean I'm any less than the others, or that I can't offer Avery the same pleasure.

My hands roam her soft thighs and midsection. Smoothing my thumbs along her ribs, I explore the line beneath her heavy breasts and she pushes her chest out ever so slightly. A low noise which could be confused with a growl passes through my chest. Pushing my hands between us, I fondle her luscious breasts, massaging and committing the shape, weight and feel of them to memory. Avery squirms, grinding my painfully hard cock against her core. The heat radiating from her center makes my mouth water, thirsty for a taste of her. Next time, when we have a bed, a more substantial lock and all the time in the world.

Returning my hand to her thigh, I drag my thumb along the inside until I reach her clit. She took me so willingly on the court, and now isn't any different. Sensing her impatience by the iron grip of legs tightening around my waist, I press down hard and rub small circles. Avery bites down on my bottom lip. Pushing both hands through my hair, her nails draw lines across my scalp. I'm a fool to think I'm the one teasing her, when it's my control which is quickly slipping.

"Avery," I rasp against her mouth, beginning to spiral. In response, she reaches between us, tilts my dick upright and seats herself on it. Our groans cancel each other out, the slow descent of her pussy over my shaft utterly euphoric. Bottoming out on the base of my shaft, we still, savoring the feeling of her stretched tightly around me. I could stand like this forever, peppering her face with kisses while she warms my cock. She deserves to be cherished and adored, but there's not enough time.

Our rhythm is instantly frantic, driven by the desperate need to devour. With every hurried thrust, a fire ignites within us, burning away any remnants of restraint. The intensity is overwhelming; each movement and each touch deepening our bond. I shift my angle, driving deeper, eliciting a gasp from Avery. Her eyes flutter closed, lips parting as she surrenders completely to the rapture coursing through her. The sight of her like this, her face contorted with ecstasy, spurs me on. I press my forehead against hers, our breaths mingling, creating a cocoon of intimacy that is sacred.

"Don't stop," she whispers, her voice a husky plea that sends a shiver down my spine.

"I won't," I promise, my voice thick with need. Avery pushes against my chest, hunting for my gaze.

"N-no, I mean-" she bites her lip as I slam hard inside of her. "Don't stop being yourself. I want you, Dax. I want you exactly the way you are." Her hips roll against mine, meeting each thrust with a fervor that matches my own. That same unfurling in my chest is back, tripled into a feeling that steals my breath. The room fades away, leaving only the two of us, entwined by the sound of our bodies moving together, our shared moans.

I feel the tension coiling in my core, ready to snap. Avery's breath quickens, her fingers gripping my shoulders with a desperate urgency. I know she's close, and the thought of her finding release pushes me to the brink.

"Avery," I groan, my voice ragged. "I'm so close."

"Come with me," she pants, her eyes locking onto mine, filled with an intensity that takes my breath away. There's no denying her, as usual. With a final thrust, we shatter, our orgasms crashing a pair of tidal waves battling to consume the other. Avery cries out, her body trembling around mine as I spill into her, the sensation embedding itself into my very soul. I immediately want to have her again, to keep fucking her until my name is the only one she knows how to gasp.

For a moment, we stand there, a tangle of limbs and sweat, riding out the waves of pleasure until we both come back down to earth. I brush a blonde strand of hair from her face, gazing at her with a tenderness that I can hardly contain. A fragile promise hangs on the end of my tongue, three tiny words that roar within my ears to be said. Whether Avery is ready to accept them is a different story.

A rattle on the doorknob reintroduces the real world. I can now hear the shuffle of feet and hushed whispers of annoyance. Shifting, I lower Avery and bend aside for my T-shirt. Giving it to her to clean up, I quickly tuck my weeping dick into my shorts, the hard-on slowly waning. For all of the jiggling on the handle, no one bangs or produces a key to open the door. This gives us time to tie our laces, right ourselves and share a knowing smile.

"Do you think the guys will know what we were up to?" Avery whispers, fluttering her lashes at me.

"I'll be making sure they do," I snort. Avery fake-slaps my chest and I pull her closer. Planting a gentle kiss on her forehead, I guide her to the door with my arm around her waist. We're leaving with our heads held high, despite every fiber of my being wanting to stay right here, where I have Avery's full attention. Not very brotherly of me, but perhaps I get to be selfish sometimes. Everyone else in our gang seems to take that opportunity without notice. Why shouldn't I?

AVERY

Walking down the street hand in hand with Dax is refreshing. Just the two of us, out in the open.

I'd half-expected the others to be arms-crossed and impatiently waiting for us to leave the storage room, but they were nowhere to be seen. Only the manager and a few disgruntled members of staff with bottles of disinfectant in hand. We were quickly handed our belongings and escorted out, much to our amusement. I reckon today was the most mischievous Dax has ever been, judging by the wide smile and air of energy about him. We're two seconds from starting to skip down the street when a hair salon presents itself. I skid to a stop, a frown pulling at my mouth.

"What is it?" Dax tilts his head. I cling onto where our fingers are linked.

"Um, it's probably silly," I avoid his gaze but Dax gives me a knowing look as if nothing I say is silly. "I've just remembered that my roots are showing. My mom has been taking me to have my hair dyed since I was adopted, in an effort to hide me in plain sight I suppose. But I don't need to hide now that Fredrick knows where I am. So...I don't really know if I should keep up the pretence or not."

Pulling me into his arms, Dax forces me to look up at his small smile.

"Forget pretences, and stop worrying about what you should and shouldn't do. How do you like your hair?" The answer slips from my tongue immeadiately.

"I like being blonde."

"Then lead the way," Dax slides his hand to the small of my back and urges me towards the open doorway. That's how I find myself draped in a protective cloak and sitting before a huge, lit mirror with Dax on a swivel seat by my side. The hairdresser works in the background, bleaching my roots while Dax's hand plays with mine.

"I just want to apologize again," I say, my cheeks flaring. The steady beat of my heart thumps within my ears. "If I made you feel insecure about the whole Garrett thing." Dax snorts, his face stretching with a grin.

"That would be ironic."

"What do you mean?" I push a strand of fallen hair aside to see his face. There's a twinkle in his crystal blue eyes, a simple shrug on his shoulders.

"Me being insecure of the most insecure person I've ever met." My head tilts before it's swiftly urged back into place. Dax's hand doesn't release mine, however.

"Garrett?" I raise a brow. A dull sense of unease blooms. Dax's chuckle is lost to the sound of a hair dryer whirring nearby, our conversation becoming masked. He's still grinning, like he's containing a secret that I should have figured out by now.

"Yes Garrett. The man who can't admit his feelings to himself, let alone voice them to anyone else. You should always be aware of the loudest man in the room, he has the most to hide."

"I just- I've never thought..." I trail off. Damn, how could I have missed it? Dax tilts my chin upwards and smooths the creases out from between my eyebrows with his thumb in the way he always does.

"Tell me, how many times have you seen Garrett with his shirt off?" My face falls. Dax nods slowly, watching the understanding dawn within me. My gaze drifts towards the mirror without really seeing, my mind reeling as if I've just tossed my heart out of the window. Garrett's insecure without a T-shirt on - why? What could be underneath that he's so worried to show, especially since he's had his hands all over my scars?

I fall into a reflective silence, the rest of the session slipping by. Dax strokes my hand until it's time to wash my hair out, in which he turns to reading some complementary magazines. Vaguely, I respond to questions when I'm asked, nod when it's polite and ignore the disquiet settling within.

Even after I'm thanked the salon's staff and credited a ridiculous tip to Wyatt's account, I walk back to the hotel by Dax's side in more of a daze.

Once in the elevator, hands are roaming again. Dax distracts me with ease, his desire piercing the confusion. Tender caresses of his knuckles against my neck. Gentle strokes of my fingers across his biceps. I lean into Dax's chest, gifted with a slow kiss. By the time the elevator pings and he leads me out, I'm smiling warmly again. I shouldn't make this revelation a big deal in my head, Garrett is still Garrett and when he's ready to open up to me, he will.

Except Dax and I both come to an abrupt halt as noise fills the hallway. Male voices yell, a concoction of curse words and slurred shouting seeps from between a door halfway down and accompanied by a loud crash. Our door. Dax tries to hold me back but I twist my grip free, running the length of the carpeted corridor. He could have caught me but I know Dax. He doesn't try to hold me back. Instead, he appears to press the keycard to the lock. As the light blinks green, I shove my way inside.

"What the hell is going on in here?!" I shout, my voice cutting through the chaos like a knife. The scene inside the room is a mess of tipped furniture, a lamp lying shattered on the floor. Huxley and Garrett are nose-to-nose, fists clenched, while Axel stands to the side, his face flushed with irritation. They all turn to look at me, the tension in the room palpable.

For a split second, there's silence. Then they all start to speak at once, a triad of voices dripping with venom and frustration.

"I was just suggesting we should visit the spa downstairs and this meathead punched me in the face!" Garrett points to a red welt on his cheek.

"This asshole thinks he can keep distracting us from the fact that we're not doing anything. Wyatt is out there somewhere, missing, and we're playing ball and-" His hand is thrown in my direction. I hear what he refuses to say as if he screamed it in my face. *And screwing around in stock rooms*. Reeling himself back, focusing on the anger burning in his eyes, Huxley's fists tremble. "Wyatt is missing, and no one cares enough to look for him."

"Wyatt left of his own accord!" Garrett shoves his shoulder into Hux's midsection, the pair of them slamming into the wall. Punches are thrown towards kidneys until Axel pushes his way between them.

"That's enough, both of you," he growls. His face is tense, his posture on the edge of snapping. Keeping the struggling men apart, his biceps and shoulders ripple but Axel doesn't falter. "We all love Wyatt. When he wants to be found, he'll let us know."

"Of course you're siding with your delusional boyfriend," Huxley roars and successfully earns himself a busted lip. I let Axel have that one. Looking over my shoulder, I nudge my chin towards some chairs in the hallway, either side of a thin table. Dax retrieves them for me, placing them in opposite corners of the room.

"Huxley, Garrett, take a seat. Axel, on the bed. If asses leave perches, Avery leaves the room - got it?" A grumble of acceptance rings out, reluctantly slumping onto the bed and chairs, still simmering with barely contained anger. The distance between each of them allows me to pace in the free space at the foot of the bed. Dax attends to picking up the lamp's porcelain pieces so I don't step on them.

I take a deep breath, trying to steady my racing heart. "Now, Axel, please explain to me what's going on."

Huxley looks away, his jaw clenched as Axel speaks up. "Gare found out there's a spa in the base of the hotel. He was setting up a surprise for us all to go down there this evening." Axel jerks his head towards an overturned paper bag on the bed, a bundle of swimwear spilling out. Garrett kicks a rogue piece of porcelain.

"I was going to bleach my asshole for you and everything," he mutters under his breath. I close my eyes to find the will of patience to ignore that statement. Axel does this with more ease than I can.

"Hux wanted to head back to the police station and see if we can find out any more information about where Wyatt went. It sparked an argument," Axel's hazel eyes slide in Huxley's direction. I twist to face the bulky man hunched in his seat, his blond waves falling forward over his face.

Huxley raises his gaze from the floor, his voice calmer but no less intense. "No one seems to care that one of our brothers is missing. We can guess where he is and pretend he's safe, but until I know that for sure, I can't fuck about playing ball and sitting in a spa."

Garrett opens his mouth to protest, but I hold up a hand, silencing him. "Not your turn." I pretend to miss the flare of desire igniting his dark eyes. Garrett's list of kinks is endless, and me taking the role as dominator must be pretty high on that list.

"Regardless of recent developments," Huxley eyes me closely and my cheeks heat, "Wyatt wouldn't leave his boys." Shifting in his seat, he faces Garrett straight on.

"Remember that time you ran away to join the circus, and we were so angry that you'd be so selfish. Axel was in pieces and no one could calm his nightmares. Wyatt spent every waking moment hunting for you with some ex-bounty hunter he hired, and every night spooning Axel. He didn't give up on you, yet you're so quick to forget about him."

Garrett's jaw is tight, his eyes darting to me.

"You may speak now," I nod. He exhales loudly, his words rushing out in a flurry.

"For the record - on that occasion, Axel told me to leave. We had that big blow-out fight about him hiding in the closet and I said I'd rather be bench pressed by the Strong Man than hide in it with him, and he was all 'go on then'," Garrett drops his voice an octave. "This is different. Wyatt left us of his own accord. He packed his bag and walked out the door without a second glance back. He didn't even say goodbye. I left a whole note detailing my plan."

"So you're not looking for him out of spite?" Huxley narrows his eyes.

"I'm not looking for him because he doesn't want to be found. His phone is always dead or off, he's blatantly ignoring us. So yeah, I'd rather spend my time in a sauna with Avery in my lap and Axel's cock in my mouth, because I'm going to live my damn life." Garrett's face splits into a smile and he shrugs. "Smoke and mirrors, baby. If you don't like the cards you're dealt, reshuffle. That's what Wyatt's done and he doesn't give a shit that he's lost a few in the process."

A heavy silence settles within the trashed hotel room. A part of me feels like a fool for becoming wrapped up in Garrett's ploy to distract us all, but another part understands why he did it. Why he always does it. Garrett is obnoxious at the best of times, but he holds our best interests at heart. He's not the asshole he tries so hard to portray.

I pinch the bridge of my nose, feeling a headache coming on. The Shadowed Souls are a gang, created by a man strong enough to lead them. They need direction from someone who understands their trauma and quirks better than I ever could. Despite Garrett's nonchalant appearance, they *all* need Wyatt.

"Huxley. I understand. I truly do. Wyatt is your leader, I'm not. I can't give you guys the strict parameters like he did, so I need you to help me out. If your gut is telling you Wyatt isn't safe, then let's come up with a way to find him."

Huxley's lips part, his surprise evident. He was prepared to have this fight with all of us, believing he is the only one in Wyatt's corner. I wouldn't put myself on Team Wyatt, but I'm not doing this for him. I'm doing it for them, the men I've become entwined with. They fight to keep me safe, so I'll fight to keep them together.

Dax steps forward, placing a reassuring hand on my shoulder. "But if we do find Wyatt and he doesn't want us anymore, you need to let it go, Hux. Whatever happens, the five of us can still find a way." My heart squeezes tightly. *We can find a way.* If Dax realizes the weight of his statement, or how much it impacts me, he doesn't let on. I gaze around the room, the twinge of emotion pricking the back of my eyes. It's them. They're my new family.

There's a beat before Huxley finally nods. "Agreed. As long as everyone makes the effort. We're a team, nothing has changed." He glares at Garrett, waiting for him to reciprocate. Garrett's expression softens slightly.

"We're a team," he repeats and nods. Axel shifts over the mattress, resting a large hand on Huxley's thigh.

"Tell us where to start."

As they start to talk, more calmly this time, a wave of relief washes over me. I lean back against Dax, feeling his steady presence behind me, and smile. We'll be okay. Whatever happens, we will manage. Whether Wyatt is in the picture or not.

WYATT

I haven't seen Ray since the evening I arrived, but the last two days have been pure bliss. Other than the small army of guards I've seen walking through the mansion, Charlton on occasion and the staff, I've pretty much had the mansion to myself. I just wish I could bring myself to enjoy it.

Stretching across the wide mattress from the ends of my fingers to the tips of my toes, I sigh heavily. When will the weight crushing my chest from the inside shift? When will the dull ache in my skull fade? Not as long as I keep waking up each morning I reckon.

A knock sounds at the door, announcing breakfast bang on time. "Come in," I call and pull the cover higher around my waist. Rachel, the lady-of-the-house, pops her head around the door with a large smile. Nudging the way in with her hip, she easily balances a tray in one hand and a glass of cranberry juice in the other.

"Did you sleep well?" she asks, her perfectly curled brown locks pulled into a ponytail at her nape. I nod to save face and accept the tray with thanks, perking up at the smell. Fried eggs on toast with sausages wrapped in bacon, just the way our cook Nancy used to make when I was a boy. Something I divulged over dinner on the first night, answering Rachel's many questions about my preferences. She hands me the glass and produces two small tablets from her apron's front pocket, stroking my hair softly as I pop them into my mouth and guzzle down the juice.

"That's a good boy. Vitamins will help that cut on your head heal quicker." Her kind smile brings my own out. I'm sure I've never heard of vitamins having healing powers but if she wants to take care of me, I'm not going to argue. I feel a sense of calm and peace in her presence.

"Ray would like to see you this morning, so make sure you freshen up and take your pick from the clothes in the wardrobe." I nod again, enjoying the warmth in her smile. She seems genuinely happy to have me here.

It's much easier to bury my head in the sand when I'm being plied with food and booze. I didn't think of myself as fickle before, but I figure this way, everyone's happy. The Shadowed Souls must be thanking their lucky stars that I'm no longer bringing them down. I was a drain on their happiness, now they've got *her* and I wish them good fucking luck. I'm on a new path, one that ends with finding answers.

Remembering the breakfast in my lap, I tuck in and moan in between mouthfuls. Rachel's cooking isn't exceptionally different from Nancy's, but I don't ever remember enjoying her food this much. Each mouthful is a burst of flavor, overriding my senses so I don't hear the sexual noises I'm making until I've swallowed, the motion making my hair bounce upon my head.

As Rachel backs out of the room, I toss my head side to side enjoying the way my hair flops from ear to ear. I've never let it grow out this long before, but now I know why Garrett does. There's freedom in not giving a shit. Man, he would love it here, being waited on with as much food as he could consume. My mood sours.

Maybe I shouldn't be so quick to think the Shadowed Souls don't need me. Is Huxley fully healed, physically and mentally? Is Dax keeping up with his studies? Even during the holidays, he can't afford to fall behind. My money is only good to him as long as he continues to pass his classes with straight A's. And hopefully, Axel's nightmares are a distant memory and Garrett isn't eating everyone out of house and home.

Reaching over to the bedside table, I unplug my phone from the charger I was provided. I don't know why I bother keeping it on since I can't bear to look at, let alone answer, it. I pull out the drawer to grab my phone. Hundreds of missed calls, voicemails and messages blink back at me. I scroll down the list, getting the gist of every message despite flicking through quickly. Even Avery's name is amongst them, causing my appetite to flee completely. She's begging me to get in touch, pretending she's worried. Even goes as far as to say she has something important to tell me.

All lies. I bet she just wants to kick me while I'm down, pull me back in just to prove that she can. She's the root of my turmoil. And still, the thought of her large blue eyes, her golden hair and lithe body in lycra, her hand on my cock, has the covers tenting in my groin area.

It's official. I'm sick, twisted, disturbed. Pushing the tray further away, I toss the phone onto the bed and rise. Crossing the room butt-naked, I enter the ensuite to shower. A punishingly cold shower.

Why does she have to crawl so deeply beneath my skin, taunting me with the life I could never have? I didn't want her as an adopted sister and I definitely don't want her as my fucking twin. I want her in the most forbidden way, the monster within stirring and clawing to be let out. I'm literally no better than the bastard who hurt her as a child, which is why I've decided I can never see her again. Pretend she doesn't exist so I can actually move onto someone else, someone perfectly uncomplicated.

Stepping into the spray, my body barely registers the icy water that the dial says it should be. My skin is taut and numb. After working shampoo into a lather into my hair, I continue to wash my body with the remaining suds. Unnerved by the lack of feeling anywhere, I start to scrape my nails across my skin in various places to try to find a spot where I'm not completely desensitized. It's useless.

Relenting, I wash out the shampoo and exit the cubicle. In the mirror hanging opposite, I assess the red scratch marks covering my body, some deep enough to draw pricks of blood. Yet I don't feel a thing. My eyes are bloodshot with haggard bags hanging darkly beneath them, my whole face appearing aged despite the fact I've never felt better. Wrapping a fluffy towel from the warming rack around my middle, I go in hunt of fresh clothes.

The wardrobe is full of dry-cleaned items in plastic sleeves filling the top rail and rows of smart and casual shoes lined along the base, fortunately all in my size. Ignoring the various fancy suits, I opt for a white polo and the only pair of dark jeans. I rub the towel over my dripping wet hair until it's in a damp mess. Smoothing it back, I shove some socks onto my feet before leaving the room.

As usual, the halls have more ghosts than tenants. I have to wonder why Perelli bothers keeping such a large home if there's no one to fill it but his guards and staff. Roaming at my leisure, I follow the sound of music. An eccentric mix of jazz and the blues. Rachel is humming along as she saunters from a room with a basket of dirty washing in her arms. My lips curve into the wide smile that appears whenever she's around. Offering to take the load off her hands, the brunette accepts and I escort her to the utility room downstairs.

Rachel must be in her sixties, and despite being introduced to me as Ray's wife, she's taken on the role as cook and maid. Clearly she takes pride in her home, but I've yet to see her interact with anyone else. Beneath her white apron, a black dress sits on her rounded frame, featuring baggy short sleeves and a white collar. Her feet are in black, flat pumps allowing her to move about the house silently. All that gives her away is her cheery humming.

She leads me past yet another unused living area. This one has a deep red corner sofa in front of a vast fireplace, filled with logs and begging to be lit. The east side of the mansion is much bigger, featuring a massive dining room, ballroom, library, indoor gym complete with pool and sauna, and even a home theater.

I'm no stranger to the finer things in life, but seeing the love and care Rachel has put into each room has me thinking. One day I'm going to own a home just like this, paid with money I've worked my ass off and earned for myself. I don't want a drop of my allowance from Nixon if it means keeping this leash around my neck a second longer.

Pulling me to a halt in front of a black door, Rachel pauses to look at me. I can't decipher her expression as she licks her lips and looks away. "Go easy on him. He's declining quickly." With that, she pushes down the handle.

Inside, the curtains are drawn, the space lit by long blue bulbs trailing the edges of the ceiling. The repetitive beeping is faint across the far side, and a strong scent burns the hairs in my nose. It's an unusual mix of sterile spray and cigar smoke, the latter emanating from Ray's mouth. Even laid in the hospital bed, hooked up to the same machines and an oxygen tube in his nose, the cigar's cherry flares and rescinds in time with his ragged breaths.

I pause, waiting for an invitation. When it doesn't come, I rasp my knuckles on the wood. "You wanted to see me?"

"Wyatt," Ray snaps out of his trance. Setting the cigar aside, he beckons me over to his bed. "My apologies for not seeing you sooner. I do hope you're enjoying your time here with us?" I nod, unsure of where to put myself. I decide on pulling up an armchair, and then uncomfortably shift forward when Ray offers out his hand to me.

"I promised you some answers, my boy. And I think you've waited long enough to get them, don't you agree?" My hand tightens in his, my throat clenching like a vice. The weight of his words is much heavier than the raspy, frail voice which delivered them.

"Agreed," I manage to grunt. Ray relaxes his head back against the pillow.

"Do you know how rich men stay rich, Wyatt? They know who to steal from. Businessmen, bankers, accountants. We're all thieves. We sell things people don't need to people who can't afford to buy them. It's all in the advertising, pitching dreams and happiness in place of the cold, hard truth. We can't escape misery. It finds us. It's ingrained in us. No matter how rich or poor you are. I found out the hard way that no one is untouchable. Nixon taught me that."

My forearms rest on my knees, my foot tapping lightly. The smoke in the room is clearing through the vents, but it's no easier to breathe when I'm hanging on Ray's every word.

"Nixon and I were those thieves once. We sold the dream. We made our fortunes too young, and we partied too hard. By the time we found our partners and eventual wives, we were on top of the world. The trashed hotel rooms and continuous holidays. I thought we were invincible. I thought nothing could come between us."

I can't imagine Nixon at my age. The image Ray is painting of a reckless, young man who parties and laughs the nights away is a distant cry from the graying man I was raised by. He's always seemed so stern, his mouth turned down into a frown whenever he looked at me. Nothing I did was ever good enough, so I learnt very young to stop trying. Ray coughs, gearing himself up for the rest of his story.

"My Rachel and Catherine Hughes fell pregnant at almost the same time. The two became just as close and we went out for dinner to celebrate. That was the first time I noticed Nixon seemed distracted. Or perhaps distanced is a better way to describe it. He didn't eat a bite and refused to join our toast. It got worse over the coming months, his mood swings were volatile and the distance grew larger. A form of depression I thought. Pre-baby blues, perhaps."

"Did you find out what was causing them?" I sit forward, hanging on Ray's every word. He nods gravely.

"Only once it was too late. Rachel gave birth first, and a few days later, Catherine had her twins." My jaw clenches on instincts. I don't want to hear this as much as I need to know. I must have the full story. Reaching over the covers, Ray hands me a photograph of my mom being wheeled into the labor unit, her face contorted in pain and hands on her stomach. The angle is askew, the edges of the image darkened as if taken from a distance. A paparazzi shot I quickly realize.

"The Hughes had been so careful to keep their pregnancy hidden. I thought it was to give them privacy, but Nixon confessed everything to me in the waiting room. He's infertile, and Catherine's twins weren't his. She'd been having an affair with a man called Fredrick Walters." I have to release Ray's hand before I crush it. Bile rises in my throat, my stomach rolling.

"No, that's not-" I hug my sides. I'm going to throw up all over the expensive carpet. Huxley showed me the news reports I purposely avoided. I knew a fraction of what happened to Avery during her childhood but I never wanted to face it. Knowing the full history and bullying her for it anyway would have made me another level of evil. Feigning ignorance was the only way I could keep living with myself. But I can't be ignorant now, not with what Ray is implying. "That bastard is not my father," I ground out.

"No, he's not." Ray shakes his head in the low lighting. I peer up, the room spinning around me. My breath is raw, all of my focus on not passing out and Ray's hoarse voice. "Catherine Hughes had twin girls. Rachel and I," he pauses, a tear leaking from the corner of his creased eye. "We're your parents, Wyatt. You're our son."

"I don't understand. I... but I've always..." My brows crease. It's a lot to process, but strangely not as far-fetched as it would have once been. I can see the truth in Ray's pale green eyes. "Did you not want me?" Ray's hand reaches out once more and this time, he squeezes me tightly.

"There hasn't been a single day we haven't prayed for you to come back to us. Rachel couldn't speak without crying for years. Everything we've built has been with the idea of you returning home." The weight on my shoulders shifts. It doesn't lessen, but becomes displaced. Those words are all I've ever needed. To feel truly loved, to be wanted. I knew there was a disconnect in the way Cathy and Nixon treated me. Like a shiny object, a stand in for the cameras. I knew it instinctively when they brought Avery home. How they doted on her, the love they had for her. It was different, special. And exactly the way Ray's glazed eyes are looking at me right now.

"I need you to tell me everything," I say, the connection through our hands becoming increasingly tender. This is my father. My old man. The beep of the machine beyond his bed becomes louder in my ears, like a gong counting down. What if they hadn't come for me? Would I have been too late?

Ray reaches a shaky hand for the decanter on his side table. He almost knocks it flying, his eyes too glazed with tears. I stand, rounding the bed and easing the glass from his fingers. After pouring the amber liquid into an empty tumbler beside the ashtray, I hand it to him and resume my seat. Ray manages to offer me a small smile, lifting the glass to his aged lips and downing the liquid.

After he gives a stiff nod, he starts talking. A tale of blackmail and kidnapping. Fredrick Walters isn't only an abusive father, but a psychopath. When Cathy refused to acknowledge him as the real father and her lover, he stole Avery from the hospital. The other girl was 'hidden', as Ray describes it, for her own safety before Walters could return. And me? Nixon wove a lie about the Perelli's which saw both Ray and Rachel spending time in federal prison and I became a ward of the state. Nixon paid off the right people to have me, placing me in his protection. I was their stand-in for the media. A poster child for those asking what happened to Cathy's baby bump.

"I've always known." I have my own whiskey now. I down it, but I don't taste it. It's so obvious now. How Avery was instantly welcomed and showered with compassion. Even though I received anything I desired, it was only material objects. She got Cathy's sole affection. Nixon's undivided attention. I was the fraud. "Instinctively, I always knew I was for show. They dressed me in the best clothes and paraded me around for the cameras. And for what?"

"To distract anyone watching." Ray's body is slumped now, his energy quickly waning. I see the affect this talk is having on him, and why it took so long for him to be able to face it. Standing, I place his hand over his abdomen gently. I tower over the bed, a stoic statue of muscle in the shadows. Ray, my father, is a fraction of the man I wish I could have met. He drank himself to death waiting for this day.

"What if Walters decided I was his other child and tried to abduct me too?" I breathe, my head swimming with questions I'm running out of time to ask. Ray smiles weakly, his low laughter quickly becoming a cough.

"That's the beauty of their plan. You were never theirs to lose." It is genius. Swallowing hard, I lean over to place a kiss on Ray's forehead and leave him to rest. My feet are wooden as I cross the room and slip out . Rachel is waiting in the hallway, not having moved a muscle. One look in her brown eyes and I crumble into her embrace. I cry into her shoulder as if I'm not at least a foot taller, holding her rounded body as tenderly as my shaking arms will allow. For Ray, I can be strong, but with Rachel, I just want to be held.

AXEL

The tightened grip on my pencil isn't enough to keep my eyes from drooping. We've been at this for hours. Listing all of the places Wyatt might go after Dax's cousin was unable to trace his phone. Either it's off or Wyatt's fiddled with the location settings. Huxley's in the process of enlisting a PI, but strangely no one works this close to midnight. Working at the table beside me, Garrett is leaning his cheek on his palm and doodling on the edge of my page. Avery fell asleep a while ago, collapsed in a heap with Dax idly playing with her hair. It takes effort to hide my jealousy, wishing I was on comfort-Avery duty.

"How come she didn't go to college with Meg?" Garrett mutters and my head jerks upright. I follow his eyeline, noting the gray sweatshirt pooling around Avery's body. It must be a special edition for the team, given the pair of crossing lacrosse sticks and ball beneath the college logo. I offer Garrett a half-assed shrug.

"Would you pass up the chance to do classes in your sweatpants?"

"I already do classes in my sweatpants," Garrett huffs through his nose. If he was expecting a more in-depth answer, he should ask me in the morning. "Do you believe she liked being alone, or do you think she didn't realize she was being isolated? She sure seemed to warm to us quickly." I frown, no longer seeing the list on my page. The words blur into one large smudge. Maybe Garrett actually has a point...

"What's happening in that head of yours?" I look him over, not liking the dazed expression on his handsome face. His hair is scruffy, hanging low over his forehead.

Garrett finally takes his eyes away from Avery and smooths a hand over my thigh. "Just thinking."

"That's dangerous," I snort. But now Garrett has powered up the train of thought, I struggle to rein it back into the station. Could it be true? Everything Avery thought was her choice, her preference, was actually part of some plan? Nixon makes the rules and she's blindly followed them. I have no doubt that her safety was paramount, and that he must have been backed into a corner to put her in Wyatt's care, but the gravity of the situation starts to dawn on me. Just how long has Avery been in danger, and if Fredrick Walters was just released from prison earlier this year, who or what exactly was she in danger of?

Tossing the pencil aside, I give up. Wyatt isn't in any of the hotels we've called, the places he used to visit with his mom on rare weekend trips, any of the police stations or hospitals in the state and definitely not back at Hughes Manor. The gates are still being watched by the press, waiting for any sign of activity. There's a webpage dedicated to live streaming it. Wherever he is, Wyatt doesn't want to be found. I sigh, lowering my head onto the desk. All the while, Garrett absentmindedly strokes my leg, lulling me into a sense of solace.

The next thing I know, a firm hand is nudging my shoulder. My breath catches and I quickly wipe away the drool from my mouth. It's seeped into my page, smudging the little progress I had made. Or lack of progress, I suppose.

"Hey," Huxley shakes me a little. "Wanna grab some ice cream?" I smile lazily, shifting the heavy weight of Garrett's body leaning against me. He continues to flop onto me until I lift and carry him over to the bed. Within seconds, he's nuzzled in behind Avery, who's still folded over Dax's sleeping body. I shake my head, wondering how many kinks I'll need to massage out of how many necks in the morning. Huxley is waiting for me in the hallway and hands me a bundle.

"What's the occasion?" I yawn, dragging the hoodie over my shaved head and stuffing my feet into the sneakers. Whether because I'm tired or just because I'm me, Huxley tucks my arm into the crook of his and walks me to the elevators.

"No occasion. Just need some air." True to Huxley's words, the fresh air is just what we needed, despite the city fumes and never-ending ruckus of noise. The ice cream parlor is down the road and conveniently, open all night. It's a quaint little spot, apparently frequented by lovers huddled at tables for two against each wall. No one spares Hux and I a second glance as he opens the door for me, our arms still linked.

At some point over the years, I think the guys went from humoring my need for physical touch to enjoying it themselves. None of us have any other family. Not a mother waiting with loving smiles, not a father to throw a ball around and share a bear hug and drink with. We only have each other and the blurred lines I've thrown us all over.

Stepping up to the waiting assistant, I'm distracted by the colorful decor, a mural spray painted by a street artist behind the counter. A sweet, sugary scent of ice cream mingles with the faint aroma of freshly baked waffle cones, making my mouth water. We're worlds away from the heavy tension of the hotel room we were in not even ten minutes ago.

"Cookie dough for my friend here," Huxley nudges his head my way. "Mint choc chip for me." He gives me a small grin and I look away. When our cones are ready, we take them to a small table near the window. It's pitch black outside, our own reflection looking back at us beneath a large neon sign. I take a lick of my ice cream, savoring the creamy flavor. Cookie dough is my favorite.

Huxley stares down at his own ice cream, swallowing thickly and breathing shallowly. I watch him closely, that familiar tension starting to creep back in. Without Avery here to force feed him, he seems to be struggling. I reach over and take the hand which is gripping the table's edge.

"Thanks for this. I needed a break."

"I figured," Huxley replies, his eyes flicking up with a mixture of concern and affection. Slowly, he licks the side of his scoop as if it pains him.

"It's a good thing Garrett isn't here. He'd have taken that out of your hand and shown you how to eat it." Huxley attempts a smile but his sigh is telling. Eventually, once the ice cream has begun to drip onto the table, he turns and drops it into a trash can. I don't comment, watching his reflection. It seems less direct that way, allowing the silence to settle and Huxley to find the words in his own time.

"I've never experienced anything like this before. I know I need to keep up my strength, to be ready for the next time Avery needs me. But I have absolutely no appetite. It's as if I know I'm going to fail her anyway, so self-sabotage is the only way. It gives me an out, to blame it on not being nourished enough rather than admitting that," he sucks in a breath and looks at a spot on the floor, "that I'm just not good enough."

My fingers twitch around his hand. The shock in Hux's own face tells me he hadn't come to that conclusion before it tumbled out of his mouth. Withdrawing from my hand, he roughs up his blond hair, a way to hide behind his good looks even though no one else is paying attention to us.

"You think I'm being an idiot," Hux tenses his jaw. I jerk back, affronted. As if I would be in any position to judge anyone.

"I think we're used to playing our roles. They're so ingrained in us, we're all struggling to break out. Who am I if I'm not Garrett's shadow? If I'm not the pet who follows him around, begging for scraps of his attention? It's an adjustment for everyone. You're so used to being the one we turn to for protection, but you're not the only one looking out for Avery. All of us are."

"Maybe that's the problem," Huxley's features harden. "She's getting what she needs elsewhere." It dawns on me that I wasn't invited out merely for a break. Hux needed someone to talk to, and he chose me.

"The only competition happening here is in your head. But I know that's easier said than heard. Take your time. She isn't going anywhere."

Huxley doesn't look convinced. I finish my cone, wiping my mouth with a napkin. Changing perspective takes time. A few months ago, I thought if I lost Garrett's attention, I would lose the foundations of who I am. The other Shadowed Souls would always be there, but Garrett is the one who's coached me through each nightmare, who's cradled my head while I've cried and who's talked me down when I thought anger was the answer. Healing is a process, and I'm finding I'm stronger than I thought I was.

"Give yourself some grace, Hux. You've been through something traumatic," I gesture towards his collarbone where a circular scar hides beneath his hoodie. "When we go back to Waversea, why don't we get you booked in with the therapist?"

"And until then?" he asks, his voice hardened. Sure, that's over two weeks away but as it stands, we don't know where we'll be day to day. Huxley's mansion and Hughes manor are off limits for obvious reasons, and the only other one of us with a childhood home to return to is me, which is a hard no on all fronts. Not while my mom still lives there.

Around us, customers arrive and leave, low chatter filling the parlor. Huxley's gaze has drifted south, his face fallen as if he might never smile again. I sit a little straighter, the faint chill from the open door keeping me awake.

"You've spent years holding us together. Take some time off, let me take the mantle for a while." I lean back in the chair, looking over my own reflection once more. Did I just offer to keep Avery safe, keep Huxley on track, keep looking for Wyatt and keep Garrett in check? Yeah, I believe I did.

"You're changing." Huxley's comment isn't an accusation, but a dawning awareness. I give him a slanted smile, feeling my dimple pop. Yeah, I'm changing and amongst the chaos, it feels good. Beneath the table, Huxley's shoe knocks against mine. It's the only sign he's heard me, his gaze distant whilst staring at the napkin dispenser between us.

"Um, excuse me?" a guy says. I twist to see his pinstripe uniform, recognizing him from behind the counter. "This was just handed in. Apparently you dropped it on the sidewalk?" He hands me a small card, seeming just as confused as I am. Glancing at it, my eyes narrow.

"Sorry, where did this come from?" The guy, no more than twenty two with a face full of acne, twists his lips.

"Some dude just brought it in. Said the two in the window had dropped it and I should make sure you got it back. I don't know," he shrugs and slinks away. I'm left with my arm outstretched, sensing Huxley's curiosity beating against my back. Keeping myself turned, I bring the card closer and quickly read the words scribbled on the back of a manilla business card from the hotel we're staying at.

'Surprised you'd leave her alone.'

"What is it?" Hux has leaned closer, eager to see over my shoulder. I tuck the card into my palm and turn back, trying to calm the upkick of my pulse. It's a bluff. Avery isn't alone. Garrett and Dax are with her. But the message is clear. Someone who knows us is nearby, watching our every move. Just when a sense of normality had settled.

"Hux," I state with a surprisingly level tone. "Calmly stand up and follow me." He does just that, his chest bumping my back as we exit the parlor. I try to be vigilant against the darkness of night, but in the street, there are too many places to hide. Too many headlights and signs blinking in my face, the world slipping by in a slur of images I can't process fast enough. Halfway down the street, I come to my senses and ask Hux for his phone. I left mine back in the room.

"Come on Dax," I mutter into the receiver, willing him to pick up. The tone rings out and I curse, trying Garrett next. The same happens and I tell myself that's good news. They're all still wrapped around Avery, blissfully unaware of the tremors taking over my limbs. Approaching the hotel, a puff of smoke appears just as I turn the corner. I slam straight into Dax, his cigarette dropping to burn a hole into my hoodie sleeve.

"What the hell are you doing here?!" I shout too loudly as true panic sets in. Dax's eyes widen, his head tucking guiltily.

"I just stepped out for a smoke," his voice trails after me as I stride across the foyer and jam my finger on the elevator button. Within three seconds, I change my mind and start vaulting up the stairs. "I was right outside. What's happening?"

Dax chases after me. I hear Huxley in tow, grumbling that it can't be good. The business card is crumpled in my hand, the edges digging into my palm as I push myself up the stairs, two at a time. My heart is pounding, each beat echoing in my ears louder than the sound of our footsteps. Dax's questions are a distant buzz, my mind focused solely on reaching Avery and Garrett.

"Explain what's going on!" Dax demands, his voice strained with growing alarm. Huxley's heavy breaths follow close behind, urging me to keep moving. Breaching the second floor hallway, I pause long enough to give Dax the business card.

"We're still being watched," I manage between breaths. Dax turns the card over in his hand, Huxley getting his first real look. Both of their faces pale. Pushing passed me, Dax rushes down the hallway whilst trepidation slows me down. Dax fumbles with the keycard, his hands trembling until the light blinks green. I wait for his face to light up with relief, for him to look back with an eye roll and curse me out for giving him a false scare. When he doesn't, I shove my way into the room.

The room is dark, save for the soft glow of the city lights filtering through the curtains. Garrett is sprawled out on the bed, Avery nestled against his side, still deep in sleep. Oh thank fuck.

Relief washes over me, but it's short-lived. Huxley flicks on the lights, and I notice the window slightly ajar, the curtains fluttering gently with the night breeze. It was definitely closed before I left with Hux, and given that there's a flat outcrop of roof where we overlook the main lobby, it's not totally ridiculous to think someone could have been out there.

"Check the bathroom and wardrobe," I instruct, my voice steady but firm. "Make sure no one else is here." Dax, Huxley, and I move swiftly, checking closets, under the bed, and eventually the bathroom. There's no one. But the unease remains, gnawing at my gut. Someone was here, and they wanted us to know.

I return to the bed, kneeling beside Avery. She stirs at my touch, her eyes fluttering open. "Hey," she murmurs sleepily. "What's going on?" I brush a strand of hair from her face, forcing a smile.

"Nothing, sweetheart. Just a little scare." Huxley grunts as if he would have given a different response, but doesn't speak. Maybe he's taking this two-week break from being in control seriously. Garrett rouses then, starting to tug at my hoodie. I hold back from his forceful invitation to join them on the bed, triggering his curiosity. He sits up and narrows his eyes.

"What happened?" Huxley hands him the crumpled business card. Garrett's expression darkens as he reads the message, and Dax nods to his unasked question, his face growing grim. "You think he...he was here?" Garrett narrows his eyes on the open window.

"Undoubtedly, but why? He was right there, so close to-" my throat closes as I look down at Avery. A tiny body lost within a baggy sweatshirt, her blonde hair is pooled across the pillow, her eyes sunken. An angel whose wings are weighed down by misery. I long to free her of those weights and watch her soar. "Why would he get so close and just walk away?"

"Because he's taunting us," Huxley huffs loudly. "Because he fucking can." Swiping his hand out, a vase of flowers flies across the room and shatters against a wall. We all take notice at the same time, eyes widening at the battered yellow roses now littering the carpet. Roses the exact shade of Avery's hair. Roses that weren't sitting on the desk when I left it. A symphony of groans echo between us.

"We're in over our heads," Dax mutters, looking at each of us in turn. He starts to pace while I remain on my knees, happy to hold Avery's hand. She blinks over at me with large, blue eyes.

"We can't ignore this," Huxley states, dropping into an armchair.

"We need to inform the police," I add. There's a few groans at that suggestion, but not from Avery. Her thumb strokes the back of my hand and she nods slightly.

"He's never going to leave me alone, is he?" She asks. Her voice is so quiet, I believe they were for my ears only. Garrett's grip tightens around her regardless.

"We won't let anything happen to you," I promise. It didn't exactly answer her question, but I can't lie to her. I don't know how or when Fredrick will strike and that uncertainty is tearing me apart from the inside. This taking charge business sucks and I glance up to Huxley. The gravity of stress is weighing on him heavily, his frown bordering on a scowl.

Garrett and Dax exchange a glance, a silent agreement passing between them. "We'll take shifts," Garrett suggests. "Make sure someone's always awake and alert."

Huxley nods. "Good idea." The tightness in my chest eases a fraction. *Finally*, some cooperation. He pushes up from his seat. "I'll inform the hotel security. We'll go to the station first thing." I agree. There's no use going now - we don't have a crime to report aside from a bit of writing which we can't prove was actually from Avery's stalker and a vase of flowers that were smashed before being inspected.

True to his word, Garrett sets up a watch rotation and double-checks the locks and windows. There's no use asking Huxley to hire a security detail; we've had that fight before. Since the phone lines at Hughes Manor were tapped, resulting in him being shot, Huxley doesn't trust that anyone is above being bribed or blackmailed. The more people involved, the more certain he is that harm will follow. I sit with Avery, pulling her close and feeling the steady beat of her heart against mine.

"I'm scared," she admits softly, her voice trembling.

"I know," I whisper back, pressing a kiss to her forehead. "But we'll get through this. One day, your biggest worry will be what to have for dinner."

"I can't wait for that day," she exhales loudly, snuggling into me. I hold her tightly, unable to let go. I've dived headfirst into the bond Avery has offered me and whereas typically I would be overthinking and freaking out, it's too easy to become wrapped up in her. I'll protect her at all costs, happy to have these moments of solace as my reward. To prove a point, Garrett nudges my arm with his head until he can also shimmy up my body. Scratch that, moments wrapped up in the three of them make it all worth it.

AVERY

The Deja vu of standing in the police station entrance ended once we were shown through to a meeting room. A box of silver and gray, a steel table and hard chairs. The officer was dubious about letting four men accompany me inside so we settled on just Dax coming in whilst the rest gave statements elsewhere.

Three hours of repeating everything from my childhood, about Fredrick's arrest, my adoption, my mom's death, the attack at Huxley's mansion and ultimately Huxley being shot. It all had to come back out, stopping short of the discovery of mine and Wyatt's genetics. Whatever reason my mom and Nixon had to keep that truth hidden, I need to respect it. Something bigger is at play which I don't want the police meddling in. Chances are I'll end up just as a case file forgotten on a desk anyway.

"So, just to clarify," Officer Dunsford repeats, leaning closely to his recording device. "You believe your biological father is stalking you, but you do not think these letters are of any concern?" He withdraws pieces of paper from his brown folder and spreads them out in front of me. Photocopies of Mr. XO's letters - all of the ones I handed over to the police anyway. A few I kept back, tucked away. The emotion that bleeds from the letters seems personal and the connection I've built in my head between those words and the author...it's not something I can or want to explain. Instead, I cross my arms defensively and sit back in the chair.

"Again, no. I know my...sperm donor," I use when 'father' seems too far a stretch. "I know how he talks." That's all I wish to say on the matter. Officer Dunsford presents a detailed timeline, pointing out the coincidence of dates the letters were received and Fredrick Walters' prison privileges increasing. The more freedom he had to writing supplies and sending mail, the more letters happened to appear in my name. But I'm not listening. There's no way a man who used to spit on me and curse that I ruined everything good in his life, would write that I'm the light on his darkest day. It's not a truth I'm willing to face.

Instead, I shift my focus. Dax is a stoic, solid presence beside me, yet to react to anything he's heard inside this room. He most likely thought they knew it all from my transcripts, but the thorough officer opposite has brought some things to light that not even I wanted to remember. I wonder if Dax will keep it all to himself, an unspoken secret between us. Or if he'll wait for a quiet moment out of my earshot to tell the others. They tell each other everything. Perhaps I want him to. It would save me repeating it all, if this unconventional relationship we've fabricated is going to continue growing and deepening. Fuck it, I'll just ask for a copy of the recording and get it over with.

"Miss Hughes?" Officer Dunsford frowns. Dax's knee nudges mine, snapping me back to the present.

"Huh? Sorry, what was that?"

"I asked if you feel safe in your present company or if you feel the need for police assistance? Given the seriousness of your father's past crimes, we could arrange a surveillance team to keep watch?" I cringe at the word 'father'. Fredrick doesn't deserve any such title. A shudder runs through me and the fight I previously held onto so dearly, vanishes. This is it. I will always be connected to him. *His* daughter. *His* victim.

"Um, I'm not..." I chance a look at Dax. His icy blue eyes are open and inviting, awaiting my response. He doesn't try to sway my decision or tell me what he thinks best. He's following my lead. "I'm not too sure where we're going to be staying," I admit. "It's something I need to discuss with..." I swallow, "with the others. We're a team, you see?" I look away from Officer Dunsford's penetrating gaze.

What must he be thinking? A naive young woman escorted into the station by four six-foot jocks in sweatpants and expensive sneakers. I glance at the mess of papers covering the table, subconsciously picking out words like abused and exploited. I must look like a poster for women with daddy issues clinging onto those who shower me with attention. I suddenly feel small, my shoulders rounding.

"We're done here," Dax announces, curling a hand around my waist. He tugs me to stand, not waiting for Officer Dunsford to stop flustering around with papers and rushed questions. Instead, Dax stops us by the door, casting a strong glance backward. "Avery is more than safe in our company. If you want to help, locate Nixon Hughes. We haven't been able to contact him for weeks."

Despite digging my heels in, Dax maneuvers me from the room to the trio waiting on a row of seats. I glance at each of them curiously. They've been trying to call Nixon for me? To come and collect me or to get answers. I dread that it's the former. Garrett is on his feet first but somehow Axel closes the gap between us quicker, grabbing me in a tight hug. Garrett tries to tackle me free but Axel turns, shielding me with his body. It's a display that probably shouldn't be happening in a police station, but I can't help the smile that melts away my worries. Being in my head for too long is never a good thing.

"It's not been that long," I murmur against Axel's shoulder.

"Longest three hours of my life," he replies, his lips against my temple. Releasing me, I catch Officer Dunsford's slightly raised brows as he exits the room, a brown folder tucked until his arm. Dax steps into my vision, blocking out all else.

"We need to talk," he addresses everyone. A lump lodges in my throat. He's going to tell them everything I said now?

While I'm standing right here and there are police officers milling around the desks at Huxley's back?

"What's happening?" Huxley stands last, creating a circle of muscle with me stuck in the middle. A cage, but not one I'm eager to escape.

"It's time to decide where we're going and what we're doing here," Dax's voice and face remain impassive. "They want to set up surveillance for Avery, but we can't do that if we keep hotel hopping. Are we even going back to Waversea after the holidays?" I gasp, stunned Dax would even consider not returning to school. He can't drop out, not after all of his hard work and not for me. My protests die on my tongue when a hand smooths around my hip. I don't even look at who it is since others are quickly joining. Soft touches giving as much comfort as they seek.

"My place is already a bust. He's been there," Huxley grunts with annoyance. "And Hughes Manor is obviously out."

"Dax and I don't have homes to return to," Garrett lifts one shoulder and twists his lips. All pairs of eyes turn to Axel. I quickly discover the hand on my hip is his, since it tightens enough to bruise.

"Fuck no," Axel shakes his head. "No, no. Absolutely not." No one speaks but their expectant looks are loud enough. Licking his lips, Axel ducks his jaw inward. "Dudes, my mom still lives there. You can't ask me to...I can't just stroll in and...She still holds her parties, you know." My heart cracks in two at the look of pain contorting his face. Turning fully, I cup Axel's cheek and bring his forehead down to mine.

"You're never going back," I breathe. Axel sighs but he leans into me, using my body to hold him upright for a moment. Then he steps away and I twist my head. "And no one is dropping out of school. I've lost enough of my life to this asshole. He doesn't get to dictate what we do."

"Here," Huxley removes his wallet from his pocket and hands it to Axel. I track the movement with suspicion. "Find us a cabin or similar. Something discreet, book it out for at least a couple of weeks and don't tell any of us the details until we get there."

"It's as good an idea as any," Dax adds, looking to me for confirmation. I nod, a determined set to my jaw.

"Agreed. We need to stay off the radar for a bit." I suppress the pang of guilt at the use of 'we', despite this whole problem stemming from my past. These men could walk away and no one would blame them, except themselves. Axel takes the wallet, a reluctant acceptance in his eyes.

"I'll get it sorted." Mentioning his home has clearly unsettled him, but he does his best to hide it. Perhaps I just know where to look. The tension between us is stifling, even though our unity in that moment is evident. These men know what's at risk, what's at stake, and they're staying with me anyway. Turning away from the officer's desks, we head for the exit.

"While Axel is sorting out accommodation, we should talk security," Huxley says, his voice firm.

Garrett nods. "Some cameras and motion sensors would be a good idea. And dare I say it," his dark eyes sweep around and his voice lowers, "it might be worth thinking about having a weapon on hand." I sense his discomfort. Garrett was visibly spooked when he found the gun at Hughes Manor. The Shadowed Souls may have a reputation with their fists, but they are way out of their league if we're thinking about strapping knives to our thighs and packing pistols. However, Dax scratches his chin in thought.

"I can reach out to my cousin. He might be able to get us what we need, quickly and discreetly." I swallow hard, the weight of the situation pressing down on me. I don't want them to be forced into people they're not. I don't want them crossing a moral line for me, but the alternative is worse. I can't let them come to any harm - again.

With the seriousness of what's to come sinking in, we push open the main doors and are temporarily blinded by a harsh winter sun. Once we step out of this station, we're on our own. Forced to face my past to secure a future where laughter and sweet kisses are an hourly occurrence. I focus on that image. A pile of limbs weighing me down each morning, of clinking wine glasses over board games and movie night huddles. We have to have a goal, and we can't afford any mistakes.

But we don't get that far. "Miss Hughes?" a voice calls out laced with urgency. I look beyond the walls of muscle behind me to see Officer Dunsford rushing forward, a phone in his hand. Raising a brow, I slip free to greet him in the hallway. "I managed to get a hold of your - of Mr. Hughes for you." Placing the phone in my hand, I just frown at it. Then my arm snaps and I press the receiver to my ear.

"Hello?"

"Avery," Nixon says with a hint of relief. I'm frozen by a flood of emotion ranging from elation to where-the-fuck-have-you-been.

"Nixon?" I question, still playing catch up. "How- Why haven't you answered any of my calls?"

"It's safer that way," Nixon quickly snaps back to his usual authoritative self. *"But judging that this call was just passed over to me from a police station, I'm guessing things have escalated."* My thoughts collide, one not able to finish before another takes over in a bid to be heard. Who's passed the call over, how much does Nixon know, what is he not telling me? I stutter over myself, turning away from the officer.

"What things? What's happening here?!" I rush to ask. I'm quickly shut down.

"There isn't any time," Nixon snaps impatiently. The surprised expression on my face is met with a showcase of darkening scowls by the Shadowed Souls watching me. *"Listen carefully. I need you and Wyatt to pack and meet me somewhere safe. I'll send you an encrypted email with the location. The password is Cathy's special place. It's imperative you drive here, no airports. Only tell Wyatt where you are going, avoid public places and hotels. You can't trust anyone."* Despite the phone being pressed uncomfortably against my ear, the voice speaking might as well be a million miles away. None of the familiarity I'm used to is present, as if I'm talking to a stranger. Nixon has never been so formal with me, which only heightens my panic.

"Okay but, um," I struggle to comprehend and I hear Nixon's frustration. Might as well just come out with it.

"Wyatt isn't actually here right now..." Nixon's scoff holds a heavy dose of disappointment.

"Well who the hell is with you?!" He asks and then groans as if he already knows the answer. Nixon may be showing many sides of his personality I've never known before, but he will always be well versed in Wyatt's lifestyle choices. His words become gritted, as if he's speaking through his teeth. *"Just tell me your safety is being taken seriously."*

"It is," I reply immediately.

"Fine. Pass me over to whichever one of Wyatt's goons you trust the most. The one you think would value your life above their own."

My eyes widen, sliding over each of the Shadowed Souls. They're all waiting, a mixture of arms crossed and hands stuffed in pockets. Garrett's smirk is a distant memory, replaced with a firm line of seriousness. It doesn't suit his handsome face. Axel's hazel eyes are glazed with worry, his shoulder leaning against Dax. Inhaling deeply, I pull my bottom lip into my teeth and make a decision. The one who would value my life over his own. Extending my arm, I pass the phone over.

"Nixon wants to talk to you, Huxley."

WYATT

Routine comes easy at the Perelli's. I wake to Rachel handing me breakfast in bed, and follow her around like a lost puppy for the rest of the day. She has a specific way of doing things, from the way she folds fitted sheets to ticking off the extensive planner on the kitchen wall. One that's filled with medical visits for Ray and abbreviations I don't understand.

I spend most days in the background, trying to make myself useful but knowing there's only so much I can do. Ray's condition hangs over the house like a dark cloud, a constant reminder that time is slipping away. Time I never had. Rachel handles it all with a calm efficiency, unaware of how her strength draws out my weakness. She's the rock I'm forced to lean on, but I see the strain in the lines around her eyes, the way her hands tremble when she thinks no one is looking.

Aside from attending to basic chores and fixing things that are in my wheelhouse, I've taken to sitting with Ray. We haven't spoken much more about Nixon. I can see the toll it has on him to voice his hatred and I don't push him. Instead, we settle into a comfortable silence, the kind that comes from mutual respect and understanding.

Sometimes, when the pain isn't too bad, he'll tell me stories about his younger days, about the deals he made and the enemies he outsmarted. His voice is weaker now, but there's still a fire in his eyes when he talks about the past, a flicker of the man he used to be. I soak it all in, desperate to know everything.

But those moments are becoming rarer. Most of the time, Ray just stares out the window, lost in his own thoughts. He can barely manage to lift his cigar to his lips and puff anymore, but I've walked in on the nurse doing it for him a few times. I suppose it's not like he's going to get any better.

Charlton's visits are the worst. They remind me of the finality of everything, the fact that no matter how much we try to pretend otherwise, Ray isn't going to be around much longer. The lawyer is always polite, professional, but there's a coldness to him that sets me on edge. I don't know what he and Ray talk about behind those closed doors, but I can guess it's about wrapping up loose ends, making sure everything is in order for when the inevitable happens.

Every day that passes, Rachel seems more distant, more focused on her planner and the never-ending list of things that need to be done. I try to draw her outside, suggest we go for a walk, but she always declines. "There's too much to do," she says, and I don't argue. We're all just going through the motions, waiting for the moment when everything changes.

And then, one morning, the routine shatters. It's a quiet day, the kind where the world feels like it's holding its breath. I'm in the kitchen, half-listening to the soft ticking of the clock, when I hear Rachel's voice, sharp and panicked. My heart stutters in my chest, and I drop what I'm doing, rushing towards Ray's room.

The nurse, who's been at the mansion all of five minutes, is fiddling with tubes and the monitor screen. She's pale as she whispers the words that hit me like a freight train. "You'd best say your goodbyes."

Rachel, for all her strength, seems to be running on autopilot. Her movements are mechanical whilst taking Ray's hand and holding it to her chest, her smile not reaching her eyes. I want to touch her shoulder, tell her I'm going to help her through this, but the words stick in my throat. Instead, I just stand there.

"My boy," Ray murmurs. I glance up and frown when I see he's not talking to me. His free hand is shakily waving at nothing in the corner. At my confusion, the nurse slips around the bed.

"It's the last stage when the delirium hits. He won't be with us much longer." I thank her quietly, swallowing past the lump in my throat.

When my mom- no, when *Cathy*- was killed and I received that phone call, I went into a numb state of shock. I thought once the shock had passed, an abundance of emotions would hit me. But they never did. I remained numb, my grief hidden behind a wall of denial. It was too easy to pretend she was still at Hughes' Manor fawning over Avery. That her weekly call would come in at any moment and she'd nag my ear off about maintaining my grades and not getting swept up with parties or girls.

There's no pretending here. I can't ignore or suppress the regret swirling within. It's one of the few times I haven't been trapped within my anger, and it fucking *hurts* like hell. Ray calls out to me again so I swap sides, taking the hand he was waving around.

"Hey, I'm here," I try to smile and fail. Ray smiles though, his glassy green eyes not meeting mine but wandering over my head somewhere.

"Ahh, Wyatt. My boy. My son," he babbles. I catch myself on a sob, using every fiber of my strength to not twist my face away. There's no running from it this time. I need to acknowledge what's happening. "Remember the lake? Our fishing boat is ready. I bet we'll catch a big one today." I squeeze Ray's hand tighter, the first hint of wetness dropping onto my cheek.

"We'll catch the biggest fish," I manage to say somewhat evenly. Despite sighing contentedly, Ray's smile slips. His head lolls and with more clarity than I thought he is capable of, he looks at Rachel. His loving and devoted wife. She doesn't offer any words, allowing the silence to be filled with her admiration for him. Small circles of her thumb stroke the back of his hand, a serene look on her pretty face. She's already made her peace with this, and I know Ray is only holding on for me to do the same.

Leaning down, I put my mouth beside Ray's ear. "It's okay, I'll look after her. I'm here now."

"Such a good boy," I hear faintly whispered back just as the heart monitor blares. One continuous noise ringing in my ears which might as well be a knife to the heart. I forget who's just died here, a crashing weight slamming down on top of me. I remain like that, hunched over and gasping for air until the nurse gently pries my hand off Ray's. I flinch and notice that crushing weight wasn't a figment of my imagination, but Rachel squeezing me tightly. I twist as best I can, drawing her into my arms.

As I hold Rachel, her body shakes against mine, but she doesn't cry. Her breaths are shallow, and I feel her fingers digging into my back, like she's trying to anchor herself to something solid, something real.

The nurse moves quietly around us, shutting off the machines, her face a mask of practiced compassion. I catch a glimpse of Ray's lifeless form on the bed, his features softened, almost peaceful in the stillness of death. A man who was a fleeting presence in my life, but has shown me more love than the bastard who raised me. The ache cracking open inside of me is akin to a void, swallowing every trace of guilt, anger, and regret I'm clinging onto. I know what's coming before that familiar numbness spreads, consuming my soul in its wake. It takes conscious effort to not take the easy road out and fully desensitize myself, for Rachel's sake. I have to keep my promise and take care of her, starting with calling Charlton. He'll need to handle Ray's assets and make sure Rachel is secure.

But for now, we stand in the quiet room, the world holding its breath once more, and just cling on to each other.

HUXLEY

"*I expect you to leave immediately.*"

Those were Nixon's last words to me before he hung up the phone and left me standing in a police station, riddled with responsibility. I know how he talks to Wyatt, and I didn't appreciate being ordered around like a piece of shit on the bottom of his dress shoe.

Neither do I need threatening to keep Avery safe. I will care for her because I have a deep and destructive infatuation, not because Nixon failed to do so. She's an addiction, consuming my every waking thought. Is she happy? How can I make her so? Yet the harder I try, the tighter I squeeze, the more she slips away and into the arms of others.

And so the spiral continues. Three days of travel thus far. An unhealthy amount of procrastination, a lack of nutrition other than protein shakes and energy drinks, the occasional cigarette from Dax's stash, and the repetitive open road passing beneath the SUV's tires. I grip the steering wheel, the stitched leather pushing against my palms. Around me, low giggles, soft snoring and the hum of music blend into one. I'm not a part of it. I'm the chauffeur. Just the driver, but at least I have a use.

A turn-off ahead becomes visible, the one I'm supposed to take. My thumbs twitch on the wheel with indecision. How can I trust Nixon's decisions from here on out? What if his safe house is anything but? These are the types of thoughts colliding in my skull, my fingers hovering over the indicator. Perhaps the true chance Avery has at safety is if I take her somewhere no one else would think to look.

Torn between my head and my heart, I push the pedal to the floor and spin the steering wheel right. A shitty Toyota sounds its horn behind as I cut straight in front, crossing the three lanes and making the turn just in time. A shudder runs through me, my arms tingling with trepidation. The image of a blue eyed, blonde hair temptress appears in the rearview mirror, her face open and curious. I'd expected a series of slaps and screams to accompany my hesitations, but instead, there's an eerie silence. An unspoken agreement to leave me in control. At least Axel tried to take my burdens, even if it was just for one night.

Coming to an intersection at the top of the ramp, I take the exit directly opposite and re-emerge onto the interstate.

A heavy pressure pushes down on my chest with anxiety. For a fleeting moment, freedom had seemed so close. We could have all run away, found a place to be whoever we wanted. As long as we were together. But like the call of a darkened cage, something was pulling me back. Or rather, someone.

I'll collect Wyatt and meet you there.

Nixon's words repeat on a loop. It's that glimmer of hope which keeps me on the instructed road. There was no time to write down Nixon's directions and he expressly told me not to. No one can know, and I'm certain that if Avery wasn't his little princess, she'd be making this journey on her own. At least with us, she has fall guys. Men that will jump in front of bullets and offer themselves up in her path. Now all we need is Wyatt back in our fold and I'll be leading the petition to get the fuck out of dodge.

Ever the diligent one, Dax turns to me from the passenger seat and looks too closely at my rigid, stiff posture. "Let me know when you need a break. I'm happy to take over so you can close your eyes for a while," he offers.

"The open road is the best kinda medicine." I reply hollowly, settling down further and attempting to spread my legs comfortably. I'm protective of who drives my SUV at the best of times but when I've got precious cargo, I don't trust anyone else. I need the control. Hands seize my shoulders with a reassuring squeeze.

"Pull over Hux," Avery purrs. "We all need a break." I shake my head.

"We'll be at our next stop soon." Catching sight of her concerned gaze in the mirror, I sigh. "I'm good guys, I promise. It's just up the road and then I'll rest." Those nimble hands stay on my shoulders, kneading gently until my spine eases. At the sight of my small smile, Avery relaxes back into her seat, returning to Garrett's shitty jokes and Axel's lingering touches. Miles of open road fly by easily after that.

The sky is a murky purple hue by the time I pull into a motel's tiny parking lot. The shabby, run down building has stepped straight out of a serial killer's catalog. Two storeys high, looming and depressing. Only a handful of curtains have a dim orange glow behind them, the rest of them in complete darkness.

Switching off the engine, Dax slips out of the passenger seat first and audibly cracks his back. His afro is getting longer, starting to poke out in all directions. In a pair of low-slung sweatpants and oversized tee, he heads to the reception. I'm last out of the cab, standing off to the side. Avery stretches, each movement tracked by the hungry eyes of Garrett and Axel lingering nearby. Her legs are hugged by green cropped leggings that clash with an orange hoodie I'm sure isn't hers, judging by the excess of material around her petite body. Her hair is trapped in a low ponytail, wisps of blonde spread over her shoulders.

Dax is back within a few minutes, his voice carrying as he approaches. "They've only got rooms with double beds. I got two and figured we'll rotate." Tossing Axel a pair of keys, Dax tries to give me the other set.

"I'm gonna hang out here for a while, stretch my legs and that." I hold my hand up, glad when Dax buys it and shrugs. Avery tries to protest but she can't hide the yawn that pulls at her mouth. "Head to bed, Little Swan." Summoning a smile, she pauses to kiss my cheek before being led away by Dax. I stare at their joined hands, a pang of jealousy hitting me where it shouldn't. Somehow while the rest of us weren't looking, Dax has stepped into the role of Avery's comfort blanket.

Once the door clicks closed behind him, I slump against the SUV and cross my arms. Exhaustion racks my body, both from being vigilant and from the mental stress I'm once again carrying. When it's quiet and I have time alone like this, I tend to wonder how things would have been if we'd all simply been students - invested in partying too hard, passing midterms and competing for Avery's attention.

Not that it matters anyway. We're here, miles from any type of world we know and secretly competing anyway. I'm surprised by the lack of fight Garrett puts up, slipping into the room next door with Axel just behind. I scoff to myself, clenching my jaw. I've been driving for nine hours straight, proving my vow to watch over her and that's exactly what I'm going to do. From this vantage point, no one can creep up on the room and no mysterious notes can be put beneath the door without me seeing them approach.

There were fifteen or so rooms on each level with metallic steps leading to the second floor. The walls probably were a fresh cream when originally painted in the 60s, but now the only hint of color is of the brick peeking through the peeling, murky exterior. Most of the windows are too dirty to see through and those earlier feelings of trepidation have come back with a vengeance.

Reaching through my open window, I lean inside and pull out the pack of cigarettes Dax has most likely left behind on purpose. I've noticed he hasn't been smoking half as much since Avery appeared in our lives and I thought he'd kicked the habit, but the small box in my hand says otherwise. We all need our vices.

Flicking open the lid, I find seven sticks and a yellow lighter inside. Should be enough to get me through the night since there's no coffee machine in sight. Leaning against the driver's side door, I pop a cigarette in between my lips and light it. The bitter taste is akin to acid but I need something to keep me going. Increasingly, the thought of digesting actual food has been making me feel more and more nauseous, so I've resolved to small scraps here and there at Avery's request. Once only the cigarette butt remains between my fingers, I flick it across the concrete and climb back into the SUV.

In the glow of a streetlamp, I shift my eyes from window to window across the two floors, checking for curtain twitchers. A brass number six hangs on Avery's door with a paper 'Do Not Disturb' sign swaying slightly around the handle. There's several cars in the car park, most of them old bangers so my white, shiny SUV sticks out like a diamond in a pawnbrokers. Another good reason for me to play bodyguard out here, otherwise my beloved vehicle would more than likely be missing by morning.

Pushing my seat back to gain more leg room, my eye-lids begin to feel heavy. I give my head a fierce shake, my wavy hair whipping around my cheeks. Pulling another cigarette from the pack, I tease my tongue between my teeth at the thought of the offending tar-like taste filling my mouth again. Of the damage I'm doing to my insides with more nicotine than nutrition fueling me.

I'm doing it again - just like I told Axel. Sabotaging myself by making sure I'm in no fit state to guard anyone, putting both Avery and my brothers at risk. As if having a reason to blame my misgivings on will make it easier. But what choice do I have? Avery needs protecting and if that means I lose myself in the process, so be it.

***

A repetitive buzzing stirs me into waking, my head suddenly jolting upright. It's pitch black within the cab, except for a glow emanating from my door pocket. Grabbing my phone, I blink against the sleep blurring my eyes, fumbling for the ceiling light.

Avery: *Are you planning on staying out there all night?*
Avery: *There's a Huxley-sized space free in this bed.*

I run a hand down my face and glance around the inside of the SUV. A perfectly rounded hole is burnt into the edge of my leather seat, the offending cigarette butt lying by my foot on the floor. *Fuck.*

Avery: *My backside is cold. Stop watching the room and come watch me sleep instead.*

I freeze, staring at the screen for a while. Apprehension fills me, a stirring in my chest coming to life. I'd forgotten what it felt like. To be desired and for me not to be doing all of the chasing. Damn, it makes me feel *wanted.*

Avery: *Please, Hux. My butt is getting frostbite.*

I snort on a laugh that had no business escaping me so easily.

Huxley: *I'm fairly sure you can't get frostbite on your ass.*
Avery: *Are you willing to run that risk? It would be such a waste of squats.*

Looking outside, there's been no change. The streetlamps glow in each corner of the building, illuminating what would be the darkest areas. There are no new vehicles, suggesting only those who had already checked in are present. It would take a psychic to have known where we were heading, especially since I didn't check into the motel Nixon suggested. My small act of defiance, just in case my instincts about Nixon happen to be right. Three dots appear on the screen.

Avery: *I'll make you a deal. You come in here or I'll come out there. I've been in your trunk, I'm certain we could both fit in it.*

It's not the worst idea, but I'm already popping the door open. Avery tiptoeing around a parking lot in the middle of the night is just asking for trouble.

Huxley: *Don't you dare move.*

The motel room door opens as I step onto the mat, but it's not Avery standing there. Dax is fully dressed with his sneakers tied. Prying the keys from my hand, he pats my shoulder. "Let someone else have a turn at being the hero." Exiting, Dax strolls over to the SUV and takes my place. I watch him with my brows furrowed. Is that what everyone thinks I'm doing - stubbornly taking on the role as Avery's hero in the hopes for some praise. Wait, is that what I'm doing?

"M-m-my butt," Avery groans from the bed. "It's s-so cold." I swiftly close the door. Two steps into the room and with my T-shirt lifted several inches up my body, Avery's hand flies into the air. "Wait! There's a cost for getting in this bed."

"A cost?" I echo, fully frowning now. The hand that halted me fists with one finger left pointing. I follow its direction, noting a Styrofoam container on a wonky plastic table.

"We were going to invite you but you were asleep. So I got you a doggy bag instead." Avery says nonchalantly and rolls over in bed. My gut drops. I was supposed to be keeping watch, and they *left*, got food and snuck back in. What a shit lookout I am.

And more than that, how could Dax of all people be so reckless? He's meant to be as level-headed as me. But then I hear Avery shuffling around, wiggling her butt in the air for my attention and I instantly know how Dax let himself slip. Avery is a minx, and she always gets her own way every damn time. I mean, look at us, wrapped around her little finger.

"You can get in the bed once you've eaten," she purrs. I hear her smirk and visualize her bobbing eyebrows through the darkened room.

"You've tricked me." My voice is thick. It's no longer just the boy's betrayal churning my gut but also the food I'm now having forced upon me. I turn to face out of the window, peering the outline of my SUV through threadbare curtains. That's why Dax left. He knew Avery could make me stop and care for myself when his demands couldn't. Best intentions or not, I'll beat him for it in the morning.

For the longest time, Avery remains in bed. Snug and safe beneath the covers, watching on intently. She doesn't rush me. Slowly, I settle into a chair that creaks beneath my weight. That's a feat, considering the muscle mass I've lost. I pop the container, instantly hit with the smell of fast food. A club sandwich and fries. It curdles my stomach, filling my senses as I try to breathe my way through it. Tentatively, I take a small bite and chew it for far too long. When did something so simple become so triggering?

"You're doing amazingly," a gentle voice comes from across the room. There's not a trace of sarcasm or judgment in Avery's tone. Only pure acceptance. My heart lifts and a grin spreads across my face, hopeful that she can keep this up. Pushing me along the road of recovery whilst I'm dragging my feet. I know I can't lean on her too hard, can't depend on her to help me if I won't help myself.

Avery waits a whole ten minutes before moving to join me, sitting opposite to eat the other half of the sandwich I've started pushing around the box. Baby steps are better than nothing, I suppose. After I fail to suppress a yawn, Avery curls her hand beneath my bicep and tugs me over to the bed. I stand beside the mattress, breathing heavily through my nose. There's no hesitation as Avery undresses me piece by piece. I don't stop her, despite my instinct to squirm and shy away. I'm a fraction of the man I used to be. Of who I'm supposed to be. Soft fingers lift to the rounded, pink scar below my collar bone.

"I'll help you heal," she declares. I take her hand in mine.

"It's already healed." Bringing her knuckles to my lips, Avery tilts her head with a hidden roll of her eyes.

"Not internally." I feel the guilt she still holds. What I wouldn't give to take it from her, to make her understand I'd take that bullet a thousand times if it means she's unharmed. The feelings we started to build on haven't lessened, but they haven't had a chance to thrive either. Avery follows my train of thought. "I'm still here for you."

"I know."

Cementing a clear boundary, Avery lifts the oversized T-shirt, which smells like Dax, over her head and leaves her underwear in place. Crawling into the bed, I take my cue. She feels incredible, her warmth soaking into my front. Slipping an arm beneath her head, I hug Avery tightly, inhaling the sweet scent of her hair and skin. She's just as smooth as I remember, just as perfect.

"I've missed this," I admit quietly. Avery shifts onto her side and leans into my chest. My hand dives into her long hair, our lovers embrace easing a lump in my chest. "Thank you, Little Swan." Slowly, brick by brick, my wall starts to disintegrate. That distance I'd put between us, thinking it was what Avery wanted, seems irrelevant now. She called and I came running straight back. "I'll make the effort to be better."

"I don't need you to be better, Hux. I just want you to be yourself again. I miss your smile. The way it lights up the lighter flecks in your eyes. I want to hear your laughter." She's not the only one. I miss smiling too.

"I'm getting there. This helps." Pressing my lips against her temple, I settle into the rhythm of Avery's breathing, surprised with how quickly sleep takes me.

AVERY

"Absolutely not."

"Oh, come on Peach, you have to! It's truth or dare, not *'truth or if you feel like it'*." Garrett whines from the passenger seat, turned all the way round to face me. I cross my arms defiantly and shake my head.

"There's no way I'm gonna sit here butt-naked for the entire journey. I'll take a forfeit." Garrett's eyes darken and I gulp loudly, wondering if I should have just done the damn dare. Axel whistles low from the seat beside me.

"Alright, fine." Garrett smirks. "Flash the next vehicle." He points at my window. Rolling my eyes, figuring it's not as bad as it could have been, I shift up onto my knees and lift my top, pushing my breasts against the cold glass. A truck passes, the driver's eyes popping out of his skull as he hollers and beeps his horn. Cheers fill the SUV, the boy's loud whooping drowning out my giggle as I re-adjust myself into my bra and settle back into the leather seat.

"Your turn, Garrett. Truth or dare." He replies dare without hesitation, practically bouncing in his seat. Looking around the moving car and across the backseat to Dax, who shrugs uselessly at me, I see a Cheeto roll out from under Huxley's driver's seat. I managed to get him to have a handful for breakfast this morning, or so I'd thought. Maybe he just hid them all under his seat. Lifting it to inspect the orange cheesy stick, there's enough hair and fluff stuck around to make it perfect.

"Eat this," I lean forward to hand to Garrett. Without a second's hesitation, he throws the chip into his mouth and swallows, making us all gag. "Ew!" I squeal, suddenly very aware I've had my tongue in that mouth multiple times and I don't know what else he's had in there. Garrett smiles widely at a shuddering Axel, possibly thinking the same, and winks back at me. It's Dax's turn to play next, to which he chooses truth.

"Pussy," Garrett mutters. "Okay then. What's your biggest regret in life?" Dax tilts his head to stare out the window, staying silent for so long I don't think he'll answer.

"Seeing the most important woman in my life in harm's way, and doing nothing to stop it." He finally says in a tiny voice. Axel's concerned gaze catches mine in a side glance. Reaching over him to grip Dax's bicep, I pull him over to rest his head in Axel's lap. That way, I can stroke his hair and bend over to kiss his forehead. I only know a little of Dax's past, the way his mother raised him to be both empathetic and strong, with a mention of various boyfriends in her life. Did someone hurt her, and worse, was a young Dax forced to watch? I swallow against the lump in my throat, not wanting the answers as much as I need to know them. Now isn't the time. Dax is quiet but there's so much torment behind his blue eyes. I'll speak to him properly when we're next in private.

For the time being, I settle for stroking his afro through my fingers, driving in silence until Garrett reaches over to turn up the radio. Dax's eyes have fluttered shut, although I reckon he's more in deep thought than sleeping, giving me a chance to study him up close. His square-shaped jaw chiseled from granite, the thick eyelashes fanning his cheeks, his skin is a smooth shade of mocha. I don't drink coffee often but I'd take a Venti of Dax any day of the week. Axel catches me staring, his expression too knowing.

Refocusing on the landscape outside, I find we've entered a small town. Each building is a different color, signs hanging from each doorway to show a particular trade. The road is tarmacked in various places, only to patch up the potholes where and when needed. There's a handful of people on each sidewalk and not many cars on the road, making our stark-white SUV stick out like a nun in a brothel. Heads turn as we pass, children staring at us like aliens.

"Last stop before we enter no man's land," Huxley announces, pulling into a gas station.

"Psst," I whisper into Dax's ear as his eyes fly open, arresting me in a cerulean prison I would gladly receive a life sentence for. A smile takes his face hostage, those full lips close enough to make me blush. The SUV pulls to a stop, breaking the moment between us as he sits up and winks at Axel. Now we're both blushing, much to Dax's amusement.

We all exit the car and stretch our legs, backs and necks. Axel takes up the position of filling up the SUV with gas, much to the female attendant's delight. It helps that this state is unaffected by the winter and he's shirtless. Rather, it's balmy with only a slight breeze trailing by lazily.

I lean against the trunk to appreciate Axel's broad chest and washboard abs too, remembering just how lickable every inch of him is, both what's on show and what's hidden in his sports shorts. His thick thighs are poking out of the bottom, well-defined calves flexing with each movement. Once finished, he heads inside the small shop to pay with Garrett right on his heels. I notice Huxley standing off to the side in the way he likes to distance himself, looking down the street. His blond hair is wisping around his face, but fails to hide the contemplative look pulling at the corners of his mouth.

"Hey," I approach, tapping lightly on Huxley's arm. "What's wrong?" Twisting his head, I see the true weight of Huxley's stress. It rings his eyes, ridding every trace of decent sleep we got last night. Snuggled in Huxley's arms felt like home, even on the lumpy mattress and singular sheet we shared.

"Nothing," he shakes his head and looks away from me again. There must be something truly fascinating about the view down the street, even if I can't see it. "I just...Never mind. Don't worry about it."

"Talk to me," I urge gently. Arms wind around my middle and I feel Dax's hair tickling my neck. Whatever look he gives Huxley, causes the larger man to sigh. I ignore the rise of his wide shoulders, and how even with minimum food and exercise, he's still a beast of muscle.

"I'm concerned about blindly following Nixon's instructions," he says sheepishly. Ducking his head, Huxley chooses not to watch the confusion pass over my face.

"You think Nixon would...trick me?" It's my turn to frown, the words feeling bitter on my tongue. "I mean, I've been wondering what we're going to find at this safe house but I have no reason to think it'll be anything less than a fortress. Nixon has always kept me safe."

"Mmm," Huxley scratches his stubbed jaw, "but why? I'm not trying to be the bad guy here Aves, but you're not...you're not his daughter. You're the product of his wife's affair. If I was him, I don't know if I'd be so," Huxley struggles to find the right word, "accommodating."

Ouch, I think to myself, but manage to withhold from flinching. I may not be genetically tied to Nixon but he's been my rock for all these years. Someone I can always rely on to look out for my best interests, even when his decision to send me to Waversea seemed questionable. I have to trust him, otherwise the fragile foundation of who I've built myself up to be will slip out from beneath me.

"What are we talking about?" Garrett appears, his inked arms wrapped around two paper bags overflowing with snacks. I note an unhealthy amount of beef jerky poking free. Dax raises his head from my shoulder but doesn't release me.

"Hux is expressing his concerns for our destination."

"The safe house?" Axel steps into Garrett's side. Now we're a huddle, all crowded on the street and blocking out onlookers. Taking my hand, Axel presses on. "Why haven't you said this earlier?"

"Yeah," Garrett scoffs, "like *before* we sat in a car for three days."

"I, um, well," Huxley clears his throat. His brown eyes settle on me, a guilty shrug lifting his shoulders. "Nixon said that Wyatt would be joining us there. I didn't want to pass up the chance to get to Wyatt, to bring him back into our dynamic. But now, the closer we get..." Huxley looks around nervously, keeping his voice low and rubbing his chest in a circular motion. "I'm worried it's a trap."

A heavy dose of reality hits us all at once. I wish the street was busier, if only to give me something to look at. A distraction. Instead, I'm left staring at the patchwork road, fixated on the unfurling of dread within. I trust Huxley implicitly, but he's wrong this time. He has to be. It's all that overthinking, causing him to see villains where there are none. Axel is first to break the silence, his chest rising and falling in a steady rhythm.

"Whatever we find and whatever happens, Avery's safety is paramount." I'm suddenly no longer a part of this conversation. Hell, I feel like I'm eavesdropping, despite being held there by Dax's arms and Axel's hand. A soft tumble of laughter escapes me.

"Guys, I assure you, it'll be fine. We can trust Nixon. I'd bet my life on it." The resulting glares I receive would be enough to make a lesser woman shrink away. Luckily, I've had years of therapy and self-defense lessons to stand tall, even when my chest is crushing inward. The safe house is in reach. Nixon will be there with Wyatt. We can finally get some answers, some clarity, and that isn't worth walking away from now. For better or for worse, I need to know what's at that safe house.

MEG

Huffing, I lean my forearms on the timber railing and stare longingly at the horizon. Another day in paradise, and I can't wait to leave. A salty breeze tingles my nostrils on a deep inhale as I try to ease the tightness of my chest. Rhythmic lapping of waves in the distance are only broken by the occasional squawk of a seagull hovering overhead and diving into the sea in hunt for its breakfast.

Rounding the porch, I hop down the steps and walk across the golden sand. My sneakers sink slightly with each step towards the shore as I enjoy the cool gentle winds before the sun rises and brings another fresh winter's day with it. The sky blends from the palest pinks to purest blues. I pull out my phone to take another photo for the 'Avery

Collection.' The day I can actually share the images with her can't come soon enough.

Avery would love it here, and I wish for the millionth time I'd begged my mom to bring her along. Every mile that stretched between us had wretched out another piece of my heart, leaving a trail from here to Waversea. With the days of driving and three motel stopovers, I lost track of exactly where we actually are, and the lack of signal doesn't give any indication either.

Checking my ponytail is secure, I adjust my sports bra and stop at the water's edge. Pushing my phone back into the hidden pocket of my black lycra leggings, I roll my neck and start to stretch my arms in large circles. The freezing water laps against my shoes, a shiver rolling through me. I'll be sweating soon enough. Stepping forward into a lunge, I continue my usual lacrosse warm-up routine, making sure every muscle is properly stretched for my morning jog.

Starting slow, my feet slap against the recoiling waves as I follow its edge along the darkened sand. Before long, my arms are pumping and breath is visible in heated puffs. My calves burn as I push harder, my mind drifting to wonder what Avery is up to right now. I hope she's managing to hold her own with a house full of men, although even Wyatt had seemed to be softening last I heard.

I skid to a halt seconds before colliding with the high metal fence marking the edge of the rental's property. I'd been so caught up in my thoughts, I almost hadn't noticed I'd already ran the two miles. Looking up, I see a bird fly overhead, having the freedom to travel beyond the fence.

Not for the first time, I wonder if this 'vacation' is more of a prison sentence.

Checking the time on my phone, the screen lights up with a notification of thirty seven voicemails and my stomach plummets. *No.* I've trekked up and down this godforsaken beach countless times trying to find a signal, and somehow I missed it. Tears fill my eyes as I desperately tap the screen but I have no bars again, I can't even listen to the voicemails Avery has left. Falling to my knees in the sand, I hover over the device and pray for a miracle. I just need to know she's okay.

As the sun peeks over the sea, I give up hoping I might get to hear my best friend's voice and rise with my mood soured. Banishing my troubles, the only way I know how, through exercise, I push myself to my limits running back towards the house. My feet fly over the sand as the sun rises higher in the distance. Returning to the spot I stood in previously, I bend to rest my hands on my knees, gulping in mouthfuls of air and focusing on evening out my erratic heartbeat.

Glancing back at the beach house, I can't help my scowl. No matter how much I've tried to enjoy myself, a niggling feeling is keeping me in a constant state of unease. In all of its luxury, something about the house feels off. Mom makes good money, but surely almost three weeks here has amounted to a small fortune, yet she still hasn't given a clue as to when we might finally return home.

Both stories of the exterior are painted a powdered blue, with the loft bedroom I have claimed poking out at the top. Huge bay windows cover every back wall, ensuites included, to allow all rooms the spectacular views of a seaside sunset. I don't know why we needed to travel so far for a rental with six bedrooms but maybe it was all that was available at such short notice. Noticing mom's shadow pass by the kitchen window, I head back inside.

"How was your run?" Her cheery voice greets me as I walk straight for the refrigerator, grabbing a bottle of water and downing half its contents. Already in her bikini top and linen shorts under a silk kimono, mom places a frying pan onto the electric hob. The rich glow to her skin from sunbathing blends with her free-flowing brown locks.

"Same as yesterdays." I answer blandly, leaning against the granite counter and deciding to keep my voicemails secret for now. With the protective way mom's been acting, she might confiscate my phone if she thinks I can use it for anything other than photos.

Contrasting with its surroundings, the interior of this place is magazine worthy. Pristine white cupboards line the kitchen wall, a double door chrome refrigerator matching the shiny appliances covering the counters. A shiny glass table fills the center of the room with enough chairs to seat twelve comfortably.

"Well don't just stand there. Fetch the bacon and eggs." She orders, despite the fake smile she's grown accustomed to wearing lately. Huffing, I take my time guzzling the rest of my water and refilling it from the filter jug. Returning with her ingredients, I hop up onto the counter beside the hob and watch her make our breakfast.

"Mom, seriously, when can we leave?" Her smile falters as she clenches her jaw impatiently.

"I will have to return to work soon, but not yet. You should be having the time of your life. No school, no stress. What more could you possibly want?"

"Avery mainly. I didn't realize we'd be gone so long and it's almost Christmas. I can't spend the entire festive season without–"

"Oh, enough of this!" my mom shouts, her brown eyes flickering furiously at me before she schools her features. Sighing deeply, her smile reappears and she leans over to grip my hand. "I'm sorry. I just want to enjoy our time away from reality. As soon as I hear we can return, we will."

"Hear from who?" I question, jerking my head back. This is the first time I've heard her speak of anyone else being involved with our beach getaway. Judging by the roundness of her eyes, she hadn't meant to say that out loud. Flicking her hand through the air to end our conversation, mom busies herself cracking eggs into the pan while I hop down to make some coffee. It's not like I have anything else to be doing.

"What shall we do today?" Mom asks. She plates up scrambled egg and bacon onto bone-china plates and carries them over to the table with a stack of buttered toast. Following with two mugs of steaming coffee, I sit beside her and open my mouth with some sarcastic reply when a sound cuts through the silence. A sound that's not the sea lapping or a seagull, not the coffee machine or water heater humming.

No, it's the screech of tires on the dirt path. Mom looks at me as if I'm about to bolt. She's right.

Flying out of my seat, leaving the screams of my name behind, I rush to the front door and fling it open. There's a monstrosity of a white vehicle looming over my mom's mini, something akin to a SUV before it was modified. A faint ringing in my ears is too delayed, because if there was any danger, I've just ran into the center of it.

Luckily, the only danger here are the rasping coughs of those falling out of a white SUV, holding their noses and wafting their hands through the air. Garrett slides out of the cab last, looking over at me innocently.

"Bad beef jerky," he shrugs, as if that explains everything. I watch the scene as an outsider, the others coming back to themselves one by one. Large blue eyes flick up to the house and then land on me, flowing blonde hair falling about her slender shoulders. My heart swells, a choked gasp escaping me. *Avery.* I'm running again, vaulting the porch steps and wrapping my arms around her middle. She's here, she's really here.

GARRETT

"**B**each!" I yell, shoving past the girl's mini reunion. Avery is stunned, asking what the hell Meg is doing here in a harsher voice than I'm sure she intended. Ignoring Huxley yelling about helping with the bags, I push my legs at top speed toward the shore. Pulling my phone and Air Pods from my pocket, I chuck them into the sand for someone else to pick up and charge into the water. The cool water splashes around the heavy pound of my sneakers, my shorts and tank top sticking to my body as I dive into the water.

It's fucking freezing. I surface on a gasp, my lungs burning as if they are shutting down, but I don't care. Flopping back, I spread my arms and legs wide like a tattooed starfish bobbing on the water. I'm the tide's bitch now. Throwing me around,

I make my way back to the sand, only to twist and toss myself back in to do it again.

"You're going to catch your death in there," Axel shouts, his bare feet sinking into the wet sand at the shore's edge. My phone and Air Pods are in his hand and I chuckle gently to myself.

"We've been stuck in a car for days. Let loose and come catch my death with me!" I wave at him, diving beneath the next current. This time, I don't fuck around. I swim hard, pushing my limbs to their limits, fighting an invisible force. Salt burns my eyes, a darkness beckoning me to carry on. It's chaotic on the seabed, rocks and sand being hurled around, small creatures not standing a chance. I only come up briefly for air and sink straight back in.

Being trapped in Huxley's SUV has been slowly chipping away at my sanity. There's only so long I can be the Garrett everyone adores. Cracking jokes, inventing games, boosting morale. I'm like a Ken doll, plastering on a plastic smile for everyone else's benefit. At some point, even my energy wains and I need a respite. A reset. This right here, swimming through the turbulence, this is for my benefit.

Some way out, I breach the surface to see a huge wave about to crash down onto my head. Being pulled underneath forcefully, I tumble and roll, fighting to find the way up. The tide steals the sneaker from my foot causing me to shout underwater and lose precious air bubbles. Finally breaking free of the undercurrent, I gulp in air and wipe the water from my eyes to look for my missing sneaker when another wave plummets onto me. Forcing my legs to kick powerfully in time with my arms, I push myself further onward until there's no longer the sounds of crashing overhead.

The beach house and Axel's outline are tiny in the distance now, my sneaker well and truly lost. I bet some fucker finds it washed ashore and shits a brick at the custom-made high-top I probably should have laced tighter. Bending to pull the left one off, I launch it as far as I can into the vast ocean. Hopefully, the lucky son of a bitch can find the other to have a matching pair.

My limbs are aching from getting to this point of calm beyond the waves. Not wanting to waste my efforts, I take my time both floating and swimming lengths back and forth towards a fence I find down the coast. The burn of exertion fills me like my own brand of adrenaline.

I love everything about the sea, mainly the freedom it holds beneath its surface. To a boy once locked in his own house without a scrap of food to eat and the electricity cut off, all that's left is to dream. To wonder and imagine. A whole world is hidden from view, mountains and volcanoes, sunken shipwrecks, stunning displays of coral and whales that could swallow me whole. Well, that's some of the best shit to wonder about right there.

Axel's whistle carries to me in the wind, a spec of a figure waving from the beach. Yeah, yeah. Reality is calling. I turn back just as a sea turtle drifts by, lazing contently under the sun's rays. A marbled effect covers his brown shell which is smooth beneath my fingertips as I stroke it. Watching the creature pass, barely having to move its limbs, I smile to myself. That's the life - no stress or commitments, just enjoying the peace each day brings until a bull shark jumps up to eat you. Deciding turtles are my new spirit animal, I start to head towards my...whatever he is. Just Axel.

Nearing the beach, the waves begin to pick up again, helping to push me the rest of the way now I'm not resisting. Realizing I can stand on the seabed, I rise to my full height and walk the rest of the way with water slapping across my back as I go. Emerging onto the beach in my soggy socks, Axel's hazel eyes assess me with a hint of amusement. I close the gap between us, I throw myself into his body and squeeze him tight, ignoring the sounds of disgust. After forcing his hands between us and pushing me away, I smirk at his now see-through white T-shirt sticking to his muscled torso.

"What happened to your shoes?" he questions.

"Sea stole 'em," I shrug. He shakes his head at me.

"Here, take these back and go fight over a room like the oversized man-child you are." Axel puts my belongings into my pruney hands with a roll of his eyes.

"Yes, Boss." I run my tongue up his cheek, seeking out the dip of the dimples that I love. I mean, like. Mildly tolerate. Ugh whatever, dimples are for douchebags really.

"Huh. Why don't I have any?" I mumble to myself, pushing my tongue against my inner cheeks.

"Have any what?" Axel frowns, wiping his cheek dry with his sleeve. Without answering, I peer up at the building. Framed by a wraparound porch, the pale blue exterior blends seamlessly into a cloudless sky, a picturesque holiday home. Nothing like the safe house I was expecting. Avery is standing in a huge bay window, her arms clasped around herself. I mentally catalog which room she has chosen. Another one I'll be crashing into at my leisure.

Striding to the porch, I leave my phone on the porch swing. After noticing there isn't a single bar of service out here, I strip out of my socks and shorts, hanging them over the railing. My boxers and t-shirt remain in place, the latter glued to every crevice of my chest and abdomen. I tug on the cotton, trying to lift it away from my body. It snaps back every time.

I pause by the back door, growing frustrated when I'm spun out of sight of the windows. Axel crowds me against the wall, yanking his T-shirt over his head, sexy-boy style. I forget what we're doing, my mouth going dry of salt water until he whips my top upwards too. I cringe, slamming my eyes shut. Axel has seen my torso before, but it doesn't lessen the rush of anguish clawing at me. Dry, soft cotton, enriched with his citrusy scent is pulled over my head. It takes everything in me not to fall into Axel's chest.

Anyone else would have said I was being stupid. To grow a pair and stop worrying about wet clothing. But not Axel. He knows the sight of my body repulses me. How I despise myself so much, I don't even look in the mirror after a shower. No matter how many tattoos I cover my pathetic, scrawny body in, I can't unsee it. I can't stand it.

"Why-" I start to ask and hastily shut myself down. Shaking my head, I blink a few times, kiss Axel's cheek and rush to get inside. I hear his sigh follow me, and sink my teeth into my bottom lip. I can't go around asking questions that will lead to trouble. Questions like, *why the fuck do you tolerate me? Why do you even care?* I'm purposely an asshat to prevent anyone from caring.

Snapping back to the Garrett I allow the world to see, I salute Huxley in the kitchen. He's put himself on inventory duty in the form of a pen and notepad, searching through the cupboards and noting what supplies we have. I suppose there's not enough for five extra people, and especially not enough for me.

I locate our bags in a heap on the living room floor. Shouldering mine, I head upstairs. I had toyed with the idea of invading the space of others, but maybe instead I should pick a room for myself and see if anyone comes creeping into my bed in the dead of night. I might be pleasantly surprised or majorly let down. Only time will tell.

Opening the door of my selected room, I frown at the floral blue suitcase upon the bed, surrounded by stacks of folded clothes. A woman walks in from the bathroom, jumping and gripping her chest in fright at the six-foot, dripping wet man filling her doorway. A floaty peach skirt with a high-slit sits at her waist, a tightly fitted white top with brown waves lying on her shoulders.

"Holy crap, you scared me!" She flinches hard. I watch her find composure, my face blank. Licking her lips, the woman attempts to smile. A fake one, I might add. "It's Garrett, right? I've just met your friends; I didn't realize Avery was bringing all of you." I shrug with one shoulder, leaning against the door frame.

"And you are?" My raised brow and standoffish stance seems to shock her. A pink tinge lights her cheeks, her throat bobbing a few times. I've never seen someone struggle so hard to remember who they are.

"Oh, I'm Keren," she offers a slender hand. I shake it once. "I'm..."

"Garrett, leave Meg's mom alone," Dax pats my back on the way past. I thought he might be going somewhere, but he just walks from one end of the hallway to the other. He paces for a moment longer, and then takes a second set of stairs to the third floor where I saw Avery standing earlier. *Typical.* Turning back to Meg's mom, I notice a toothbrush and paste clutched in her hand.

"Are you leaving?" I ask, trying not to sound too hopeful. This is the biggest room with the best view. She smiles sadly, opening the suitcase to pack the items spread across the mattress with expert organization.

"I'm afraid so. Nixon thinks it's best that I return to keep up appearances - act normal." Her tone suggests she doesn't believe him. First Huxley, now Keren. I wonder how many members of the Distrust Nixon club we'd need before making it an official gang. I'd join just for the matching jackets.

"Well, I have no idea what you're talking about, but I call dibs on your room." I saunter inside, setting the black duffel bags by the bay window. Axel is back out on the beach, having removed his shoes and socks to wander along the water's edge. Smart man. He repeatedly runs a hand over his head, meaning he is deep in thought, worrying or both. I'll beckon him up here shortly and help him forget about any concerns that might be troubling him.

"Ahh," Keren says beside me, making it my turn to flinch. Sneaky little devil. "I know that look. How long have you two been a couple?" I choke on my own inhale, spluttering and spinning around to face away from the delicious view.

"Oh, no, no. I don't do monogamy." I state gruffly. Deciding to help fit the rest of her clothes into her bag, I haphazardly move this conversation swiftly along.

"And why is that?" Keren tilts her head, not bothered that I'm crinkling her perfectly folded skirts. Call it clarity or the chance to put the bullshit aside for once, I find the answer easier than expected.

"I suppose the notion of being tied to one person for the entirety of my life is ridiculous to me. People are constantly changing. Whoever I may or may *not* fall in love with now won't be the same person in five, ten years. No one will stick with me for that long anyway." Zipping her suitcase closed, I place it onto the wooden floor.

"Does being with Axel make you feel trapped?" Her brown eyes pierce my skull, reading my thoughts.

"Well, no but he's...," I chew on my lip for the second time in the last ten minutes. "Axel is precious. Far too special for someone like me to keep dragging him down. He has a chance to be free of his past traumas. I'll never escape mine."

"You're right," Keren nods slowly. My brows shoot up. No one ever agrees with me so easily. "You do seem far too damaged for a relationship. It must be terrifying to know people are constantly changing when you seem adamant to stay exactly as you are. Axel will outgrow you quickly."

My chest halts mid-breath. I stare into Keren's brown eyes, a fierce wave of resentment washing over me. I resent every fucking thing she just said. Kicking the wheeled bag towards her, it halts at her feet, my intentions clear that she has overstayed her welcome. I'm not a gentleman by any stretch of imagination but I can't stand people trying to worm their way into my head.

"You don't even know me, and you sure as shit don't know Axel. If there was someone I could see myself staying with, it would be him. But that's not who I am and he knows that. It suits us both just fine."

"Does it?" Keren doesn't look convinced, twisting her head to the window. The defensive part of me wants to whip the curtains closed, blocking her view in fear she can psychoanalyze him from here. Fuck my own; Axel's issues are sacred. I scoff to regain her attention.

"You know what, unpack your bag and stick around. I'll show you. I can be whatever Axel wants me to be to him." The words tumble from my tongue, punctuated by the thumping of my heart. The mere thought of staying in Axel's life, of being worthy of him, is uncharted territory. I know he'd accept me without question, but I also know he wouldn't push me away when I'm hurting him, and therein lies the problem.

"See, people are constantly changing," Keren smirks whilst using my own words against me. "For some, it just takes a little push." Taking the bag's handle, Keren holds back her smile as she wheels the suitcase out of the room. I stand there, gut punched with revelations I can't begin to understand, feeling like a complete simp. Three minutes of conversation and Keren has me reevaluating the walls I've spent years putting in place. Sneaky little devil indeed.

AVERY

Elation is the last thing on my mind. I want to be happy, to hug my best friend tight and not let go. But her being here only brings more confusion. As soon as she ran up to me, with her windswept ponytail, tight fitting leggings and skin damp with sweat, I knew something wasn't right. She didn't just get here like the rest of us.

"Is he still in the water?" Meg asks from her perch on the bed. I don't move a muscle, still standing in front of the large bay window, arms crossed and face tense. Although, my eyes refocus, searching for a bobbing head of dark hair in the sea beyond.

"No," I answer stoically. Garrett must have left sometime between my dark thoughts taking over and the numbness creeping up my legs, pinning me in place.

The waves break steadily, pushing the crystal blue water to roll onto a blanket of sand. I wish I could have shared Garrett's excitement and ran straight in with him. Instead, once again, I'm left feeling like I'm an outsider to my own life. The punchline of a private joke. When I came up here to seek solace in the tide, I only found a striking resemblance with the murky depths and unknown monsters lurking within.

Meg sighs heavily, shifting and approaching me cautiously as if I might jolt and make a run of it. "Aves, I'm just as clueless as you are right now."

"Are you?" I raise a brow, taking her in suspiciously with a side glance. My best friend. The girl who has been by my side every chance she could. She knows everything about me, so why am I suddenly worried I'm looking into the blue eyes of a stranger. Meg recoils in surprise, anger flashing in her delicate features.

"Are you being serious right now?!" She takes a step back from me, the distance between us seeming much more vast than a few inches.

"Yeah, I am. You were supposed to be at college, wrapping up loose ends for the holidays. Patting your team members on the back and having festive drinks with the swimmers. I needed you! I've left so many voicemails," my voice rises, accusations tumbling free. "But instead, you've been hiding in Nixon's safe house the whole time. I just don't get it."

"Now rewind for a second," Meg tugs my arm to spin me roughly. There's a subtle shift of feet in the hallway, the ghost of sneakers underneath the door jamb. I know instinctively Dax is lingering for my emotional support, trying to gauge when and if I might need him. Meg, however, is visibly annoyed by his eavesdropping and lowers her voice.

"I didn't even know this was Nixon's place until you told me. I've been stuck here with no cell reception and no idea of when I can go home. Apparently, I'm in this mess just as much as you." Meg's words sting, despite not holding as much bitterness as they could have. Sighing and looking towards the window, the ghost of a tear trickles down Meg's cheek.

All following arguments leave me with a heavy fall of my shoulders. Sensing and seeing my deflation, Meg wraps her arms around my waist.

"I think I should be the one comforting you right now," I frown, but lean into her anyway. Meg laughs, lacking all traces of humor.

"Let's press pause. I'm just glad I'm not alone anymore."

"Oh fuck, Meg." Grabbing my best friend, I tug her to me tightly. "I'm sorry. I've been so selfish. You've been stuck here while I've had...well, the guys. Now I'm giving you a hard time about it."

"It's okay," Meg tries to reassure me. Epic fail. Pulling back, I raise an all-knowing brow. Shaking me off, Meg plants herself on my side, our arms crossing around each other's backs. "Nixon has a lot to answer for."

"I'm starting to think the same," I scoff. I may be the last passenger to board the 'Nixon Speculation train', but that's only because I so wanted to believe he had no ties to this mess. I've been delaying pulling the thread that leads back to my mom's death or my traumatic childhood. I don't want to think Nixon has been aware, possibly involved, and the last truth I'm refusing to face is that my mom should have told me all of this herself. Now it's too late.

We stand together, lost in our thoughts and wishing the tide would wash away our problems. Dark, ominous clouds are creeping forward, bringing the promise of rain. That same shuffle sounds in the hallway and Meg's head tilts to the side.

"Let him in. I'm going to shower anyway." I watch Meg stride into the attached bathroom, just barely keeping the stomp from her steps. Regret clenches around my heart.

As soon as the sound of the shower hits my ears, I call out for Dax. He's by my side in an instant, strong arms lifting and carrying me to a small armchair in the corner, still facing the window. Seating himself first, Dax waits for me to curl up like a tiny creature on his lap before exhaling and stroking my hair. We slot into place, as if we've synced back into each other.

"Are you okay?" His chest rumbles beneath me. I give a small shake of my head.

"I was a complete bitch."

"She'll forgive you. We all need some clarity." I don't want to let the sadness subside so easily. It's not fair that I have Dax, that I have all of them, and Meg doesn't. In any other instance, she would wave off my concern and tell me

I deserve the way they make me feel all warm and gooey inside. That it's my time.

Twisting further into Dax's body, my face finds the curve of his neck just in time for the first of my tears to splash against his collar bone. He holds me gently, soothing my back, careful not to touch the place where he knows my linear scar is. Every so often, his lips press against my head.

The rain begins to fall, soft at first, then steadily increasing in tempo until it's a full-on downpour. The sound of water hitting the windowpane seems to echo the steady rhythm of Dax's heartbeat beneath my ear. I let the warmth of his embrace anchor me as the storm outside mirrors the one brewing in my heart. Why can't it be simple, this being happy thing? Why do I always seem to lose as much as I gain?

"I've got you, Little Swan," Dax says after a while. I lift my head, taking in his icy blue eyes.

"I know," I nod. The warmth radiating from Dax blooms through my entire body, from head to toes, a furnace coming to life. We stare silently. Dax parts his lips to say something, and he quickly bites down on his cheek and closes his mouth again. I feel like I know what it is. I can feel it, taste it. Those three tiny words are so obvious in his glimmering eyes, I can practically hear them being roared in my ears.

"Say it." I beg quietly. I need to hear it, grasp onto it. The tremble in my voice is at odds with the tightening grip of my fists in his T-shirt. "Please."

"As if you don't already know," a small smile breaks across Dax's face. He's so handsome and utterly unique, his mocha skin and blond afro. Winding my arms around his neck, I drag him the rest of the way to meet my lips.

Dax's breath hitches as our mouths meet, his warmth sending a shiver down my spine. His kiss is gentle at first, exploring. A tender touch that belies the unspoken intensity simmering beneath the surface. A slight wobble of Dax's lip, a tiny squeeze of the hand at my waist. He's savoring every second. My arms unwind from his neck for my hands to cradle his jaw, my thumbs brushing the rough stubble that Dax has procured over the past few days. It's endearing when he's not perfectly put together, when he lets his carefully-constructed walls falter. When he lets me seep further in.

The kiss deepens, and Dax's hold on me tightens as if he's afraid I might slip away. There's something both tender and desperate in the way he kisses me, as though he's pouring the words I want to hear into the press of his lips. My fingers weave into his soft, blond curls, and he groans softly into my mouth, the sound vibrating through me and igniting a fire in my core.

When we pull back, we're both breathless, our foreheads resting against each other. Dax's eyes search mine, his icy blue gaze now molten with emotion. To emphasize the words I know are coming, his hands glide beneath my shirt to rest on the circular scar littering my ribs. For once, maybe for the first time ever, I don't flinch. I'm not triggered by the pain they symbolize, by the past which can no longer hurt me. My scars may have molded me, but it's Dax who has helped me heal.

"I love you Avery," he whispers, the words finally escaping, so soft I almost miss them. But they're there, hanging between us like a lifeline, and my heart swells with a fierce sense of joy.

"I love you too Dax," I reply, my voice breaking with the sheer force of the truth. It's like a dam has burst, releasing everything I've been holding back.

Dax's smile is slow, warm, and it melts the last of my doubts. He leans in, capturing my lips again, this time with a passion that speaks of all the promises we've yet to fulfill. And as we kiss, I know, without a shadow of a doubt, that I'm exactly where I'm meant to be, in the arms of one of the men who will never let me fall. My suffering hasn't been senseless after all. It's led me here.

AVERY

The shower shuts off, bringing me back to the beach house. Back to reality. I'm practically floating as Dax rises and sets me on my feet. "Let's head down," he refuses to let go of my waist. "If I can smell food from three floors up, Garrett definitely has too."

We slip out just as the bathroom door opens. I don't see Meg exit, thinking she would rather not see my face for a little while. She waited so long to have company. She showed me that her cell didn't have any service, told me how she clung to the device each night just in case something happened to come through. And all I've done is given her a hard time and accused her of colluding with Nixon. I don't think I want to see my own face for a while either.

Following Dax's lead, we descend the two flights of stairs and do in fact find Garrett already at the head of the dining table. It's a huge slab of polished mahogany, big enough to seat us all comfortably. I take a seat next to Garrett, Dax lowering on my other side. Axel is directly opposite and after placing down a final bowl of salad, Huxley sits on his left.

"Thanks Hux, this all looks delicious," I smile warmly. Given that Keren and Meg weren't expecting us, he's managed to make a meal of buttery fried potatoes, roasted cauliflower, stuffed mushrooms and a green leaf salad. It smells incredible, infused with vinegar and garlic. I didn't realize until this moment how sick I am of fast food and greasy diners. Standing, I pick up the plate in front of Hux and start to load it with a small portion from each bowl. "I'd hate for you to miss out on any of it."

Smirks are passed around with the cutlery. Hux stabs a piece of potato with his fork and does his best to nibble on it, clearing his throat. "Are the others joining us?"

"Keren used some sort of voodoo on me and left," Garret says in time with chewing. My eyes widen and fly to him.

"She's left?! But I was in Meg's room. She didn't even come to say goodbye."

"Did she say what was so urgent?" Axel frowns. I'm trying to ignore the fact he's topless again, the panes of his chest a firm distraction. Garrett, who is currently sitting in Axel's T-shirt, is also having a hard time keeping his eyes on his food as well, which is a feat in itself.

"Something about Nixon wanting to keep up appearances. It was hard to hear while she was prying open my soul."

"You know Keren is my childhood therapist, right? That's how Meg and I met." I raise a brow. Garrett stills, fork halfway up to his open mouth. He looks like he's been struck with a blunt object, staring dully into space.

"Well," he sits upright and clenches his jaw. "That makes sense. I knew there was something witchy about her." I can't decipher the way Garrett glances at Axel, a hidden spark of light behind his dark eyes. Axel's hazel eyes are humorous and focused on me.

"Garrett has an aversion to therapists."

"She raped my mind," Garrett is starting to raise his voice when Meg appears.

"Guys! My mom is gone?! I went to check in and there's clothes and shit all over the floor!" Everyone glares at Garrett and he simply rolls his eyes. I stand, opening my arms out to my best friend.

"I know, Meg, I just heard too. I'm so sorry. Apparently your mom is following Nixon's orders too, but she should have said goodbye. That was really shitty of her."

"Yeah I know, but that...I don't," Meg shakes her head, pushing out of my hold and gripping her temples. "I've been here for two weeks. There's no phone signal. How the hell did Nixon get a message to her? And she's taken the car. What am I supposed to do when we can leave? Hide in the trunk of the SUV?"

"Don't be ridiculous," Garrett turns, dabbing his mouth on a napkin. "Avery can ride in the trunk. She loves it in there." I smack the back of Garrett's head. Now is not the time. Coaxing Meg to come and join us, Dax scoots over a seat so I can keep her under my arm. I watch Meg, picking at a lettuce leaf, and once again that clawing worry settles in.

We eat in silence. It's deafening, despite the downpour pounding against the windows. Apparently Keren felt that she would risk the slippery mud trail leading to the beach house, rather than sit with us and wait for the rain to pass. How is Nixon's influence so strong? Are we all just puppets, hooked up to his strings? Huxley's warning from the gas station rings in my ears. I should have listened to him, but at least Meg isn't isolated anymore. She has us now.

I glance at Huxley, who manages a few forkfuls of food. All for my benefit I assume. I finish my water and place my glass down with a light thud, just as a firm hand pushes down on my bouncing knee. I hadn't realized I was outwardly showing the stress building within. I peer up at Garrett from beneath heavy eyelids.

"Don't feel down Peach," he winks at me. His thumb strokes small circles on my outer thigh. "We won't be here forever, and I'll make it my personal mission to ensure you're thoroughly entertained." I find a small smile for him, marveling at how Garrett also knows the right thing to say. "With my cock."

I take it back.

"Ew," Meg suddenly perks up. She's managed to shake her anxiety for a moment, the spunky girl I know and love shining through. "Keep it behind closed doors."

"Ugh, just when I thought I liked you." Garret throws a carrot stick in Meg's direction. She snorts, lifting her spoon. I manage to talk her down from the edge just before she flings a mass of stuffed mushroom back. We need to be sensible with our food. There's no telling how quickly Garrett will eat through everything. Settling back in her seat, Meg eyes each one of my men in turn.

"So this is still happening," Meg waves a breadstick at everyone, ending with me. I smirk and nudge her shoulder. There's the overprotective bestie I've missed for weeks. Dax pushes back in his seat, humbled to high heaven since our exchange upstairs.

"It's still happening," Dax chuckles gently.

"And it's working? Like the whole sharing thing," Meg looks at each of the boys suspiciously. Axel's boyish grin reveals his dimples and I swoon. His handsomeness should be illegal.

"It's working just fine." He pulls his bottom lip between his teeth, almost giving me an aneurysm. Meg assesses the expression on my face and the rest of her unease melts away.

"Well, good. I'm happy for you all." I raise a knowing brow and Meg laughs. "I mean, I'm surprised - don't get me wrong. It's odd that there's no arguing or possessiveness."

"Oh," Huxley snorts, "there's definitely possessiveness." His chocolate eyes slide to Garrett. "Some of us struggle to get a look in sometimes." The man in question is taking a questionably sized bite of cauliflower. Shrugging, he mumbles around his food.

"I am who I am. Deal with it."

"Well," Meg rolls her neck so it clicks. Oh, she's going into full defensive mode. The breadstick turns on Garrett sharply. "All I'm saying is, if you ever put Avery in a position where she is going to get her heart broken, it'll be you who is *dealing with it*. Because my foot will be so far up your-"

"Axel sweetie, could you help me clear the table?" I flutter my lashes sweetly, belying the fact my fist is thumping Meg beneath the table. Axel smothers a laugh and immediately obliges. In fact, I think he takes great pleasure in taking Garrett's plate out from beneath him.

"Hey! I wasn't finished!" Garrett gives an impressive pair of puppy dog eyes but we're already clearing away and heading to the kitchen counter. All leftovers are either stored in tubs or covered and put into the refrigerator for later. Leaning on the counter, I stare out of the window. Slanted rain obscures the view of the sea and soaks through a pair of forgotten shorts and socks hanging over the railing. The walls suddenly feel closer, now that leaving isn't an option. It never was - Nixon has made sure of that.

Behind me, there's vague talk of board games and the sound of movement. I thought they'd all moved into the living area until a firm body steps in behind me. The height, the strong arms that round my front, the smell of citrus and spice. I exhale and lean into Axel. He doesn't say anything, simply holds me across my chest, his large hands curved around my shoulder blades.

The world around us fades as his warmth seeps into me, grounding me in the moment. A silent strength I've come to expect. After years of building myself up to not depend on others, a few months with the Shadowed Souls has brought it all crashing down. I know for a fact, I'll never be able to go back to being alone again. I won't survive it.

Axel's steady heartbeat against my back is a silent promise. I can always count on his unwavering presence. In this small pocket of calm, I let go of the tension I didn't realize I was holding, breathing out the weight of the day as he holds me close.

Sometime later, we emerge in the living area with a bottle of vintage wine in each of our hands. We'd found them in the pantry, all replicas of the ones I'm used to from Hughes Manor. I picked out a Merlot, my mom's favorite, for me and a white option for Meg. She can't drink red without passing out, and the board game covering the coffee table looks complicated enough. I don't need her drooling against my shoulder as well.

To my surprise, Meg is laughing. Garrett is sitting cross-legged on a mound of cushions, holding on tightly while Dax and Huxley try to wrestle a few free for themselves. It's a humbling scene, if only it was so simple. As soon as the rain stops, the cover of noise will fade and our awareness will return tenfold. How long will we really be safe here?

Garrett, now dethroned from his cushion tower, frowns at my lost expression. "What's up, Peach? Not a fan of strategy games?"

"This is all so fucked up," I blurt, not thinking first. Five looks of stunned confusion met my face. I chastise myself, knowing I should have kept my thoughts inside but it's been a long day. My emotions feel erratic, turbulent like a wrecking ball smashing from one side of my psyche to the other. Just when I think it's done enough damage for today, it rotates and crashes back through. Too late to take the words back now, I sigh to myself.

"You should all be free to come and go as you please. None of you would be stuck here if you weren't associated with me." Garrett is saying what a boring life that would be but my ears perk up at Huxley's deep voice. He has settled on a low armchair, but his steepled fingers and narrowed eyes command my attention.

"You wouldn't be here if we weren't associated with you, either." Tugging on his white T-shirt, Huxley bares the circular scar on his collar bone. "You'd have been kidnapped and who knows what else. It pains me to even think about it. There's nowhere else we should be."

"He's right," Dax nods from his spot on the floor, cushionless, and Axel chimes in.

"We're not going anywhere you aren't, Little Swan." He's placed down his wine bottles and removes mine from my hands. Sitting in the free space, Axel pulls me down into his lap, not seeming ready to let go just yet. My heart squeezes, fighting against beating. I could burst with the amount of love I feel for everyone currently in this room. My guardians, my saviors. My family.

"It's cute that you call her that. The whole ballet and Swan thing." Meg softly chuckles to herself, attempting to change the subject. For once, Garrett is suspiciously quiet, his gaze anywhere that I'm not. He fiddles with a small metal character on the game board, twisting his lips this way and that. Meg picks up on the shift in the air too, raising a brow at those sat opposite her. "That's why you call her that, right? Like Swan Lake?"

"Um, well," Huxley swallows thickly. My own eyebrows lift.

"Wait - it isn't?!" I don't waste my time looking around at Axel's sheepish face or listening to Garrett's weak '*of course it is*'. I lean forward to get the truth directly from Dax. He wouldn't lie to me.

"It's kinda, maybe not exactly where the nickname came from," he clears his throat and looks to be struggling to phrase his thoughts properly. "There was a time, before we knew you or what you looked like, that Wyatt used to refer to you as....the ugly duckling," he winces as he says those last three words. The guilt on his face is apparent, his fingers twitching as if he's yearning to take my hands in his. My mouth drops open. "But then we met you and it was like..."

"Fireworks." Garrett finishes for him. Abandoning his game piece and his cushion stack, Garrett slides across the floor to kneel beside Axel and me. My hand is wrapped in his in the next instant. "Beautiful fucking fireworks that burst into our lives. We expected you to realize you were meant for better than a group of tormented jocks. We thought you'd spread your wings and fly away, leaving us behind in the dust, but for some strange reason, you stayed. Our precious Little Swan who loves like there's no reason not to and dances like the world doesn't exist."

While Axel nuzzles my neck from behind, Garrett lifts my chin with his thumb and forefinger. I can't be angry with his playful demeanor and lovable smirk. I smile back and let him take a chaste kiss from me.

"You know that's all bullshit charm to get his own way, right?" Meg mutters beneath her breath, yet loud enough for us all to hear. I nod, my eyes not leaving Garrett's gleaming dark ones.

"You get used to it."

AVERY

I lie awake, staring up in the pitch black room. Meg's deep breathing is occasionally interrupted by a soft snore, probably disturbed by my fidgeting. Where are they?

It's been hours since I said goodnight to the boys, but I didn't actually believe I wouldn't see any of them until morning. We haven't slept apart in weeks. I don't even know if I can drift off anymore without heavy limbs thrown over my legs and firm chests pressed against my arms. Sure, I'm sharing a room with Meg - at her request - but I figured at least Garrett would accept the challenge with vigor. It's why I made up a cot bed beneath the bay window. I wouldn't put it past him to attempt screwing me beside my best friend.

It would likely unlock a new kink. But there's not a sound beyond the door.

"Screw it," I mutter, throwing the covers aside. Meg jolts but doesn't wake. My footsteps are silent on the carpet, and I untwist my shorts and cami as I go. Slipping out of the door, I've crept halfway down the stairs when movement reaches my ears. *Here he is*, I think to myself, anticipating meeting Garret on the stairs. Instead, a body rushes past the hallway below, not sparing a glance in my direction and definitely not seeing me flinch out of my freaking skin. Hushed voices soon follow. Stopping on the bottom step, I stand within the shadows and listen in.

"Here, I got water." Huxley whispers, slightly panting. Must be tiring being a man of his size, on barely any food, trying to creep around like a ninja.

"Is it cold? Cold is best." Garrett doesn't keep his voice so low. In fact, his tone causes me to frown further. I peek around, seeing him accept a tall glass.

"It's cold, asshole. Just give him the glass already." The pair disappear into the bedroom Garrett and Axel have claimed. I almost move to follow when another figure appears in the dark, the fuzzy outline of Dax's hair catching the low light emanating from the bedroom before he disappears inside. Now I'm the only one missing from this impromptu sleepover. I push aside my pout and step out of my hiding space with a straightened spine.

"Any improvement?" I hear Dax ask on my approach. There's a grunt, followed by Garrett's harsh tone once more.

"It's really bad this time."

My heart clenches. My feet move faster, instinctively taking me to the bedroom door. It's unfair for my mind to make the sudden jump to Huxley's presence in that room, singling him out. He's never kept anything from me, not even when I wanted him to, and the secrecy stings. I don't dwell on it as the concern in Garrett's voice sends a jolt of worry through me. His hushed murmurs continue, although I can no longer make out the words. I hesitate for a split second at the threshold, the sound of labored breathing reaching my ears.

I push the door open without knocking, my presence announced by the creak of the hinge. The room is dimly lit, the bedside lamp casting a warm glow over a chaotic scene. Axel is sitting on the edge of the bed, his head in his hands, chest heaving with shallow breaths. Dax is beside him, a hand on his back, rubbing soothing circles. Huxley stands nearby, holding the glass of water once again, his face etched with unease. Garrett is kneeling between Axel's legs, his usual jokey demeanor replaced with a frantic concern.

The moment they see me, all movement stops. Garrett's head turns and his eyes widen slightly, but it's Dax who speaks first, his voice low and calm, "Hey Little Swan, you should go back to bed. We've got this." It's like a slap in the face.

"Got this?" I repeat, my voice trembling with anger. "What happened to being a team? Axel needs me, and you want to shut me out?"

Axel's chest heaves, breaths coming in shallow, desperate gasps. Sweat beads on his forehead as his hands tremble uncontrollably. His wide eyes dart around the floor, unfocused, searching for something solid in the chaos. He clutches his chest, the sheer terror in his expression making the air feel heavy. I forget to breathe myself.

"Peach, we didn't want to worry you," Garrett says, running a hand through his hair in frustration. "Axel had a nightmare, that's all. We thought we could handle it."

"He's having a damn panic attack," I snap, moving to Axel's side. His whole body is shaking, a fine tremor that ripples through him like a wave. My heart breaks at the sight. "Axel, sweetie," I say softly, reaching out to him.

His head lifts, and I meet his hazel eyes—wild and unfocused, but when they land on me, something shifts. "Hey, I'm here," I whisper, sitting beside him on the bed and pulling him into my arms. His body is tense, muscles coiled tight like he's ready to snap, but I hold him close, stroking his head. There is a millimeter of dark hair covering his scalp. I feel it at the same time Axel does, the spikiness beneath my palm causing him to release a pain-filled groan. Anyone would think I was torturing him, and in Axel's mind, I probably am.

Shifting across the bed, I pull open a few drawers and check through the black duffle bag on the floor. The guys ask what I'm doing but I block them out, fully focused on finding the rounded head shaver that's in the bag's side pocket. Returning to the bed, I kneel behind Axel now, flicking on the same device. Working his head in small circles, I slowly but surely remove every trace of hair. I'm careful around his ears, gently tilting his head this way and that. He allows me to, his harsh breathing starting to ease as I announce it's done.

Shuddering, Axel tries to thank me. I wind around his front, my arms around his neck. His three best friends are now all standing, looking sheepish and backing towards the door.

"We'll give you guys some space," Dax breaks the silence first.

"I'm not forcing you guys out. Stay with us." Garrett shakes his head, his eyes downcast. I can't make out the misery in his expression, but I hear it in his voice. It cuts through me like a knife.

"No, Peach. You were right. Axel needs you." The three of them leave. I tighten my hold on Axel slightly, wavering on whether I should go after Garrett. He should be here. I didn't intend to take over or to force anyone out, I just wanted to be included. Axel shifts, recapturing my full attention.

"I don't-," he chokes out, voice raw with emotion. "I don't want you seeing me like this." I close my eyes briefly, a lead-like ball dropping into my stomach. It didn't occur to me that I wasn't called upon at Axel's own request. He was trying to shield me from his pain.

"I never want you to hide from me, Axel. Not ever." I murmur, pressing a kiss to his temple. Axel's breathing is deep now, his grip on me tightening as he grounds himself in the moment. I remain still, letting him draw strength from my presence. After a few minutes, the shaking subsides too.

"Do you want to talk about it? Your nightmare?"

"Fuck no," Axel bites out harshly, instantly regretting it. Pulling a strand of my hair from behind my ear, he twirls it around his finger absentmindedly. "It's hard enough reliving it in my dreams. I couldn't put it into words. They used to be memories, but more and more lately, they feature you."

"Me?" I reel back to scan Axel's face. Guilt hits me like a truck. I'm causing Axel anguish just by being in his life. "But nothing happened last night. We were all just chatting and relaxing. There was nothing to trigger..." I gesture to all of Axel. "This." Despite the state he was just in, unable to catch a breath or hold himself upright, Axel smiles. A sad, longing smile, my hair still curled around his finger.

"It doesn't work like that, Aves. The nightmares just creep up on me, usually when I least expect them. Usually when I'm at my happiest." I twist away so Axel can't see the tightness of my jaw, the harshness of my frown. Well, that's not fucking fair. My sensitive, sweet Axel. He deserves so much better. His large palm cups my cheek, turning my face back towards his.

"This is just a tiny part of my life. I refuse to give it any more of my time than it already takes. That's why Garrett is adamant on staying with me. I've normally exorcised my demons by screwing him through the headboard by now. It's the only time he's submissive to me." A blush hits me hard. I instantly warm, suddenly aware of my closeness to this stunning, muscled man, sitting in his boxers. My nipples instantly push against the thin fabric of my vest.

"Um, so," I lick my lips. "Tell me what you need."

Axel's smile grows and my heart flutters. Lowering my hand, I press it against the smooth rise and fall of his chest, reveling in it. He's okay. He's come back to me. His lips lower to my ear and I shiver.

"Dance for me, Little Swan." Blinking wide in response, Axel slips his hand into my hair and tilts my head back. His eyes are ablaze, hazel swirling in the low light. "The world doesn't exist when you dance."

I suck in a breath as Axel reiterates Garrett's words from the previous evening. The intensity in Axel's gaze holds me captive, and I nod slowly, letting the tension in my spine melt away. His fingers untangle from my hair as I rise from the bed, heart pounding with every step I take toward the dresser. I pull out a pair of fluffy socks and slide them onto my feet. The soft fabric cushions my toes as I turn back to him, finding comfort in the relaxed curve of his posture.

Axel watches me intently, shuffling back to lie in the large bed. He's propped up by cushions, his fingers steepled over his six-pack. The earlier panic is gone, replaced by a calmness that only deepens as I move into the center of the room. The space is small, but it's enough. I take a deep breath, closing my eyes for a moment, letting the familiar sensation of ballet flow through me.

There's a sudden sound, my eyes popping open to see Axel place his phone down on the mattress. A simple melody led by a piano bleeds out of the speaker. My heart catches as I recognize it as the practice music I used for the showcase during those days we were trapped in the frat house by the paparazzi. Those long afternoons confined me to dancing in the dining room, then afterward heading upstairs for an ice bath drawn by Dax and a massage awaiting from Axel.

"You kept the song?" I whisper, a lump blocking my throat. A faint, knowing smile plays on his lips as Axel gestures for me to begin. I swallow hard and start with a plié, my knees bending as I sink gracefully into the movement, feeling the strength in my legs. From there, I rise, lifting onto the balls of my feet, my body stretching upward as if reaching for something beyond the ceiling. My arms glide through, framing my face before extending outward, a fluid motion whilst the fluffy socks glide over the wood flooring.

My body spins in perfect balance, the room blurring around me as I focus on a single point—Axel's eyes, steady and unwavering. As the spin slows, I land softly, extending my leg high in front of me, toes pointed, every line of my body taut with purpose.

The room fades away as I focus on the stretch of my arms, the pointer of my toes, the way my body feels light and free, and the way Axel's eyes follow every movement. His expression softens, the remaining tension draining from his muscles. I see the weight ease from his shoulders, the nightmare retreating into the shadows where it belongs.

I let myself dance for him, just for him. The music is soft, carrying us both away from the darkness. I glide into an arabesque, my leg extending behind me, arms reaching forward as if to gather all the fear and pain, transforming it into something beautiful. The movements are gentle, soothing, meant to ease Axel into a place of peace. As my feet skim across the floor in quick, tiny steps, I feel the connection between us like a living entity. This dance is my way of telling him everything will be alright, and I know he understands.

As I finish, I see Axel's eyelids growing heavier, exhaustion finally winning over. I approach the bed, climbing in beside him, and he immediately pulls me close, his head resting on my chest. I run my fingers along the curves of his muscles, stroking the strong V disappearing into his waistband. His grip on me loosens as sleep starts to take him, the last remnants of his stress fading into nothingness. I force myself to stay awake a little longer, listening to the steady rhythm of his breath, feeling his warmth against me.

"Thank you," Axel murmurs, his voice barely audible.

"I'll always be here," I whisper back, pressing a kiss to the top of his head. "Always."

HUXLEY

I shouldn't have done it, I already know that. Avery will tear me a new one, not to mention how my brothers will react when they find my bed empty. But I can't shake the sense of relief filtering through me with each passing mile. My hair billows wildly, my arm casually tossed out the driver's side window. I hold the steering wheel in my other hand, tensing and relaxing my grip periodically.

It's the first time I've felt true freedom since waking in the hospital, a dressing wrapped around my chest and shoulder. That was the moment I realized none of us are safe, no matter where we went, and no one is off limits. Those masked men viewed us as collateral damage in order to get to Avery. The real Hughes child, as they called her.

They laughed in Wyatt's face, the mocking echo of it trapped inside my skull. They knew even then that we're still playing catch-up to understand. We're playing a game with only half of the pieces.

Approaching the small town, I pull into a street behind the main row of shops and switch off the engine. A stark white SUV isn't ideal for discretion. Running a hand through my hair, I comb back the waves into some sort of acceptable fashion and emerge in a nondescript black hoodie, camo green baggy shorts and sneakers. An empty backpack sways on one shoulder, my head kept down for the most part. I needn't bother trying to blend in. The street is just as quiet as the day we stopped here for gas, tourists just passing through. I hoped we wouldn't be sitting around, twiddling our thumbs long enough to become regulars, but Garrett's stomach isn't built for rationing.

With a plan in mind, I head towards the bank first. The small building is disguised by a brick front, a large potted plant on the one step up to the open front door. A swinging metal sign labels it's business, and once stepping inside, I see that I'm the only current customer.

I don't loiter, approaching the walnut counter. Through the glass divider, a small graying man with glasses gasps at my request, quickly directing me to a side room. The woman behind the desk there, previously filling in her account books by hand, rises in a fluster. I provide her my bank card, one linked to an offshore account, asking how much money she keeps on the premises. A quick check in her ledger provides a meager sum by my standards but I understand resources are limited.

"I'll take all of it." Twenty minutes later, I'm back on the street, my backpack weighed by stacks of cash. While the others have been occupying their time drinking themselves stupid and playing kiss chase on the beach, I've been strategy planning. What account do I have that is least traceable back to me, how can I keep us afloat without drawing attention? I've thought about it from all angles, maintaining my promise to Nixon. Avery's safety is paramount.

Next is a hardware store and it doesn't take long to fill a shopping cart. Locks, chains, and a powered drill are first. This so-called 'safe house' has yet to prove to be anything other than a standard holiday home, aside from the lack of cell signal. At least the solar panels provide electricity. I wander down the aisle, stopping at a back counter.

Behind a man with hair the same length as mine, although thinner and darker, heavy wooden shelves line the walls. Tools hang in neat rows—hammers, wrenches, and saws, each one gleaming under the flickering fluorescent lights. On one shelf, camping gear is haphazardly stacked. Bear traps, their sharp teeth glinting, are displayed ominously beneath boxes of ammunition. The metallic scent of the traps mixes with the earthy smell of leather gloves and canvas. Faded hunting posters dot the walls, adding to the rugged, utilitarian atmosphere.

I mentally catalog each one. Pointing out items to be passed over and added to the cart, I soon have a collection from tents to ropes, and a few lanterns for good measure. Call it paranoia, but I'm not naive.

Those who want Avery will be coming, even if she's a little harder to find now. We can't sit in the beach house indefinitely, praying Fredrick Walters is found and sent back to prison in the meantime. He has connections at the very least, men on his payroll. His apparent fascination with our Swan won't end just because he's incarcerated.

Weariness bleeds into my soul. I'm just a guy who wants to love a girl. Back at Waversea, the Shadowed Souls liked to pretend they were the big bad wolves. Everyone wanted to be us or be with us, but in the real world, we're nobodies. A bunch of unloved boys looking for solace in each other.

The aging man behind the hardware counter watches me suspiciously whilst holding onto either side of his opened tactical vest. I avoid his stare, eyeing the rows of tools. The small-town vibe is evident in the limited selection of items. No high-tech surveillance gear, no advanced security systems, and that's exactly what I need. An escape plan, something truly off-grid.

"Need something?" Tactical Vest asks, squinting up from the counter. His voice is raspy, like he's smoked a pack a day for the past fifty years.

I clear my throat and gesture behind him. "Yeah, I need those." I point to the row of bear traps hanging on the wall. "Four of them."

"What kind of animal are you hunting?" There's a slight edge of curiosity in his voice, but I hold his gaze steady, unflinching. I don't owe him an explanation, and the tension in my jaw warns him not to ask for one.

"The worst kind."

"Huh, bear trouble I take it?" Tactical Vest turns his head, revealing a thick mangled scar on his neck. It tugs on his skin from beneath his hair to shoulder in angry, pink welts. I swallow hard and just nod. He retrieves the traps and places them on the counter with a loud clunk. The metal teeth gleam under the store's harsh fluorescent lights, and for a moment, I imagine those same teeth sinking into one of the masked men who dared put Avery's life in danger. The thought is fleeting but satisfying.

"You'll also be needing this then." Reaching beneath the counter, he produces a length of thick chain. Each link is the size of my open hand, as if this guy actually expects me to wrangle the imaginary bear and ride it like a bull. He chuckles to himself, almost manically.

"And if you happen to come across a grizzly with a slash across his nose and a limp, tell him I want my ear back." He whips his head, hair parting to reveal that he is definitely missing an ear. Continually nodding, I take the chain and head directly for the cashier, my steps too quick to be considered casual. An older version of Tactical Vest rings me up without much fuss, and I slide the cash over to him. He eyes it suspiciously but counts it anyway, his wrinkled fingers working through the bills.

Shouldering my backpack, the weight of the bear traps and chains presses down on my shoulders, but it's a comforting weight—solid, real. Something I can control, unlike the chaos swirling around us.

An hour later, I'm back at the SUV for the second time, unloading an ample amount of grocery bags into the trunk. I've been lenient with the alcohol supply too, knowing everyone needs their own escape. Nestling the glass bottles between a tent and several layers of tarp, a sense of grim satisfaction settles over me. For the first time in too long, I feel prepared, and it feels damn good.

Once finished, I'm pleasantly surprised to feel my stomach rumble. A faint tremor, but I felt it nonetheless. I've been trying so hard over these past few days, nibbling on a sandwich or attempting some soup a few times a day. I barely taste any of it, nor do I feel the desire to eat, but Avery flashes me the proudest smile every time she catches me. As if I'm a child who deserves a gold star.

Keeping my bag of cash with me, I stop by a cafe. There are a total of four tables, each with a singular flower sprouting from a thin white vase in the center. I take a bench seat in the back, giving me a sweeping view of the window and door. The young waitress, a girl no more than fifteen, asks for my order. I inhale the scent of coffee, asking for a caramel latte. She returns in no time, after the woman training her has filled the small space with the grinding sound of the machine, and places a cup and saucer before me. The tiny packeted biscotti on the side causes me to smile. That I can manage.

I wait for the waitress' attention to be back on her boss before opening my backpack and taking out the only item left in there from the compact local supermarket. A burner phone. It takes several minutes to set up and find a signal, and my heart judders when those tiny bars appear. Thank fuck. I'm immediately typing in the phone number I memorized, hoping for this exact outcome. The ringing is music to my ears. His phone is on at least.

"Come on, you bastard," I mutter under my breath. "Pick up. Pick up." I curse as the voicemail starts to play, yet I can't bring myself to hang up. Hearing his voice steals the air from my lungs, my hand clenching on the edge of the table.

"You've reached Wyatt. I'm either busy or I don't give a fuck about what you have to say. Leave a message if you want but it'll be a waste of time."

I cling to the phone as Wyatt's voicemail plays, my pulse racing. The familiarity of his voice stings more than it should. I don't know how the others can forget him so easily. They're too wrapped up in what's new and exciting. After everything Wyatt has done for each of us, he deserves better than that. My thumb hovers over the "end call" button, but I don't press it. Instead, I swallow hard, trying to gather my thoughts. I need him to hear me. I need him to understand.

"Wyatt, it's Hux. Look, I know you're pissed. And I get it. But I just wanted you to know, we miss you. I...I miss you. There's a huge chunk of me missing and I know it won't be right until you're here. I really hope you're on your way. I don't know how much longer I can hold the fort. You do it so effortlessly." I pause, biting my lip, the weight of the distance between us physically aching.

"I need to stay close to Avery, I made a promise." My throat tightens. "But it would be so much easier if you could help me. I can't keep carrying the boys alone. And when you do get here, all I ask is..." I blink hard to keep the tears at bay. "That you don't shut me out. We can handle this together, like a te-"

The beep sounds as the message ends, leaving a hollow silence in its wake. I lower the phone, staring into my untouched latte. Outside the window, the sun dips lower, casting long shadows over the quiet street. I've been gone too long. I've enjoyed my freedom enough to contemplate if anyone would miss me if I didn't return at all. Even so, I take the small packaged biscotti and place a few notes of cash on the counter, far more than the amount of my bill, and exit. It's time to head back to my brothers, to my Little Swan, and to deal with the consequences of leaving without an explanation.

WYATT

A pitch-black moonless sky looms through the windows, but I can't close my eyes whilst knowing what's waiting for me out there. An unforgiving world of lies and deceit. The vibrations that woke me have long since gone silent, but sleep won't come again tonight.

Rubbing a hand down my face roughly, I pace in a circle at the foot of my bed, scuffing my slippers against the wooden floor. An old-fashioned clock on the chest of drawers ticks insistently, reminding me of the ungodly hour. *Tick. Tick. Tick.*

It's not the clock's fault. My life is a sham and every second that passes is a reminder of time lost. Of what I could have had if one man's selfish need to save his own daughters didn't change the course of my life. Nixon chose to protect them. Avery and some other brat, safely stashed away, whilst my face was splashed across the papers and paraded around on TV. I thought the Hughes liked to show me off. Their poster boy. Their perfect son. And none of it was real.

Groaning, I stride for the door. I can't stay in here another minute with that fucking clock or else it will be smashed into a million pieces. I refuse to be reckless in Rachel's home. Supposedly I'm the man of the house now, but I can't claim to be. Pride and love is etched into every polished surface and well-coordinated curtain. Rachel has worked too hard for a practical stranger to enter and lay claim to it.

Wrenching the door open, I decide to hunt down some of those pink pills I'm given every morning. Since Ray's passing two days ago, I started taking them in the evenings too. They must be herbal or some shit 'cause they work wonders for my stress levels, but they don't keep the nightmares at bay.

Speaking of nightmares, as I reach the top of the blackened staircase, a recurring one becomes visible at the base. The uneven shadow of a body is cast across the bottom step. A shiver rolls through my spine, a slight tremble shifting into my fingers.

At this distance, I merely see a black shape that's growing darker by the second but in my mind's eye, I can image every tiny detail. His thinning hair and gaunt cheeks, endless glassy eyes that I will forever see staring back at me in the mirror. The images get worse every time, turning him into more of a corpse. Intensifying my desire to hide under my covers and never leave.

"It's not real, it's not real," I whisper to myself as I creep slowly down the stairs in a set of plaid pajamas. As soon as my slippers hit the cold flooring, I turn right and half-run for the kitchen at the back of the house. The terrace outside the glass doors is swallowed by the night, casting everything around me into darkness. There isn't another soul about, just me and the visions that refuse to leave me alone.

Walking through the kitchen doorway, the eerie outline has moved to appear by the fridge. I know I can't outrun my own mind, but I flinch anyway. Gritting my teeth, I stride past and yank the fridge door open, the delusion disappearing in the bright light which glows from within. Pulling out the other half of the meatball sub I couldn't stomach earlier, I close the door and lean against the counter. Glancing around, I cautiously eat, suddenly realizing how hungry I am.

Cooking is another one of Rachel's fantastic traits, along with keeping this huge house spotless. I don't know why she does it. Even before a few days ago, Rachel has the money to never need to lift a finger for the rest of her days. She should be relaxing by the heated pool and being waited on by the hordes of staff she could employ. My only guess is she invented ways to distract herself from her son's missing presence. She's the one who lost everything.

Devouring the sub in record time, I turn to rinse off the plate when a burst of movement explodes against the window. A bird propels itself into the air, all feathers and wings, sending my heart into overdrive as I reel back on instinct. The plate in my hand slips and smashes against the floor.

"Fuck's sake!" I yell, spinning away only to find the darkened shape sprawled across the floor again. This time, his legs are twisted unnaturally, a look of horror on his pale face. I'm losing my mind, splintering from the inside out.

Gripping the sides of my head hard enough to crack my skull in two, I clench my eyes shut and slide down the cupboard to hunch on the floor. Voices spring to life in my mind, swirling and shouting. They grow louder and louder, blurring into a whirlwind but one voice stands out amongst the rest. Ray's crackled tone bleeds through, full of conviction.

He stole you from me.

I barely knew Ray. Not enough to mourn him, but that's the point. I'm mourning a life I could have known, a family I should have had. Whether I convince myself that Ray held on just long enough to meet me or not, I treasure those few days. It wouldn't have been the same being shown a photograph and expected to create a connection which wasn't there. At least I got to hear his voice, feel his hand wrap around mine, to see the admiration in his eyes. He was proud of me. I choke on a sob. A man that didn't even know me was proud, yet the one I've been trying to please for twenty-one years looks at me with disgust.

I've never wished death on anyone. But I would have swapped out Ray for Nixon any day. In what cruel world should Nixon, who abducted me and blackmailed my real parents from getting me back, carry on winning? Ray will never breathe another breath, see another sunset or have another chance to kiss his wife. I throw my head back against the cabinet, not registering the pain. It's so unjust, but one thing is clear. Ray wanted revenge, and it's become my duty to get it for him.

Something touches my shoulder. On instinct, my hand lashes out to catch the wrist in a tight grip. At Rachel's whimper, my dampened eyes shoot open and I jump to my feet.

"Oh shit, Rachel I'm so sorry." I babble and fuss over her forearm but she takes my hand in hers gently and smiles. I slide up her sleeve to check for a mark anyway, despite it being too dark to see properly but needing to check she's okay.

"Don't worry, Love. I'm fine. I shouldn't have snuck up on you." The worry etched into her face for *my* well-being brings more tears to my eyes. I just assaulted her and all she cares about is me. Some invisible dam inside me is breached. Rachel pulls me into her shoulder and holds me while I cry like an infant with a grazed knee, running her hands over my back and stroking my hair. Her sweet scent envelopes me, the fluffy material of her dressing gown brushing against my cheek.

"I'm so sick of crying," I whisper as my warring emotions start to ease in her presence, "But Ray won't leave me alone." Rachel stands me upright to assess me with her brown eyes, complete understanding shining in them. She doesn't need an explanation, nor does she tell me to man up. Just lifts my hand to kiss the back of it and pulls me across the kitchen to a cupboard on the far side.

Pulling a key from her large front pocket, she pushes it into a tiny lock in the cupboard I hadn't noticed before, wedged into the corner. Rising to her tiptoes, she pulls a long box from the middle shelf. The box is split into seven sections, each one with the initial for the day of the week. Flicking open the 'W', Rachel picks out two of the small pink vitamins and places them into my palm. As I chuck them into my mouth without hesitation, Rachel reaches up to cup my cheek lovingly, the warmth radiating from her palm allowing my body to finally relax.

"Let's get you some warm milk and back to bed. Everything will seem better in the morning, I promise." Mimicking her smile, I can't help but believe her. Watching her rounded frame move around the kitchen, not a single shadowed illusion tries to find me. Soon enough, she is escorting me back to my room with a steaming mug nestled between my hands.

"How are you so strong?" I whisper, fighting against the vulnerability pouring off me in waves. Rachel has just lost her husband, yet she's caring for me like I'm a fraction of my age. Perhaps it's what she needs, what she's been waiting for.

Opening her mouth to answer, a thundering boom sounds across the foyer. We pause on the bottom stair, an instinctual need to protect Rachel forcing my back to straight. The booming comes again, heavy pounding against the front door. Taking a step away, Rachel tugs on my arm and shakes her head. Within an instant, two security guards dressed all in black storm from the side wing. Hints of metal gleam from their hips and their boots are neatly laced. They were on duty, lingering in the shadows I was recently screaming at. I don't have time to ponder on that as the lights are flicked on.

"Get out of my way," a rough voice barks as soon as the door is cracked open. The vitamins Rachel just gave me aren't enough to suppress the sledgehammer of emotion that strikes my chest. I grip my T-shirt, choking on a gasp. No. Not here. Not yet. But there's no stopping the man who stomps into the foyer, flanked by the guards with their hands on their guns.

"You have no right to be here," Rachel steps forward, her hands free of the steaming mug. It's been forgotten on a side table. I'm warm at the way she tries to stand in front of me, but I gently move her aside. I'm scared of a great deal of things and the aging man opposite me is not one of them.

"I knew exactly where you'd run off to," Nixon spits at me accusingly. As if I've been caught out for being at Ray's mansion. His voice is like a bucket of ice water has been thrown over my head, washing out all of the confusion I was so recently drowning in. I see with clarity now, and that clarity is twinged with rage. "It's time to leave. Avery needs you."

Laughter bubbles out of me. A stream of hysterics, the irony tickling me in the bitterest of places. "That's fucking rich!" I hold my waist. Nixon doesn't see the funny side. Standing at my height in his slacks and button down shirt, his graying head pushed back in the same way I like to wear mine, I start to notice the differences between us. Where the learnt behavior and the natural genetics differ. He's no father of mine and never has been, but that doesn't stop his disappointment flaring.

"Seriously Wyatt, I gave you one simple task and you can only think about yourself like usual." I'm stunned silent for a second, before my eyebrows crease and the anger seeps back in.

"I've already told you. I'm not a fucking babysitter." I seethe, wanting to call him out for all the lies so badly but needing to hold my cards close to my chest. I'm going to avenge Ray and take back control of the life I was meant to have, but a quick outburst in the foyer won't do it. I need to be strategic. I need to bide my time. I need to be like Ray.

"We have to go, Wyatt," Nixon repeats, quickly losing his patience. "Avery is on her way to a safe house of mine. I'll take you there."

"You think I'm going to leave Rachel to look after Avery?" I roll my eyes. I'm not leaving, and to prove it, I reach out and take Rachel's hand. Nixon tracks the movement and sighs loudly, his tone relaxing slightly.

"I figured you'd feel differently considering this." Withdrawing a piece of folded paper out of his pocket, Nixon reaches across the space to hand it to me. The guards at his back tense, veins popping out of their arms with the tight grip on their guns. It's then I realize, they're waiting for my command to remove Nixon. They think I'm their boss now.

Taking the paper, I unfold it for the briefest moment and instantly snap it shut again. I don't need to read it to know what it says.

"Where did you get this?" I crumple the page in my hand. My heart is jackhammering in my chest, a rush of adrenaline fighting with the pills I recently took. Perhaps I'm paranoid but the chain reaction of those two components takes root until my hand is shaking around the paper and blood is roaring in my ears. I'm going to vomit, faint and/or die - probably all in that order. Nixon smiles then, an eerie expression on his aged face.

"You have your sources, I have mine. Get in the fucking car. We need to talk." Turning on his heel, Nixon leaves. The security guards follow him out, keeping close and vigilant. It allows me a brief moment to look at Rachel, who's already smiling sweetly.

"Do what you have to do. I'll be here when you're ready to come home." If only she knew that those words nearly brought me to my knees with the desire to hug her legs. Not trusting myself to linger, I place a quick kiss on her cheek.

"I'll be back. I promise." Without a second look, I walk out of Rachel's world, regretting every step I put between us.

AVERY

"Garrett!" I chastise, tugging him back from the kitchen by his T-shirt sleeve. He pauses mid-bite, looking down at me guiltily. "We're supposed to be mad at him." I stand tall, arms crossed and shoulder to shoulder with Dax and Axel. We all glare at Huxley, casually leaning against the kitchen counter.

"Sorry guys, he got me doughnuts. I have no issues here." Garrett sinks his teeth into the cream dessert and slinks away. The rest of us aren't so easily assuaged. The central island between us is covered with food, ending with a crate of wine and several bottles of pink gin.

"Ohhh, ice cream!" Meg appears then, instantly drawn to a tub of cookie dough poking out of the top of a paper bag. I clench my jaw, allowing her to retrieve the tub and a spoon. Sensing the tension rippling between us, Meg suddenly looks around and excuses herself, retreating to the living area.

"Some of us can't be bought so easily." I glare at Huxley. He's unaffected, his ankles crossed and hands leaning against the worktop behind him. He was fully expecting this reception.

"What if something had happened to you?" Dax says, followed by a sharp huff. Huxley rolls his tongue between his teeth.

"Then only one of us would have been harmed, and the rest of you would still be here to look after Avery."

"You're out of your mind if you think we'd be able to restrain her from coming after you," Axel grits out. It's true. Huxley has taken a bullet for me once. Never again. I was preparing to climb out the window and go after him when the SUV pulled up outside the beach house. Hux's chocolate brown eyes darken and he stands straighter.

"You'd better find a way. I'm doing the supply runs. It's non-negotiable." Pushing away from the counter, Huxley attempts to storm away until Axel slams a hand into his chest. A moment of uncertainty passes when I can fully envision a fight breaking out. Moving swiftly, I put myself between the two of them.

"Why are you acting like this?" I frown up at Huxley's stone-like expression. At some point, for some unknown reason, a wall has been slammed down between us. Just when I thought we were getting back on track with his eating and our relationship. Just when I thought our dynamic was going back to how it used to be, he's shut me out.

"I'm saving your damn life," Huxley snaps. I feel Axel and Dax tense behind me, offended by his tone. I manage to hold my ground, despite the sinking feeling that I'm losing him. He's drifting away from me, despite our bodies being barely a few inches apart. A long exhale comes through Huxley's nose. "Go back to worrying about who will share your bed, Swan. I'll be in the background, doing whatever it takes to keep you safe and I'm sorry to say, I don't even need you to like me for me. Maybe it's too late for us." He leaves then, snatching my heart from my chest and stomping all over it in the process.

The slam of the door echoes through the kitchen, leaving a hollow silence in its wake. My breath catches in my throat, and the weight of Huxley's words sinks in, dragging me down with them.

Maybe it's too late for us.

The words play over and over in my mind, each repetition cutting deeper. After everything we've been through and all of the progress we've made? That's it? I stand frozen, staring at the spot he just vacated, my chest tight and my pulse thrumming in my ears. A thousand things I should've said, could've said, race through my head, but nothing came out when he clearly needed to hear them.

I feel a warm hand settle on my shoulder—Axel, always grounding me—but even his touch can't ease the ache clawing at me. Dax is on my other side, quiet as usual, his easy going grin replaced by a somber frown.

"He didn't mean it. He's just stressed." Axel's voice is soft, his concern clear, but all I can do is shake my head. Because no, it's not just stress. We're all freaking stressed here, and no one else is cutting themselves off. Quite the opposite in our search for reasons to keep living and laughing. In terms of excuses, I do not accept Huxley's. If he's so concerned with keeping me safe, he should start with protecting my heart, not leaving it as an open fissure bleeding out. The man who has always had my back, who's taken a bullet for me, has decided we're no longer worth fighting for, and didn't even give me a chance to tell him he's wrong. Or perhaps he did and I've just held my tongue for too long.

Garrett whistles low from his position on the sofa. I half-turn, seeing how he's finished his doughnut and is pushed up against Meg, sharing her ice cream one spoonful at a time. "What crawled up Hux's butt and convinced him to become a martyr?"

I bite down on my lip, hard enough to draw blood, but it's nothing compared to the pain coursing through me. Huxley has been my rock. And now, he's bashing about upstairs, slipping further from my grasp with every passing second. The last man who was slamming around on the floor above appeared with a bag in hand and walked out of my life for good. I felt Wyatt's loss like a knife to the gut and silently cried myself to sleep that night. So why aren't my feet moving to run upstairs and insist Huxley talks to me, that we work this thing out before it gets worse?

Because I'm stubborn and I'm fucking furious with his sudden change of heart, that's why.

Snatching a bottle of pink gin, I twist off the cap and take a long swig, feeling the burn spread through my chest. Dax raises a brow but doesn't comment, his arms hanging loose by his sides as he watches me. Axel, too, stays silent, his hand still resting on my shoulder, his thumb brushing soothing circles that do nothing to quell the storm inside me.

"That's one way to deal with it," Garrett mutters, his mouth half-full of ice cream. Meg elbows him sharply, sending him a glare. He shrugs, unbothered.

"I'm not dealing with it," I snap, wiping my mouth with the back of my hand. "I'm actually going to do what it takes to not deal with any of this shit right now. Especially not trying to figure out when exactly Huxley decided we weren't worth the risk anymore."

Axel's hand tenses on my shoulder. "You know that's not what he meant." I turn to face him, the heat in my chest spreading like wildfire.

"Then why did he say it? Why is he pushing me away? I can't—" My voice cracks, and I hate it. I hate how vulnerable I feel, how raw I've become. "I can't keep losing people like this." For a moment, no one says anything. The room feels suffocating, the silence thick and heavy. I stare at a spot over Axel's shoulder, my eyes unfocused and my throat tight with unshed tears. "Leave Huxley for a while," Axel says softly, though the tightness in his voice betrays his own frustration. "He'll come around. He always does." I'm not so sure this time.

"Fuck this," I mutter harshly. Crossing the room, I hand the bottle of gin to Meg. "Get drunk with me." She doesn't need to be told twice.

***

Fun fact, pink gin gives me the giggles. Another fun fact, I'm terrible at Monopoly at the best of times, and this is the worst I've ever played. Somehow, I'm three million paper dollars in debt, trading favors and dares just to see myself pass Go one more time. I should give up, but then I wouldn't have a focus. Well, not one that isn't my festering anger with the blond broody bastard upstairs.

The dynamic between Meg and the guys is steadily becoming easier to navigate. Alcohol helps, loosening lips. Some conversations are uncomfortable, like Garrett telling Meg how I left teeth marks all over Wyatt's dick. I really shouldn't have gone into detail with him about that.

Logically, I now know Wyatt is not related to me. Physically, my body can't deny its reaction when thinking about that evening during the showcase interval. I felt something that night which has been denied to me for so long, and Wyatt didn't willingly give it. I took it. That night, I felt like I was in control.

With those flashbacks vivid in my mind, I grab Garrett's hand and lead him to the back porch. It's dark out, the only light coming from the soft glow of the moon reflecting off the rolling waves. The air is cool and salty, goosebumps breaking across my arms. The sound of the sea laps against the shore, filling the quiet space between us.

I release Garrett's hand as we step onto the wooden boards, turning to face him. His eyes, dark and intense, catch mine. For a second, we just stand there, the breeze brushing against my skin, his presence anchoring me in a way that's comforting yet electrifying.

"You need something from me, don't you Peach?"

I bite my lip, shame washing over me. Attempting to step away, Garrett grips my arms to hold me in place.

"Ask and it's yours." Garrett murmurs, his voice low and soothing as he steps closer. His floppy dark hair hides his forehead and brows. I tiptoe to brush it back, smoothing the straight lengths into a different style. One he would never wear by choice, but seems only too happy to keep for now.

"I shouldn't," I turn my head away. This thought, this stupid tiny thought that crept up on me, is so incredibly selfish when sober me knows Garrett's struggles with his own insecurities. I shouldn't ask this of him, but he's staring at me so openly, coaxing me to speak. I let out a shaky breath, feeling the tension still coiled tight in my chest. He reaches up, cupping my cheek and causing the world to fade, leaving only the two of us and the quiet rhythm of the ocean.

"I need you to be him for a while," I admit, my voice barely a whisper, but he hears me.

"Who exactly?" Garrett asks, his thumb brushing against my lower lip. A hint of a smirk lifts his mouth. He knows who.

"Say his name out loud." Something about his tone, so easy, so accepting, makes the last bit of my restraint snap.

"Wyatt," I breathe, swaying slightly from the alcohol I've consumed. The smile on Garrett's face deepens.

"Finally," he breathes as if a weight has been lifted from his shoulders. As if he's wanted to do this for the longest time. Before I can second-guess myself, I rise on my toes, pulling his mouth down to mine.

The kiss is slow at first, tentative, a testing of boundaries. Giving me a chance to back out, I reckon. But when Garrett groans softly against my lips, his hands sliding down to grip my waist, something inside me ignites. The heat flares, and suddenly, I'm pressing myself closer to him, deepening the kiss, desperate for more.

His body responds immediately, his grip tightening as he pulls me flush against him. His tongue teases mine, the kiss growing hotter, more insistent. Everything from Huxley's declaration to my confusion disappears in the heat of the moment. There's only him, or rather, who he's pretending to be. My mind slips too easily, conjuring the scent of expensive cologne, reliving his warmth, the way his hands explore my body and sends shivers racing down my spine.

I gasp when his lips leave mine, trailing hot, open-mouthed kisses down the side of my neck. My hands tangle in his hair as he nips at my skin, his breath ragged against my throat. He lifts his head, his eyes dark and filled with a hunger that mirrors my own.

"Use me, Peach. That's what I'm here for," he whispers, his voice rough, his forehead resting against mine as he catches his breath.

"No," I shake my head. "He wouldn't call me that." For some reason, it has to be right. My mind needs to believe it's real, because this is the closest I'll ever come. Garrett is the only one who can give this to me. Without a trace of hesitation or uncertainty, Garrett's hand slips into my hair and he pulls back roughly.

"Strip, Little Sis. Show me how fucking beautiful that pussy is." My heart skips a beat. With trembling hands, I lift my sweater over my head, unclasp my bra and push down my cycling shorts and panties together. A smile tugs at his lips before he kisses me again, harder this time, deeper. The lust between us is a living entity, taking on its own lifeforce. The more wrong it should be, the hotter the fire within me burns. I'm ill, sick in the head, and horny as fuck.

Walking me backwards, my thighs touch the porch swing. Using his tight grip on my hair, he lowers me down onto it, nudging my thighs apart with his knee. There's a slow, assessing tilt of his head, which is so typically Wyatt. I bite down on my bottom lip, heart pounding in my chest. He doesn't comment, but I can feel his stare lingering, his dark eyes roving over me in the moonlight, memorizing every inch of my body.

His fingers slide gently along the line of my jaw before trailing down to my collarbone, leaving a heated path in their wake. The intensity between us is thick, almost tangible, as he watches me with a predatory focus. Then his hands are on his waistband. My breath comes in short, uneven bursts as a hard, thick cock juts out in front of my face.

"I'm going to feed you my cock. Don't forget how I like it." The hand at my jaw clenches tightly, tugging my mouth wide. I don't get a moment to prepare myself as his smooth length glides over my tongue. Desire already pools at his tip, the taste causing me to groan. Opening my throat, I permit him full access. Thrusting in deeply, a frustrated huff comes on his next withdrawal.

"Where are those teeth? Show me how much you hate me." Oh. *Oh*. That's right. This is Wyatt. The man who's hated me for as long as he's known me. Who stole my therapy transcripts and used them against me. Who stuck me in a bird's cage because he thought it would trigger a panic attack, and who thought I'd come running when he decided he wanted me.

Flaring my nostrils, I grab the base of his shaft and squeeze hard. My nails dig into his flesh where his body meets his cock, my mouth tightening around his girth. Pulling back, I drag my teeth upwards until I reach the tip. "That's better," he hisses. I do this several times over, steadying myself on his thighs. Taking his plump head between my lips, I suck hard. Hollowing out my cheeks, I prepare to suck the soul from his body when he pushes me off with a pop.

"Bitch," he groans, the desire thick in his voice. Shoving me to sit back in the porch swing, he sinks onto his knees and leans in, gently inhaling my pussy. "My turn." Delving his tongue into me, I arch and stifle a groan. The kitchen window is closed but not too far away. Anyone could watch on, but this time, I don't want an audience. This is private between me and Wyatt. A hidden fantasy that will never see the light of day.

That devilish tongue is quickly replaced by two fingers, his lips finding my clit instantly. Every sensation is sharp, hateful and filled with spite. He plays his role perfectly. I let go of all inhibitions, grinding into his face, the roughness of his stubble grazing my skin. Ripples of heat course through my veins. One strong hand grips my hip, tilting me further into his assault. I'm kept on the precarious edge of pleasure and pain, just enough to remind me of his control. His rules.

I can't help the way my body responds, arching and squirming for release, my fingers threading through his hair, tugging as he sucks and drags his tongue firmly over my clit. The rhythm of his fingers increases, pumping in and out of me in sharp, short thrusts. There's no gentleness. Each movement is precise, calculated to draw me in, higher and higher. It's maddening and intoxicating how much I want this. The sound of the waves lapping against the shore is distant, drowned out by the rhythm of my own heartbeat pounding in my ears.

I can't take it anymore. I tug at his hair again, drawing his gaze up to my flushed face. His shimmering eyes are dark with focus, catching the light just enough to be believable. My heart races as I picture the face to match those eyes, that swept back hair. The intensity between us climbs to its peak, a quiet storm in the night.

And then, when I think I can't hold on any longer, he pulls back slightly, just enough to whisper against my skin, "Cum for me, Little Sis." His voice is low, rough, and it undoes me completely. Curling his fingers inside of me, I clench around him, convulsing as his lips close around my clit once more. He draws wave after wave of pleasure through my body, the sound that escapes me slicing through the night. There's no denying him.

As soon as I come down, blinking away the spots covering my vision, I'm twisted and lowered onto the sand. A heavy body lowers onto me, his mouth hovering just over mine. There's a delicious pause, a quiet moment where our breaths mingle. Then, like a dam breaking, his mouth crashes onto mine, punctuated by the taste of my own desire.

His kiss is demanding, his tongue teasing mine, his grip in my hair tightening as he presses me down into the swing. I gasp against his lips, my hands finding his shoulders, pulling him closer as I arch into him, my thighs parting further beneath the pressure of his knee. He breaks the kiss, his lips trailing fire down my neck as his hands roam lower, fingers tracing the curve of my hips. His breath is hot against my skin, and every nerve in my body is on high alert, aching for more, for him.

"You drive me insane, you know that?" he growls softly against my ear, his voice thick with need. I let out a soft moan, threading my fingers through his hair.

"Good," I breathe, the word barely more than a whisper as I tug him closer. I want to lose myself. I want to forget our troubled past and see what we could be if he let us. But to my dismay, he pulls back. The coldness that hits my body is a sudden shock, embarrassment coating my cheeks. In true

Wyatt fashion, he takes what he wants and then stands to leave. I know in reality, this is all a game. A new form of role play we shouldn't make a habit of, but the rejection hits all the same. I lie naked, exposed, filled with desperation and self-loathing. Can't we play for a little longer?

Rolling his head, his neck cracks and a shudder rolls down his spine. I make a feeble attempt to cover myself when he suddenly swoops down, lifting me with ease. I swallow hard, my frown evident.

"Where are we going?" I ask. Long strides carrying us down the few steps onto the beach, further into the darkness.

"I'm sorry," Garrett kisses my temple. I search his face for answers, an unfamiliar tremor beating within.

"What for?" I frown.

"I'm a selfish bastard. Being Wyatt is fun, but when I fuck you, it's my name I want to hear you scream." Garrett lowers us onto the sand, me straddling his lap as he sinks his cock into me. I gasp at the sensation of being stretched and filled, clinging to his neck tightly.

"Oh Gare," I groan against his skin, peppering him with kisses. "You'd better earn it then." A smile graces my lips as Garrett barks a sharp laugh. He twists me in an instant, flattening me on my back.

"Challenge accepted, Peach."

AXEL

"Garrett! What the hell-" Avery's voice cuts through the usual beach house noise. I tilt my head back on the sofa, unable to see her or Garrett.

"I'm sorry, Peach, but I'm going to need you to step aside. I know exactly what I'm doing," Garrett fires back, his tone all smug confidence.

"Clearly not!" Avery retorts. "You can't just stuff it all in like that."

My brows shoot up, interest piqued. Putting down the magazine Hux picked up on his last supply run, I drape my arm over the backrest. I've always been more of a gossip column kind of guy, the newspaper is full of depressing shit that I don't need spoiling my morning.

"It's the way I've always done it. I've never had any complaints before," Garrett counters, voice muffled slightly by the sound of him wrestling something into submission. I snort. In fact, I have complained about Garrett's habit of steam rolling ahead with no prep work, but he chooses not to listen.

"I'm telling you," Avery grumbles, "that load is way too heavy. It's not going to fit."

"I'll make it fit," Garrett grunts back. There's a metallic bang, the floor shudders slightly, and I start to wonder if I should intervene. "Just hold still, it's almost in-"

"Here, just give it to me, I'll do it," Avery insists, her voice taking on a no-nonsense tone which will have absolutely no effect on Garrett.

"No, I'm fine. I've got this," Garrett grinds out, clearly in the middle of another epic struggle. A loud clatter follows, and then comes Avery's shriek.

"Ew, Garrett! It's everywhere! Ugh, and I just washed my hair!"

Curiosity gets the better of me, and I haul myself off the couch. Rounding the corner, I spot the chaos. Avery and Garrett kneeling on the floor of what we generously call a laundry room. It's really just an alcove with a washer and dryer, and right now, it's also a warzone. The smell of fabric softener hits me first, the liquid spilt all over the floor and splattered over Avery's face as if she lost a tug of war battle. Between them, Garrett is trying to force a couple kilos of washing into the machine while Avery is fighting to drag it back out.

"Erm, do you, um, need any help?" I ask, trying to sound casual but failing to hide my grin.

"Tell him he's going to break the washer, and we're all going to suffer for it!" Avery angrily wipes at the softener on her cheek and uses her huge eyes to plead with me. Garrett tilts his head, lips pursed as if to say, *don't bother telling me shit.* I lean against the doorway, crossing my arms, a smirk tugging at my lips.

"Avery does have a point. If you break that washer, none of us are going to enjoy living in our own filth. Especially you, if you have to walk around naked." I give him a knowing look now, hitting home that he above all others would feel the repercussions the most. Garrett glares at me, beads of sweat dotting his forehead.

Garrett stills for a second, sighing as if the weight of laundry is suddenly the most dramatic obstacle he's ever faced. "Fine," he mutters, reluctantly pulling some of the clothes back out. Avery exhales in relief, flashing me a quick, thankful smile. I wink back.

"I'll grab the mop." Avery stands and steps aside, her eyes roving over my arms and shoulders as I clean the floor.

"Honestly, how does he survive?"

"He has us," I say with a shrug. Avery giggles, swiping more of the gloopy liquid off her neck. Garrett puts an acceptable amount of clothes into the washer and switches it on.

"There," she says, glancing at Garrett. "That wasn't so hard, was it?"

"I'll give you hard," he mutters under his breath. Grabbing his laundry basket, he attempts to leave when I block him with the mop's handle.

"Where do you think you're going?" I cock a brow. An instant shift happens in Garrett's features, his eyes brightening at my tone. He acts like he prefers being the Dom out of the two of us, but he loves it even more when I turn the tables on him. "Our girl needs another shower. You made the mess, you need to help clean it up." I gesture to her hair, sticky and tangled. Garrett grins, grabbing a towel and holding it out to her.

"You heard the man, Peach. Let's get you cleaned up."

We make it all the way to our private bathroom before the reality of what he's agreed to hits. I watch Garrett hesitate, torn between wanting to walk away and realizing that he's cornered. He lets out a resigned sigh and reluctantly moves into the bathroom, the towel slung over his shoulder. Avery follows after him, wringing out some of the softener in her hair.

I lean against the doorframe of the bathroom, arms crossed, curious about how this is going to play out. The dynamic between the two of them changes. Garrett, usually so cocky and brash, suddenly seems completely out of his element. Avery, on the other hand, seems unfazed by it all, not noticing the turmoil taking place behind Garrett's dark eyes. I see it, but then again, I know where to look. She tugs at her shirt and sweatpants, baring herself to both of us.

Garrett clears his throat, avoiding her eyes as he grabs the showerhead, turning on the water. Avery raises a brow at his gym shorts and white T-shirt.

"Are you not coming in?"

Garrett doesn't answer, too focused on adjusting the water temperature and busying himself with unnecessary tasks. I can't help but chuckle under my breath. I rarely get to see him flustered, and if I was a better man, I might offer to shower with Avery to save him the trouble. Alas, I'm enjoying this far too much.

Once the water is at the right temperature, Garrett indicates that Avery should step into the shower. She does, waiting for Garrett to hose her down like a prized pig before she turns on him. Grabbing his shoulders, she yanks him into the cubicle. There's a struggle with the shower head, resulting in Garrett's front becoming soaked before he can grapple back some control.

Seeming satisfied, Avery gives him her back, arching so that he can rinse the fabric softener from her hair. The water cascades over her head, dripping down her stunning body. Shifting her hair aside, Garrett's fingers trail the arrow tattooed at the top of her back, causing her to shudder.

His own discomfort becomes more apparent as his drenched T-shirt sticks to his frame, and nothing he does helps. In the end, he glances at me, giving the best puppy dog eyes. I slowly shake my head.

"This is good for you," I clarify. I'm right here, a few feet away. This is a safe space and until Garrett is put in situations that he can't back out of, he'll never start to heal. So much focus is spent on me fighting my demons while he's happy to ignore his, but I won't let him anymore. Garrett's throat bobs as he looks down at the fabric molded to his body, outlining the tattoos inked across his chest and abdomen.

Avery's attention shifts at the same time, turning back to face him. She assesses the wet material. "What's that one?" She points to a tattoo on his chest, just above his heart.

Garrett stiffens, glancing down at where she's gesturing. "It's a rabbit's foot," he mumbles, his tone suddenly shy.

"For luck?" Avery tilts her head, water droplets gathered on her lashes. Garrett releases a harsh bark of laughter.

"None of my tattoos have any meaning, Peach." Her eyes flick back up to his face but she doesn't remove her finger from prodding his chest.

"So what's the point of them?"

"To hide me," Garrett answers immediately. He's unusually devoid of all emotion, standing statue still and holding the shower head over Avery's shoulders to keep her warm. "They're just illustrations I picked off a wall. Once, I donated my legs to a bunch of students, letting them do whatever they wanted. It's not about the images, it's about the coverage." Avery glances at me and I nod.

I was with him for that entire weekend. Some of the artists were more promising than others, and anything that the tattoo shop owner didn't deem up to quality was offered a free cover up. Gare never took the offer. He doesn't care about being a walking piece of art or his skin telling a story. Garrett simply wants to disappear beneath the ink.

To her credit, Avery doesn't pursue the conversation that could have followed. She doesn't tell him that's stupid or try to give compliments he would have refused to hear. Instead, her finger trails lower.

"What's this?"

"A paper bag of daisies."

"What's that?" Avery squints, shifting her face closer to Garrett's ribs. He sucks in a breath, going even more rigid before looking down.

"A naked woman in a scuba mask walking a fish on a leash."

"And this one?" She points lower, just above his hip, where another tattoo peeks out from beneath his soaked shirt.

"That's Bart Simpson's butt with 'Eat My Shorts' written across it." Avery snorts a laugh. She's smiling wide, and soon enough, so is he. It's a beautiful sight, something I'm thankful I got to witness as an outsider. Avery is helping Garrett in ways he can't fully comprehend.

Reaching for the shampoo, Avery busies her hands working up a lather and massaging it into her scalp, her eyes still appraising Garrett's muscles. "Do you think you'll ever get a tattoo that has meaning behind it?" Garrett pauses, the vulnerability flashing across his face as he answers.

"I'm contemplating it." Avery misses the longing look he gives her, too busy washing her hair and peering through the material at the rest of his artwork. His body is fascinating, and this is the closest she's ever got to fully seeing it.

"I like them," she says quietly, her hands dropping to her side. "They suit you."

Garrett lets out a breath he'd probably been holding. "Thanks." The tension between them shifts, becoming more intimate. Garrett slowly turns her to finish washing out the shampoo, his movements gentler now, more focused. Avery closes her eyes, leaning into the sensation of his hands working through her tangled strands.

I stay quiet, watching from my spot by the door, not wanting to break the spell they're under. Garrett, for all his bravado, isn't used to being seen like this; exposed, vulnerable. He doesn't even like me pressing him too hard to open up. But with Avery, it's different. She doesn't judge him, doesn't pry too hard, but she sees him. Really sees him.

The water runs clear, and Garrett shuts off the shower. "You're done," he says, his voice softer than before. He reaches for the towel and drapes it over her shoulders, his fingers brushing against her skin for a brief moment before he pulls away.

Avery looks up at him, smiling softly. "Thanks, Garrett."

He nods, his usual cockiness muted. "Yeah. No problem." As Avery stands, wringing out her hair with the towel, Garrett steps back, giving her space. His shirt clings to him, outlining every muscle and tattoo, but he doesn't seem to care as much. Maybe he's starting to get comfortable in his own skin around her. Around both of us.

Avery looks over her shoulder, her voice, light and teasing. "You know, you should really wear your tattoos with pride, Garrett. They're kind of hot." I grin, knowing that comment is going to stick with him for a while. Garrett finally laughs, coming back to himself.

"What do you mean, kind of?" he nudges her, a smirk dancing across his lips.

"Come let me dry your hair for you, Beautiful," I hold out my arm. "A Princess deserves pampering after all." Instead of giving me shit for that princess comment, Avery approaches me, shooting back the wink I gave her earlier.

Turning us both towards the bedroom, I slowly and silently clap for a job well done. She's a sneaky one, even if she doesn't know the extent in which she just helped Garrett through multiple demons he faces alone. Just letting her scratch the surface of his trauma is a feat that took me years.

But maybe that's because Garrett doesn't realize he's already falling for her. It's just a matter of time before he admits it to himself.

AVERY

Breaching the salty surface, the burn in my lungs starts to fade as I gasp in mouthfuls of clean air. Seagulls fly overhead in the sky, heading towards the heavy gray clouds rolling this way. A deep rumble in the distance is a sign I need to get out of the sea before the storm hits. Diving back into the icy water, I kick as fast as my nearly frozen legs will move, coming up for air every few powerful strokes of my arms. The beach is in sight when the rain hits, pelting mini bullets of water down onto me. Finding the seabed beneath my feet, I push myself up and wade the rest of the way to shore.

Not slowing once back on land, I grab the towel I'd left on the sand and force my legs to carry me towards the beach house. Leaving the violent crash of waves behind, the calm sea I had entered turning turbulent, my feet hit the wooden porch steps.

Taking a second to collect myself, I lean against the blue exterior and watch the dramatic weather shift from the safety of the porch's timber cover. A dense sheet of rain hides the sea from my vision, a bright flash lighting the landscape briefly. The back door beside me flies open and a hand flies around the corner to latch onto my arm, dragging me inside.

"What the hell were you thinking, swimming in that?!" Huxley whisper-shouts. By his hunched demeanor and low tone, I conclude that the others are still asleep upstairs. He crowds me against the now-closed door, his bare chest heaving beside my face. I glare up at his chocolate brown eyes, hidden within the curtain of his wavy hair.

"What? You're allowed to decide when you come and go alone but I'm not allowed to take a swim without permission?" I snap bitterly. Hux holds my gaze, his chest heaving. "Obviously it wasn't raining when I initially went into the water. I just needed to think for a while." Huxley's brown eyes narrow in the way they do when he's about to lecture me, so I try to shove past him to leave. A puddle starts to form at my feet, my hair dripping onto the Lino floor. Thunder rumbles around the building, rivaling the rain's noise.

Hux is like a whippet, snatching the towel in my hand and creating a cage around my middle with his strong arm. I buck as if I would be able to escape, even if I wasn't dripping wet and slippery. In a battle of wills, Huxley holds me tight and drags the towel through my hair with the other hand, squeezing tightly at the ends. My elbows are flying and a few times, my feet leave the floor.

"Hey!" Huxley jerks me roughly. "I'm not your enemy here! I'm fighting too damn hard for your safety, for you to go and catch pneumonia in the early hours." I continue to throw myself around like a rag doll, as if the act of him drying my hair is burning me. In actual fact, I just needed a break from being cared for. I'm not some precious princess who can't look after herself - this morning's swim is exempt from that notion.

"No! My enemy is a real father who won't let me be free of him, an adoptive father who sent me here to hide away and a mom who never told me anything of importance until it's too late and now she's not here for me to defend herself but if I'm angry with her, I'm the asshole because she's dead!"

My limbs drop, hanging loose. If it weren't for Huxley's hold around my middle, I'd have collapsed on the floor. His chest pressed against my back, wet hair forgotten over my shoulder.

"Avery," Huxley slowly turns me and plants his hands on my waist. I refuse to look at him, shame lacing my cheeks. "Hit me." My eyes fly upward, widened as I snort.

"I'm not going to hit you Huxley."

"Yes you are. You're either going to fight me or fuck me, but either way, we're not leaving this kitchen until you've found whatever release you were searching for out there." He jerks his head to the door. The rain is roaring now, punctuated by flashes of light and rumbles of thunder. The storm is crawling closer, beating as viscerally as the pounding of my heart. The cold seeps in then. The water clinging to my skin creeps beneath the rage bubbling inside. I'm so fucking cold. The sea water was freezing, and it did nothing to freeze the thoughts plaguing my mind.

Drifting my gaze back to Huxley, my hands ball into fists but there's no weight behind my thumb to his chest. Instead, my forearms settle against his abs and I fall into him.

"How can you see me when I have no idea who I am?" I breathe, voice hitched. Strong fingers tilt my chin upward, the tenderness in Huxley's movements too much to consider.

"You're Avery Hughes. An incredible, strong and stunning woman. You dance without fault and you love without limitations. You're our Little Swan."

"I thought you didn't want to be with me anymore." Weakness leaks into my voice, and I don't have the energy to care anymore. Huxley already knows I'm broken. Deft fingers tuck a loose strand of my hair behind my ear.

"There hasn't been a single day since meeting you that you haven't held my heart, Aves. I just needed to take a step back to think logically. If anything happened to you because of my infatuation, I wouldn't be able to live with myself."

I can't contain my tears now, the saltiness of my sadness and the sea mixing between the soft mouth which seeks out mine. Huxley's lips are sturdy whereas mine are wobbling. I hate crying, especially in front of people.

"Get on the kitchen island," I groan through our kisses. No doubt Huxley would have kissed me until my toes curl and I can no longer breathe, but I can't give into the swirling whirlpool within. I can't learn to lean on others, I can't lose sight of my independence after years of building it up, brick by brick. If I only exist when the Shadowed Souls acknowledge me, what will I do when I'm left alone with my own thoughts for company? The prime example is what happened this morning, driving me out into the sea without any consideration of the elements around me.

Huxley assessed me for a moment before lowering his hands from my face. "Whatever you need, Angel." He moves across the kitchen with long, easy strides. There's no light source in the kitchen, only daybreak looming and the occasional flash of lightning. Just before he reaches the high marble surface, I stop him with a command.

"Shorts off and lie on your back." He obeys without hesitation. Power thrums through my veins. Shedding his shorts, the outline of Huxley's cock is visible, half-mast and thick with need. Seemingly, our scramble for control affected both of us. His biceps flex as he pushes up onto the counter, his ass pushing back across the marble. He's the image of an Adonis, a Greek sculpture chiseled to perfection. The muscles in his back ripple, the length of his torso tenses as he lies back. Blond waves spill over the gray marble and if he's affected by the cold surface, he doesn't show it.

I stride towards him, my eyes locked on the steady rise and fall of his solid chest. The storm outside rages, the wind howling and the rain pounding against the windows, but in this kitchen, there's a different tempest brewing. Standing beside the island, I let my gaze roam over his body, drinking in every detail. He's focused on controlling his inhales, his muscles taut with anticipation. My fingers trace over his smooth skin, feeling the warmth beneath and the faint shiver that follows my touch.

Leaning over, I capture his lips in a fierce kiss, my hand tangling in his hair. Huxley responds with equal fervor, his hands gripping the edge of the counter. This is nothing like the gentle reassuring kiss from moment's ago. This is a desire to feel alive, an invisible force driving me to seek another type of comfort from Huxley. Not tender touches, but a feverish need for control. Control over him, over my emotions, my thoughts. Breaking the kiss, I move lower, trailing my mouth down his neck, over his collarbone, savoring the taste of his skin. He lies still while I explore, a meal laid out for my consumption.

I stop at his chest, my tongue flicking over a hardened nipple, drawing a low moan from him. His hips lift slightly, seeking contact, but I keep my pace slow, savoring the power I hold over him. My hand wraps around his length, feeling him harden further at my touch.

"Swan," he groans, his voice thick with need. Ignoring his plea, I continue my exploration, my mouth and hand working in tandem to drive him higher, to make him harder. His shaft is solid in my hand, throbbing as I stroke him, keeping him tethering on the edge. The storm outside hammers on the beach house, pounding to be let inside. Lightning illuminates the room in brief, brilliant flashes, each flicker of light revealing the raw desire in Huxley's eyes. His body tenses and relaxes with every touch. "Please use me."

"I will," I smirk. My wet hair trails his chest, leaving a wet trail across his gorgeous body. I near his plump head, pausing over it to blow gently. He jerks beneath me, watching closely. Opening my mouth, I exhale and shift my head aside, kissing his hip bone. Huxley groans.

"Fucking tease." I smirk against his upper thigh, dragging my lips over his smooth skin. It should be illegal for a man to be this toned, this gorgeous. He shouldn't be dominated, yet he's given me that power over him. He doesn't rush or guide me. My nails drag up his thigh and over his balls, which tighten on instinct. My mouth brushes over his shaft and he twitches. "You're driving me crazy."

To prove a point that I can, I release him and step back completely. Huxley's whine is drowned out by a bout of thunder. A smile stretches across my face. Peeling the black straps down my arms one at a time, I strip from my bathing suit. It hits the floor heavily. Using a stool, I move to straddle his hips, positioning myself above him. His hands find my hips, gripping them tightly as I slowly lower myself onto him. The wetness between my legs and weeping at his tip create an effortless glide between us, our matching groans filling the room.

I don't stop until I bottom out. The feeling of being completely filled and stretched is electric. At a jerk of his cock, a jolt of pleasure radiates through both of us. His eyes never leave mine, the intensity of his gaze matching the storm outside. I set a slow rhythm, each movement drawing us both closer to the brink. The marble beneath him grows slick with the water dripping from my hair, over the valley of Huxley's abs and onto the countertop.

With Huxley's dick pushed deep inside, I push my hips forward and roll my body. It's torture, and I do it several times over. The world outside ceases to exist; there is only us, caught in the eye of our own private storm. Leaning forward, I slip my hand around Huxley's throat. His breath catches, his eyes widening with lust. Bracing myself on both his throat and his chest, I lift my ass high in the air until just his tip is inside me. I wait, hovering and waiting until Huxley's jaw grows tight.

"Do it," he dares. "Fuck me. Use me like that pretty pink dildo you hold so close."

"*Held* so close. You took it from me and I never saw it again." I tilt my head, the weight of my hair winning a battle with my neck. Hux raises his hips, struggling for more friction.

"I gave it to Garrett. Pretty sure he's been using it on Axel." I was able to lower myself but I pause and Huxley's face falls. "You don't need it, Angel. You've got me." I smirk, thrusting down on Huxley's dick. His groan by my ear is everything I needed to recharge my desire. Again and again, I lift and lower, riding him, strangling him. Our breaths come in ragged gasps, my pace punishing across both him and my thighs. His hands move to my waist, his hips snapping upwards to match my rhythm. Our connection deepens, a bond forged in the heat of our passion.

My climax is undeniable. Inevitable. The thunder crashes in time with my thrusts, empowered by mother nature. The heat between us is palpable despite the chill in the air. Like a wave, the orgasm that hits is powerful and all-consuming. Huxley is right behind me, unable to hold back from the torment I've put him through. Our cries mesh, our bodies shuddering in unison.

In the aftermath, we collapse together, hearts racing, skin flushed. The storm outside begins to wane, the rain easing to a gentle patter. In the silence that follows, I rest my head on his chest, feeling the steady beat of his heart beneath me. His arms wrap around me, holding me close, and for a moment, I allow myself to savor the warmth and security of his embrace. He gave me this. Complete control over his body. A full release from my own mind.

"It doesn't have to be me," Huxley murmurs beside my ear, "but can you please take someone with you next time you want to swim in the sea during a storm before daybreak?"

"Again, it wasn't storming when I went out there." I roll my eyes. I feel his glare rather than see it. "Okay. Okay, I hear you. I'll take someone with me." Pushing up on his chest, I notice too late how Huxley's eyes slide away to look out of the far window. My chest clenched. "No. Hux, I'll take you with me."

His smile is everything, the brightest thing I've seen all morning. Sitting upright, Huxley holds my ass to shimmy down the island and move to stand. He holds me as if I weigh nothing, bending to collect his shorts and using them to clean up the mess between us.

"Go clean up. I need to disinfect the kitchen island."

"I don't mind," a voice bleeds through the darkness. I jolt at Garrett's intrusion, spotting his outline at the dining table, eating a bowl of cereal. I didn't even hear him pour it, nor do I know how long he's been sitting watching us. Breakfast and a show, lucky man. Dismissing him, I kiss Huxley long and slow, savoring the taste of his mouth. Warm and sweet as ever. I leave the kitchen without a second glance at the man smirking from the shadows.

My limbs are languid, my brain otherwise occupied as I climb the stairs back to my room. Sleep clings to the bedroom walls, the lump in the bed breathing heavily. Meg is still dead to the world, oblivious to me slipping into our shared bathroom. The packaged bar of soap that set this entire morning into motion is still sitting beside the basin. When I woke in the early hours, I was suddenly plagued with the date. It's Christmas Eve.

The first Christmas without my mom, and it's nothing like what I envisioned. In a strange place, my life is a mess of rumors and lies. At least Meg is here, but when I was rummaging through my luggage, hunting for anything that could substitute as a gift, this shitty bar of soap is the best I came up with. I don't know if the ribbon I've tied around the yellow packaging is better or worse; a humble attention or an insult to Meg's body odor. That's how my costume ended up in my hand and I was racing through the house, seeking an escape within the fenced boundaries.

I hadn't intended to cause myself any harm, and least of all worry anyone more than they already are. Huxley was right. Everyone is caring for my safety and I have absolutely no concept of it. I need to be more careful, even if it's just out of respect for those around me.

Leaving the soap present where it is, I switch the shower to scalding hot. Steam thickens the air, fogging the large oval mirror above the basin, as I push my damp hair back and step into the spray. Warmth immediately soaks into my skin, drawing the chill from every cell in my body and swirling it down the drain. Taking my time, I wash the shampoo from my hair and smooth a handful of conditioner through the long lengths. Leaving it to soak in, I shave my legs and wash my body twice before rinsing it out.

I'm stalling. I know that, yet I can't decide why. Turning the shower off, I emerge thoroughly scrubbed, my skin reddened. At the dull ache between my legs, I chew on my bottom lip. My relationship with Huxley isn't as easy as with the others, because he always tells me the truth, no matter how ugly it is. He doesn't shy away from trouble, but holds my hand and helps me wade through it. There's an intensity to our connection, despite all the times I've pushed back. Huxley is a good man. A solid presence in my otherwise turbulent life.

Combing through my hair in the mirror, an edge of sadness lines my pale blue eyes. A rounded window in the slanted roof shows the rain has stopped, the sun poking through the clouds to brighten the bathroom. Meg is still fast asleep when I return, the bed a mound of crumpled covers and soft snoring.

After I hunt down some tracksuit bottoms and don the orange hoodie I can't bring myself to bury in the sand and forget about, I slump downstairs. I should be happy we're all here together and safe. I should be so much more thankful than I currently feel. Yet my feet are heavy and when hushed whispers meet my ears, I brace myself on the railing.

I can't handle any more bad news. Perhaps it's not too late to run back upstairs and hide in Meg's unmade bed. I could resurface in the New Year and pretend my biggest worries are returning to school and shifting through the stack of agent's offers from the ballet showcase.

As if sensing my turmoil, an arm winds around my waist. Dax appears on the step beside me, evidently freshly showered and ready to face the day. He smells amazing as always, his sea mineral body wash blending into the environment perfectly. His smile is contagious, a glint in his blue eyes. He doesn't speak, but gently guides me down to the lower level. Movement distracts me from staring at his gorgeous face and when I see the living area, my heart slams to a halt in my chest. What the fuck?

DAX

Seeing Avery's face light up far surpasses the new addition standing tall and proud in the center of the living area. A Christmas tree so wide, it almost touches the ceiling and is held in place by a thick metal stand. The pine needles are incredibly thick, dark green branches stretching wide and filling the room with the fresh scent of winter. I'm surprised they managed to get the monstrosity onto Huxley's SUV and through the doorway, but if there's one thing that can be said about Garrett's plans, it's that they usually work out.

"Where the hell..." Avery whispers, still standing in shock. Garrett rushes over, grabbing her waist and twirling Avery away from the bottom step - and me.

"Axel and I went out on a sneaky mission at dawn," Garrett announces proudly. "Although given the scene I returned to, I wish I'd stayed behind instead." A mischievous look is passed between them, Avery blushing furiously and Huxley choking on his slurp of coffee. I've definitely missed something.

"Would have been cheaper," Axel chimes in with an eye roll. He gestures to the piles of food crates and wine boxes stacked high on the dining table, ready for a feast. Or perhaps those are just Garrett's provisions.

"But how?" Avery asks, still dazed by the sight of the enormous tree. Axel's face lights up then, clearly proud of himself. "That little town we passed through the other day - I spotted a Christmas tree farm on the way out." He beams, smugger than I've ever seen him. "I'd barely finished telling Garrett about it, and he'd already hatched 'Operation Merry Mayhem.'"

"My best idea yet," Garrett declares, refusing to set Avery back on her feet. He spins her one last time, her laughter ringing through the air before she lands with a soft thud on the hardwood floor. "Where's Megera? We need everyone to join in!"

Avery shakes her head with a grin. "You won't get Meg out of bed before lunchtime if it's not for sports, and especially not if she hears you calling her Megera."

Garrett's eyes twinkle with mischief. "Challenge accepted." He rushes up the stairs, providing us a moment of quiet without his boyish, boundless energy. Axel, Huxley and I all gravitate to Avery now standing in the center of the room. Her eyes sweep across the tree, to the boxes of decorations. These aren't new, in fact they're covered in thick layers of dust and cobwebs.

"Dax found them in the attic. We figured they were brought here and forgotten about." Axel strokes his fingers down Avery's arm, just as much for his benefit. Garlands of holly, strings of fairy lights and cozy blankets have been draped over the sofa. "We did talk about surprising you by decorating the room before you woke up, but Huxley thought you'd like to be a part of it."

Avery turns then, allowing us all to see the unshed tears gathered in her eyes. A slither of worry blooms inside of my chest until her mouth breaks into a wide grin. My shoulders visibly relax. Huxley, who has been silently watching from the corner, steps forward, his expression as serious as it always is these days but there's a touch of warmth in his chocolate eyes.

"It's our first Christmas together. We wanted it to be special." Avery's face lights up even more, if that's possible, and she pulls Huxley into a tight hug.

"It's perfect," she whispers, her voice cracking with emotion.

Suddenly there's a scream piercing the upper levels of the house, quickly followed by a stampede of rushed footsteps. Garrett flies down the stairs, almost stumbling as he seeks refuge behind Avery's back. Meg appears next, slower stomps juddering the banister. Her hair is wild, a brunette mess around her shoulders, her expression like that of a crazed lion and a shoe clutched in her hand.

"I just thought you might want to join us," Garrett cries out defensively. Meg's blue eyes zero in on the lingering silhouette of a six foot three inch man trying to crowd behind a lithe ballerina. Meg's jaw clenches.

"You threw me off the mattress, squatted down and farted in my face!"

"Early Christmas present?" Garrett offers, barely holding back his own laughter.

"There are poo particles in my mouth!" Meg continues shrieking, scraping her tongue with her nails. Avery tuts and rolls her eyes.

"Sometimes I really don't know why I'm attracted to you." She steps aside, leaving Garrett in the firing line of Meg's shoe. It hits him hard in the chest.

"I was just thinking the exact same thing," Axel adds, already grabbing a box of ornaments. I chuckle as Garrett brushes himself down, bravely grabbing Meg around the neck and rubbing his knuckles over her scalp. He has a death wish. Huxley starts rummaging through the decorations, carefully removing baubles and placing them in piles depending on color. Avery moves to help and the rest of us follow suit, except for Meg. She's been drawn in by the scent of Huxley's coffee, heading off into the kitchen to wake up properly.

A short while later, everyone has been assigned jobs. Garrett is trying to untangle the endless mess of the fairy lights, Axel is decorating the fireplace and hanging the wreath. Huxley and I are Avery's tall servants, hanging tinsels and baubles on the exact branches she points to. Once the tree is finished, minus the star, we shift it back into the corner and drop onto the sofa beside Avery to appreciate it. Axel lights the fire when he's done, the warmth of the room enveloping us amongst the twinkling lights and sparkling ornaments.

"Okay, it actually looks so homely in here," Meg returns, her mood seemingly shifted. She's managed to tame her hair, while water droplets speckle her college sweatshirt. She hands us all a bottle of water in turn, marveling at the tree for a while longer. Having finished with the lights, Garrett joins us, a look of distant serenity on his face. It's calm moments like this that remind me Garrett was robbed of a real childhood, left to fend for himself. I doubt he even knew when Christmas was as a child, each day blending into the next.

Unscrewing the cap of his water, he slings an arm around Meg's shoulders to call a truce and takes a large swig. Suddenly spitting the water back out in a prolonged spray that covers us all, Garrett scrapes his tongue with his nails, choked gagging noises coming from his throat. "What the fuck is that?!" he croaks and retches. Meg loses herself to a fit of cackling hysterics, delivering back the knuckle polishing to Garrett's head.

"Sea water," she manages to rasp out. We all look at our own bottles, noticing that the safety caps are still attached and only crystal clear water sits inside. Huxley hides a rare smile behind his hand while Axel shakes his head, clearly amused by the scene unfolding before us. Avery's laughter bursts out, a beautiful, melodious sound that fills the room and sends warmth spreading through my chest. It's infectious. The joy in her eyes, the way she lights up at even the most chaotic moments—it's why I love her more than anything in this world. My heart beats a little faster just watching her, completely captivated by the moment, and ignoring Garrett's fit of cursing.

"You little-" he makes a grab for Meg and she manages to evade him. The pair tear through the kitchen, out the back door and onto the beach. We can't see them, but we can hear the squeals and screams. I hope Meg likes the taste of sand.

Inside the house, we're all falling over each other howling. A stitch pulls at my side, not having laughed this hard in so long. Beside me on the sofa, Avery turns to me, her eyes shining with happiness, and my heart skips a beat. She wraps her arms around my waist, her head on my chest. "This has turned out to be a great day," she murmurs, her voice full of contentment.

I brush a kiss to the top of her head, holding her close as Axel also leans in, eager for Avery's touch. Huxley cleans up, stacking the boxes on the stairs before he returns, handing Avery the star.

"Want to do the honors?" he asks. Taking the star from his hand, Avery stands for Huxley to lift her onto his good shoulder. She secures it in place and amongst the smiles, Axel's fingers snake into my hand. I squeeze them, a silent agreement that we did it. We made her happy.

The rest of the day is filled with just as much laughter, the air thick with the scent of pine and cinnamon. The sun climbs higher in the sky, but none of us seem to notice. Axel had the good sense to pick up a few candles, which added to the lit fireplace creating the perfect backdrop of a glass of wine and well deserved rest. Every light, banister and spare surface has been adorned with tinsel and garlands. Nothing matches. It's what I'd imagine the inside of Garrett's brain looks like, all a mismatch of color and textures exploded over the room.

The man in question has had it out for Meg, and she gives as good as she gets. As Avery pulls out a deck of playing cards, I jerk my head discreetly to Axel and we slip upstairs.

"Did you get it?"

Axel nods, a grin tugging at the corner of his mouth as we head into the quiet of his bedroom. "Of course I did," he whispers, pulling a sleek, rectangular box wrapped in deep green paper and tied with a crimson ribbon out from beneath his pillow. "The jeweler was just opening the shop but he wasn't going to turn down the cash we offered. Bank of Huxley," Axel chuckles softly.

I'd only been filling my time exploring the house when I happened upon a thin stairway to the attic. Somewhere Huxley had apparently already found, because he'd stashed his cash-filled backpack there. Suddenly a few tattered boxes of decorations became the spark for a Christmas I thought we were going to pretend wasn't happening - with Huxley's permission, of course.

Axel flips open the velvet box to reveal a delicate bracelet, thin strands of silver woven together like vines, studded with tiny diamonds that catch the light. In the center sits a charm of a compass with intricately etched directions.

"There wasn't much choice but I thought this might be fitting. Like she can always find her way back to us. Think she'll like it?"

"Are you kidding? It's stunning. She'll love it." Axel's hazel eyes sparkle, devotion rolling from him in waves. Finally, he's found someone to love who will return his affections. Taking the bracelet in his large fingers, he carefully turns it over.

"And it turns out, the jeweler had an engraver on hand. I got him to add this." On the back of the charm sits a tiny, dainty outline of a swan above the initials S.S. *The Shadowed Souls.*

"Oh, Axe." I pat him on the back, overcome with emotion. "She's going to cry, you know." Hell, I think I'm going to cry just imagining her response.

"Yeah," he says, grinning. "That's the plan." Tucking the bracelet back into the box, he slides it back beneath his pillow just as shouting sounds from downstairs. Not the kind of Garrett driving Meg crazy, but the panicked kind which drags my attention to the doorway. Rushing from the room, we take the stairs two at a time. Huxley is barking orders at Avery and Meg to go upstairs, leaving no room for argument. His tone is harsh, laced with concern and my own gut twists. The girl's sulky faces push past me as I hop down from the bottom step. "What's going on?" I ask no one in particular.

"A car has pulled up outside." Garrett answers for me, everyone standing around the living room poised for some kind of attack. Sweat lines Huxley's brow as he flexes his hands beneath the cuffs of his sweater. Axel and I are hanging back by the staircase, panic closing in. The weapons Huxley bought have been hidden all over the house and I'm already calculating which one is closest.

Shooting through the kitchen, a shadow on the other side of the blind follows me. My heart beats wildly, emotions I can't pay attention to rising and guiding my actions. From the cupboard beneath the basin, my hand curls around the cold, metal handle of my chosen object.

Pausing with my palm hovering over the back-door's handle, the figure steps in line with me, their face obscured by a black hood. Huxley shouts for me to get back but there's only so many times I can hide behind his bravado. I love Avery just as much as anyone in this house, and I have to be prepared to protect her safety like any other. Grabbing the handle, I twist and throw the door open, holding a hammer high above my head. Green eyes widen at the sight, Wyatt's eyebrows cocking in surprise.

"Hey Dax, nice to see you too."

WYATT

Footsteps pound against the wraparound porch, a heavy weight collides with me from behind and sending me flying into Dax. Initially thinking I've been attacked; I elbow and squirm until I recognize Garrett's fingers pushing in my hair and forcing my hood down. Dax pulls us both into a tight embrace, my bones threatening to crack under the pressure. It only hits me now how much I've truly missed my boys, a feeling that was much easier to suppress when they weren't around. Releasing me so I can breathe again, I find Axel approaching to clasp my hand.

"Welcome back, I hope you're staying?" His crisp hazel eyes watch me closely as I slap on the relaxed smile I've been practicing the whole way here from the passenger seat of

Nixon's navy Sedan. Not having the words to lie to him, I nod and move into the modern kitchen, removing my backpack and placing it on the mahogany dining table. Blond waves catch my attention, the saddest brown eyes I've ever seen glancing across the room but he makes no move to greet me. Walking through the kitchen, I initiate the hug this time, having known seeing Huxley would be the hardest part of this whole charade.

"Hey Hux." Gripping him tightly, he buries his face into my neck and squeezes me with the same vigor.

"Why didn't you return any of my calls?" His voice is muffled against my skin, moisture pooling in my collar-bone from the few tears which have escaped him. I swallow down my guilt, forcing myself to remember the real reason I came here. For answers. For revenge. "I've really needed you," he whispers, clearly not wanting the others to hear. *Fuck*, I didn't expect my resolve to crumble so easily.

"I know, I'm sorry man. I'm here now." I pat him on the back, my heart breaking as I say the words that I know aren't true. Needing to distance myself, I step back and my eyes land on my father standing uselessly in the living area. He came in the sensible way, through the front door. No longer trapped in his close proximity and pointedly ignoring him, I glance over his hair which has more gray in the temples than he's ever permitted before, disappointment etched into his pale blue eyes. Stubble lines his tense jaw which is at odds with his overly smart attire.

"We need to talk. All of us." There's no fondness in his tone until he approaches the staircase and looks up longingly. "I'll get the girls." I clench my fists until he's disappeared from sight. Hatred has kept me more company than Nixon has, the man I used to crave praise from barely uttering two words to me during the entire private jet and car ride. It was preferred really. I don't think I would have been able to make small talk without screaming at the top of my lungs, demanding answers.

Not in any rush to start this non-family reunion, I take in my surroundings. A charcoal gray sofa large enough to seat five, faces a lit fireplace with two matching armchairs parallel. A dark coffee table divides the room with a similarly colored cabinet by the window, and absolutely nothing else. No TV or games consoles, no entertainment in the slightest. I can already feel the boredom settling into my veins already.

Four pairs of eyes follow me as I wander around the room and take the armchair that's facing Huxley. He's rigid, his open hands placed on his jean-clad thighs. Thighs which look thinner, much like the bagginess of his T-shirt hiding a lack of muscle within. Dark circles frame his eyes and his hair is limp, in need of some deep conditioning. The Huxley I left behind would have never let himself get in such a state. What have they been doing to him?

Twisting his head to look at me expectantly, I blurt the first thing that comes to mind. "You look like shit." Huxley doesn't react, nodding with slow acceptance. Axel is quick to sit at his side and jump to his defense.

"Speak for yourself," Axel narrows his eyes at me.

I look down at my black hoodie, dark jeans and Timberlands. I look exactly the same as I always do. "Not your clothes," Axel clarifies. "You. Your eyes are bloodshot to shit. Are you on drugs?" Scoffing and refusing to answer such a stupid question, I hold out my empty hand towards Dax and Garrett lingering in the kitchen.

"Is someone going to get me a whiskey or do I need to do it myself?"

"You won't find whiskey here, Riot. You know it triggers Avery."

"Of course. Silly me," I roll my eyes. The expressions, which so recently were overjoyed to see me, harden. I knew it wouldn't take long. Footsteps sound on the stairs, beating in time with my dead heart. This is the part I've been truly dreading. Seeing *her* again. But it's not Avery who's trailing Nixon first. It's Meg.

"What the fuck is she doing here?" I scowl. No one answers. Avery has a whole support system under one roof while I've been cast aside, floundering on my own. I just buried a parent I didn't get the chance to know, while she's been surrounded by the men who are supposed to be mine. Ignoring me, Nixon steps aside for Meg to pass, closely followed by Avery. Fluffy white socks, long legs in leggings and an oversized orange hoodie swamping her upper half. I glare with malicious intent.

Is that my hoodie?

Ordering us to all congregate at the dining table, Nixon taps his foot and checks his watch for added effect as I slowly make my way over last. I'm numb to his glower, no longer a pup on his leash. I'm my own kind of pit bull now. I stride purposefully towards the furthest chair, ready to get this over with as quick as possible. Ready to hear Nixon's lies.

Avery and Meg huddle together at the top end of the table, Garrett and Axel doing the same opposite them. Dax and Huxley are on each of their sides, leaving a clear gap between them and me. Pulling his own chair back, Nixon lowers and rests an ankle over the opposite knee. For a moment, he doesn't speak. In the bright overhead light, shadows of creases pull at his eyes and mouth showing how much he has aged in the past few months.

"There's so much I need to tell you all but I'm afraid I can't stay long. An extremely dangerous man is searching for Avery so I need to keep moving, to keep throwing him off her trail."

"It sounds like your ghosts are catching up with you, Nixon." My voice echoes against the walls, my use of his real name not going unnoticed by those present. They have no idea what I've discovered, but they will. I won't let Nixon put his spin on what I now know.

"Wyatt, I need you to hear every word I'm about to say." He focuses on me with every ounce of his attention, something he hasn't gifted me with for an exceptionally long time. I nod for him to continue. "Cathy and I adopted you at four days old to cover up the fact we had twin girls. It's a long story I don't have time to dive into-" My laughter is a callous slap in his face, jarring him from the script he's probably been rehearsing during our entire car ride.

"Why don't we try that again?"

"Wyatt, what's gotten into you?" Dax raises a brow. He might as well be addressing a stranger, and I suppose that's what I am to all of them now. But they need to know this.

"Who, me? Oh nothing. I just thought this meeting was supposed to be worth the journey. At this rate, I might as well not have bothered coming." Picking at my nails, I hide the true anxiety creeping through me. I could have stayed with Rachel, focusing on rebuilding a life where I'm not used as a pawn.

"Well since you're so knowledgeable, why don't you take the lead, Son?" Nixon challenges me. I see what he's doing, provoking me into spilling all I know so he can lie his way out. I'm not fooled, but I'm not in the mood to play coy either. Jetlag is a bitch at the best of times.

"Fine. You didn't adopt me, you stole me. My real father was your best friend and business partner. You blackmailed him into giving me up, forcing him to choose between his newborn son or his wife."

"Is that true?" Avery gasps, her head whipping back to Nixon. I'm confused by the rigidness of her spine, acting as if she actually gives a shit about me. No one gives a shit about me anymore, except Rachel.

Nixon unhooks his ankle and leans back to steeple his fingers. This is the disapproving man I remember growing up with, the one who looks at my grazed knees as if it offended him that I bled. Who only cared to address me in public. Nixon hasn't been that man since Avery was brought back to the manor, which all makes perfect sense now.

"Ray Perelli was a crook. He made the wrong deals with the wrong kind of people. I did you a favor removing you from him and that scatterbrain wife of his. I don't know what Cathy got out of being friends with such a ditsy woman."

"Don't you dare speak of Rachel that way! You have no idea how she's suffered because of your mistakes!" I fly into a rage, standing and kicking my chair back against the wall. Huxley is before me in the next second, those dormant instincts flaring back to life.

"Hey man, it's okay. I've got you," Hux mutters into my ear, his large hands braced on my shoulders. It's only his weakened state that holds me back from shoving against him, searching for a way to vent my frustration. "He's not worth it." I catch Hux's serious stare. Has he been able to see Nixon's true colors too? Grabbing my seat, I swivel it on one leg and plant myself on it backwards now. The backrest acts as a barrier.

"The Perelli's are good people," I grit through my clenched teeth. "It wasn't just them you robbed of a son, but me of a loving family." Nixon sighs, a dramatic fall of this chest which makes me tighten my fists by my sides. One of these days, I'm going to ensure Nixon feels the anguish I've been forced to live with. In my peripheral vision, a shadowy figure nods.

"We loved you Wyatt. Even when you made it impossible to."

"You used me." I spit back. The tension between us hardens, so much to be said but it's all redundant. I will never be able to understand and I will never forgive him.

"Sorry, 'scuse me," Garrett raises his hand like a school child. "Can we just hit the rewind button for a second? Before you started robbing cribs, if you please." A flutter of warmth hits me unexpectedly as Garrett shoots me a sly wink. Nixon isn't amused but when he glances upon his precious, innocent Avery, his expression softens.

"Cathy was having an affair," he begins, oblivious to the fact we already know this. Huxley showed me the diary, it's detailed in undisputable black and white. "And she fell pregnant with twins. I knew they couldn't be mine because I have...fertility issues," he clears his throat. I snort, reveling in his embarrassment.

"Maybe it was the world's way of telling you nothing good would come of being a father." My response is ignored, his entire focus on the two girls huddled together at his end of the table.

Nixon continues to speak, detailing how he and Cathy were looking into adoption when she broke the news. How she begged him to stay with her, that she'd break it off with the other man. Freddie Walters, Nixon called him. There are many things to be said about Cathy, but nothing tops her need to maintain her public appearance. I've heard the rest of the story from Ray, how Freddie became obsessive, impulsive. How he threatened to take the girls if Cathy wouldn't be with him.

The longer Nixon speaks, the quieter his voice becomes in my ears. A white noise takes over as I follow his eyeline to the girls and back. The shadow lingering around me makes the connection at the same time I do, dragging itself closer to the pair.

Two sets of blue eyes look ahead, varying in shade beneath perfectly arched eyebrows. Side on together, their profiles are identical, button noses smeared with light freckles above full lips that they are both biting subconsciously. Wearing matching hoodies and leggings, only the colors differing like the long hair upon their oval shaped heads, the truth of their genetics is so clear I can't believe I've never seen it before. My stomach plummets.

"-Cathy had trouble breastfeeding, she could only handle one baby at a time. She was with a night nurse when Walters made his move. He only found Avery asleep in the crib and stole her from us that night. We didn't know what to do, so the best idea we could come up with was to hide our other daughter with a woman we'd met at the infertility clinic."

Nixon briefly closes his eyes, the picture of guilt and sorrow. What a fantastic act. "It took us ten years and hundreds of private investigators to track down Walters. He may be insane, but he knows how to keep a low profile. As soon as we found out his location, we drove sixteen hours to bring you home," Nixon's voice cracks, his hand outstretched to rest on Avery's. "You were right there, so frail and skinny, darting out in the road. We almost hit you with our car."

I return to the present, my heart too tight to beat properly. I can't listen to these twisted versions of the truth that make Nixon sound so innocent. He leaves out the part where neither he nor Cathy couldn't risk their precious reputations, so they decided to trick her deranged lover by sending their best friends to prison on bogus fraud charges and claim the right to their baby. I bite the inside of my cheeks at the thought of Ray and Rachel's pain, their devastation at losing me. And what do any of us even have to show for it now?

Dax has inched closer to Avery, her hand now hanging low in his. Her other arm is wrapped around her best friend, clinging onto her for support.

"Okay," Avery nods, absorbing every word. "So who is she - my twin? Is she in danger too?" My head pulls forward on its own accord, my ears pricked. I want to hear him say it. Keeping his head low, avoiding all eye contact, Nixon's answer travels across the table on a low breath.

"It's Meg," Nixon confirms. I knew it was coming, but I still feel like a sledgehammer has barreled through my chest. She's been right here, under our noses the entire time. The brunette herself looks like she's about to vomit. I almost pity her, having been a bystander to Avery's pain to now being thrust into the center of it. It's shit finding out your mom isn't really your mom and nothing you believed is true.

Avery's face has tilted, her expression lost to me by a mass of blonde hair. "I- I don't understand."

"It was always our intention to leave you girls and let you grow up to lead happy, comfortable lives. But after we found you in that state, Cathy thought it would be helpful to introduce you to Meg. So we hired Keren to be your therapist and encouraged Meg to stay over every weekend."

I notice how Nixon is yet to speak to Meg directly, speaking over her as if she isn't even here. As much as the notion is intriguing, a wave of fresh anger washes over me.

How dare he ignore her now, his full attention still centered on Avery. The daughter he loves above all others, the only one he truly wanted.

"Address her," I growl, my brows pinched. Nixon flashes me a warning glance that has no effect. "Meg is sitting right there. The least you can do is talk to her." Nixon's mouth twitches in frustration, but he doesn't meet my eyes. Instead, he shifts uncomfortably in his seat, the tension thickening in the air. Meg sits motionless, her hands clasped around Avery's arm. Her face is ashen, her eyes wide with disbelief. She's absorbing everything, but she's clearly drowning under the weight of it all.

"Meg," Nixon finally mutters, his voice lower, as if forcing out her name burns his throat. "We did what we thought was best for both of you." He speaks slowly, deliberately, as if every word might shatter the delicate balance of truth now teetering between them.

Meg doesn't blink, her gaze locked somewhere distant. Her lips tremble, but she doesn't speak. I can see the fear and confusion mixing with her anger, swirling in her expression like a storm brewing just beneath the surface. I can't blame her—finding out everything you knew about yourself was a lie, all in one conversation? It's enough to break anyone.

Avery is struggling too. Her hand tightens around Dax's, her knuckles white. She glances at her sister, really seeing her for the first time in a new light.

"This whole time..." Avery whispers, the words barely audible. She looks back at Nixon. "How long would you have let these lies continue if your hand wasn't being forced? Forever?"

Nixon lowers his head. "It wasn't meant to be like this."

Meg finally finds her voice, though it's ragged and thin. "You use people," she reiterates my words from earlier. I suffer with her then, my pulse beating in my ears. Someone finally understands my pain. Meg turns to Nixon, her voice shaky. "Everyone at this table aside from Avery is expendable to you."

Nixon shifts uncomfortably again, but he doesn't deny it. The silence is his confession. The room becomes suffocating. Nixon looks ready to speak, but I see the indecision on his face, unsure how to move forward. Meg is just another problem he can fix with a few carefully chosen words.

"I'm sorry," he finally says, the words brittle in the heavy air. "But the damage is done. What matters now is Avery's safety." I don't know why I expected anything different from the same old familiar tune. Nixon has shut himself off from anything aside from his tunnel visioned goal. His words wouldn't have fixed anything anyway. The truth has already torn through our lives, and no amount of apologies can piece it back together. "Cathy made these choices on all of our behalf. I'm just following through with her wishes. I'm not to blame."

"What a cop-out." Axel scoffs, excusing himself from the table. He's had his fair share of parents playing puppeteer. He doesn't need to sit through it again. Garrett gives Nixon his best glare face before following his lover out onto the back porch. I should leave too. Make a scene of storming out and smashing a few things, but the numb sensation has taken up residence in my body once again. Ray's shadow clings to me, my hands starting to tremble.

Pushing up from the table, Nixon rests his hands on the mahogany surface. "I will be leaving shortly. Walters seems to be on my trail wherever I go. I can't risk him finding me here."

"What's the plan then?" I raise my hands into the air. "Are we supposed to wait here for you to return or shall I send a carrier pigeon when another one of my friends has been injured?"

"I don't have a next step yet. I'm living day to day as it is." I see it then, the weariness in Nixon's eyes, the weight in his stance. He's exhausted, and I can't bring myself to give two shits. "There's no signal at the safehouse but the closest town is forty miles away. Drive down every few days to check your emails. I'll update you when I have any information."

Well, that's that then. I'm stranded with two women who hate me and a gang that doesn't know me anymore. Huxley is sitting beside me but he might as well be miles away, watching the pair across the table. Avery and Meg are clinging to one another, and Dax is hovering on the edge, ready to swoop in and be Avery's prince charming. There's just one burning question I can't leave unanswered.

"Why did you even bring me here?" I ask, hating that the way the words sound leaving my mouth. They taste bitter like ash. Nixon raises his gaze, a harshness there which reminds me of the piece of paper burning a hole in my pocket.

"Wyatt, more than anyone, you know you're the only one who can truly protect Avery. No matter what's happened before now, you're still her best chance."

"Gee, thanks a bunch," Huxley mutters. Watching Nixon leave, I scowl at his back with all of the anger I've been suppressing. The weight of his words lingers, but it feels hollow, just another burden dumped on us without a plan. I can feel Huxley's frustration radiating off him, his arms crossed tightly against his chest like a shield. The tremors in my hands increases, finally pushing me to rise from my seat and leave the kitchen.

Grabbing my bag, I hunt for the first bathroom I find, slamming the door closed with my back. The shadow follows me everywhere I go, a comforting presence in my blind spot. Tipping my bag upside down, the contents spill out but it's only the small plastic tub Rachel gave to me before I left that I'm interested in. Thirty pink circular pills rattle inside. She calls them vitamins but I've come to realize they're much more potent.

Removing two, I swallow them dry and sink into the floor, my back pressed against the wood. Instantly, I feel the world slip away and only the pieces of myself I choose to cling onto remain. My anger at Nixon, my sympathy for Meg, my grief for Ray, all float away on a cloud of relief. I inhale as if my lungs have never expanded so much, the lightness of my limbs bringing an easy smile to my lips. *Finally*, I can let go and remember what's important. I'm Wyatt Perelli, and I'm such a good boy.

MEG

Leaning my head on Avery's shoulder, I watch Nixon retreat upstairs. The entire time he was speaking, the weight of his secrets were visible in the stress lines etched into his face. He's retiring for a shower and nap before he leaves once again. Leaves us here to fend for ourselves.

How have I been so blind? So willing to accept inconsistencies over the years. My first instinct is man, I sure caught a lucky break. Watching Wyatt glare at Avery across the table, listening to Nixon try to justify his actions. Then came the dawning that Avery's birth father, *my birth father*, is stalking her, intent on bringing her more pain and suffering.

Whereas, I had a mom who raised me with more love than I could have ever asked for. She gave me all of her time, her full attention and that's something the Hughes' money could never buy. This is why she left so quickly without saying goodbye. Like ripping off the band aid, she thought after I heard Nixon's truth, I would disown her. The opposite couldn't be more true. All I want to do is wrap my arms around my mom and thank her.

Once the weight of the day settles, Avery and I retreat to our room. The guys wanted to comfort her, offering me small understanding smiles. I just wanted my head to stop spinning. Dropping onto the bed, I shudder as Avery digs her backpack out from beneath the bed. She pulls out Cathy's old diary and nestles in close.

"I've read this cover to cover a hundred times," she tells me. "But maybe now we know, you should reread it with me?" I nod tentatively. Creaking the spine, Avery opens the first page, settling into my side. We fit together like missing halves of a whole. It's so obvious, so natural. Something we've done a thousand times before, but has never held so much meaning. Swallowing hard, I gaze upon the words of a woman I only knew as Mrs. Hughes up until now.

I'm pregnant. With twins. And they aren't Nixon's.

It feels harsh to admit, but it's my reality. From the outside, my life seemed perfect—successful career, beautiful home, a husband who once adored me. But our marriage has been crumbling for years. Nixon withdrew long before this, spending more time at the office than with me. We've become strangers, barely touching on anything beyond appearances.

Then Freddie came into my life. It wasn't supposed to happen, but he made me feel alive again—seen, desired, like the woman I used to be. I know it was wrong, but I can't regret it completely, especially not with the babies growing inside me. I already love them more than I can explain.

Nixon knows the twins aren't his, though he hasn't said it. There's a coldness in his eyes, a distance between us that feels permanent. We're both avoiding the inevitable conversation, neither willing to start it.

I don't know what happens next. I want to beg him to stay for the sake of the children, but how can I ask that knowing the truth? I made my choices, and now I have to live with them. All I can hope is that these babies will one day forgive me for the mistakes I've made.

Avery kisses my forehead, jarring me from staring into the distance and refocusing on the page. Cathy makes it sound so simple. An ignored wife, an accidental pregnancy. Except nothing about Cathy's life was simple. She's known worldwide, her reputation carefully crafted to seem warm, content and charitable. And all she cared about was if Nixon would stick around to continue that illusion.

"*Freddie,*" Avery shudders. "It makes me physically sick to know she actually fell for that psychopath."

"Mmm," I purse my lips. "And to know that psychopath is our dad." A moment of dreaded silence falls, suddenly lifted by a small smile to Avery's lips.

"Fuck me, you're my sister Meg." As if the notion has just hit her, Avery squeals and throws herself onto me. The diary hits the floor with a thud, instantly forgotten. I suspect it isn't needed anymore, not when the past Avery has been chasing is right here. I'm right here. The other half of her soul, the sister she always wished she had.

Wrapping her arms around my neck, she peppers kisses in my hair. I can't help but laugh, the sound muffled in Avery's shoulder as she clings to me. Her excitement is infectious, even though the truth that has just been uncovered is still sinking in. The sister I never knew I had. The father we never wanted. The mother whose perfect life was anything but.

Avery pulls back just enough to cup my face, her eyes glistening with unshed tears. "We're in this together now, okay? No more secrets."

I nod slowly, playing catch up on the implications of what 'we're in this together now' really means. Avery's expression is filled with joy and hope, and that's how I know she hasn't fully understood what this means for me. If my birthright becomes public knowledge, I'll be in Fredrick's firing line too. He's been looking for me.

It feels like everything has shifted in an instant. The life I thought I knew, the family I thought I had—it's all been rewritten by one man's declaration and a few crumpled pages. But to Avery, she's no longer alone in this. She has someone to share the burden with, someone who's soon to be in the exact same position of being forced out of college and chased across country.

I don't want that. I love my life.

Avery wipes a tear from my cheek with the pad of her thumb, mistaking it for the hollow realization that it actually is. Her voice is softer now. "I wish things were different. I wish Cathy had told us everything from the start, that we could've been with each other sooner."

I lower my gaze, my heart heavy. Is it selfish of me to understand why Nixon wanted to keep us apart, to keep the attention off of me? Yeah, it really fucking is. "I know. But we're here now." My chest expands and falls but I feel nothing but hollowness inside.

We sit there in the artificial light of our bedroom, surrounded by the ghosts of a past we didn't ask for. The air is thick with everything unsaid, my stomach knotting from the tension. My mind keeps drifting back to Nixon, though. The burdens he's carried for twenty-one years and is still trying to run from.

"What do we do now?" I ask quietly, more to myself than Avery. The gravity of the situation presses down on me, and suddenly, I feel small again, like a child lost in someone else's nightmare.

Avery takes a deep breath and shrugs, a familiar defiant smile flickering across her face. One I've seen in the mirror many times. "To be honest, I could eat."

I laugh again, this time a little less hollow. As if I forgot how brave my twin is. How used to these turbulent twists and turns she's become, that now it's second nature. She's still the exact same person she was this morning and will continue to be. Considering I'm normally the more confident one out of us, I really need to step back and take Avery's lead on this.

"Okay, yeah. Let's get food." It feels good to shift the focus, even just for a minute. Avery hops off the bed, her infectious energy pulling me along as I follow her down both flights of stairs. We step into the kitchen, where the air still feels heavy and stale from our recent family meeting. The faint scent of old coffee lingers, toying with me. Except I can't get to the machine because Wyatt is leaning on the counter in front of it, holding a cup in hand.

His sharp, unreadable eyes flick up as we enter, and the tension thickens instantly. The weight of his judgment settles over us like an invisible fog. I watch him intently as he moves like a predator, retrieving his bag and stopping in front of us. A vein protrudes from his temple, his jaw clenched tight enough to crack a tooth. Pure hatred is swirling in his green eyes, and it all seems to be directed solely at me.

Leaning close, Wyatt puts us nose to nose. "Don't expect my protection to extend to you. I can only handle watching over one helpless fake sister at a time."

I don't know what Wyatt was expecting, maybe a curtsey or for me to scurry away in floods of tears, but the shock in his face says it definitely wasn't the full powered shove to his chest making him take a step back. Even Avery gasps and grabs for me, knowing I'd take a swing if I felt like it. I understand his world has been flipped upside down and he's no longer sitting high up on his titanium pedestal, but I'm not meek and it's best he realizes that from the start. Wyatt can't intimidate me.

Dax materializes between us, holding Wyatt at bay as he tries to advance on me again. He rams his shoulder into his friend, those haunted irises glued to me the whole time. Something has changed within him. Avery and I have always known he's a moody shitbag, but physical violence has never been one of his traits.

A hand wraps around my wrist, Axel gently tugging me away. Wyatt growls like an animal, practically frothing at the mouth as I allow myself to be removed from his firing line, pulling Avery with me. As soon as we are clear, Wyatt twists to throw his fist into the nearest wall before shoving past Dax and storming upstairs on thunderous feet.

"And here I was, thinking he'd be rolling out the welcome banner for his new sis," I deadpan. Realizing Axel is still holding my wrist, I shake out of his grip and eye them all suspiciously. Dax has moved into the threshold between the two rooms, his hands clasped in front of him like a warden overseeing his prisoners. And then there's Garrett, the polar opposite as usual, swinging his legs back and forth whilst sitting on the kitchen counter. A huge grin reaches from ear to ear, his dark eyes sparkling with excitement.

"Here," Avery hands me a banana and ushers me into the living room. "Keep Huxley company while we make dinner for everyone." I only now notice him sitting on the long sofa since he is unnervingly still, staring at the opposite wall. His pale cheeks are surprisingly hollow, no hint of the smile he used to permanently wear. Crossing the room, I take the armchair on the far side so I can watch Avery and Dax's dynamic. Looking over to my companion he doesn't acknowledge me as I clear my throat.

"Rough couple of weeks, huh?" is all I can think to say. No response. *Wow, someone is a barrel of laughs.* Sitting back against the cushions, I unpeel my banana and turn my attention to Avery instead. She is currently washing lettuce while Dax's biceps ripple in time with his vigorous cheese grating. He flicks a strand of cheese at her, landing in her hair as she giggles and flicks water onto his face.

A topless Axel hops down the stairs, only to find himself in the middle of a food fight. Grabbing her around the waist from behind, Avery squeals as Axel spins her in time for a handful of coriander to hit his bare back. Arming himself with a chopping board as a shield and a spatula as a sword, Axel advances on Dax who fails to dodge the spatula spank he receives on his backside.

Huffing at the sound of Avery's giggles, Huxley pushes himself to his feet and leaves swiftly.

"It was nice talking to you," I call after him, unable to resist. He doesn't glance back, opening the front door and slamming it shut behind himself. "Well, fuck me I guess." I mutter. Garrett jumps over the back of the sofa to land on his side, his hand beneath his head as he watches me take a bite of my banana.

"A few months ago, I would have taken that as an invitation," he smirks.

"What changed?" I ask out of curiosity. His eyes slide to the group messing about in the kitchen, his attention pinpointed on Avery in the center and I have my answer. Drawing my legs beneath myself and covering them with a blanket, I settle in to watch as well. None of this evening's revelations are evident in her sparkling blue eyes, in her wide smile. That's what sets Avery apart from everyone else. Her whole world can be falling into chaos, but she'll find happiness in the smallest of places. I truly believe it's what pulled her through the horrific childhood I was seemingly spared.

"She's always been like that, you know?" I mumble. Garrett doesn't look my way but his ears prick up.

"Like what?"

"A paradox. Avery says she hates crowds and people, hiding away any chance she gets, but everyone she meets is drawn to her. She's magnetic." The outline of a smile tugs at Garrett's cheek as he slowly cracks his knuckles.

"Well as long as those drawn to her keep their hands to themselves, I won't have to become a master at breaking fingers beyond repair." Turning to face me at last, Garrett's grin has taken on a manic edge.

I try not to smile back but I can't seem to figure Garrett out. Usually, I'd write him off as a self-centered jackoff. But for some reason, I like him. It's the way he breaks all of his own rules for Avery, how he listens to her, adapts for her. How much he clearly has feelings for her, even though I doubt he's recognized them yet.

The others in the kitchen have returned to preparing a meal. In record time, they are transferring plates to the dining table so I move over to the table. Garrett rushes past, shoving me off the chair I try to take at the head of the table. Opting for the next one closest, the smell of spices and onion fill the room. A stack of fajitas takes pride of place, surrounded by chopped salad, both meat and veggie fillings and a range of condiments.

While all of the men present take a seat with me, Avery remains standing, preparing a plate and carrying it outside. Tracking her beyond the windows, I watch Avery sit with Huxley, who is now on the wooden swinging seat. He still doesn't smile or outwardly show any type of joy, but he leans in and takes a bite of the food she offers him. They eat together in silence, quietly sharing and enjoying each other's company.

My scoff and eye roll doesn't go unnoticed. My cheeks heat as the three men around the table immediately shift their attention toward me. "I'm sorry, I know he's your friend and everything. I get the appeal with the rest of you but...I just don't get what Avery sees in him. He's so different from the man who was so full of life at Sweetwater Creek."

"Don't be too hard on Huxley. He wasn't raised with love and affection like we were." Dax's voice drifts across the table with a calm understanding that catches me off guard. I suck in a breath, noticing how Garrett has swiftly diverted his attention to his plate, while Axel's thigh presses firmly against Garrett's under the table, a silent show of support. Axel's hazel eyes meet mine, softened with a quiet sorrow.

"When Hux cares about someone, nothing else matters but their wellbeing. He'll do anything to ensure their happiness, which, in his mind, often means he's better off keeping his distance. We've all been through it." A round of low grunts circles the table. "He just takes a little more convincing that he's worthy of love."

Forcing myself to plate up and act normal, I take a bite of my fajita, noting how I barely taste anything now. The first tremors of a headache are beginning to settle in the base of my skull. I was fully prepared to be here to support Avery, providing a woman's touch when the testosterone became overbearing. I figured Fredrick would be located and thrown back in jail for a basic parole violation, then we'd all go back to school and carry on.

But none of that is true. Nixon believes there was foul play with Cathy's death, that Fredrick has plans to capture Avery and her twin. To torture and kill us both.

"We're so happy you're here with us, Meg. Avery's been so lost without you." Dax interrupts my spiraling, smiling kindly just as I lift my food to my mouth and take a large bite. I force myself to swallow, Dax's words having an opposite effect to what he intended. If anything, he's just torn a larger hole through my chest. I'm sitting with a group of men who are openly in love with my best friend, my twin, and a dull thud in my ears whispers that they'd sacrifice me for her.

Avery would never allow it, but that's only if she knew. Dropping my food, I suddenly stand. Those three pairs of eyes are on me again, watching too closely. I'm trapped in a safe house with no phone signal, no mode of transport and nowhere to go. I'm a lamb being led to the slaughter.

The back door creaks open, and the soft sound of Avery's voice tugs at me. "Meg?" Her words are tentative, unsure, but I can't stop. Her plate clatters on the counter behind me as she rushes to follow. I'm moving faster, trying not to break into a full sprint, my chest tightening with every step as I rush upstairs.

In the bedroom, I collapse into her arms, burying my face in her neck as though I could disappear. My fingers cling to her shirt, and she holds me back just as fiercely. Her hand strokes up and down my spine, each movement a soothing balm to the storm raging inside me.

"Aves, I love you." The words come out in a hoarse whisper, muffled against her hair.

"I love you too." Avery pulls away so she can see the miserable look on my face. "But?"

"I need to leave." I rush the words out, hoping they don't slice through her as sharply as they do me. We've just truly found each other, after all of this time. Her body stiffens, her face a mixture of confusion and fear. "I'm asking you to please let me go. The only people who know about me are in this house, and my mom. I know it's selfish, I'm sorry, but I....I still have a chance. I could go back to my life and now I understand the dangers, I can be careful."

Her face crumbles as the impact of what I'm saying hits her. I've just found her, and now I'm tearing myself away again. "But we're together and the guys will keep you safe. It's all going to be okay." I can see by the tears in her eyes, she doesn't believe that. She knows I'm right.

"The men downstairs are here for you, not me. They will do whatever it takes to keep you safe, and that's amazing. Please understand that you've been fighting this unknown evil for months, but I've just found out about it. I need some time, and I need my own support system."

Avery's arms loosen, though her hands still grip my shoulders. Her eyes glisten with unshed tears, and her bottom lip trembles.

I step back, breaking the physical connection between us, though it feels like ripping a part of myself away. Her arms drop limply to her sides, and I see the moment her hope falters. "Nixon has kept us apart for a reason," she sighs. "I was speaking to Huxley outside, wondering why Nixon sent me to Waversea instead of Cedarbrook with you. He didn't want to draw attention to us as a pair. And until this is all over, I think he might be right."

Her face crumples. The tears fall freely now, the quiet sobs wracking her shoulders. Avery has always been so strong. But now, standing here, vulnerable, there's nothing she can do to fix this. Nothing that will hold us together when I'm the one walking away.

"This is my choice, not Nixon's," I manage to get out, my voice hoarse. "It's my only chance of freedom." This seems to sober Avery in an instant. That strength is back, straightening her posture. I've resonated with a desire she's had stolen from her. She's been living in this storm for months, while I've just stepped into it, unprepared, raw.

That night, in the cover of pitch black, I hug my twin goodbye. She turns into the chests of the men waiting to comfort her as I slip into the back of Nixon's car, the tears silently falling and my heart cracking in time with the engine starting. I look at the clock on the dash, watching one minute strike past midnight.

"Merry Christmas, Aves." I whisper into my knees. "Thank you for letting me go."

AVERY

To my pleasant surprise, the Shadowed Souls let me sleep most of the day away. Christmas Day. A day that should have been filled with joy and laughter, yet I couldn't bring myself to face it. The weight of the past, the mess I'm tangled in, feels too heavy to bear right now. Throughout my slumber, I faintly felt the shift of bodies around me, someone always staying by my side. There were countless moments I could have let myself wake, but I chose not to. Dreaming seemed easier.

Behind my closed eyelids, I could pretend Meg was still here, laughing by my side. I could pretend Nixon hadn't stolen his business partner's baby to cover up his wife's affair. Pretend I hadn't ended up in Fredrick's clutches anyway, despite everyone's attempts to keep me safe. Memories of those darkest days tried to claw their way into my dreams more times than I care to count, but each time, the warm arms of whoever was holding me chased them away.

At one point, I was certain I could smell remnants of Wyatt's expensive cologne. It's a powerful thing, dreaming, because I swore I could feel his arms tighten around me as if to anchor me here. There was even a faint whisper, telling me he would keep me safe. What a cruel lie for my mind to conjure up. But in the haze of sleep, I almost believed it.

Eventually, I rouse as the sun begins to set, casting the room in a warm, golden light. I shift, my limbs heavy from sleep, and find myself staring directly into Dax's icy blue eyes. His gaze is soft, all the usual sharpness muted. Somehow, his presence chases away the last remnants of the coldness I woke up with.

"How long have you been watching me sleep?" I ask, raising a brow. Dax gives me that half-smile of his, as though weighing up his answer.

"Long enough to be considered endearing but not creepy." I let out a soft laugh, nudging him with my shoulder.

"I can see why you took English lit for extra credit."

"Best thing I ever did," he says, wriggling closer, until there isn't an inch of space between us under the covers. His breath is warm against my lips as he murmurs, "Because it brought me to you."

His kiss is slow, deliberate and unhurried, like he's savoring every second. I melt into him, my body responding instinctively, though my mind still feels like it's catching up.

Dax always knows how to make me feel seen, even in my messiest moments. As his lips move against mine, I allow myself to fall into the sensation, letting it drown out the lingering shadows.

But the peace doesn't last. The moment we pull apart, the weight of everything comes rushing back—the tangled web I can't escape, the lies, the danger lurking on the edge of our world.

"Dax," I whisper, pulling back just enough to search his face. "What if I can't fix any of this? What if Wyatt never forgives me?" Dax silences me with another kiss, this one firmer, more urgent, before pulling back to look me dead in the eyes.

"You don't have to fix everything and you certainly aren't asking for forgiveness," he says, his voice low and steady. "None of this is your fault, and you're not alone, okay? We're here. I'm here."

For a second, I want to believe him. Want to let the comfort of his words wash over me and erase the fear gnawing at my gut. But I know better. Fredrick spent years teaching me that I'll always be his victim, even when I thought I'd found freedom. Tracing my fingers along his jaw, I try to hold onto this fragile moment for just a little longer.

"Come on Swan, the boys will be ready soon."

"Ready for what?" I ask but Dax decides he's said enough. Instead, he tugs me up, cradles me in his arms to the bathroom and proceeds to shower with me. I'm not complaining, sighing at his gentle touches and chaste kisses. He lathers body wash all over us both, slipping and sliding, taking intimate care to wash between my legs. Moving onto my hair, Dax honors me like his queen, his lips finding the crook of my shoulder on multiple occasions. Every time I try to reach for his hardened cock between us, he eases my hand away.

"This is about you," he whispers. Thoroughly cleaned, Dax takes a warm towel from the rack and wraps me in it. I step back into the bedroom, halting at the sight of Axel standing beside the vanity, a paddle brush in one hand and hairdryer in the other, like it's the most natural thing in the world.

"My turn," Axel declares, his voice smooth and calm, but the intensity in his eyes makes my heart skip a beat. Dax gives my lower back a gentle push, and I find myself walking toward Axel without even thinking, the soft towel wrapped around me like a shield.

I glance over my shoulder at Dax, but he's already slipping out of the room, leaving just the two of us. The door closes with a quiet click, and suddenly, the space between Axel and me feels charged with something unspoken. His hazel eyes are heavy with emotion as he looks me over, freshly scrubbed and standing in the center of the fluffy rug. Not just desire, but something deeper. It makes my breath catch.

Axel gestures to the chair in front of the vanity, and I sit, my legs curling up under the towel. I can't help but shiver a little, not from cold but from the feeling of being cared for like this—like I'm delicate, precious.

"Relax," Axel laughs softly, running his fingers over my tense shoulders. "I might not have hair but I'm not totally inept." I smile at him in the mirror, although it wasn't his skills I was questioning. It was how much longer I can go without throwing myself into his long arms and declaring the depth of my feelings for him. For all of them, because apparently I can't be satisfied with a typical relationship.

Oblivious, Axel gently untangles the damp strands of my hair with his fingers first. I close my eyes as he begins brushing through my hair, slow and methodical. Each stroke of the brush pulls me further from my swirling thoughts and deeper into the present, the weight of the past momentarily lifting. Axel's touch is hypnotic, grounding. It makes me feel safe.

He works in silence, drying my hair with precision, the soft hum of the hairdryer filling the space. I feel his gaze on me, the heat of it making my skin tingle, but he doesn't rush. He's always had this way of making everything seem like there's no urgency, like time bends around him.

Setting the dryer down, Axel runs his hands over my now-silky golden hair. I pause to assess the brown roots pushing against my scalp, barely a millimeter but now I know why Cathy was so desperate for me to be blonde, I have a decision to make. Should I continue to dye it or become a brunette again like Meg?

"Beautiful," Axel murmurs, stepping back to admire his work. A faint knock sounds on the door.

"How's it going in here?" Garrett pops his head around the door. Axel smirks and gestures for him to enter. For a moment the pair of them stand shoulder to shoulder, sizing me up like their next meal. A wave of heat flushes my skin, my nipples tightening under the towel as my mind flashes back to memories of them sharing me and dominating me. As if sensing my thoughts, Axel's grin widens, a dimple flashing before he turns and slips out of the room. Garrett steps closer, his hands resting on the back of the chair, spinning me to face him.

"Don't tell me," I roll my eyes, "all of this is part of some plan you've concocted. Using the others to get me ready for you." He chuckles, the deep, rich sound making my stomach flip.

"I like the way you think, Peach, but not quite. I'm your fairy Garrett-mother, here to help you put clothes *on* for once." True to his word, Garrett turns to the dresser and ruffles through the clothes folded neatly inside. Some are Meg's that she left behind, figuring I'd have more use for them than her. Garrett pulls out a soft cashmere sweater in a shade of light gray and a pair of black leggings.

"Here," he says, turning to face me. "Something comfortable but cute. You'll thank me later." I narrow my eyes at him as I stand, the towel wrapped around me slipping slightly.

"Do I get any underwear?" Garrett roars with laughter this time, slapping his knee and wagging a finger at me as if I'm a comedy genius. Whipping the towel aside, he helps to guide my feet through the leg holes, pausing to inhale my pussy before pulling the leggings up over my hips. I should probably feel a trace of embarrassment but there are some things you just expect with Garrett. His audacity is one of them. He slips the sweater over my head, the fabric sliding over my skin like butter. Garrett brushes the back of his tattooed fingers over my nipples through the fabric, his gaze hungry but restrained.

"We'd better get out of this room before I undo everyone's hard work," Garrett licks his lips suggestively.

"Where are we going?" I ask. Garrett winks, opening the door to present Huxley standing on the landing outside. The blond beams as he spots me, probably thankful Garrett stuck to his job. The latter jogs downstairs, leaving Huxley to pull me into the cage of his arms.

"Hey," I breathe. His brown eyes sparkle.

"Hey." The tension between us has dissipated since yesterday morning, where I kind of blamed him for everything that's wrong in my life and then screwed him on the kitchen island. Both of those things were needed to get over the hurdles separating us, evidently hitting the reset button on our relationship. "Merry Christmas, my love." I turn to liquid at the name, leaning against Huxley's solid chest for support. It's almost too much, the intensity of care they're all showing me. How they've once again understood exactly what I needed and proven why I was right to fall for them all so quickly.

"Why are you all doing this for me?" I lean back, stroking a strand of Huxley's hair away from his stubbled chin. His lips twitch into a small, lopsided smile and his hands rest gently on my arms.

"There isn't much we could do about Nixon's...intrusion yesterday, and salvaging the festive season seemed like a lost cause. We agreed the least we could do was make you feel safe and wanted. This is just a fraction of what you deserve."

His words hit me hard, breaking through the last of my defenses. I've spent all night trying to stay strong, to keep it all together. What I so easily forgot is that I have four men who will gladly carry my burdens on my behalf, shouldering the weight of the world so I don't have to. I bite my lip, trying to keep the tears at bay, but it's no use. One escapes, slipping down my cheek. Huxley catches it with his thumb, wiping it away gently.

"No crying on Christmas. That can be your present to me."

"I can't make any promises," I manage to smile. We stand together, content to stare at one another for a while. Then Huxley tucks my arm into his and escorts me downstairs, the anticipation building with every step. Surprisingly, the house is entirely still. No signs of life cross our path until we reach the kitchen and I can finally hear the faint sound of laughter nearby. Huxley leads me through the back door, onto the porch that overlooks the beach.

The air smells of salt, smoke and burning wood, the familiar breeze is cool against my skin. A large fire crackles and pops a few hundred feet away, its flames dancing wildly against a pastel-streaked sky. The waves crash softly in the distance as an orange glow illuminates the beach, casting long shadows across the sand, and there, gathered around the fire, are the others.

Axel is sitting cross-legged on a blanket, a beer in hand, his striking hazel eyes softened in the light. Dax is poking at the fire with a long stick, the muscles in his arms flexing as he adds another log to the flames. Garrett, of course, is stretched out on his back in the sand, one arm thrown behind his head, his smile lazy and content as he watches the flames flicker against the darkening sky.

Blankets are spread out across the sand, bottles of wine and beer scattered around. Off to one side, a circular barbeque is gently warming, smoke trailing from the metal rack.

"Here she is," Garrett pushes up onto his elbows. All heads turn my way. "Merry Christmas Peach! We hope you like it."

Axel lifts his beer in a toast as Huxley and I approach the fire. I stare at them, at this moment they've created for me, my heart swelling with gratitude and something deeper—something that feels a lot like belonging.

"Come sit with us," Huxley says, lowering down and patting the blanket next to him. I hesitate for a moment, the warmth of the fire licking at my skin as I take in the scene. It's almost too much; the thoughtfulness, the way they've pulled this together last minute to give me some semblance of normality after everything that happened yesterday. But then Huxley squeezes my hand, a silent reassurance that it's okay to accept this, to take the good while we can.

So I do. I sit between Axel and Hux, leaning back into the warmth of their bodies and the fire, and for the first time in days, I feel like maybe, just maybe, everything will be okay. Until the back door slams open.

"Riot! I was starting to think you'd gotten lost." Garrett sits up fully now, digging a beer bottle out of the sand and offering it up to the approaching figure. Framed by the light he's left on in the kitchen, his dark silhouette seems to suck all of the air out of my lungs. I avoid looking at him, preferring the dancing flames of the fire as a focal point.

Wyatt strides toward the fire, brushing off Garrett's offered beer with a dismissive wave. Catching sight of the movement, my eyes dart to the side and I immediately regret it. Ignoring the handful of packaged food he's carrying, Wyatt is dressed in casual shorts with large pockets and a thin button down which has been left open to reveal the dragon tattoo spanning his muscled torso. His dark hair is tousled from the wind and those eyes, a shade of startling green, lock onto mine. I instinctively tense, my stomach knotting. It's been so long, I don't know how to act around him or on what terms we left things.

"Alright, let's get this thing over with," he says, his voice low but carrying through the cool air. His gaze flicks over the fire, the blankets, the guys, before settling back on me. There's always an edge in his words, always something sharp beneath the surface.

I open my mouth to shoot something back, to meet his hostility with my own, but then he does something unexpected. Wyatt shoves his free hand into his pocket, his expression softening just slightly. Not much, but enough that it throws me off.

"I'm in charge of dinner. Are burgers okay?" he mutters, almost as if the question is painful.

I'm thankful that I'm sitting or I might have just collapsed. Blinking, utterly caught off guard, my mind trips over itself, playing a delayed game of catch up. Wyatt is cooking for me?

The same man who's made it his life's mission to remind me how much he resents my existence? I glance around the fire, but no one else seems as stunned as I am. Axel takes a sip of his beer, Dax keeps poking at the fire, and Garrett's already gone back to lounging in the sand.

I narrow my eyes, trying to gauge whether this is some kind of joke or setup. "You're in charge of dinner?" I repeat, incredulous. "And no one is concerned you're going to poison me?"

Huxley makes a humorous sound in his throat. "Everyone was given a job to make your day special. Wyatt's on dinner duty."

Wyatt's eyes flicker with something I can't quite read, but it's not anger. He sighs, the sound barely audible over the crashing waves. "Yeah. It's the only way I didn't have to come in your close proximity."

Ahh, that makes sense. I relax my shoulders now that Wyatt is once again the calculating dick I'm used to. All is right in the world again.

Wyatt moves toward the small barbeque setup, pulling further packages of meat and buns from his deep cargo pockets and placing them beside the grill. My eyes continually flick up, curiously watching him work while the others try to distract me with gentle conversation.

I turn my attention towards the sea, catching the last speck of sun peering over the horizon just as it sinks out of sight. The sky has quickly gone dark, only a strip of clouded red visible in the distance as if mourning the loss of light. The loss of a day that should have been filled with laughter and joy, but I can't resonate with the guilt that threatens to take over. In Huxley's arms, Axel pressed up against me, Dax just beyond and Garrett relaxing, singing a gentle song to himself, I can't regret a single thing. This is perfect. They are perfect.

The smell of sizzling meat quickly fills the air, mixing with the salty ocean breeze and the smoky scent of the fire. I can't stop glancing at Wyatt, quietly flipping burgers, his back to me. To an untrained eye, he might appear at ease, but I know better. Wyatt is never at ease around me. He stands with his back ramrod straight, his movements are slightly robotic and every once in a while, his hand shakes slightly. He quickly shoves it into his pocket, doing most tasks with just his left hand.

"Food's ready," Wyatt announces flatly, handing out the stacked buns without a plate in sight. His tone is all business, but when he passes one to me, his fingers brush mine. I feel the briefest spark of heat before he quickly pulls away.

I wait for the others to take a bite first, still not certain Wyatt wouldn't take great satisfaction in trying to kill me off and save himself the hassle of staying here. Sitting opposite with his own burger, Wyatt's eyes spear me expectantly. A small pause stretches between us, the crackling fire filling the silence. I take a bite, praying the others will revive me should anything go wrong, but all that explodes in my mouth is flavor.

"Damn, these are really good Riot!" Garrett exclaims around a mouthful. I have to give credit where it's due and nod along in agreement. Turning away from our praise, Wyatt looks out to the sea, his breathing even and controlled.

"I've been cooking with Rachel these past two weeks, she's a big fan of garlic salt," he smiles into the distance. A sudden reality hits me. Wyatt has left someone behind, someone he clearly cares for. *His biological mom.*

"What's she like?" I ask tentatively. A flash of emotion crosses Wyatt's face and for a moment, I think he's going to tell me to mind my own damn business. But then it passes and he relaxes once more.

"She's wonderful. We've spent more quality time together in two weeks than I think I ever did with Cathy. Instead of hiring help, Rachel likes to take care of her home herself. She takes such pride in every detail and taught me how she likes it. I tried to relieve some of the workload where I could."

All of us let Wyatt's admission soak in. Dax responds first, his tone lighter than the frown marring his handsome face.

"You must miss her."

Wyatt shrugs, putting his burger aside. I think most of our appetites have subsided, except for Garrett's. "We've been apart for twenty one years. A little bit longer won't hurt."

"What about your dad?" Axel asks, tilting his head. Goosebumps have risen over his arms but I doubt they're from the chilled winter evening. Once again, Wyatt surprises me by not avoiding the question.

"Ray was already sick when I got there and he declined quickly. It was...difficult trying to create a bond with someone who wasn't going to be around for long, but both of them made it easy. After Ray passed, I didn't really leave Rachel's side. She asked me to help sort his belongings, showed me photo albums and trinkets from their time together. She helped me to realize I could still build that relationship even though Ray isn't here anymore."

I can't be sure in the light of the fire but I'm sure Wyatt's eyes dart to the side and his sad smile grows. My chest tightens, the weight of his words settling over me. He met and lost his father in a matter of weeks. I can't even imagine the turmoil he's been through, yet he's not angry. In fact, there's something raw in Wyatt's tone that makes me wonder if this is the first time he's ever let his guard down. I almost forget about the years of tension between us, the biting remarks, the cold stares. In this moment, there's only Wyatt, and for once, he's not lashing out. He's... reaching out.

I sit there, the fire's warmth battling the chill that's crept over my skin. Wyatt's gaze drifts back to the flames, and he says nothing more, but it's enough. Enough to remind me that underneath, there's something else. Something that might be worth understanding.

The others seem to sense the shift too. Garrett shoots me a knowing glance, a faint smile tugging at his lips. Meanwhile Dax leans closer, his arm brushing against Axel's in a quiet gesture of support. Huxley remains draped over my shoulders, his presence alone grounding me.

Not too long after, Wyatt leaves to fetch a garbage bag and returns to clean up. I finish my burger, not wanting to seem ungrateful now that he's decided not to be a gigantic prick today. Small wins and all that. Once satisfied the beach is clean and his duty has been filled, Wyatt leaves us with a tray of s'more ingredients and skewers before retreating inside. I track the lights through the house, lighting and darkening until he reaches his bedroom. I can't believe that I'm thinking this, but he didn't have to leave. We could have hung out or whatever.

"He'll be okay," Axel nudges my shoulder. I catch myself staring at the bedroom window and return to those around the fire, noting that their attention is now squarely on me.

"We have something for you," Dax says across Axel's far side. I'm already protesting that this evening has been enough, all I could possibly want and need, when Dax pulls a long gift box out from beneath the blanket. Garrett pulls up to his knees, watching intently with a boyish grin on his face. I blush beneath the scrutiny as I accept the box, pulling at the ribbon and revealing a delicate bracelet nestled inside. Dax explains the meaning of the compass, Axel shows me the inscription and as Huxley is putting it on for me, he leans forward to whisper in my ear.

"You mean the world to us." Huxley's breath is warm but I shiver regardless. Dax reaches over to take my hand, his thumb stroking my skin in small circles.

"All of us." My heart stumbles. I glance down at the bracelet, the small silver compass glinting in the firelight. It's delicate but carries so much weight, tethering me to the love I'm constantly being surrounded by. I run my thumb over the engraved inscription, a wave of tears threatening to spill over. I promised Huxley I wouldn't but now I'm certain he set me up to fail.

It's too much. This whole night has been a whirlwind of emotions I wasn't prepared for, and now this—a symbol of connection, of permanence. A promise. I suck in a breath, willing the air to fill my lungs. For so long, I fought to keep everyone at arm's length, to keep them out of harm's way. Then I gave in, allowing them to surround me with affection, but this—this is more than I have ever dared wish for.

"Thank you," I breathe, glancing at each of them in turn. Every pair of eyes is so different, but the reverence in them is the same. My throat closes with emotion and I swallow hard, pushing myself to say what I feel. What they deserve to hear. "I'm so thankful for all of you. Seriously, I never saw you guys coming."

"Yet we've seen you coming oh so many- ow!" Garrett receives a sharp thump to the thigh from both Dax and Axel. I burst out laughing, reaching out and grabbing them all, dragging them into me. I want to be surrounded, a pile of limbs weighing me down. It's the only type of comfort I've come to desire these days.

Garrett laughs softly, clambering over to plant a fierce kiss on my lips. He doesn't hold back, his hands cupping my cheeks while I'm certain he's elbowing the others out of the way. I laugh against his mouth, twisting so Garrett drops onto the blanket in the center of us.

Axel takes the opportunity to scoop me up, cradling me in his arms. It doesn't stop Dax from leaning forward to kiss me next. My chest swells. Finally, Dax isn't waiting in the background for his turn. Finally, Dax is taking what he wants.

"That's enough," Huxley physically breaks us up, tugging me free and lifting me to stand on wobbly feet. Like a pack of hounds, the three on the blankets crawl after me, hands on my ankles, pleading eyes begging me to take pity. Huxley bends, hoisting me over his shoulder. I squeal, surprised by the strength he displays as he starts to run. Not towards the house but further down the beach, away from the warmth of the fire.

"No you don't!" Garrett yells. He, Dax, and Axel scramble to follow, tripping over blankets and bottles in their haste. Laughter trails us as I scream to be put down, lightly pounding my fists on Huxley's back. My hair flies wildly, and I'm giggling uncontrollably as we seem to do a circuit, a bright flash of light cutting through the dark. Huxley stops for just long enough to wrench his SUV car door open and toss me inside. Slamming the door shut, his body weight is on me as a familiar click of the locks sounds, the key fob dangling from his hand.

"Oh, you are so naughty," I gasp. He chuckles, ravaging my neck.

"I'll pay for it later," Huxley murmurs by my ear, and from the banging and screaming on the outside of the truck, I believe he's right.

WYATT

Slamming the bedroom door shut, I barely make it two steps before falling to the floor. Tremors rake through my entire body, and in complete contrast, my mind is numb. Pushing the heels of my palms into my eyes, I try to erase the past few hours from my mind. The way Avery totally captivated all of my boys. How they looked at her like she's the most important person in the world. I was an outsider, encroaching on their private moment and not for the first time, I really wish Nixon hadn't brought me here.

I wish I could disappear. Leave this world behind and fade into nothingness. More of late, it seems inevitable. Whatever I used to mean to people, whatever impression I used to give when I entered a room no longer exists.

I miss Rachel. She makes me feel like a young child desperate for the end of the school day to run into his mom's arms. Something I never had, the majority of my upbringing handled by nannies and employees.

When Nixon delivered me here, I thought Rachel and I would still be able to speak regularly enough for her to keep me centered, but the lack of signal here prevents that – another one of his tricks to ruin my life. Instead, I feel completely isolated and without her to anchor me, each night I drift further away.

The group downstairs were all the family I needed up to two months ago, but so much has changed since then. I'm not the same person I was, and I have no idea how to open up to them. They wouldn't accept me this way even if I could. Once the threat to Avery is no more, I'll be a distant memory, hiding away in Ray's mansion to live out my days in peace. That's the best I can hope for these days.

My despair has fizzled marginally, so I stretch my legs out and roll onto my back, focusing on breathing evenly. Drifting my eyes closed, I inhale and exhale deeply the way a normal person might to relax. Although, I'm so far removed from normal it's laughable I'd even try.

Knocking sounds on the door, jolting me upright. Taking another moment to compose myself, I push up onto my feet and twist the handle. Axel is standing on the other side, his hazel eyes trailing over my shaky hands before I have a chance to hide them in my pockets. The concern in his expression already has me wanting to slam the door in his face. I don't need his pity.

"Hey, you made a quick exit back there. Thought I should check on you." He fists his hands, no doubt trying to refrain from pulling me into a hug.

"I thought you would be too wrapped up in Avery to realize." I have to look away from him, hating the bitterness that spews from my tongue every time I open my mouth. Why can't I just let it go? Let her go?

Before Axel even opens his mouth, I can already hear his voice in my head, telling me it doesn't have to be this way. Urging me to let go of my hostility and join the group. To save him the effort and the chance of anyone else overhearing, I drag him into my room and swiftly close the door. Axel halts just a few steps inside.

The blackout curtains are drawn, as they have been the entire day. Clothes are strewn across the floor, my bed a mess of twisted covers. Evidence of a mini meltdown I had yesterday lies heaped in the corner, broken wooden shelves and a fan that got in my way. I'm just thankful the bathroom door is closed so he can't see the state of the oval mirror, or now lack thereof.

Axel's eyes narrow on the small pill box Rachel gave me sitting on the pine dresser, already popped open and ready for my next hit. Not wanting to explain, I spin him by the shoulders and give him the damn hug he wanted.

There isn't a moment's hesitation before Axel is embracing me. The weight of his comfort is almost enough to make my knees buckle. It's easier to keep the Shadowed Souls at an arm's length, to deny myself their acceptance than face the harsh reality. Once Avery is dealt with, I'm gone and this time, I won't be returning. They need to learn to manage without me.

Closing his arms around my middle, Axel rests his cheek on my shoulder. After resisting at first, I ease into the support he's offering, the rest of the world briefly fading away. The fight I've been clinging onto evades me, allowing for a moment of weakness to slip through the crack. My life has been flipped upside down, tossed side to side and back again since the last time I permitted Axel to hug me like this.

But for a singular split second, I wonder if Axel might be able to help dust me off when I eventually stop falling and eventually crash into the ground.

"How did you do it?" I ask softly into his ear. His chest rumbles against mine, our closeness too comforting to be considered alien.

"Do what?"

"Find yourself again after..." A part of me feels terrible comparing my situation to his. Axel's been through a type of hell I can't even imagine, but maybe he could offer some advice on how he rebuilt and moved on. He doesn't answer for a long while, the cogs turning in his mind. Stepping back for his hazel eyes to assess me, I'm stunned by the resentment held within.

"What makes you think I've found myself? Look at me Wyatt. I'm a man who can't survive without affection, who relies on everyone else's moods to get by. I live through others to avoid the pain that still plagues me. I'm as fucked up as I was seven years ago, you just can't tell as easily."

Axel steps away from me and leaves the room in a swift movement.

I remain, frozen in place and stunned by his admission. My eyes focus on the spot where Axel had been standing, trying to understand how to turn his words into something I can use. I don't know what answer I had been hoping for, one that will magically give me a light to strive for. But instead, all I heard was *'you're never coming back from this.'*

Throwing my foot against the edge of my bed with a cry of rage, the wood splinters and the end of the mattress dips slightly. If all I was destined to be was a rich couple's decoy, then I wish I'd never been born at all.

The shadow in the corner of the room draws closer, cloaking itself over my back. I know it's not real, that he's not really with me, but I absorb Ray's comfort anyway. A lump lodges itself in my throat. What would he say if he were really with me? That he's proud of the man I've become? I scoff, turning away. Grabbing two small pills, I storm into the bathroom. Remnants of the shattered mirror still cling to the wall, dissecting my face into a hundred mini reflections. I hate every single one of them, I think as I toss the pills into my mouth and swallow them dry. The effect isn't as instant as I'd like, leaving my chest heaving and my green eyes piercing my own soul. How did it all go so wrong?

High pitched laughter somewhere within the house drags me back from the brink of self-destruction. A sweet sound, so filled with careless joy. Avery's life is in danger, more so with every passing day, yet she's running around playing kiss chase with my friends. She manages to find the good in every situation, but there's no good in me to be found.

Crossing the room with powerful strides, I swing the door open to see Avery huddled at the far end of the hall, looking around for whoever is hunting for her. A feeble attempt to conceal herself with a curtain is ruined by her large blue eyes and flushed cheeks peeking out. She blinks up at me, a trace of excitement lacing her expression. Surely she's not expecting me to play again, or I haven't been doing my job well enough. One burger and she's practically melting at the sight of me, clearly hoping I'll offer to hide her in my room. Fuck that.

I bare my teeth, feeling every bit the animal I probably look. My clenched fists hang by my sides, no clear plan in mind other than to strap her to a chair and scream in her face - 'why?!' Why was I dragged into her mess? What makes her so special that my life had to be used to defend hers? Instead, I throw my fist into the wall, causing her to flinch and leave, hating myself for it all the more.

My strides don't slow until I'm beyond the porch steps, the numbness of the pills finally settling in. I hate to think I'm so far gone that I'm becoming immune to them, because then I'm truly fucked. The air is twinged with smoke, a faint pathetic glow all that's left of the campfire Dax spent over an hour coaxing to life. Judging by the screamed laughter and squealing filtering out of the second floor windows, it did the job.

I walk across the sand until reaching the ideal spot to sit, a few feet from the water's edge. Waves roll lazily, not having the energy to break properly in the moonlight. I know how they feel. Once in a while, a light breeze carrying mist passes over me, the saltiness filling my senses. Pushing my fingers into the soft sand, I grab and release handfuls in an attempt to feel grounded, not that it works. My feet sink deeper, my body sinking further into the blackhole growing within. Ray stays close as always, a flicker of movement on the edge of my vision but when I look, there's nothing really there.

Turning my attention back towards the landscape, the moon shies away behind a cloud, plunging me into almost pure darkness. I would grieve the loss of light, if it wasn't perfectly resonating with how I'm feeling. Now I can wallow in peace, shrouded by the shadows and cut off from the beach house. That distinct numb sensation has taken over my limbs, my mind. The questions that plague me slow, but never fully stop. Is this it? Am I supposed to keep slipping away until only a shell of a man remains?

My actions are no longer my own. I'm trapped inside my skull, muttering the consequences but unable to stop myself from shuffling out of my shorts and tossing my shirt aside. I wobble to stand and through distant eyes, watch myself walk into the water in my boxers. Icy coldness seeps across my feet, creeping up my legs with every long stride.

Walking further into the inky depths, the water level rises over my thighs, stealing all sensation on its way. Only stopping once my chest is fully submerged, a sense of calm finally settles over me. My heartbeat slows, the low temperature surrounding me biting at my skin. I stand there for a long while, desensitized to the sharp sting prickling my body. The notion of staying right here is almost too tempting, allowing the sea to draw the life from my pores and carry me away. I wonder who would mourn for me, but on closer inspection, I have to wonder why do I even care? I've given everything to those I love, ensured they will have futures that far outlive me, and not once have I ever felt truly indispensable. Wyatt is always discounted as the asshole, he's easy to toss away.

I stare into the dark, into the nothingness. It's all I've got left. The icy water presses against my skin, seeping in like it's trying to extinguish whatever remains of me. I step deeper, the cold climbing up to my neck, each movement slow and mechanical. There's a dull hum in my ears, the world blurring at the edges as the pills sink deeper into my system. I barely feel anything now—just the water, just the pull on something better waiting somewhere beyond my grasp. The tide tugs gently at my body, urging me forward, welcoming me like an old friend.

I wish I could say I fought it, that I wrestled with the thought of disappearing, but it's not a fight when you've already surrendered. I don't feel like fighting anymore. I'm tired. Tired of pretending that tomorrow will be any different. Tired of being the one who gets left behind, the one everyone expects will be fine because I'm supposed to be the guy who can take it.

I can't take it anymore.

My breath fogs in the cold air as I sink lower into the water. The sea cradles me like it's been waiting, patient and calm. For the first time, the questions stop. No more asking if I'm good enough or wondering when it'll all fall apart. No more pressure, no more weight on my chest. I can just... float. Disappear into the deep, drift away until I'm nothing but a ripple on the surface.

My knees give way, my body falling forward and my face slipping beneath the water. The glacial water rushes over me, closing in on every part of me, but it's not so bad. The world above disappears, muffled and far away. It's finally quiet. The silence is so peaceful that for a second, I think maybe I was always meant to end up here, suspended between the surface and the deep, where no one can reach me. Maybe I was never meant to resurface.

But then her face flashes in the dark. Rachel, waiting for me at the kitchen table, her tired smile, the worry she tries to hide. She's already lost so much, how could I let my selfishness bring her any more pain. The weight of it settles in my chest, heavier than the water surrounding me. I think of her sitting by the phone, probably wondering why I haven't called. She still believes in me, still thinks I can pull myself out of this spiral. She's the one person who's never stopped wanting me, who looks at me like I still matter. Like I'm more than the mess I've become.

The cold starts to bite harder, and my lungs beg for air. Despite the screaming in my mind, my limbs are only growing lighter. I clench my fists beneath the water, fighting the instinct to stay down, to let it take me. I hold onto the thought of making it back to her, back home, but my body refuses to obey. Panic flutters against my deadened heart. I'm too late.

Suddenly, arms crash around me like a steel band. I'm hauled against the tide, a willing and warm body forcing me upwards. Breaking the surface, a gasping rush of air hits my chest, causing me to splutter and cough. The frigid air stings even more now, but it's real. The air, the pain, the world—it's all still there, waiting for me. And somehow, I'm still in it.

I'm dragged back toward the shore, my savior saving my heavy and shaking legs from failing me. I can't stop shivering, the cold water drilled into me, all the way to the bone. The numbness isn't gone, not entirely, but it's been pushed back by something stronger. Someone that won't let me go, not yet.

"How many times am I going to have to drag one of you out of the fucking water?!" A gruff growl filters into my ears, a hard hand slamming into my chest. I splutter up water, the burn of the salt in my throat causing me to heave long after there's nothing left. I collapse onto the sand, staring up at the sky as the moon peeks out again from behind the clouds. Blocking my view, a head of long hair drips onto my face, Huxley's face hidden by shadow.

"I swear to fucking everything, the next time we take a vacation, it's going to be far, far away from the sea," he's rambling whilst checking me over. Once deeming me alive, Huxley eases me upright. "Wyatt, what the hell?!"

"I-" my throat is still raw, my body shivering beyond reason. I'm near enough naked, relying on my arms wrapping around myself. A towel is lowered over my back, more bodies appearing in the night. Dax throws my arm over his shoulder to lift me up, saying nothing in that silent, reassuring way he always is. Axel has a second towel that he wraps around my midsection. That rising panic from before grips me in its hold firmly now.

"I-I don't want...A-Avery to-"

"Relax," Axel rubs my back. "She didn't spot you out the window like the rest of us did. Garrett is on distraction duty." My teeth clench together to stop from juddering. I want to push myself free, to insist I'll walk myself back but it's useless. I'm too weak and shaken from what I nearly did, from what I nearly put Rachel through, to not lean into their hold.

Huxley shoots me a look, one that's sharp enough to slice through the fog still swirling in my head. "You're lucky Axel raised some suspicion about your mood a while ago." His voice is tight, not with anger, but with fear masked as frustration. I don't blame him. Hell, I don't even have the strength to argue. The guilt sits heavy in my chest, thicker than the cold in my bones.

They came for me. My brothers, my men holding me up when I can't stand on my own. And instead of feeling grateful, I feel hollow. How many more times will they have to pull me back from the edge? Dax's grip tightens around my arm, as if sensing the darkness creeping back in, but Axel's steady voice cuts through.

"I'm sorry, Wyatt," he murmurs. "You reached out to me earlier and I shot you down. We're all battling our demons, but you're never alone. We've got you."

And for the first time, I might just let myself believe him. Maybe I don't have to fight this alone. Maybe, just maybe, I'm worth saving.

AVERY

"Seriously, Peach, this is not what I thought you meant by a morning workout," Garrett grumbles, lagging behind. I barely contain my laugh, wondering how he would even have another round of sex in him. Since the guys ditched us last night, Garrett had the job of filling in for three others. There's a delicious ache between my legs as I continue on, jogging along the dirt path. We cut left just before the road, heading into the forest that surrounds the beach house.

The sun filters through the dense canopy above, dappling the dirt path with patches of soft light as I jog ahead, the salty tang of the ocean still lingering faintly on the air. Pines and firs tower overhead, their branches woven together, forming a natural ceiling that casts the trail in cool shade. A layer of pine needles crunches softly beneath my feet, and the earthy scent of damp soil and moss fills my lungs with each deep breath. It's peaceful out here, the only sounds are the rhythmic thud of my sneakers against the path and Garrett's trailing behind.

"Come on, slowpoke. One more lap around to the beach and I'll make you lunch."

"One...more," Garrett gasps in desperation. No one said entertaining me would always be wine and card games by the fire. In fact, coming here on the back of grueling back-to-back ballet practices and a showcase, I've never felt so unfit. There's a type of adrenaline only the burn of my limbs can provide and I didn't realize until this morning how much I've missed it.

"How do you manage with early morning basketball practices?"

"Well, I normally wake to Axel jerking me off," he calls out, his voice tinged with a mix of amusement and exhaustion. I bite back a laugh, glancing over my shoulder, dragging his feet through the fallen needles. His hair is still messy from last night, and he has that disheveled look that comes from too many hours tangled in bed with me. If it weren't for the fact we need to get our fitness levels up before heading back to campus, I'd almost feel guilty for dragging him out here. Almost.

"Thought you had more stamina than this," I tease, picking up the pace. In a flash, a six foot three man in crumpled clothes rushes past me with his arms pumping furiously.

"I'll show you stamina."

We leave the wider dirt path and head into a narrower trail that winds deeper into the forest, a slight incline leading us towards the metal fence edging the territory. The thick trunks of the trees loom closer now, the dampness soaking up the morning mist. It's cooler here, the air fresher, and the sound of the beach looms ahead of us.

Garrett slows near a boulder, leaning back to catch his breath. Despite my reservations about stopping a run halfway through, I take the bait and come to a stop in between his open legs.

"It's confirmed," Garrett sighs, wistfully looking over my shoulder. "You're trying to kill me."

"I would never try to kill you," I tilt my head to the side, brushing his messy hair back with my fingers. "If you weren't around, who would do that incredible thing you do with your tongue?" Garrett's grin is blinding, his hands sliding over my hips.

"Oh Peachy, it pays to be gay sometimes." My laughter causes some birds to flee a tree nearby. Raising a brow, I toy with my tongue between my teeth.

"I'd love to see what else Axel has been teaching you."

"Some secrets I'll have to take to the grave."

"What a waste," I sigh. Lowering my hands to settle on Garrett, I lean into him, the heat radiating off his sweaty body. His T-shirt is starting to cling to his chest, not that I'm looking. Something tells me he wouldn't want that. Instead,

I wait for our breaths to mingle, our lips to brush and then I push away from him. "But since there's no chance of you getting me off again this morning, we can finish our run."

I'm gone before Garrett's rumbling curses can reach me, only glancing back to check he's following. He is, and I just about resist the urge to call him a good boy. It'd be difficult to run with an erection. Breaching the tree line, I follow the fence to the edge of the ocean. The wind whips through my ponytail, my lycra tank top and leggings clinging to my body and the compass bracelet circling my wrist. A few months ago, I would have hid behind a baggy hoodie. A few months ago, I didn't have the endless affection of four men who fill me with confidence.

My legs are already burning but I push on, savoring the feeling of my muscles working, the sharpness of the air filling my lungs. This is true freedom, or the most I can have anyway. I'd built up so much anxiety about Christmas, and now it's passed, I need to focus on what's next. Returning to Waversea refreshed and ready for the pressure of classes and exams. I'm done being a bystander in my own life. It's time to take back control.

Garrett gives me a playful shove as he catches up, breathing heavily. His shoulders have curled inwards as if he's fighting to stay upright. The sound of the waves encases us, faint but steady, a reminder that the world is still there, waiting for us to return. But not yet. For now, it's just us, the beach ahead, and the rhythm of our feet moving in sync, carrying us forward.

I could have gone for another lap or two but Garrett is gasping by the time we reach the porch steps. He clings onto the banister, dramatically pulling himself up and into the house. It's just as quiet as when we left this morning, nothing touched or out of place. I honor my promise and head straight for the refrigerator, taking out eggs to whip up some omelets for Garrett and myself. The man in question has collapsed onto the sofa, his head tilted back and eyes closed. I should take pity on him; it's not like he got much sleep last night. Then again, neither did I.

In no time, I have two plates in hand and I'm kicking Garrett awake. He eagerly accepts his, despite the redness in his dark eyes. Placing mine on the coffee table, a chill rolls down my back, dried sweat clinging to my skin. The shower is calling my name but with the smell of food making its way around the room, it's overruled by the growling of my stomach.

"I'm gonna grab a hoodie. Don't eat my omelet!"

"I make no such promises," Garrett calls behind me. Chuckling and shaking my head, I take the stairs up to the second level. Passing the middle door along the hallway, a low groan barely catches my ears.

I freeze in place, waiting for another but only silence follows. Yet a niggling feeling I can't place tells me something is wrong. Slowly twisting the rounded handle, I crack the door open a tiny bit to peer inside. Everything is dark, only a tiny slither of the light cracking through the curtains allowing me to see the perfectly made bed and tidy space inside. Huxley's denim jacket is slung over the back of a wooden chair, his white and blue Air Jordans tucked beneath the matching desk. Pushing my head further into the room, I notice a shine bleeding out from beneath the bathroom door.

Tiptoeing across the space, I press my ear against the timber separating us. Inside is silent. Knocking softly, I wait a second before entering the room. I gasp at the body on the ground, more so because it's not Huxley. A shaved head is leaning back against the bathtub, his legs strewn across the tiled floor like an afterthought. Edging closer, he doesn't open his eyes and I note that his face is a bright shade of red, sweat is covering his forehead and chest.

"Axel?" I whisper, giving his arm a nudge. The limb falls lifelessly at his side, panic seizing me. Grabbing his face in my hands, I shout his name and give him a rough shake. His lids crack open ever so slightly, but his hazel eyes remain unfocussed. "Fuck. Axel, what happened?" I ask but his only response is a twitch of his nostrils. Glancing around, I don't find evidence of anything suspicious so I'm going to hazard a guess that he's had another panic attack. I leave him, flying around Huxley's bedroom. After turning the fan on and directing it towards the bed, I return to the bathroom and fill a cup on the side of the sink with cold water.

"Drink," I order, lifting Axel's head forward and pushing the cup against his lips. He flinches as the cold-water splashes over his chin and chest, the moment rousing him enough to take a few sips. He groans as his head lolls back. Looping a towel beneath each of his underarms, I lean Axel against the cotton strap I've created across his back. It takes a few tries to prepare myself, clutching the towel tightly. Then I'm heaving, walking backwards, one effort-filled step at a time. I use all my strength to drag him the last distance towards the bed.

Tugging him back up into a seated position, his weight rests against me. "Axel, I'm going to need you to help me here." I grit out whilst knowing he's in no position to do anything. Axel mumbles incoherently.

After counting down three, two, one – mostly for myself - I start to lift him upwards. His weight is crippling but I force myself to hold on, despite his trembling limbs. Gripping his arm and throwing it around my waist, I urge him to hold on and I heave upwards again. Drawing Axel to his knees, I feel him start to slip so I give the back of his head a smack.

"Stay with me, you heavy sack of shit," I grumble into his ear. Using my shoulder in his chest, I push him upright with all my might until he is just about on the edge of the mattress. "Okay, good." I praise myself.

I feel the second Axel zones out again. A scream escapes me as he topples over, his weight doubling over my shoulders. My own legs threaten to buckle but I persevere, throwing his floppy top half back onto the mattress. Breathing heavily, as if I've just run a marathon, I move the fan onto him and retrieve the cup of water. After a few failed attempts to rouse him, I change tactic and move across the bed. Rolling his head and shoulders up, I use my body to stop him from sagging back down and force him to drink at least half of the water I'm pushing against his lips. After I'm satisfied he's beginning to cool down, his face returning to its usual beige color, I leave him to rest against my front.

I'm exhausted, weary to my bones with worry. Stroking my fingers across his head, my thoughts tumble and clash. Where are the others and why the hell isn't anyone caring for Axel?

Stirring, his head shifts as he glances around the darkened room while I continue to stroke his shaven head. He groans, attempting to push himself upright and I use my flattened hands against his back to help. I give him a whole minute to come around before shouting a little too loudly.

"Axel, what the fuck?!"

"I'm sorry," he mutters, hanging his head. I gently smack his shoulder.

"Don't apologize," I frown, remaining in place to support him. Gradually, Axel's frame starts to relax and he shifts further up the bed. Crawling beneath the sheets with him, we lay together in the dark, propped up by pillows that smell distinctly of Huxley. "I'm worried. Talk to me."

"It was just a rough night, that's all. I didn't sleep because I was watching-" Axel sharply cuts himself off. "I was just heading to my room when it hit me out of nowhere."

"What did?!" I blanch, visually checking him over as far as I can see. I should have checked for a wound before moving him.

"A panic attack. I wasn't thinking straight and the tremors started. I ducked into the nearest room and...well, I must have blacked out. That's never happened before." His voice is a desperate, yet resigned tone. "It's not normally that bad."

"And you still won't tell me what's causing them?" I ask softly, now drawing gentle circles on his chest. Axel puts his hand over mine, halting my movements and flattening my hand over his heart.

"It's random. There's no telling why or when." Axel must feel the stiffness of my body along the length of his. He presses a kiss against my forehead. "Just stress, sweetheart. It all affects us in different ways."

Hmm, not buying it. We've all been stressed for weeks, and whether Axel's panic attacks are new or he was just better at hiding them, it's clear they are escalating. But there's nothing else I can do or say. If Axel won't share his burdens with me or anyone else, he needs to find his own way to rise from the darkness he's trapped himself in.

"I'm just saying, whatever you're currently doing to handle this, it's not working. You should talk to someone." I ask softly, feeling like I'm about to poke the beast. Axel doesn't react, laying statue still.

"I'm doing what everyone else in this house is doing. Trying to be strong for you." His voice is barely a whisper, his shoulders tensing like that confession caused him physical pain. I chance a look up at his face, his strong jaw clenched and hazel eyes glazed over.

"I don't need you to be strong for me. I need you to take care of yourself. In fact, that's all I want and the rest will follow."

"I will try." His chest rises and falls on a large breath, his fingers moving to link with mine. "For you, I'll try." I push myself up so I'm hovering over him, my ponytail falling limply to one side.

"No, not for me. I won't always be around. You need to do this for you or it won't work. You're so special, Axel. Sweet and loving and funny, you light up every room and the guys out there love you. That's the Axel you need to hold onto."

"What about you?" he asks, his hand curling around my arm. I resist the urge to look away from his penetrating gaze. Even in this darkness I feel the weight of it spearing through me. When I don't respond, Axel's hand rises to my shoulder and then neck. Using my nape, he lowers me until I'm leaning directly over his mouth. "Do you love me?"

I have to fight not to throw myself into his kiss and body. My arms shake with the need of it, my breathing growing thin. I want to shout yes, to give Axel that anchor to cling onto, but it's not the right time. It would go against everything I've been through with Huxley, encouraging him to work on himself first. It would make me the world's biggest freaking hypocrite.

Cupping Axel's jaw, I sway my head and press a trembling kiss to his cheek. The weight of emotion behind that connection is enough to break me, but I'm practiced in patience. Settling back into Axel's side, I speak directly into his ear, hoping it eases the sting of rejection.

"The only love that matters is the one you have for yourself. I'm not going anywhere and I will help you every step of the way, and once the panic attacks are a thing of the past, you can ask me again."

AVERY

I lie with Axel until his chest is rising and falling steadily. Not a single tremor has passed through him, whether from exhaustion or my presence, I'm not sure.

Slipping out from beneath the cover, I tiptoe into the bathroom for the shower I've desperately needed since this morning's run. I tidy as I go, straightening the crumpled bathmat and righting the stack of toilet rolls which was kicked over in our haste. Axel hid for a reason, so I do my best to cover up any remaining evidence of his panic attack and shower quickly. He's still sound asleep by the time I creep back through the room, dressing in some of Huxley's clothes and making a silent exit.

"Hey Peach, bad news," Garrett's voice explodes through the hallway. I spin to see him striding closer, a smirk pulling at one corner of his mouth. "A rabid dog ate your omelet."

"I assume you mean yourself." I scowl, a sudden flash of resentment sparking within. "An apt description, Garrett, because you are a dog." I stab my finger into his chest. Garrett's eyes fly wide open at my tone and he allows me to push him back into the opposite wall.

"Peach, I'll make you another one." He blinks, giving me his best puppy expression. I don't melt as he's expecting, recent events at the forefront of my mind.

"I don't want another omelet. I want you to stop hiding behind your ego and settle things with Axel once and for all."

"Things are fine," he scoffs, brushing my finger aside. Forget resentment, a flare of burning hot anger takes over. Things are the opposite of fine when I find Axel, *his lover*, collapsed on the bathroom floor. Something needs to change, to ease Axel's mind and I have a funny feeling I'm staring into the dark eyes of his biggest insecurity.

"No, Garrett, they're not. He's unsettled. How can a man who is desperate for affection and the need to feel loved be fine with you playing hacky sack with his emotions?" I move to leave but Garrett is too fast, grabbing my wrist and tugging me back into his chest.

"Now hold up. I've never pretended to be anything other than an asshole. I've owned that shit. And I've actually been trying lately, giving extra snuggles and being at the bottom more often than not. What else do you want me to do? Propose? Would that make you happy?" My lips purse, drawing Garrett's attention briefly to my lips. *Bingo*.

"You figure it out, Garrett. But just so you know, until things are smoothed out with you and Axel, I'm withholding sex."

"*WHAT*?!" Garrett's grip of my wrist loosens, as if touching me without the possibility of me dropping to my knees physically burns him.

I pat his cheek with a smug smirk of my own and turn away. I leave Garrett as a flustered mess banking incoherent sounds and struggling to piece a sentence together. Maybe withholding sex was a step too far. My intention was to back him into a corner, not break his brain.

Returning to my original mission, I slip into the mini library at the end of the hall. As an extension onto the building, possibly added much later on, the room is modern in its circular shape and holds no windows. Instead, a glass domed skylight floods the room with sunshine. Plush, leather armchairs face one another, situated beside floor-to-ceiling bookcases. To some, the rich mahogany and rows of dust-bound books might feel imposing. But to me, the thick scent of leather and paper just reminds me of Nixon. This would have been his design choice, his domain.

As a man of business, it makes perfect sense that the library heavily leans on the side of non-fiction, organized in perfect rows, books alphabetized by agenda. I imagine the times Nixon spent here without cell reception, he would stand here, stroking his chin, deciding which new venture he could pursue. I can almost hear the click of his polished dress shoes against the wooden floor.

But I'm not here for nostalgia. Axel needs help, and I need to find something, anything to guide him through these panic attacks which only seem to be getting worse. I should have noticed it sooner. The way his hazel eyes dart around as if searching for an escape, how the cracks are starting to show despite holding himself together for my sake.

I run my fingers over the spines as I browse. Self-help, psychology, mindfulness. Where would Nixon have stashed something like that? The shelves are packed with books based on smart investments, seizing business opportunities and reading the stock market for profit. Even on vacation, it seems my adoptive father never truly took a day off.

Then, a glimmer of gold trimming catches my eye. Wedged between two thick tomes of philosophy is a slim book with no title on its spine, but the faint sheen of its leather cover suggests it's been well-used. I grip the aged cover gently and try to remove it from its dusty spot. Albeit stiffly, I manage to wiggle the book a quarter of the way out before it jams. A faint click echoes through the quiet room. I freeze, still gripping the book, unsure of what just happened. My nerve-endings jolt into hyper awareness, the room suddenly seeming too cold, too quiet.

Then, with a low mechanical whir, one of the mahogany panels across the far side begins to shift. My heart jumps into my throat as the panel slides smoothly to the side, revealing a dark room behind the bookcase. I step back, blinking, unable to process what I'm seeing. This is a joke, right? Some sort of trick to freak me out? Well, mission accomplished.

But sure as shit, the panel stops moving. Dim, recessed lights flicker on within, illuminating a high-tech safe room. The walls are lined with reinforced steel, thick and imposing. The floor is made of polished concrete, smooth and gray underfoot. Against one wall is a large metal table with a few sleek monitors on top, their screens black and a bank of servers hums quietly underneath. I already know what the rest of the room will look like because I've seen it before. It's an exact replica of the one in Hughes Manor.

I glance around the library, half-expecting someone to have felt the gentle tremor of the wood shifting over the floor. When no one comes, I flick my focus back to the passageway, forgetting how to breathe.

I should step away, should call for someone. I do neither of those things because lo and behold, I have a freaking death wish. I step cautiously into the room, seeing the small bunk beds and plastic drawers that I knew would be there. Shelves hold food provisions and lined along the floor underneath are stacks of bottled water. There are no windows, no hint of the world outside. Everything is controlled, precise, and impenetrable. It's Nixon down to a tee.

On one wall, I notice a series of locked cabinets, their surfaces smooth and featureless. Above them, what looks like an advanced ventilation system silently whirs, keeping the room cool. A faint chemical scent hangs in the air, sterile and clean, like a hospital or a lab.

"You sneaky bastard," I shake my head at myself. He came here, that night after he'd dropped the bombshell that Meg is my twin. He went upstairs to 'prepare' for the journey back home, but he checked on his well-kept secret instead. Did he expect me to find it, knowing that I would spend hours curled up in the library at the manor?

I stop to close the door, concealing myself inside. Something tells me this room isn't meant for public knowledge. Moving further inside, I stop beside the cot-style bunk beds, neatly made up with crispy, white sheets. A small nightstand sits to the side, with a lamp and a few personal items—a framed photograph of Nixon, Cathy and I, a well-worn black book with a button clasp. Inside, I find jotted coding and a list of passwords I presume will gain me access to the computer.

Holy shit, the computer! I rush across the room, my mind suddenly catching up. Is there reception in here? Could I check in on Meg? My fingers hover over the touchpad, hesitating. I've stumbled into another one of Nixon's secrets, and that hasn't worked out well for me so far. Taking a long and loud inhale, I press the touchpad and the monitors blink to life. At first, they display a series of codes, lines of text scrolling too quickly for me to make out. I type in the passwords when prompted, working my way through layers of security. Then, slowly, the screens shift, revealing a grid of security camera feeds.

My heart drops out of my vagina.

Each screen shows a different room of the beach house—the kitchen, the living room, the bedrooms, even the bathrooms. There are cameras everywhere, hidden so discreetly I never would have noticed. My skin prickles with unease. Did Nixon turn these on that night too? Is he watching remotely and if so...oh god. My eyes dart to each room, each surface where I've screwed around with the guys. I had Huxley on that kitchen island, Garrett pinned me against a wall in the laundry room, I may or may not have gone down on Axel on the sofa and Dax has been my bed partner more often than not.

I glance at another one of the screens and see myself—standing there in the safe room, staring up at the very cameras I'm watching now. I quickly look away, feeling exposed despite being completely alone in here. My pulse quickens as I flick through the various camera angles. The guys are lounging around, Axel and Wyatt are lumpy mounds hidden within their bed covers, Dax is reclined in a clawfoot bathtub. Huxley is in the kitchen speaking with a dejected Garrett.

There's one feed that catches my eye—a shot out the front, facing the dirt path beyond Huxley's SUV. Someone's standing there.

A small shriek escapes me. The figure is tall, disguised in a black hoodie and shadowed by the late afternoon light. Even without the hood pulled up, I doubt I would be able to make out their face through the grainy resolution of the camera. My heart thuds wildly in my chest, an uneasy rhythm syncing with the sudden surge of panic.

Who the hell is that? My mind races. I can't tear my eyes away from the screen, every instinct in me screaming to lock myself in the safe room and never leave. But I can't leave my boys out there. Preparing to run through the house screaming, I watch as the figure shifts slightly, stepping closer to the SUV. Their posture is tense, deliberate, like they're scouting for something—or someone. The minutes stretch out in painful silence. I watch through tremors of panic as they touch Huxley's car, doing something at the back, and then turn and walk away. I track them all the way down the path until they're out of view, but there's no sense of relief.

I sit down heavily in the chair at the desk, my mind racing. I grip the edges of the metal in an attempt to steel myself, although my knees are knocking together. Think, Avery, and breathe. Breathing is good.

I'm in a replica of the safe room Cathy used to take me to. A place she wanted me to be familiar with and comfortable staying in. She's been conditioning me to hide for so long, preparing me for the day Fredrick was released from prison. And she was right to be concerned, given that she was killed not even six weeks later. I cast my mind back to just before that dark time.

Cathy had been traveling more, apparently needing to fulfill a work contract on a deadline. Nixon was present in her absence, spending as much quality time with me as possible but whenever she was due back, he would leave. I remember thinking it was odd but it wasn't unheard of. I frown, wondering why I hadn't picked up on there being heightened security around the grounds. They knew. They all knew and as always, kept me sheltered. Kept me naive.

I'm not naive anymore. I've learnt that darkness thrives when we mistake loneliness for strength, allowing it to root itself in the cracks of our hearts, unseen but ever present. The Hughes conditioned me to be a fragile princess, hiding away in a tower. They told me that's where I'm happiest. But they're wrong.

I've broken free, spread my wings and flown into the love of four incredibly damaged men. Their traumas are as raw as my own, and somewhere between patching each other up, past wounds have started to heal. The Shadowed Souls don't treat me as something weak and breakable. They've taught me that I'm headstrong. That I'm their Little Swan.

Switching off the monitors, I leave the safe room and push the panel closed with a click. I don't pass anyone as I descend the stairs, hearing Garrett and Huxley still speaking in low, hushed tones. Avoiding the kitchen, I remain close to the wall, silently putting one socked foot in front of the other. Somehow without raising suspicion, I need to get outside.

What if it was one of Fredrick's men putting a bug on the car, or even worse, *a bomb*? I can't let the guys use the truck until I'm certain but equally, I've decided against sharing the safe room's existence for the time being. Should there be an attack on the house, I can't depend on Wyatt not blabbing its location. He'd do whatever it takes to return to Rachel, even if that means getting rid of me.

"Fine!" Garrett growls, smacking his hand against the corner. I'm silent beside the Christmas tree, gradually slinking behind it. The back door is thrown wide open, punctuated by Huxley's sigh.

"You can't run from this forever, Gare." Following Garrett outside, I take my chance at dashing out the front door and down the steps. Reckless, I know, ending up alone when I know there's a stranger somewhere in these woods. In my defense, I vowed no one else would get hurt because of me so in theory, if there is a bomb on the back of the SUV, the guys will just have to hate my chargrilled corpse.

I feel every small stone through the socks, the dirt part unforgiving as I hobble closer. Briefly pausing myself by the headlight, I all but throw myself around the corner, already winced for an inevitable *boom*. Instead, I just look like an idiot, cracking one eyelid to see an envelope tucked into the rear wiper. My name is written in a familiar cursive and my heart judders for a whole different reason. It's him. He was here.

MR. XO

My Dearest Avery,

I know I shouldn't be sitting here, writing the words I'll never have the courage to speak aloud. I know I should leave you to move on with those you are now surrounded with. But I also know, I don't only write these letters for you. They are for me too.

There's a peculiar comfort in transferring my thoughts into ink, watching it dry on the paper and become permanent. There's an intimacy in knowing that you will read these words and finally know the truth, even if it will forever remain an unspoken vow between us.

You have always been my light. My life has been cloaked in shadows for so long, the kind of darkness that threatens to swallow a man whole. It creeps in around the edges, suffocating joy, erasing hope. Before I knew you, I wandered in that endless night, searching for something—anything—that would make it worth continuing. And then you appeared.

I recall the exact moment I first saw you. Huge blue eyes on an angelic face, blonde wisps that refuse to be tamed. You will never know the power you hold, how your mere presence pulls me from the abyss. Every time I catch a glimpse of your smile, hear your laugh—it's as if the weight I carry lifts, if only for a fleeting moment.

I wonder, sometimes, how someone so full of life can be so unaware of the effect they have on the world. You radiate warmth, kindness, and something else—something that is yours alone. Something that emanates from you when you dance, a sense of power invisible to the eye but has the force to bring grown men to their knees.

I have spent years observing you, waiting for the right moment to step forward. But every time the thought crosses my mind, fear claws at me. What if my presence taints that light? What if, when you finally see the real me, you turn away? I could not bear that. I wouldn't survive it.

And so, I will remain as the man who has loved you from afar, who has cherished every moment you were unaware of. Every letter I send is a piece of me, a confession of love that I am too afraid to speak aloud. They have become the only way I know to reach you. In these letters, I am brave. In these letters, I am whole.

I am not perfect. I am flawed, and my life is far from easy. But you have given me reason to live, to keep fighting through the darkness, because somewhere out there, you exist. And for that alone, my heart beats.

I do not ask for you to love me in return. All I ask is that you allow me to share your light from a distance, and know that in you, I found my salvation.

Always Yours,
XO

AXEL

Trying to catch Garrett's eye, he continues to ignore me, just as he has during our entire supply run. Huxley drives his SUV with practiced ease, knowing the route by heart now. Even before a guy at the supermarket counter gave me a strange look for tucking a strand of Garrett's hair behind his ear, he was tense. Uncomfortably quiet. In my head, there's no issue. I don't give a shit what people say or think about me, it can't be worse than what I already think about myself.

We return to a gloomy looking beach house, no visible lights on. I had no qualms about leaving Wyatt behind with just Dax as mediator between the two others. Avery has spent all day in the library whereas Wyatt has been a ghost since we rescued him the night before last, other than the occasional crashing and smashing inside his room.

No one said withdrawal is easy, especially since I stole his pill stash. It was an impulsive decision in an effort to hide them from the others, but it quickly became apparent that I'm not a suitable candidate for such a task. I couldn't confess to anyone that I'd caved and taken one, wanting to feel the release he was so desperately seeking.

Lest to say, drugs are not the answer for a panic-attack sufferer. I thought my heart was going to burst out of my chest, only just managing to crawl into Huxley's bathroom before someone found me. I wish it had been anyone other than Avery.

Huxley is quiet as he parks, picking up on the tension in the back seat. The three of us empty the bags from the trunk, lining them onto the kitchen island. Hux does all he can to keep his distance, his head in the refrigerator as he organizes and makes room for the items we pass him. All the while, the other male in the room seems to be absorbing all of the air out of the room.

"Go upstairs and relax. I've got it from here," Garrett finally breaks the silence between us and jerks his chin towards the stairs. I freeze, a tub of ice cream in hand. He relieves me of it and instantly turns his back before I can get a read on his expression. He might as well have slapped me across the face. Huxley avoids my confused gaze, so I take a few steps away. It's like ripping my heart out of my chest. What did I do wrong?

I drag my sorry ass up the stairs, pausing outside a few doors along the way. I could seek comfort in someone else, but not even that feels right. I don't want to see anyone, or moreover, I don't want anyone to see me on the verge of tears and start asking questions. Entering mine and Garrett's room, if it even is that anymore, I head straight into the bathroom and lock the door.

We're breaking up. That's what this is. I don't know if we were ever really together, but the finality of it hits me like a ton of bricks. Stopping in front of the mirror hanging on the far wall, I close my eyes at my own reflection. I can't look at myself right now, from the eyes that have received one too many compliments to the shaven head I cling to like a smooth teether when life seems to evade my grasp. Just when I thought the panic attacks were my only concern, Garret has gone and done what he always promised. He's thrown me away, trusting Avery to pick up the pieces.

That's all I am. What I've always been. An object to be passed around. I swallow hard, mentally preparing before flicking those hazel eyes open once more. Whatever I was hoping to happen, didn't. All I see is that weak, fourteen-year old boy I once was staring back. Some days it's easier to pretend he's a distant memory, and today is not one of those days. I pace back and forth across the fluffy circular mat that sits beside the bathtub.

The ensuite is almost as big as the bedroom. Aside from a shower cubicle tucked into the corner, the overly large tub sits proudly in the center, facing towards a huge window. Being on the end of the house, the forest stretches across the horizon, thousands of glimmering stars covering the midnight blanket above. Being this far from a busy city life is an ideal break from glaring artificial lights and noisy crowds. Add in the campfire, the small town and simple way of living, a part of me would gladly stay here for good. But I know better than anyone, my nightmares will follow me anywhere. The view doesn't matter if the turmoil I carry lives inside my head.

I should have done a better job at guarding my heart. But the way he looks at me sometimes steals the breath from my lungs. He knows me better than anyone else. He knows what I need without me having to ask.

I switch on the shower and strip out of my jeans and polo top. Entering the cubicle and closing the glass door behind me, I relish the cool spray of water raining down upon my shaved head. Using the shower gel, I lather the back of my neck and shoulders, trying to conjure happy images before the impending reality of what awaits in my room hits. Namely, an empty bed and all of my hopes crushed to dust.

In every scenario I can imagine, from a basketball game to picnics in luscious green parks or dinner at five-star restaurants, Garrett is in each one with me. With his wide smile and floppy brown hair that doesn't have a favored side to rest on. His endless dark color of his eyes and contractionary lighthearted humor. Garrett can hide behind his bullshit jokes, but he was the first person to ever truly see me. I thought that meant something.

Stepping out of the shower, I pull a brown towel from the folded stack on a nearby shelf, roughly rubbing the material over my head. By the time I secure the towel around my waist, I'm feeling no less defeated and exit into the main room.

Garrett is waiting for me. Clothes have been laid out on the bed, which he gestures to before running a hand into his floppy brown hair. His dark eyes downcast, shifting nervously on the other side of the bed separating us. I stop, my heart slowly sinking. This is really it.

"Don't overthink this, don't ask questions. I hate labels. Just get dressed and meet me on the porch," he says bluntly, shifting towards the door already. I frown, not taking my eyes off his. I want him to look at me, to explain.

"What's happening?"

Garrett sighs in frustration and closes the gap between us so quickly, I fight the urge to step back. Covering my mouth with his hand, his pained eyes finally land on mine. "What did I just say? No questions."

I swallow, attracting attention to my Adam's apple. I can't get a grapple on Garrett's expression, but he's not smiling so it can't be good. In fact, he seems strangely on edge; his body language is rigid and breathing slightly labored. Stepping back and lowering his hand, he holds up his palm with all fingers stretched out.

"Porch, five minutes." With that, he disappears through the doorway in a rush. I stare after him for a moment, then down to the clothes he's laid out on the bed. Nothing fancy, a pair of navy tracksuit shorts, plain gray T-shirt and no boxers. My frown has yet to lift. Pulling the items on, I throw the damp towel into the laundry basket in the corner and sit on the edge of the bed to wait the full five minutes as requested.

I don't think I've ever seen Garrett flustered. He's usually the most confident of us all. He hides himself deep inside to stop others from seeing his vulnerable side. Even I barely see it. Waiting an extra minute for good measure, I leave the room and head down the staircase. It's late evening so the rest of the house is silent, only the groan of the wood beneath my feet penetrating the air. Passing through the living room and kitchen, I emerge onto the back porch where a faint flickering light catches my attention.

Small lit candles trail the banister leading to the built-in porch swing. A thick blanket covers the seat with a bowl of popcorn placed in the center. Garrett walks up the steps, a meter-long indent in the sand that shows I'm not the only one who's been pacing. Avoiding my eye contact, he points to the swing for me to take a seat but I remain where I am.

"Sit in the swing, Axel." He tries to use his Dom voice on me. I cross my arms and raise a brow.

"Why?"

"Because I-" he blurts out, almost angrily, before quickly regaining his composure. Rolling his tongue over his teeth, Garrett exhales and tries again. "I would very much enjoy it if you sat your ass on that fucking seat so I can casually sit next to you."

I bite the inside of my cheek to stop from smiling. This isn't a breakup. Garrett would never put so much effort into it if it was - he'd just jump out of a window and start a new life in a different country. To him, that would be easier than explaining himself.

"Is this a date?"

"No!" Garrett flinches and finally looks up at me. He appears to be in a state of anguish, his eyes sunken and hair even more wild than usual. "It's just a mutual gathering between two b...bros." I take my bottom lip into my mouth, that smile fiercely trying to creep out but I'm having way too much fun. Ten minutes ago, I was waving my life goodbye. Now I'm trying my best not to explode with laughter.

"Okay, *bro*. You can guide me to my seat." I hold out my hand like a princess, and Garrett's stunned expression is so worth it. Anyone would think I just offered to run him through with a machete.

"Can you not just-" Garrett groans, jerking his chin towards the swing a few times. I shake my head. Cursing under his breath, Garrett stomps up the wooden steps dividing us and takes my hand. I make sure it stays up in the air like a real lady, and when he lowers me into my seat, I hold it up until he kisses the back of it.

"Was that so hard?"

"Fuck off." I chuckle. Not the best etiquette for a date but I am one hundred percent certain this is the first date Garrett has ever been on so I'll let him off. Lifting the blanket, Garrett settles us both beneath it. The bowl is resting in Garrett's lap, where I would expect it to be, as we face the landscape in silence. It's too dark to see the sea, but the sky looks like a monotone Jackson Pollock painting, flecks of starlight filling the sky. The quiet lapping of water can be heard and as

Garrett kicks off for the swing to gently rock, a slight breeze is cast over me. It's nothing short of pure romance.

Gare lifts the bowl of popcorn and moves it towards me, intending for me to take the first handful. I blink in shock, although he will not take his eyes away from a particular candle on the timber railing in front of us. To anyone else, this would seem like the lamest evening ever, but I know better. Garrett doesn't willingly share food, nor does he do dates.

Without pausing any longer, fearing he may think I'm freaking out inside the way he clearly is on the outside, I snuggle down further to rest my head on his shoulder and take a cluster of popcorn. Popping it into my mouth, it crunches loudly between my teeth. Slowly, as I keep eating, Gare's body starts to soften and he joins me in his midnight snack. I dare not tell him I'm not a big fan of popcorn, nor am I hungry but I keep on eating, realizing this is about more than just food.

We sit together, swinging and sharing body heat until the bowl is almost empty. Garrett reaches over to place it on the railing and I gasp. There was still some popcorn left. Oh no, is Garrett sick? Is this one big ruse to tell me he only has a few days left to live? Luckily, when he sighs and starts talking, that's not the revelation he says.

"I don't do romance or flowers. I'm an asshole that pushes people away so I can never be hurt again. I don't like to count on others and I'll probably fuck this up too. Really soon. But you make me want to be better, Axel."

He's definitely dying. I sit upright and face him properly. That look of pain is still there, as if none of this is actually what he wants. As far as I knew, he was rather content being the asshole.

"Gare, you don't need to do this if it's just for my benefit."

"Is that what you think?" Garrett's eyes darken, his voice low, almost a growl. He runs a hand through his messy brown hair, visibly struggling to find the right words. "I don't know how to explain...ugh I knew I'd fuck this up. I'm trying to figure it out because—" He pauses, swallowing hard as if the truth might choke him. "Because you make me want to try. And that scares the hell out of me."

The soft creaking of the porch swing fills the silence that follows, the night air cool against my skin. I let his words sink in, unsure how to respond at first. Garrett, always the impenetrable, sarcastic wall, is now crumbling just enough to let me glimpse the vulnerability underneath. He's trying, and that alone shakes me more than I thought it would.

"I know you're not perfect," I finally say, my voice gentler than I'd intended. "It's actually what I love about you."

Garrett exhales sharply, my words taking him by surprise. His eyes drift away from mine, focusing on the darkened horizon where the ocean whispers quietly to the stars. The tension between us is palpable, thick with unsaid things, but it's different now. Less suffocating and more honest.

"You deserve better," he mutters, almost too quietly to hear. "You know you do. That's why this is so hard, Axel. Because you damn well stay anyway."

My heart clenches. Like me, Garrett has always seen himself as broken, someone who could never be enough. If only he'd let a trickle of my affection in and then he might realize he's worth so much more than he wants to believe. I reach out, taking his hand in mine in a solid grip. He flinches, but doesn't pull away.

"I don't want someone better, Garrett. I want you. I always have."

The raw truth hangs between us, heavier than the stars overhead. His hand tightens around mine, the pressure reassuring. It's not easy for either of us. I've got my own demons, and Garrett's past is filled with a much different kind. Just like the home his parents neglected him in, he's built a structure around his heart and shut himself inside. But right now, for the first time, it feels like we're finally on the same page.

Garrett lets out a humorless chuckle, shaking his head as if he can't believe what he's hearing. "You say that now, but—"

"No," I cut him off firmly, leaning in closer. My breath skates over his clenched jaw. "I say it because it's true. You think I haven't seen all the messed-up parts of you by now? I know who you are, Gare. And I still choose you. Every damn time."

He looks at me then, really looks at me, his dark eyes searching mine for something. Maybe he's hunting for lies or doubt, but he won't find any. I hold his gaze, willing him to believe me. The silence between us stretches on, and I can almost hear the gears turning in his head, the battle he's fighting within himself. Then, finally, he releases a long, shaky breath.

"You make it sound so simple."

I smile, just a little, trying to ease the tension. "Maybe it is simple. We're the ones making it complicated."

Garrett lets out a soft laugh, but there's no humor in it. "Simple," he echoes, the word rolling off his tongue like it's foreign. Closing his eyes for a moment, he steels himself whilst the porch swing rocks us gently. When he opens them again, his expression has softened, the storm in his eyes calming just a little bit.

He reaches for me, sliding his arms around my shoulders and closing the last few inches between us. Pushing my lips against his, the entire world falls away. Our lips meet in a slow, burning glide, soft yet insistent. His breath was warm against my skin, sending a shiver down my spine as a connection instantly sparks between us with all of the words we can't say.

The gentle pressure of his mouth deepens, his tongue poking out to lick my bottom lip. It's an invitation I've had many times, but my heart hasn't been so close to bursting out of my chest before. Opening up, Garrett ravages my mouth, his tongue quickly dominating mine and tasting every feeble movement I try in retaliation. He kisses me until I'm rigid beneath his hold, a slave to his desire. I'd give Garrett anything he wanted right then. He has the ability to cause my pulse to race as soon as his hand strokes my head, grounding me in the moment. Our chests are heaving, mirroring a steady rise and fall one after another.

A breathy laugh fans over my face as Garrett leans his forehead against mine. We huddle under the blanket for the rest of the night, our limbs tangled as we force the night's cool air to stay out.

"You know I'm going to screw this up, right?" he murmurs, his lips brushing the top of my head.

I smile against him, the warmth of his body grounding me in a way nothing else ever could. "Probably," I reply, teasing lightly. "But we'll figure it out."

We sit in comfortable silence for a while, the tension between us dissipating into the night. The candles flicker gently, casting soft shadows around us, and for the first time all evening, I feel a sense of peace wash over me.

Eventually, Garrett breaks the silence. "Axel," he says, his voice soft and tentative. I lift my head to look at him, and the vulnerability in his eyes almost undoes me. Garrett, the man who hides behind jokes and sarcasm, who's spent his life pushing people away so he doesn't get hurt. But here, with me, he's trying to face his demons head-on. "With whatever remains of my splintered soul, I love you."

"I know," I whisper, pressing a kiss to his jawline. It's a quick evasion tactic to hide the welling of tears behind my eyes. Like I said, Garrett isn't perfect and neither am I. But in this moment, under the starlit sky, it feels like maybe we don't have to be. We can finally have validation. We can finally feel like we're enough.

AVERY

Lying on my stomach across my bed, my legs swing to and fro as I mindlessly scroll through my phone's old photos. I rarely take pictures, given that most days at the manor were a carbon copy of each other, but it's a habit I plan on breaking.

At least Meg had no such qualms. She often took my phone hostage, snapping photos from our perfect summer breaks and endless weekend sleepovers. It's a wonder we didn't get bored, but there was always a new series to binge, reading marathons to do, picnics to have on the grounds. In our later years, Meg started to introduce me to her friends and that's when the mischief started.

I smile at one of those photos now, our huge smiles beaming out from a crowd of basic strangers. Everyone is in their swimwear, dripping wet from a mass body jump in the pool. It was just an excuse really to slip and slide against each other, hands roaming and crotches brushing. A cesspit of horny, tipsy teenagers who were manhandled out by security. I don't even know who snapped this exact photo before the party was hastily shut down, but the next weekend, we were all back at it again.

Another image is from the stargazing event Meg and I put on, which was basically a hundred beanbags spread across the lawn and enough weed for everyone to convince themselves they saw a UFO. Meg lazily looks towards the screen, red eyed with a joint hanging loose between her fingers. I'm in the forefront, sober as sin with a goofy smile and a thumbs up.

I've stared at these photos so many times, I've memorized each detail. But I'm going back with fresh eyes. I'm hunting. The letter I found on the SUV is burning a hole through the bedside table drawer. The letter that revealed something new - I've met him. I know him. He described the first time he saw me, which is why I'm now scouring through any evidence I have, searching for a familiar face in the crowds.

It's been four days. Four days of sitting at the safe room computer, waiting for him to reappear. Four days of rereading the words he gifted me, building a connection with a complete stranger. Four days of keeping a secret from those who vowed to keep me safe. I wish I was strong enough to light another campfire and burn the letters once and for all.

I wish my curiosity didn't always have a death wish. But no. I'm more sure now than ever these letters weren't penned by Fredrick. The burning need to know who is carving me up from the inside and the little voice in my head is growing louder.

Why are the heart achingly beautiful men in this house not enough for you? Why are you so selfish?

A soft knock barely reaches my ears before the door bursts open, the low murmur of Axel's voice chastising Garrett. I roll over on the mattress, and my breath catches in my throat. They stand there, a vision of dark desire, both in fitted slacks and polished dress shoes, shirts molded to their sculpted torsos with the top buttons undone. Garrett's pebble-gray shirt is rolled at the elbows, the muscles in his forearms taut beneath the fabric, while Axel's is a navy polo.

It's the closest I've ever seen Axel to wearing a collar, knowing how jarring he finds the feeling of it closing in around his neck. A noose his mother used to dangle him from in front of all of her horny friends. The fact he's sporting a cotton collar now, albeit pushed wide open, renders me immobile.

Garrett's eyes are dark, bordering ravenous, as they travel over me, lingering on the oversized T-shirt and panties I'm wearing. I know that look. He's found his prey and is preparing to strike. Axel grips Garrett's forearm, holding him back from doing just that.

"What's happening here?" I ask, my voice rough, my throat suddenly dry. Whatever they have planned, I'm already in. Their gazes drift, hot and deliberate, to the exposed skin of my thighs, the goosebumps rising in response to their attention. Garrett licks his lips in a way that I imagine he's practiced in the mirror a million times, while Axel's voice finally breaks the tension.

"We've got a surprise for you," he says, his tone thick with promise. "Meet us downstairs when you're dressed." Presenting a box from behind his back, Axel opts for leaving it on the dresser instead of allowing Garrett to move further into the room. I quickly glance at the box, pale blue and wrapped with a ribbon in a darker shade.

My pulse quickens. I rise slowly from the bed, and Garrett, as if by instinct, steps forward, drawn to me like a magnet. Axel pulls him back, his grip firm as he draws them both back through the door, Garrett whining like a dog the entire way.

Waiting until they reach the lower level, I rush forward and tear at the box. Lifting the lid and opening the tissue paper, my brows rise. A hunter green bodycon dress is folded on top of a pair of black heels. At the bottom, there's another tissue paper package in which I find my underwear for the evening, or rather, lack of. Nestled in the corner, there's a douche with clear intent.

I barely make it into the bathroom before I'm tugging the T-shirt over my head. Excitement courses through my veins, reigniting a feeling that had gone dormant. I shouldn't have forced a distance between the guys and myself, insisting that I wanted to be alone to sneak off and watch the surveillance cameras instead. A part of me thought it might be easier that way, because when they find out I've been hiding the fact Mr. XO was right outside the house, they're going to be *pissed*.

After taking care of business, I stand the douche in the shower and move back to the box. The lingerie is exquisite, despite consisting of merely a few straps of lace. I ease the black thong up my legs, relishing the feeling of unaltered sexiness. Baggy hoodies and leggings have been killing my vibe lately. The bra is more like a harness, crisscrossing over my back, winding over my shoulders and creating an open triangle around my breasts. The lace connects in my sternum with a flower motif. Then comes the dress.

Slipping the green one-piece over my head and pulling it down, my nipples graze the material and I bite my lip. I'm instantly aware of Garrett's plan to sexually torture me, an effort to break our no-sex arrangement, no doubt. Turning to face the mirror, I brush my hands over intricate black beading sewn into the dress, creating a swirling pattern over my hips and sides, accentuating my curves. The color causes my mind to shift to Wyatt and dammit if my nipples don't harden more.

Emerging from the bathroom, I sit down at the vanity and take the time to apply makeup for the first time since we arrived here. Not one for contouring, I apply a mineral powder to my face and work carefully on a smokey eye like Meg would have done on me, before adding mascara. Using a dusty pink color on my lips, I brush out my long hair and finish with a light sprinkling of hairspray. Pushing my feet into the skinny, black heels, thankful I was bored enough to shave my legs this morning, I leave my room and descend the staircase.

Only Axel is on the level below, waiting for me patiently. Gliding down the staircase with as much grace as I can muster in these neck-breaking heels, Axel extends his hand to help me down the last step.

"Wow," he breathes, raising his eyebrows as he looks me up and down. Pulling me into his body, he gently tucks my hair behind my left ear and bends to place a kiss on my neck. "You look...,"

"Stunning? Gorgeous? Beautiful? Pick an adjective Axel," I grin against his cheek. His grip tightens on my waist, barely withheld restraint causing my breath to catch.

"Bewitching," he whispers in my ear. I shudder. Stepping back, Axel takes a hold of my hand and guides me along the corridor. I start to pause at the next staircase, expecting us to descend but Axel continues to pull me along with a knowing smirk.

"Where are you taking me?" I ask, but he doesn't answer. Instead we continue on, my heart sinking with each step as we near the door at the end. The library. Do they know? No, surely not - unless this is all a ruse to make me beg for forgiveness. I can never be sure what goes on in Garrett's head. But Axel doesn't seem to be hiding any anger, his hazel eyes alive and sparkling as they continue to glance at me. I catch his gaze lowering to my breasts before snapping back up and facing forward. It gives me the chance to appreciate him instead, the harsh cut of his jawline and cheekbones enhanced by his shaved head.

Bringing me to a halt outside the library, he raps his knuckles against the wood and clutches my hand a little tighter. From the stiffness to his shoulders, I'd say he's nervous. That makes two of us. Inside, the thumping of heavy bass starts to vibrate through the floor, apparently being our cue to enter. Axel opens the door to reveal Dax, Huxley and Wyatt standing in similar formal attire.

My throat restricts at the sight of them. Dax's hands are in his dark slack's pockets, his shirt a dazzling white and clinging to his tanned chest. His piercing blue eyes trail my body in a similar way Axel's did, his cheeky smile growing even further. Huxley is beside him, thick arms crossed over his shirt, another appraising expression raking over my body that leaves me feeling naked and exposed. I honestly wish I was.

And then there's Wyatt. Brown hair pushed back, a suit that he wears like a second skin, black ink poking out at the base of his throat. A blind nun would have caught the expression he gave before quickly shutting it down. Leaning against a bookcase, his ankles crossed, he tries to pretend he doesn't want to be here but those haunting green eyes deceive him. They land right on my nipples, that are pushing against the dress' fabric in a bid to be noticed by *him*.

My libido is calling out for attention as I step further into the room, tearing my eyes away from those now surrounding me.

The library has been converted into an improvised night club. Void of the usual furniture, black fabric panels cover the bookcases, flashing neon lights trailing the edges of the wooden floor. The bulbs in the lamps have been replaced with ones that turn from one color to the next, giving the room its own strobe light effect. A pop-up DJ stall is against the curved edge beside the door. Garrett has taken pride of place behind the booth, my name on an LED screen rolling across the front on repeat. A table draped in black along the right side holds the entire house's stock of alcohol by the looks of it, and white bean bags have been placed around the makeshift dance floor.

"What...What's the occasion?" I ask over the music, walking further inside so Dax can shut the door, stealing away the glare of the hallway's artificial light. Garrett rushes up behind me, the length of his body briefly cemented against the curves of mine as if we are one being.

"It's New Year's Eve, Peach! I want my kiss at midnight," he mouth dips to my ear, "and then some." My knees are weak as the urge to say 'yes master' toys with the tip of my tongue. Turning my head, my temple clumsily connects with a chunky headset covering his ears. Returning to the DJ booth and fiddling with switches, his brown hair flops back and forth as his head nods to the beat.

Axel strides towards the drinks table and pours a round of shots, clearly ready to kick this party into gear. He hands us each a vibrant green shot and carries the other over to Garrett, us following behind. My shoulders bump between Dax's and who I presume is Huxley, until the hand holding the shot glass extends. Wyatt's chest lowers on a silent sigh, his jaw ticking. But he's here. Garrett reaches over his booth to clink his glass with the rest of ours, shouting into the microphone despite us standing right in front of him.

"To making Avery smile," he winks at me as we all down our first shot of many. Setting both of our glasses onto the booth, I reach deep into my cleavage, much to everyone's excitement and produce my phone. Flicking the camera to selfie mode, I twist so Garrett is in the background in his DJ get-up and pull Wyatt back from walking away. This once, we're doing this. Locking my arm around his, he raises an unimpressed brow at the screen whilst the others all shift into any space they can. Once everyone's in the frame, I use the tiny buzz from the shot to slip my hand south and grab Wyatt's junk so a shocked, huge smile spreads across his face as I snap the shot. Gotcha.

Giggling to myself, I plant my phone down on the booth and turn towards the dancefloor. Dax slips his hand into mine and leads me into the center of the room as Calvin Harris' 'We Found Love' starts to blast through the speakers. Pulling me into the cage of his body, I can't hide the smile he draws from me so easily. My steady, reliable and knowing Dax. Placing my hands on his firm chest and looking up, the colored patterns passing over his face lure me into our own moment, away from the rest of the library.

Hands find the dents of my waist from behind, Axel's fingers trailing over the bead work on my sides. Dax pulls away, clearly not in the mood for sharing, my hand stretching after him as he turns away. My pout is quickly retracted when he returns a second later with a bottle of champagne in one hand and rosé in the other. Opting for the wine, I raise the bottle to my lips to take a long swig whilst Axel grinds against me.

The mix of alcohol and flashing lights quickly affect all efforts of rational thinking, giving myself into the beat of the music and escape the guys have provided me with. It can't be more than an hour later when my hair is sticking to the back of my neck and my shoes have disappeared, although I can't remember removing them. Huxley has fabricated in front of me, his shirt unbuttoned as he too lets the rhythm take over. I smile openly at him, loving that he's letting loose for a change. His body moves fluidly, his face relaxed and eyes closed, a bottle of rum gripped in his hand.

Garrett walks over, headphones and all, delicately holding another shot in his tattooed fingers with a smirk in place, magnified by the neon lights. I stop bouncing on my heels as he trails a finger up my throat and gently pushes my chin upwards, lifting the glass and pouring its contents into my open mouth. Licking my lips after swallowing, Garrett bends his head to trail the same path with his own tongue. My dulled senses come to life, electricity humming through the air, so potent I instantly feel wetness increasing between my thighs.

Needing to distance myself from the girl who's about to throw herself at these hot and sweaty men, I signal for a timeout and edge away from the dance floor. Collapsing onto a beanbag, my chest heaves as I try to catch my breath around a fit of giggles. My head is woozy in the best kind of way as I watch the guys jump enthusiastically to a new beat. Axel has loosened up more than I've ever seen him, his arms thrown around his best friend's shoulders as they sing 'I'm the real Slim Shady' at the top of their lungs. A smile is glued to my face, my cheeks starting to ache from holding it in place.

Movement at my side catches my ear, Wyatt on the beanbag next to me and lifting a beer to his lips. My eyes are already heavy as I watch him swallow, his Adam's apple bobbing. Trailing lower, the light catches a steady rise and fall to his chest, controlled as always. His abs are tense beneath his pale shirt, the ink underneath bleeding through the fabric. My gaze reaches his belt buckle when his fingers click right in front of my face, jarring me back to his face.

"Stop that," he frowns. I purse my own lips, the alcohol loosening them and suddenly, no thought in my mind is safe. Oh god, here it comes.

"It's really not fair you know," I knock his hand away. The action causes me to tumble closer. His expensive cologne hits me like a ten-ton truck.

"What isn't?" Wyatt looks at me as if he's humoring me, doing me some sort of favor.

"You being so fucking hot. Why couldn't I get a stepbro who's fugly as shit and doesn't infuriate me at every turn?"

"We're not related, remember," Wyatt taps one finger on my forehead. I lunge, grabbing his wrist.

"Then why don't you want me like they do?" My eyes widen at my own admission. I didn't know I still cared what Wyatt thought, but here I am, holding his wrist like a lifeline, begging for him to admit that he likes me. That it doesn't always have to be like this. Wyatt's throat works again, his green eyes dancing between mine. When he doesn't answer, I release him and sink further into the bean bag.

"Whatever Wyatt. I can't be bothered to do this with you anymore. It's exhausting. I relinquish all resentment between us." I flourish my hand in the air, repeating that last part in my head as I'm not sure the syllables all made it out of my mouth. Who knew I was so eloquent when I'm shitfaced? Suddenly, I'm being spun, my shoulders gripped until Wyatt is all I can see. His face hovers over mine, his fingers digging into my skin a tad too harshly.

"I need you to hate me," he states, voice low and harsh, every word hitting like a punch. His glare pierces through me, cutting deep, but I can see the tremor in his jaw, the flicker of something softer buried beneath the hardness.

"Why?" I demand, my voice cracking. My breath catches in my throat, his cologne flooding my senses. He's so close I can feel the heat radiating off him, the sharp rise and fall of his chest syncing with my own. "Why do I need to keep hating you all the time?"

Wyatt's fingers tighten, and I flinch, feeling the sting. He doesn't pull away. "Because," he growls, but there's a hesitation. A crack in the facade.

"Because what, Wyatt?" My voice is louder now, more insistent. I slam my fists into his chest but make no effort to put any distance between us. "Why do you keep doing this? Why do you keep creating reasons to push me away?"

His breath hitches, and for a split second, his grip loosens. He looks away, his jaw clenched so tight the muscles are twitching again. Then, as if the words are ripped from him against his will, he leans into my ear on a rough, strangled whisper.

"Because if you don't hate me, there's nothing to stop me fucking you into ruin, leaving my brothers to deal with the wreckage. I will shatter you, Avery. I'll destroy every piece of your soul and piece it back together in a way only I know how to pleasure. You'll crave my cock, scream my name when they slide into your tight cunt. Nothing good will come from this, only a devastation none of us can fix."

The room stills, the music fading away into nothing. The air between us is so charged, it feels like a thread about to snap. I'm about to snap. His harsh eyes meet mine again, raw and exposed. Wild and desperate. "I nearly made that mistake once. I won't let you get the better of my control again."

Multiple heavy weights chuck themselves onto bean bags around me, and I blink up, realizing the music has in fact stopped. The guys are laughing at some private joke, panting from their dancing. Only Wyatt knows why my own cheeks are so flushed, my heart trying to tear itself free of my chest. Returning to his beer like nothing has happened, Wyatt downs the remainder of his bottle and chucks it aside.

"I'm out," he announces, rising and moving to leave. Garrett chuckles, saluting Wyatt's back.

"Avery will be butt naked and strapped to my bed in five minutes if you want to watch the show. She's going to squirt so beautifully." Garrett reaches over to brush his thumb over my bottom lip and I almost climaxed right then and there. The smile drops from his face, the sudden seriousness of his features reminding me that there is a monster lurking beneath the surface. A monster I've denied sex for four days, and I'm about to pay for it.

At the door, Wyatt has stilled, his back rigid. I hang on the precipice, waiting for the moment he walks up and slams the door closed. Waiting for the finality of it to hit my soul and break it, just like he promised but not for the same reasons. Instead, whether from the drunken buzz we're all sporting or just drained from our constant to and fro, Wyatt turns back to face me. His expression is still unreadable as he approaches, the most lethal type of predator in this room because he's the most unpredictable.

Sauntering over at a casual pace, my eyes are drawn to the shift of his powerful thighs through the tight material of his slacks. I swallow loudly to my own ears. Holding out his hand, Wyatt raises a brow. I don't hesitate to accept and allow him to pull me to my feet.

GARRETT

This is better than I could have planned. Although I did plan it, and the evening is progressing to a fucking tee.

Last to exit the library, I still can't believe Wyatt led Avery to my bedroom for me. My blood is raging at a fever pitch with the need to have her again. Axel has kept me sated and things between us are better than ever since our date, but knowing Avery is actively withholding her sweet cunt from me is a type of crazy I've never known.

Fisting my hands at my sides, I try to keep my legs from running down the hall. Knocking my bedroom door open hard enough for it to bang loudly against the wall, I find her waiting on my bed patiently, Wyatt in an armchair in the corner. Axel lowers onto the bed, his fingers playing with

Avery's hair, her chest lifting and falling with anticipation. He's barely touching her, yet her eyes are frantic with need. Exactly how I want her, I smirk to myself.

Planting a fresh beer in Wyatt's hand, I give him a side wink. "Take a swig every time she cums," I tell him, just to make sure he pays enough attention. We haven't come this far for him to pussy out and pretend he doesn't want to watch anymore.

As I near the bed, Axel and Avery stand together and wait for my instruction. I shiver, my dominant side roaring to life, a voice in my head screaming to bend and break them both. However, I promised Dax and Huxley I would play nice. The pair are lingering by the window, not knowing whether to sit or stand, but simultaneously deciding to cross their arms.

"Undress her," I order, forcing my back to press against the wall. Axel takes his time, giving us all a show as he draws a path up her legs with his fingers. Reaching the edge of her dress, he eases it upwards, revealing her creamy skin bit by bit until the green material is pushed over her head. We all inhale sharply at the same time. The black lace framing her breasts push them up ever-so-slightly, her perfect nipples pink and pebbled. The curve of her hips are also enhanced by the high straps of the thong, tilting over her thighs and disappearing between her legs.

Avery stands tall, unashamed, undeterred by those only gawking at her. The circular scars on her ribs don't matter to her anymore. She knows she's flawless in our eyes. Not waiting for my next command, Avery takes her turn, unbuttoning the few buttons at the base of Axel's collar bone, stripping him of his navy polo shirt with painful slowness. Rising onto her ballet-perfected tiptoes, she pushes it over his head, kissing a path over his jaw.

"Who said you could kiss him?" I ask but there's no anger in my voice. Avery mutters against Axel's skin.

"I did." I grin, catching a similar look in Huxley's eyes. We move at the same time, my hand curling into Avery's hair whilst Huxley grabs her throat. She's spun and trapped between us, her back to my front, her wide blue eyes blinking up at Hux.

"You're not in control tonight, Little Swan," he breathes and then ravages her mouth. Avery arches against me, a moan filtering through their kiss. I can only imagine how delicious it feels being trapped between mine and Huxley's erections, the roughness of our slacks rubbing against her sensitive areas. I grind into her ass, tightening my grip on her hair to pull her head back gently. Just enough to force a gasp against Huxley's lips. Her body is trembling but not in fear, in anticipation. There's a commendable tension in her muscles as she fights to keep control. But she won't win tonight. Not against us.

"You're going to do exactly as you're told." I lean down, brushing my lips against Avery's ear. Beneath me, she straightens, the trembling subsiding in an instant. I look over her shoulder, catching the defiant gleam in her eye and I meet it with my own. *Oh please defy me, Peach.*

Grabbing the clasp of Huxley's belt buckle, Avery smoothly pulls it free from his trousers and turns between us to face me. Threading the tail into the buckle, I watch in fascination as she pulls the loop smaller and repeatedly winds the leather back on itself. Pushing her hands into each hoop she's managed to create, Avery takes the loose end of the belt in between her teeth and pulls securely. The strap tightens around her wrists in makeshift handcuffs, the quick snap of it like an arrow of pleasure to my dick. I'm throbbing painfully behind my zipper.

"I may not be in control, but I can still manage my own pleasure," Avery tells me with a reassured tilt to her head.

Huxley grins against her neck, placing firm kisses trailing her shoulder. With each one, he grows more possessive, marking her with his teeth. I stare at her self-bound hands, her vulnerability wrapped in strength, and it only stokes my hunger for her more.

"Okay, Peach," I grin, taking a hold of her arms. "Where would you like us to fuck you? On the bed, the floor or in the shower?" Avery raises a challenging brow.

"Against the windowsill, and Dax goes first." Behind me, Dax shifts to uncross his arms and clear his throat, his eyes locked on the scene unfolding before him. I give him a long side glance before relenting, stepping aside to drag Avery towards him. Huxley moans at the loss of his plaything. The lines blur between who's really in control as Avery places her bound hands onto Dax's chest and pushes him to sit on the ledge. Then she lowers to kneel between his legs and I see my opportunity.

Whilst Dax obeys her every whim, unfastening his slacks and pulling his cock out for her, I grab Hux and Axel, taking them over to the dresser. The top drawer is filled with the sex toys I purchased during today's supply run with Hux, while we concocted this entire evening in the front of his SUV. I thought we'd find a butt plug at best, but a bit of charming the local hairdresser and she told us of a sex shop at the far side of the small town. It did not disappoint.

Resting near the front are a pair of polished stainless steel butt plugs, medium and large, each adorned with a sparkling gemstone at the base, glinting under the light. Next to them are glass dildos in varying sizes and textures—one smooth, one ribbed, and another with a curved design intended to tease every sensitive spot imaginable. A bright pink vibrator sits in the corner, the one which Huxley confiscated from Avery a while ago. I was hoping she'd come begging for it eventually.

My fingers brush over the soft velvet restraints, although it doesn't look like we'll be needing them anymore. Avery has created her own type of binding. Alongside it lies a box of vibrating cock rings and silver nipple clamps on a delicate chain. What can I say, I'm a greedy bastard.

Axel's gaze flickers between the toys, his grin widening as he reaches for a pair of feathered ticklers and a tube of flavored lube. A hand lashes out to knock the ticklers aside.

"No, this one," a gruff voice cuts through the air. Wyatt lifts the handle of a leather paddle and hands it to Axel. All three of us bend forward to look at him with questioning gazes but he just shrugs and returns to his armchair, beer still clasped in hand and untouched. Okay then.

I take the paddle from Axel, swapping it out with the larger butt plug. Axel made it clear back at the sex club that he has no desire to punish Avery in the ways he might have taken his sexual frustrations out of other women, even more on occasion. I have no such issue, testing the weight of the paddle in my hand. Huxley doesn't take anything but follows us across the room, stripping down to his boxers as he goes. I order Axel to do the same whilst I shed my slacks.

The three of us lower around Avery's kneeling frame, her head lowering as she takes Dax's cock deep into the back of her throat. I merely sit and watch for a while, admiring the sight of how well she takes him, how long she can buckle down and hold her breath until Dax is squirming. His head knocks back against the glass, eyes squeezed shut. Poor dude isn't going to last.

Squeezing lube onto the butt plug, Axel meets Huxley's eye and the pair nod. My blackened heart lifts at the sight, watching my boys divide and conquer the girl we've chosen to belong to us. After easing the thong down to her knees, Axel rubs the plug around Avery's puckered hole, Huxley slides his hand around her front, instantly locating her clit.

Avery jolts, her throat constricting around Dax's cock and drawing a groan from both of them. I smirk, running the paddle along Avery's curved spine.

"Who liked that more, I wonder?" I smirk. Sweat beads across Dax's forehead. When Huxley rubs at her clit again, Avery jolts once more and I bring the paddle down on her asscheek, hard. She cries out, releasing Dax with a pop. Twisting her head to glare at me, I grip her chin.

"Keep still, or you'll get another one." Turning her back, I pull open her jaw and lower her onto Dax, helping to bob her head a few times. Huxley's arm flexes as he moves once more and this time, Avery remains still. I use the paddle to rub the reddened spot blossoming on her ass. "Such a good girl. Go ahead and fuck her with your fingers, Hux." He does just that, sliding his fingers inside of her. I'm jealous, but my time will come. I want her tender and used, believing she can't give anymore until I squeeze another climax out of her wrought body.

With her remaining in place, Axel is now able to work the butt plug inside, a centimeter at a time. Avery whines beautifully, her thighs trembling. I watch closely, anticipating the moment she tenses, and rises up a little higher on her knees, clenching so Axel can't make any more progress. Huxley's fingers keep up a steady pace but it's not enough to coax her to relax. Instead the surprise of the paddle cracking against her flesh is enough to shock her into baring down, taking the entire butt plug at once. I drop the paddle then, drawing her head over her shoulder.

"Doesn't that feel good, Peach?" She nods with Dax's cock filling her mouth. I stroke the column of her throat with one finger. "Since your mouth is full, I'll make the decision of who gets your sweet pussy first." She doesn't argue, her brows knitted together as she continues to work Dax into a frenzy.

Huxley's arm is pumping now, the veins popping from his forearm as his pace increases. Axel and I help him along, with Axel reaching around to harshly rub her clit whilst I'm pinching and rolling her nipples until she's jerking on a muffled scream.

"Oh fuck!" Dax moans, the vibrations of Avery's throat too much for him to handle. I push down on the back of her head, forcing her to take every drop of his cum as he explodes in her throat. His knuckles are white, clenched around the window's ledge until he's slumping against the glass. I release Avery's head, allowing her to come up for air whilst looking over my shoulder to Wyatt.

"That's one." He raises his beer towards me and drinks down a quarter of the bottle. His dick is tented in his slacks but otherwise, he remains impassive. We'll see about that.

"She's all yours Hux," I jerk my chin. The blond looks up in shock, clearly expecting to be left until last. Avery slumps into him, still catching her breath while I grab the back of Axel's head. Slamming his mouth into mine, his hands skim up my thighs, thumbs tracing over the edge of my boxers. I draw my tongue along the seam of his mouth, asking him to open up to me and he does instantly. My darling, submissive Axel.

I slowly coax him over to the bed, taking our party away from the show Huxley and Avery are going to put on for Wyatt. Every time I glance over, he's staring intently, not missing a single detail. He'll need them for when he retreats to his room to jerk off later. Avery has taken back control, her stubborn nature shining through. Hux is only happy to let her straddle him, gazing up at her with chocolate brown eyes filled with awe and wonder. He'd do anything for that woman. We all would.

"Focus on me," Axel drags me down onto the mattress with him. He gets it. I need to take out my pent-up frustration on him first. When Avery decided to withhold sex from me, she effectively sent me into an unstoppable frenzy to fuck some sense into her. Whilst battling that urge, I had to do the thing I hate most and dig down into my feelings, allowing myself to be vulnerable with Axel. Sure, I never would have without the push, but now that beast inside is clawing to burst free and sink my teeth and dick into Avery simultaneously.

Covering Axel with my body, we fight for control, ending up on our sides with our legs tangled. Smashing my lips against Axel's, sure there will be bruises left, I push my clenched fists against his exposed abs as his nails deepen into my nape. It's a feral display which Axel neutralizes in an instant when his hands lower to the buttons of my shirt. I freeze along the length of him, the first of my own tremors juddering down my back. Our kisses turn softer, a gentle plea from me to stop but I don't attempt to push his hands aside. Axel has been testing my boundaries all week and I no longer have the energy to deny him.

Working his way down to the bottom, the shirt material opens. A shiver of cold air hits my chest and abdomen so I nudge closer to cover myself in Axel's shadow. His hazel eyes search for mine, an open kindness waiting there.

"You look beautiful like this," he whispers, the words so soft they almost get lost in the tension-filled air.

"Not now," I shake my head, a flare of embarrassment lining my cheeks. But he ignores me. Placing his lips on my collar bone, Axel kisses my skin in places I've never let him go before. My chest, over my heart, my sternum. He stops at each nipple to slowly flick his tongue over the bud. I gasp, silencing a groan. If he knows how incredible that feels, he'll want to do it all the time.

Moving lower, I brace my hands on his shoulders to stop him. Axel lifts his head, searching my eyes again. When I don't object, he kisses my sternum and shifts over to kiss each of my ribs, then moves to the other side.

I lie frozen, trapped in a shell of myself. If I order him to stop, the others will hear and wonder what's wrong. The soft press of his lips are excruciating, gliding over the parts I hate most about myself. The ribs that used to stick out like a skeleton, the stomach that used to growl for food I didn't have.

As Axel's lips continue their slow, deliberate path down my torso, my body feels like it's shutting down. The weight of his affection, his tenderness, is unbearable against the parts of me that scream imperfection. His touch is gentle, reverent even, but in my head, all I can see are the harsh angles, the bones that once protruded grotesquely, and the softness that has returned, a reminder of all the years I fought against my own reflection.

I press my palms harder against his shoulders, not to push him away but to ground myself, to stop from spiraling. His lips trace over the sharp lines of my ribs, and I flinch. He doesn't stop, doesn't pull away. My breath comes in shallow bursts, each kiss sending waves of discomfort crashing over me.

"I can't," I whisper, my voice barely audible, but Axel hears it. He pauses, his lips hovering just above my skin, waiting. I know he's giving me a choice, waiting for me to push him away, but I can't. I'm trapped in this moment, torn between wanting to let him in and the deep-rooted fear that he'll see me the way I see myself—broken, ruined.

Just when I think he might stop, he reaches up, gently cupping my face in one hand. I can hear his voice in my head, his reassurance drowning out the voices that plagued me.

You're safe with me. I know you don't see what I see, but you're not that person anymore. You're more than your scars.

He's wrong of course, but Axel has a way of peeling back the layers, of seeing straight through me. I hate it, but at the same time, I need it. I need him. I close my eyes, and release my hands from his shoulders. I remain tense, anticipating the next press of his lips which doesn't come.

"You've done so well," Axel's breath fans my abs. The hand on my cheek shifts, grabbing for a pillow which he covers my front with. Then his hands are on my boxers, my cock springing free before his face. Desire rushed back through me with renewed vigor, the weight of a dam bursting open releasing from my chest. Swirling his tongue around my tip, I moan, fully relaxing into the mattress.

In the background, Avery's moans have taken over the room. Skin slapping flesh pounds against the hard flooring as she screams, falling apart in a display I can envision perfectly in my mind. I roll my hips, trying to gain more friction from Axel's mouth but he's playing hardball. His hands clench my thighs, pinning me in place. God, I love his strength. I hear the dull knock of glass on wood as Wyatt places down his empty bottle and leaves.

At the same time as Axel stops toying with me, taking my cock fully into his mouth, Huxley lifts and lowers a shaky Avery onto my face, the taste of his cum spreading over my tongue.

"Happy New Years," Hux chuckles, tapping my arm as he and Dax also leave. And with that, the line between control and surrender dissolves entirely.

AVERY

Sleep clings to me, repeatedly dragging me under while those either side of me flinch and shift. A bone-deep exhaustion pins me down into the mattress, dreams flittering in and out. Images of glistening eyes, full lips curved into smiles. Someone kisses my head.

I remain a dead weight pressed up against a strong back, my limbs too heavy to move, too weary to care. The scent of citrus flickers at the edge of my awareness, but it's hard to hold on to anything for long. I lean myself closer to who I know instinctively is Axel. From behind, an arm snakes around my waist and tugs me back. I don't bother fighting, not even when a hand covers my mouth.

"Hold still," a distant voice penetrates the darkness, although the brush of lips is hot on my ear. I don't have the energy to do anything other than remain still, not after Axel and Garrett were finished with me.

They spent hours lavishing my body with pleasure, taking me savagely at first and then worshiping me with longing kisses and tender licks. The three of us ended up lying vertically, the gentle rhythmic thrusting of them both inside of me akin to making love and I'm fairly certain I was asleep before they'd even withdrawn their cocks. It was glorious.

Now, in true Garrett fashion, an erection pushes insistently at the curve of my ass. Someone get this guy a medal for stamina. I attempt to mutter something along those lines but the hand on my mouth tightens.

"Shh. Don't wake Axel." I huff into the hand, surrendering to the cock pushing its way between my thighs. I try to shift, acting as an accommodating host, when the shaft brushes my pussy and I gasp. A shot of tender soreness bursts to life, causing me to jolt. I squirm more now, attempting to protest that it's too much. I can't take anymore. The mouth beside my ear places gentle kisses against my hairline. "Relax. This is for me."

Slowly rocking his hips back and forth, he uses the apex of my thighs to stroke himself. His breath hitches, his hips jerking with slow, controlled thrusts.

The hand stays firm over my mouth, muffling the whimpers that build at the back of my throat as his cock slides between my thighs. He's using me—my warmth, my softness—to state his need. It shouldn't be so erotic considering what we were doing a few hours ago, but somehow a different kind of need has awoken within me. One which wants to let my sleepy state hide how much it turns me on. I'm just an object for pleasure.

Biting down on my ear lobe, I clench my ass in response, squeezing him tightly. His harsh breathing picks up, a lone sound in the darkness as he pumps back and forth. The slick, heated friction between us intensifies, each stroke teasing me in ways I can't ignore. The quiet rhythm of his body, the subtle desperation in his movements, builds a tension that coils low in my belly. The soreness between my legs throbs in protest, but there's a strange thrill in the powerlessness of it all, in being pinned down and used so deliberately.

His hand slips from my mouth, brushing down my neck before cupping my breast, his fingers rough as they tweak a sensitive nipple. I stifle a moan, biting my lip, but he hears it. He knows.

"That's it," he murmurs against my skin, his voice low, reverberating through the darkness. "I can feel your heat. You'd take all of me if I decided it."

Axel shifts beside me, still asleep, his even breathing a stark contrast to the hungry gasps on this side of the bed. He drapes an arm across my waist and tightens possessively, as if even in sleep Axel can sense what's happening, what's being done to me. It only makes my attacker bolder. He thrusts harder, pushing himself closer to the edge. My body betrays my exhaustion, my soreness, as desire curls deep inside me.

"You're going to make me come," he groans, my breast being roughly groped in his large hand. His rhythm falters, becoming erratic. My breath catches, the tension too much to bear. I grip the sheets, biting back the sharp cry rising in my throat as my body, drained as it is, responds to him with a sudden pulse of pleasure.

His hand flies back to cover my mouth just as I arch into him, and his groan is a low, broken sound as he spills against me, warmth spreading between my thighs. He stills, his lips brushing my neck, and for a moment, the room is filled with nothing but our heavy breathing.

"Good girl," he whispers, his voice rough with satisfaction. His hands release my mouth and waist, and in the next moment, he's gone.

I lie there, now too wired for sleep, as the click of one door closes and the bathroom one opens. Light floods the room, the rough movements of a towel being tousled over a head of dark hair and a T-shirt being pulled on. Garrett doesn't even try to slip in quietly, dropping himself onto the mattress with a soft bounce. He grabs for me instantly, his hand curling around my thighs and suddenly jerking away.

"Holy crap, Peach. I hope you're dreaming about me because you are *gushing*." Heat floods my cheeks, a delayed response stuttering in my brain. What the fuck just happened? In front of me, Axel's hazel eyes blink open, his voice void of any grogginess.

"Wyatt just dry humped her against my back."

"What the hell?!" I instantly push against his chest and shoot upright. No, that can't...there's no way...Oh god. "You were awake the entire time, and you didn't say anything?!" Axel pushes himself upright too, leaning against the headboard with a boyish smirk.

"It beat the nightmare I was having," he shrugs. "And if I gave any signal that I was awake, he would have run off. You're welcome." My mouth drops open. That was Axel *doing me a favor*? I throw my face into my hands, finally catching up with what just happened. Wyatt was here, using me as a human sex doll. His kisses still linger against my neck, the heated press of his hand on my breast. The twisted reality of it only makes it that much more erotic, even if I'm convinced I can never look him in the eye again.

Curling his hands around my shoulders, Garrett encourages me to lean back against Axel's chest. I don't have the energy to resist. I'm too embarrassed that I was so easy, even though something didn't feel quite right and I allowed it to happen anyway. Plain and simple - I'm a slut. That's my destiny now. Once I'm reclined, Axel strokes my hair while Garrett's attention drifts lower.

"Let's put this where it belongs." He widens my thighs, his fingers sliding through Wyatt's cum until he reaches my most sensitive area. I tense on instinct, attempting to clamp my thighs shut but Garrett is already positioned in between my knees.

"Relax, Peach. I know you're sore, but this has to happen."

"Why?!" I half-screech, my brows knitted together.

"Knowing all of our cum is inside of you sends me feral." For the second time, my mouth drops open and I'm speechless. I don't know how much more of these blurred lines I can take, and I one hundred percent blame Garrett.

He's spent months filling my head with these fantasies, switching up normalized dynamics that I don't even question it anymore. Anyone else want to slide into my bed and come on me? I'm fair game to the Shadowed Souls, no exception.

Axel's chest vibrates beneath me. "Technically, Dax didn't cum inside her." Garrett's expression falls. There's an instant gut-punching moment where I'm sure he's going to hunt poor Dax down and milk him just for this occasion. This warped bonding initiation he's conjured up. But then, his easy going nature returns and he rolls his eyes.

"He came inside her throat. Don't challenge me on logistics right now."

Without any argument, Garrett holds my gaze as he uses one hand to spread me open and the other to push two cum covered fingers inside of my pussy. I wince at the contact but he doesn't stop, scooping up the next bit and tenderly pushing it into me. The more he does it, the more the pain subsides, opening the gateway for pleasure to crash through. Scratch being a slut, I'm a full-on cum bucket now. Garrett's fingers work their way inside of me, curling, twisting and pulling back in a rhythm I'm soon lost to.

Throwing my head back against Axel, I twist my head so he can kiss me. Just like our love making earlier, his lips are full of reverence and passion. Garrett scoops the last of the cum from my thighs with a satisfied grunt.

"That's the last of it," he says, pushing those long fingers back into me. On his withdrawal, my own hand lashes out to grab his wrist, holding him in place. Axel's tongue dips into my mouth, my nerve endings alive as I start to work

Garrett's wrist back and forth, fucking myself with his fingers. I shouldn't have anything left after last night, but with Wyatt at the forefront of my mind, I manage to quickly draw myself towards another climax.

Especially when Axel's mouth lowers to the spot behind my ear that Wyatt kissed and he whispers, "Such a good fucking girl."

Avery

Suffice to say, I skipped my run this morning. The soreness between my legs has somewhat eased after an hour in the bath with Dax, given that he's gentleman enough to not trick me into another round of sex like Garrett tried to this morning. Axel drank his coffee by the window and watched a physical fight break out on the bed, my fists flying as Garrett pinned me down. Luckily, Dax came to my rescue, announcing a bath was ready and we've been lounging in the huge, jacuzzi tub ever since.

The warm water laps gently as Dax shifts behind me, his chest a solid, comforting weight against my back. Beneath the layer of bubbles, his arms are draped lazily around my waist, fingers tracing soft patterns across my stomach, his touch soothing rather than teasing. There's no urgency, no hunger simmering beneath the surface. Just peace.

I tilt my head to the side, resting it against his shoulder, and he presses a soft kiss to my temple. "Feeling better?" he murmurs, his voice low and familiar, a sound that always makes my heart flutter.

"Much better," I sigh, sinking deeper into his embrace, wrapped in a languid contentment I haven't felt in days. "You have no idea how grateful I am."

"For the bath?" he tilts a brow. I smile.

"For you." Dax's blue eyes crackle with love, his chest swelling beneath me. Moments like this, the calm between the storms, remind me how lucky I am that Dax will always be in my corner. Stoically waiting on the sidelines to pick me up when I fall and dust me off. He's my go-to for comfort, the man who is holding onto my heart and keeping it safe until I'm ready to cross the next barrier. To cut it into pieces and offer it out to the rest of the men in this house.

Mistaking my silence for tiredness, his hand slides up to brush a wet strand of hair behind my ear. His lips graze my shoulder. "After last night, you deserve a break." I nod in agreement. It's not often all of the guys get involved with me in the same evening, and when they do, it's intense. If only Dax knew about my late night visitor.

We fall into a comfortable state, the soft splashing of water and the faint hum of the world outside the only sounds filling the room. We're facing a huge bay window that overlooks the ocean. Our last day in paradise, which I decided about twenty minutes ago.

I didn't expect anything of this festive season, having no home to go to and a stalker chasing me around the country, so the break we've had has been incredible. I was gifted a real Christmas, and I finally got some answers. But we can't hide from the world forever. We can't put our lives on hold, allowing them to be dictated by others. We're going out on a high before something goes wrong and ruins the peace we've found here.

I glance over to see Huxley leaning against the doorframe, his torso bare and accentuated by the crossing of his arms. He catches my gaze and a slow, knowing smile curves his lips.

"You two look cozy," he remarks, his tone teasing, but there's warmth behind his brown eyes.

"Join us," Dax suggests, his voice lazy and inviting. My own brows hit my hairline and I look up at Dax's open expression. He chuckles against my back. "I'm taking a leaf out of Garrett's book. There's no use in us fighting each other for your attention when we can just share it."

"Yeah, I get that," I lick my lips, searching his face for any reservations, "but...naked?" Both of them laugh at me now, Huxley stripping out of his pajama pants. My eyes immediately drop to his cock, impressively thick and swaying.

"I find it adorable how you can ride me in front of four people but you're shy about sharing a bath."

My pulse quickens at the sight of his lean, muscled body walking toward us. In the mirror, I catch a glimpse of the kneeling angel tattooed across his back, her huge feathered wings shifting in time with his movements. He's filled out more than before, his shoulders wide and filled with the quiet confidence he carries. It's the swagger that gets me more than the shape or size of his body, and the way he devours me with his eyes that has my heart beating a little faster.

Dax shifts, making space for Huxley in the tub as he steps in, the bubbles rippling as he lowers himself across from us. His leg brushes mine under the water, a casual touch that still manages to send a thrill through me. He reaches for my hand, lacing our fingers together, and tugs me gently until I'm leaning toward him.

"How's my girl doing?" Hux asks, his voice soft, his thumb brushing tender circles against the back of my hand.

"I'm good," I say quietly, my gaze meeting his. "Better now." Dax makes a mock noise of disagreement and we all smile. Hux's eyes soften, and he tugs me closer, pulling me out of Dax's arms and into his lap. I don't protest, settling against his chest, the warmth of his body wrapping around me like a blanket. Huxley's hands slide up my arms, massaging the tension from my shoulders, and I can't help but melt into him, the love and tenderness between us enveloping me.

"You're all so good to me," I whisper, feeling the warmth of his affection sink into my bones.

"Not all of us," Hux comments. My thoughts tumble back into last night, how my dreams after the fact played Wyatt's intrusion on repeat whilst filling the imagery. I could perfectly envision the crazed flicks of his brown hair against

Garrett's pillow, the tick in his jaw as he tried to withhold from spilling all over me, then the release of tension when he did. It's all there, locked inside my mind, ready to be called forth at any possible moment.

I expected to feel that same embarrassment when I woke, but it had vanished. Instead, something much more potent was laying in its place. Power. Wyatt, once again, has given me an insight to his true desires and now, anytime he tries to push me away, tries to give me a reason to hate him, I can call him out on his bullshit. All he's done is give me ammunition.

Huxley kisses the top of my head, his lips lingering there as Dax watches us with a small smile, his hand still resting on my leg under the water. Their legs intertwine to settle me between them, leaving only the steady rhythm of their hearts against mine. I was right. This festive break has been exactly what all of us needed, so I decide it's better to just rip the band aid off.

"Now might be as good a time as any to tell you I've come to a decision..."

***

"Family meeting!" Garrett runs through the house hollering. I blow out a breath, rolling my eyes. My decision did not go down well. In fact, it blasted a hole through the serenity which had settled. "Dining table, five minutes!" He bangs on several doors as he tears through the lower level, even though he was one of the last to find out.

Zipping up my bag, I collect Mr. XO's letter from the bedside drawer, briefly holding it against my chest before pushing the envelope in the front of my bag. I've decided I know what my problem is. I'm a hopeless, endless romantic and I blame the books I've spent years curled up reading. They were my sanctuary away from the world, and now I can't let go of the notion that Mr. XO is simply some crazy super fan who will forever remain a stranger.

Once I'm fully packed, I lug my bag down the two flights of stairs and approach the dining table. My ponytail of wet hair is heavy, slowly seeping through my sweater. Choosing to stand behind my chair, I lean on the back of it and look over those already seated. Wyatt saunters in last, completely avoiding my gaze - as expected. He heads over to lean on the kitchen island, keeping a clear distance between us.

"It's really not a big deal," I address the guys. Garrett throws his arms in the air, an incredulous yet sarcastic look on his face.

"Not a big deal, she says," he throws an inked hand in my direction. "Totally upheaving our lives and putting herself totally in danger but it's totally not a big deal."

"Stop saying totally," Hux huffs, physically man-handling Garrett's colorfully-marked arms back down to his sides. Axel steeples his fingers on the table, hazel eyes imploring mine.

"It does seem rather reckless. What's the rush?"

I look to Dax for back-up, figuring he's my best chance but even he is skeptical. My back is immediately up in full defense mode.

"School will start again soon. We can't just rock up the night before. We need time to settle back in and I didn't want to be the one to say it," I spear Garrett with a narrowed look, "but some of us are starting to let ourselves go." Garrett's hand flies to his chest, his mouth dropping wide open and then slamming shut.

"How very dare you." I refuse to drop his offended stare. Coming from the man I watched inhale a whole bowl of chicken wings intended to be shared between four people yesterday, I'm not fazed. Huxley takes charge to bring us back under some form of control.

"We haven't heard from Nixon yet. Wyatt has me check his emails each time I go into town. There's no further instruction."

"Fuck Nixon's instructions," I half-shout, exasperation fueling me. Garrett pretends to gasp and faint, and I take a banana from the fruit bowl to throw at him.

Dax leans back in his chair, arms crossed over his chest, watching me with those ever-calculating blue eyes. He's quiet for a moment before asking, "What if going back puts us in more danger? What if Fredrick's men are just waiting for us to resurface?"

"None of Fredrick's men have even come close to the beach house since we got here. They're too busy chasing Nixon and Meg is safely hidden in plain sight."

"How can you know that for sure?" Dax frowns. I'm caught in the web of his gaze, biting down on my bottom lip. I can't let on that I've been watching secret footage and scrolling back through to hunt for any sign of danger. Even when it was just Meg and Keren here, there wasn't a single incident that would lead me to think the safe house has been compromised.

Then there's the fact that whoever watches those surveillance tapes now will be treated to the image of me being screwed in every position possible by a group of well hung guys. I knuckle down, biting on my inner cheeks to keep the realization from showing in my face.

"We're coasting here. Getting too comfortable. We can either wait for the boredom to settle in and eventually start to resent each other, or we can go back to our lives and show we won't live in fear anymore." Taking a deep breath, I push off the back of the chair and stand straighter.

"I'm not asking for permission," I say, my voice holding firm. "I'm telling you what's happening. We're going back to Waversea. Together." The silence that follows feels suffocating. It's a heavy, loaded silence, one filled with the weight of a thousand unspoken fears and arguments. But none of them say anything.

"I need all of you with me," I add quietly, eyes moving from Garrett, to Axel, Huxley, Dax and finally over to Wyatt. "I can't do this alone. But I am doing this." I swallow thickly, pushing away the lump of nerves that had been building in my throat. I really didn't want or think this would warrant an entire intervention. If anything, I figured someone would be on my side. "Besides, Wyatt is on my side with this."

"I am?" Wyatt speaks up for the first time. I barely spare him a glance.

"Yes, because you know as well as I do that Dax cannot miss a single class without good reason otherwise it will hinder his scholarship." A long pause follows, the tension in the room thickening. I'm preparing the next part of my argument when Wyatt crosses the room to stand at my side.

"She's right. We can't risk a blemish on your record, Dax. You have to go back." Wyatt holds up a hand when Dax starts to protest. "You've spent too many years and worked far too hard to let it slip now. I promised I'd always keep you on the right path." Turning to face me, I blink up at Wyatt's glistening green eyes, doing my best not to show the thoughts running through my mind.

You fucked my thighs in the dark, you naughty pervert. When can we do it again?

"I suppose it's useless trying to persuade you to stay behind whilst at least Dax leaves?" He asks, a knowing tilt to his brow. I nod.

"A complete waste of breath."

"I thought so." He stares at me like I'm an odd jigsaw piece that won't fit in the perfect compartments in his mind. For a moment, no one moves. The air seems to buzz with tension. And then, slowly, Axel rises from his seat, walking toward me. He stops just in front of my chair, hazel eyes meeting mine with a look of determination.

"Then we'll make it work," he says, his voice steady. "But don't expect me to be happy about it." Huxley follows suit, standing and giving me a small nod of agreement.

"I guess that's that then," he mutters. Garrett still looks like he wants to argue, but when Wyatt shoots him a look, he shuts his mouth, throwing his hands up in resignation.

"Fine whatever, but for the record," he points his index finger at me, "I am not getting fat."

Through it all, Dax's piercing stare doesn't leave my face, but eventually, he stands and moves around to my side. "I will never stand in your way, Avery. You know that." His fingers tangle with mine and he brings my hand up to his lips for a brief kiss. "But if there's one hint of trouble, Wyatt is to take you somewhere safe without a single argument. Even if we need to be separated for a while. My scholarship doesn't come before your safety."

For the first time all morning, my resolve wobbles. I wouldn't know what a day without them would even look like. I've become so attached - no, *so dependent* - on them. I trust Dax implicitly, but he is putting my life in Wyatt's hands.

But if this is the reassurance Dax needs, then I will give it to him. "I promise," I reply softly, leaning into his embrace. I cling to him as much as I cling onto a small slither of hope that Wyatt doesn't care about me enough to separate me from the other Shadowed Souls. Once we're back at Waversea, he becomes so focused on returning to his own life, he'll be oblivious to mine.

WYATT

It took longer for Garrett to say goodbye to each element of the safe house than it did for all of us to pack. *Goodbye bed, goodbye Christmas Tree, goodbye refrigerator.* The sea was the worst one, as Axel had to drag him away weeping and promising to return one day. Garrett can always be trusted for his melodramatics, but also for being easily distracted. Given that there is one more person to seat ratio, a giggly blonde in his lap was enough to get him down the driveway without looking back.

Rolling my tongue between my teeth, I hang my arm out of the driver's side window. My other hand grips the wheel, smoothly gliding Huxley's SUV between lanes with the man himself tensed in the passenger seat. There was no way I could sit for hours on end, listening to the bland chitchat in the backseat without a distraction.

Since Avery made the decision to leave on our behalf, we took no arguments in the logistical planning of heading home. Home. I roll that word around in my mind, buffered by the sweeping wind hitting the side of my face and hair. The Waversea frat house used to be the one place I'd ever felt accepted. *Seen*, if only for the rich fuckboy facade I put on. Now that word holds a very different meaning, with Rachel patiently waiting for me. As we turn into the hangar where Huxley's jet is waiting, I switch off the engine and manage to sneak off and find five minutes to call her. The phone rings twice before she picks up.

"Hello?"

"Rachel, it's me. Wyatt." My voice cracks on her name, my sneaker rolling over a small rock behind the hangar.

"Oh, Wyatt," she gasps. Relief floods her voice. *"I've been so worried. Are you well? Are you eating?"*

I choke on a lump locking in my throat. Fuck, just hearing her voice, hearing how much she cares, is enough to buckle my knees.

"I'm okay," I say shakily, barely convincing myself. I clear my throat and try again. "Yes, I've been eating. I..." My cheeks heat from the confession working its way out of my mouth. "I went a little hard on those...vitamins...you gave me. My brothers storm-rolled in and stopped me before it went too far."

There's a beat of silence on the other end, and I hear her breath hitch like she's about to cry. My gut twists painfully.

She's not supposed to cry. I'm the one who screws up. I'm the one who deserves to feel like this. But her voice is trembling now.

"Oh dear. I'm sorry, I'm so, so sorry."

Throwing one fist backwards into the hangar's exterior, I look up to force my own tears back. I hate that I'm causing her more suffering after everything she's already been through. It doesn't matter that she gave me drugs under false pretenses. She was doing her best to guide me through twenty one years of trauma in a matter of weeks. But it didn't work. I'm still broken, and all I've done is hurt her more.

"It's not your fault," I murmur, blinking back the tears as one of Huxley's staff appears, signaling we're almost ready to take off. I shoo him away with my hand. They can wait. I can't step foot on that plane until I know Rachel is okay. "You were just... trying." Trying to love me the only way she knew how. But that doesn't make it hurt any less—for either of us.

"I just wanted to give you a way to escape. I...I need to escape sometimes."

"I know that. You're not to blame. In fact, I have so much respect for you. You've been so strong for so long. I can't wait to come back."

"Does that mean you're coming home?" She gasps, so full of hope that I'm about to crush into dust. Why do I always have to be the asshole? Why can't I seem to just...be?

I swallow hard. There's that word once again. Home. A tugging pulls at my chest, a physical draw back to her. I know Rachel would love me like no other, that she'll never let anything come between us again. But something holds me back.

"Not yet," I push my fist against my mouth. "I have something I need to do. It shouldn't take long."

"Is this about the girl?" Rachel asks bluntly, twisting my gut into a knot. I forget that I'm the only one late to this party. Rachel has known the truth all along, and she's been forced to live with it.

"Yeah, it's about her." I nod to myself. It's always about Avery. Every damn aspect of life has always revolved around her, even before I knew she existed. Inhaling, I close my eyes and let the dam crack open for a moment, spilling the words I've never dared to speak aloud before. "She's been tossed around in this mess as much as me. Call it my redemption, but I need to see this through."

"I understand." A quiet sigh sounds on the other end of the line. *"But remember, Wyatt, you haven't done anything that's worth a redemption. If Nixon can't see that you are owed the world, then I will happily get it to you."*

A frown pitches my brows at the sudden steel quality to Rachel's voice. Was that a loving threat or a dangerous promise? I have to remind myself that she's not only the shy, quiet housewife but the gangster's wife who will do anything to protect her only son. Unfortunately, I'm long past the point of letting people protect me. I've been through too much not to see this through for myself.

"Rachel. Thank you for caring, but let me handle it. I know what I'm doing," I lie. I haven't got a fucking clue, but I'll figure it out. Eventually. An understanding sigh travels into my ear.

"I'm not without my uses, Wyatt. I have my own set of connections and resources. If there's anything you need, promise me you'll call straight away."

"I will. Thank you." The uniformed employee appears around the corner to beckon me again, the sound of the jet roaring to life behind. I'm out of time. "I have to go, I love you." I call into the phone, pressing the device against my ear to barely make out her answer.

"I love you too, my boy."

Choking on my own sob, I lower the phone, every vein in my forearm popping into full effect. My knuckles are white while I stall long enough to level my breathing. I've always had a singular objective. One destination in mind, and it was as far from Hughes' Manor as possible. For the first time, I'm torn between where I long to go and need to be.

A dark shadow lingers over my shadow. The drugs may have painstakingly ebbed their way out of my system over this past week, but Ray refuses to vanish. I won't let him. I imagine his presence, powerful and imposing. It fills me with the same notion.

Rolling my neck, I stride around the hangar to see that same employee standing within earshot. Has he been there the entire time, listening into my conversation? The thought that Rachel wasn't the only one to hear my vulnerability hits me like a wrecking ball to the chest, throwing my guard back up in full effect.

He straightens upon seeing me, eyes wide as if he's been caught out. Fuck yeah, he has. Ray leans into me, pressing the weight of his suspicion into me. I force the man to look me in the eyes, daring him to reveal his secrets.

"Who the fuck do you really work for?" I glare, stepping into his space. He's a few inches shorter than me, a man of around thirty. His blue eyes flicker to the family crest embroidered into his jacket, feigning confusion. I grip his lapels and slam him into the white metal at his back. "You like listening to phone calls, do you?" My voice is raised over the roar of the jet, my impatience quickly wearing thin. After the emotional backlash Rachel has unknowingly dealt, I have nothing else to fall back on but rage.

The fool shrinking away from me is muttering words I can't hear. Lies, I'm sure. Yanking him closer and throwing him back into the metal again, I get right into his face.

"You don't repeat my conversation with anyone, you understand? Nothing I say is of your concern." He's nodding so fast, his blond hair falls from its neat slick-back. Whoever he is, he's pathetic. I toss him aside, and Ray prims with pride. He'd want me to be strong, to be the sort of man Rachel needs. By the time I make it back to her, I'll be fit to bear the Perelli name.

The employee, who clearly has a death wish, jumps back into his job role instantly. Attempting to usher me towards the jet, his hand brushes my back and I don't even consider my reaction. Red coats my vision as my arm snaps back and plummets forward, my fist connecting with his jaw. He hit the floor this time, dirt marring his jacket and slacks. Without a second thought, I push my hands into my pockets and stride towards the jet. No one dares to rush to his aid until I've ascended the stairs, and no one tries to rush me again.

Once inside, five sets of eyes hit me like daggers. Huxley is on the right side by the window, the one with the best view of just what happened. I keep my face relaxed, dropping into the seat furthest away from the rest and instantly reaching for an eye mask. My intent is clear - leave me alone, go back to giggling and fucking around with each other.

Darkness settles over my mind, keeping me company for the remainder of the journey back to Waversea. I manage to go the entire day with only a series of grunts and shrugs, keeping up the pretense that I'm the monster they should fear. That I no longer exist in their world.

Stepping into my old bedroom, my resolve shatters. Everything has been left exactly as it was the night I stormed out. A path of destruction carves its way from one side of the room to the other. A visual portrait of confusion and hatred. Those emotions flood back now, as if they've been lingering beneath my broken bed and waiting for me.

However, there's clarity.

The man who caused this mess couldn't see a future worth living. He didn't know he had a family who would never give up on him, and I don't mean the Perelli's. The Shadowed Souls. The men who have fought their own battles and day after day, continue to tolerate me through mine. Love is a powerful thing. It's enough to replace the emptiness I've been clinging to. The validation I've been seeking from those who were never going to give it willingly.

They could have tidied the clutter, replaced the broken furniture, and figuratively swept the evidence beneath the rug. They could have sat around waiting for me to return and pretend that everything was normal. But doing that was never going to help. I need to tidy this mess for myself. I need to take responsibility for the damage I cause, and I know exactly where to start.

AVERY

A cold wind nips at my cheeks as I make the short journey across campus, tugging my cardigan tighter around my leotard and leggings. The bag slung over my back holds my ballet slippers and compression socks, and Dax holds my hand. He gives me a small smile every time I look up at him, wondering how he's unaffected by the sudden winter clinging to Waversea. We were lucky that Nixon's safe house was in a warmer climate, and I completely took it for granted.

But nothing can lessen the excited tremors building in my chest as we near the dance studio. My first class back. I'm practically giddy with the thought of being a normal university student again, cementing my decision. I needed to return to my life, to take back control.

There's not too many students around this early, none as visibly eager to get back into a routine as I am, but those who pass throw us curious looks. I suppose a lot has changed in the last few weeks, and Dax's claim on me is clear.

Crossing the uneven mound of frosted grass, we take a shortcut to the studio where he openly kisses me goodbye, wishing me a good day. The smile on my face is touching ear to ear when I push open the heavy door to the familiar room of wood and glass. Warmth and brightness hits me all at once. The smell of rosin, wood, and sweat feel like a familiar friend, welcoming me back.

As I make my way inside, there's a chorus of hushed voices. I pull up short at the expression on many of the dancer's faces. A mixture of disgust and jealousy hits me, reflected in each of the mirrors circling the room. Madam Nightingale crosses the dance floor on light feet, a long white skirt floating around toned legs and a smile on her face that shows she's the only one pleased to see me.

"Avery! How was your festive break?" She air-kisses my cheek, her hands clasping my frozen ones. Those at her back return to their warmups, but are no less evident in their eavesdropping.

"It was good, thank you. And yours?" I respond, barely aware I'm speaking. My attention is on my peers, actively ignoring my presence whilst lingering close by. Madam Nightingale waves me off, whisking me towards the rear door where the dressing and storage rooms linger. She leads me into a dim office, the blind half-mast and paperwork strewn across an aged desk. My chest tightens. "Am I...in trouble?" I frown, thrown into a spin of confusion. Madam Nightingale rifles through her paperwork, blinking up as if she doesn't understand my question.

"You tell me. These are letters I received over the holidays on your behalf." Cocking her brow, she holds out the folded papers, totally unaware that my heart just fell out of my ass.

Letters? Here? It wouldn't be the first time Mr. XO approached me at the studio. Perhaps he wasn't aware I'd left for the holidays, and when he did find out, he tracked me to the safe house. But that doesn't make sense. If he could find me, surely Fredrick Walters could too. Growing impatient by my stalling, Madam Nightingale rounds the desk and plants the folded papers into my hands.

I quickly scan the typed words, latching onto the formality of the language. The breath I didn't know I was holding rushes through my lips. They're acceptance letters into some of the country's most prestigious ballet schools, offers from agents to represent me and some are simply commendations from well-known names in the business, stating that they will be keeping an eye out for what I do in the future.

"The showcase was a huge hit! You can take your pick of schools, of careers. You're going to be a star, and don't forget who gave you the small push into dancing publicly," Madam Nightingale breaks her usually strict character to wink at me.

She's gushing, her eyes alight with possibilities. Suddenly, the looks when I entered the studio all make sense now.

Placing the letters back onto her desk, I smile warmly and take a step back towards the door. "Thank you, Madam. I'm flattered you saw potential in me, but I'm happy where I am. I'd like to just stay here and dance for you."

The shift in the senior dancer's demeanor is sharp, bordering vicious. All joy is erased from her face, leaving only the stern lines and sharp stare behind. No longer floating around on air, Madam Nightingale stands painfully straight, her lips pursed tightly.

"Avery, listen to me. You've had the best private tutors, been given the best shot at making a name for yourself beyond just being a Hughes' heiress. These are opportunities any other dancer would die for. Please don't squander this because of some boys."

I recoil another step towards the door. What does she know of my connection with the Shadowed Souls? Regardless, the protective streak within is quick to respond. They aren't just some boys. They're men. My beautifully damaged men who have seen the light in me. Not because I'm good at dancing or because of whatever claim to money I have. They've seen the version of me who was bursting to break free of her cage. And besides, they are no one's business but mine.

"Like I said, I'm finally happy and settled here. I won't be pushed out by any fancy offers, agents or otherwise. I just want to dance." I leave the tiny, barely-used office with a deflated, yet aggravated sigh.

Why does no one get it? Ambition is the death of passion. As soon as I start giving my craft to the world, it will no longer belong to me. Endless hours of practice, of pain, of pushing myself to the next extreme height and taking no joy for myself. I might as well hand myself back to Fredrick if the people's puppet is all I'm destined for.

Re-entering the studio, there's a ball of nerves in my gut, festering into a physical stomachache. I don't waste time with crowd control. Dropping down beside my bag, I pull on the compression socks and slippers, rolling my ankles until warmth seeps through the cotton. Standing at the barre, I fall into the same warmup that the others are leading, figuring the best way to tackle their jealousy is to show I'm not a threat. I'm not the enemy, trying to use them as steppingstones to a higher purpose. Especially Nikko, who's eye I try to catch but is actively avoiding me.

The tension in my shoulders soon melts away as I move through pliés and tendus, my body remembering exactly what to do. Theo slips in last, setting up at the piano for today's lesson. He fumbles with his sheet music, red cheeked as if he's woken up late and ran here. Again, he refuses to acknowledge my presence, but that's fine. I'm just another student amongst the masses.

Beginning a steady cadence over the piano keys, the soft brush of pointe shoes scrapes against the floor as Madam Nightingale appears. Having composed herself, she gives nothing away in her expression, but her voice cracks through the room like a whip. Oh, she's pissed.

Snapping orders like a drill sergeant, we're thrown into a vigorous workout that quickly burns through our muscles, and then some. I try to lose myself in the flow of the music, in the simple joy of moving again, but it's near impossible when I'm greeted with looks of hatred on either side. They all seem to know this change in attitude is my fault, and I quickly realize I never could have won. Either I accept the offers I received and they despise me for it, or I upset Madam Nightingale and we all pay the price.

We're forced to pirouette on the spot again and again while Madam hunts for imperfections. No one escapes her narrowed glare, but I seem to get the brunt of her shouting. We work through the combinations being barked our way, repeating the movements until everyone is in sync. She pushes me harder than any other, holding me to a higher standard.

"Miss Hughes!" she shouts, declaring us no longer on first name terms. "Keep up. Correct your posture, extend those hands. My God, what is happening with your alignment? Do put some effort in." Sweat quickly beads across my forehead, my legs shaky from lack of practice.

I love ballet. I need ballet. I wanted this, I chant in my mind. It's that mantra alone that sees me through to the end of the lesson. My entire body is aching as I drop down against the mirror, slowly tugging my slippers free of my sore feet. I'm definitely going to need one of Axel's sport's therapy massages tonight.

Madam Nightingale leaves first, throwing her hands up like she's lost the will to live before disappearing out back.

Most of the students barge out of the main door as soon as they can, but several remain, lingering around for something. I finish packing my bag when I hear the door open again, and my blond archangel enters. I smile up at Huxley, sighing sweetly at the sight of his handsome, chiseled face.

"Hey." I reach up for him, wanting to feel his arms banded around me. A little dramatic, I must admit, but Huxley swoops down onto his knees to put my sneakers on. My very own Prince Charming. His basketball jersey and shorts are baggier on his frame than they used to be, although he's never quite lost the fine definition to his muscle. I watch his arms flex now, as he ties my laces, lost in my own thoughts until a voice penetrates my mind.

"I told you," a girl nearby, Jenna, scoffs, huddling in with her friends. They mutter amongst themselves but given that the studio has an echo, I catch every word of it. "She's screwing all of them."

"Whore, much? Save some for the rest of us," another twitters back. Nikko leans in, only too happy to encourage the nasty giggling.

"Stacey said she saw her sneaking into the dressing room with Wyatt during the showcase interval. Surely that's illegal, right?"

"That's daddy issues for you," Jenna tilts her head on a small laugh. All fight leaks from my shoulders, my face tinted red. I'm dumbstruck, my mind an empty space where no thoughts formulate. It wasn't the offers that everyone was hung up on, it was *this*. This gossip that I can't even deny.

Huxley's hands have stilled on my sneaker. A moment of silence passes, thick with the weight of their rumors. I glance at Huxley, his jaw clenched tight, his normally calm demeanor cracking. He rises slowly, his height towering over me now, his brown eyes dark with a protective fire. The other dancers still loitering freeze as his gaze sweeps across the room, landing on Jenna and her whispering entourage.

"You've got something to say?" His voice is low, controlled, but there's an unmistakable edge to it.

"Hux, just leave it," I scramble to my feet. Tugging on his arm, he's unmovable. Jenna's friends shrink back, but she doesn't. Instead, she smirks, stands and crosses her arms.

"Just calling it like we see it."

"Like you think you see it," he mumbles back, the veins in his throat strained. The rigidness in his back scares me. This isn't some armed thug threatening to cause us harm, it's a big-mouthed bitch sticking her nose in my business. I tug on his arm again.

"Come on, they're not worth it." I implore him with my eyes, although he's not focusing on me. An hour ago, I was so hopeful that this was the right decision. Now I'm looking at Huxley, who's contemplating getting himself thrown out of college and my nails dig into his forearm. I can't handle the thought of us being separated, not for a day, not for weeks at a time. Eventually, Huxley allows me to drag him closer to the door, although his eyes don't leave Jenna's.

By the door, so close to freedom, he stops to address the entire studio. I shrink behind his back, not wanting to see their faces. "None of you know a damn thing about

Avery. What she's been through, what she means to us. But keep running your mouths, and you'll find out exactly what happens to people who disrespect her."

My heart races and I finally manage to get him out into the cold air. Snapping back to full protective mode, he hastily tugs my cardigan higher up my shoulders and draws me into his side, despite not wearing a jacket himself. Our breaths puff in front of our faces as we hastily walk towards the SUV, parked on a nearby road. Once satisfied I'm safely in the passenger seat with my seat belt clicked in place, he closes the door and rounds to the back. I watch his silhouette in the rear view mirror, how he stalls to collect himself, rolling his neck to and fro. Once ready, he joins me in the driver's seat.

"Don't listen to them," he murmurs, reaching across to tuck a stray strand of hair behind my ear. His face is taut, pained somewhat, but there's also an overriding glimmer of love there. "They don't know you like we do." Huxley's tone sends a jolt of comfort through me. He captures my lips for a quick kiss before twisting the key in the ignition and speeding us down the road.

"Where are we going?" I ask as the campus grows smaller behind us and we turn into the long street of frat houses. I've only had one class so far and surely Huxley has places he needs to be. Hux shrugs one shoulder, his mouth finally tilting upwards.

"Garrett sent me to fetch and bring you to the gym. He was whining that he missed you and wanted his little mascot to watch our basketball drills."

"So, why are we here?" I clarify as we pull up beside the house we share. Huxley leaves the SUV half on the driveway at an angle, twisting in his seat.

"Because Garrett's not the fucking boss of me," Huxley states, stubbornness shining in his chocolate brown eyes. He unclips my seatbelt as an indication to follow him out of the car and through the front door, where he promptly smacks my ass. "Get changed, Swan. We're going out."

"Hux, it's the first day back! We can't ditch class already!" I laugh, smacking his arm lightly, but before I can say anything else, Huxley moves with a familiar, swift grace. In an instant, he sweeps me off my feet, spinning me around effortlessly. I squeal, my giggles bubbling out as he nuzzles my neck, his breath warm and teasing against my skin.

"We're not ditching. I'll have you back for English Lit at two-thirty," he murmurs, voice low and playful, "and I don't start until tomorrow. Wyatt just wanted to run some drills to get back into form."

He sets me down gently, but his hands linger, sliding down to my waist. A shiver runs through me, the ache in my toes forgotten the moment his touch electrifies my skin. His fingers tighten slightly, as if he can't bear to let me go, and I find myself leaning into him, wanting more.

"And you're defying the big boss man for me?" I tease, batting my lashes and pressing a hand to my chest dramatically. "I'm flattered." His smirk grows, eyes twinkling with mischief.

"You should be. I don't make a habit of blowing off basketball for any old chick with daddy issues," he says, and before I can protest, he's tickling my ribs. I can't help but writhe against him, my full belly laugh echoing around the entrance hall as I try to escape his relentless fingers.

"Huxley!" I gasp between laughs, swatting at him, but he just pulls me tighter against him, his playfulness melting into something warmer, deeper.

"I missed this side of you," I whisper, as the laughter fades and the space between us closes. His forehead rests against mine, and the world narrows down to the feeling of his breath on my lips, his hands gripping me like he's afraid to let go.

"Me too," he murmurs, his voice quieter now, his brown gaze locking onto mine with an intensity that makes my heart race. "You're incredible, Avery. All of those whispers, the rumors—it's all bullshit. They don't know you like we do. They don't see who you really are."

My throat tightens, my heart swelling. I'd give him anything he wanted in that moment, absolutely anything. "I don't care what they say," I breathe, trembling slightly. "As long as I have you. All of you."

Huxley's lips curve into a slow, tender smile. "You always will," he promises, his tone thick with emotion. "I'll make sure of it." Without another word, he leans in, capturing my lips in a kiss so soft it feels like a whisper against my soul.

Time stops. All the noise, the chaos, and the doubts vanish. All that remains is the steady rhythm of his heart against mine, the way his fingers curl into my waist, pulling me closer as if he's afraid I might slip away. His mouth glides over mine sensually, every brush carefully placed to communicate the depths of emotion we've yet to speak. Deepening the kiss, Huxley's tongue dips in to coil with mine, filling me with a need that matches my own, silently vowing to never let me go.

When we finally pull apart, breathless and dazed, Huxley's eyes search mine, filled with a softness I've only ever seen when it's just the two of us. "We shouldn't waste any more time. I need to get you out of here before Garrett comes looking for you."

I smile, nodding as he steps back, but his hand remains on my waist, unwilling to lose contact. As he guides me toward the stairs, I marvel at the man standing before me. The Huxley I fell for, the one who chases away my worst fears and holds me through my darkest nights. He's back. After everything he's been through, he's struggled and suffered and found his way back to me.

HUXLEY

A very looks beautiful. Not just pretty in the way she always does, but softer, more relaxed. Her golden hair is pulled back, a few loose strands falling to frame her make-up free face as she reads the thick paperback in her hands. She's opted for a cozy sweater that hangs off her shoulder, showing just a hint of what I know to be underneath. I tried to be a gentleman when escorting her into this tiny, corner café, but keeping my eyes off the roundness of her ass in those jeans was hard damn work. I deserve a medal for even attempting it.

We've found this spot on the edge of town, just far enough away from the campus crowds. The place smells like coffee and fresh pastries, our table tucked into the back with a simple pinecone ornament separating us. Avery is gently tapping her foot against my leg beneath the table, lost to her reading as she absentmindedly stirs sugar into her tea. I could watch her like this all day.

"Here we are," an older woman arrives at our table with a plate in hand. Her gaze flicks back and forth between us, wondering where to put it until Avery snaps into action, moving the ornament aside and gesturing to the middle of the table. Once the plate has been placed, the woman hovers. "Are you sure that's all I can get you? We have a range of sweet treats, all baked by myself."

"They look delicious," Avery agrees, glancing at the glass cabinet. "We'll definitely take some to go but this will be great for now. I had a big breakfast," she lies. She barely had time to grab a granola bar after Garrett spent all morning trying to convince her to climb back into his bed. Once we're alone again, Avery's warm smile turns back to me. "Eat whatever you can manage, I'll have the rest."

My gaze drifts down to the steak sandwich and fries that don't look half as intimidating as they used to, and that's because of her. Avery doesn't push me, doesn't make it into a big deal. And thankfully, she doesn't watch, preferring to go back to her book. It was a tactful plan on her part, once I announced we were going out for lunch. I wanted to do this for her, to be like a normal couple without all the baggage we carry. More specifically, without the others breathing down our necks now we're out of the safe house.

I do as asked, picking at the sandwich and fries until I've managed just under half. I was already semi-proud of myself, but when I push the plate towards Avery, her smile is everything.

"You did so good," she says softly, her voice like music to my ears. That's all I need. Quiet words of encouragement as she accepts the leftovers. My chest tightens, the kind of feeling that makes the air around me lighter. These last few months have been a slow, festering torment which I didn't know existed. A form of self-sabotage that was beyond reason, a type of pain I couldn't explain. But with Avery, it's different. She doesn't treat me like I'm broken or like I need fixing. She just...gets it.

"Yeah, I guess I'm getting there, huh?" I rub at my nape, ducking my head. Her smile widens, and she reaches out, her fingers tracing the back of my hand in a slow, gentle motion.

"You're more than getting there. You're fighting and you're winning." Those blue eyes swallow me whole, so large and filled with purity. I feel like there's more she wants to say, but she holds herself back. Baby steps and small wins. That's where we're at right now.

"I suppose I deserve a reward then," I smirk, instantly causing Avery to perk up. She pops a French fry into her mouth, raising one slender eyebrow at me.

"I completely agree. What kind of reward did you have in mind?" Pushing the plate closer to her, I jerk my chin at the food.

"Eat up and you'll find out." Avery takes another fry, her eyes sparkling with curiosity as she hands me the book. It's another one from Dax's extensive romance collection. I lean back in my chair, stretching my legs beneath the table and open to the bookmarked page, continuing where Avery has left off. I don't need to know the premise since she's apparently reached a sex scene that is enough to make even me blush. She giggles knowingly, watching me read and tilt my head, trying to visualize the tangle of limbs this particular mutant and ghost have gotten themselves in. Kinky.

Once she's finished, we purchase some pastries as promised and take them to go, heading out of the café. The crisp air brushes against our cheeks, slicing straight through my leather jacket and ripped jeans. I take her hand in mine, guiding her down the street until we come upon a nail salon near the parked SUV. Avery gives me a side-eye, but doesn't ask anything. She trusts me, and I love that.

Stepping inside, warmth instantly wraps around us, the scent of lavender and citrus circulating. The decor has been geared towards creating a space for relaxation, the back wall covered in fake grass with an LED sign displaying the salon's name - *'Nailed It'*. A few women are scattered on plush chairs, having their nails done whilst serene music plays in the background.

"Can I help you?" the receptionist asks, her eyes lingering too long on my body to be considered friendly. I doubt they get many men in here, especially ones over six-foot and clearly athletic.

"Two for pedicures if you're able, and a manicure for my girlfriend." I tug Avery closer into my side. The receptionist's eyes snap back to my face, her cheeks twinging with pink that she's been caught gawking. Swiftly leading us to the high-backed leather seats, she begins to prep the warm water in the foot spa with various salts. Avery's full attention is on me, a teasing smile playing at her lips.

"Your reward is to get me a mani-pedi?"

"My reward will be seeing your fancy, new nails wrapped around my cock later," I reply, shrugging off my jacket. The attendant testing the water jet slips, fumbling around to get the faucet back under control. Avery gives me a pointed look.

"You've been spending too long with Garrett." Avery rolls her eyes. Being directed to soak our feet in the warm water, we shed our shoes and socks, and I catch the first glimpse of her reddened toes, instantly frowning.

"Fine, that was just a ploy to get you to take care of whatever is causing you to limp around. You're not as sneaky as you think you are." She doesn't even try to deny that I caught her wincing multiple times, just sinks further into the seat and closes her eyes.

"That's a lie, I'm incredibly sneaky when I want to be. But Madam Nightingale did go really hard this morning. I pissed her off." As the technicians wheel over two tiny stools, I reach over to take her hand.

"Tell me about it." And she does just that.

For the best part of half an hour, Avery confesses about the offer letters, her reasons for turning them down, how her ballet teacher used it as a reason to push her to her limits and then moves onto the gossiping. I knew it was coming, even though I did my best to shut it down quickly. I'll need to regroup with the others later to discuss it, but for now, I simply sit and let Avery work it out of her system, whilst my feet are being attacked with a harsh, porous rock.

"So yeah, that's that," she shrugs, seemingly deflated but also finally relaxed. "Never a dull day."

"Not in our world," I manage a smile. Our feet are patted dry with warm towels and fitted with disposable flip flops before Avery is led to a nail station, with me trailing to remain by her side. I don't ask if I can sit at her side, nor do I wait for permission to lean over and pluck a nail polish bottle from the wall of hundreds. Avery immediately approves, turning the red bottle over to read the name.

"Crimson Desire," she bobs her brows. The same technician who did her feet sits on the opposite side of the table, quietly busying herself with filing and preparing Avery's nails. The tranquil music washes over us, carefully stealing us away from the real world. I notice there are no clocks in here, and the windows are covered with heavy blinds. Avery tilts her head for her blonde ponytail to tickle my forearm. "This might just be the best idea you've ever had."

"I have my moments," I say, trying not to look smug. Truthfully, I'm just happy I managed to swoop in when I did and whisk her away from campus before things got ugly. I didn't expect returning to be easy but for very different reasons than her classmates turning on her.

My palm glides over her thigh whilst her hands are occupied, just as my pocket begins to vibrate. I tug my phone free and glance down at the screen flashing with a group call. I was wondering how long it would take. Declining the call, I push the device back into my pocket and ignore it when the vibrating starts up instantly. Avery hears the repetitive buzz, her eyes flicking over to me.

"Aren't you going to get that?"

"Nope." I shake my head, reaching over to take her hand. "I'm not ready to share you again just yet."

"It could be important," she twists her lips.

"It could be," I shrug, my intentions clear. Nothing is going to take away the precious time I have left with Avery all to myself. Her eyes soften how they always do when I've managed to get my own way. It's those small looks, those tiny traits I've memorized that fill me with bursts of love at any given moment. I hold it inside, letting it blossom and grow until I've done as Avery asked - to learn to love myself again first.

For now, I'm content. In this little bubble of peace, nothing else exists. No threats, no responsibilities, no rumors. Just us, creating pockets of time to reconnect and remain united. I won't let a distance form between us again.

AXEL

"Told you he wouldn't bring her back," I scuff up Garrett's hair. He finishes tying his laces and straightens, hair wild and lips twisted.

"I swear no one respects me around here." At this, we all start laughing and the locker room echoes with mockery. Packing up our sweaty gym gear, I throw an arm around Garrett's shoulders when he looks at his phone again.

"Leave them be," I murmur, plucking his cell free of his hands and putting it back in his sweatpants' pocket. "We won't clip her wings, remember?" Garrett sobers in an instant.

It was one of our sweeter occasions, after a particularly horrible nightmare of mine. Instead of burying myself inside of him to banish the ache carving out my chest, I asked Garrett to talk to me. And he did, until the sun started to rise, he whispered pretty fantasies and made tender promises. How he'd always care for me, how he'd make sure Avery never left us behind. I made him swear then and there that he wouldn't hold her back, no matter how hard it might be. To see her soar would outweigh the pain of losing her.

We leave the locker room and wander the stone hallways back to the main gym. Dax hangs back behind Wyatt, keeping a close eye on our quiet leader. I'm sure Wyatt didn't have the same sense of separation anxiety that we felt, but he didn't protest when Garrett ordered Huxley to fetch our Little Swan either.

Pulling open the heavy door, I'm instantly hit with the heat from the gym, a heavy scent of sweat in the air. Pounding footfalls slam against treadmills, occasional grunts radiating from the weight bars. Usually Wyatt would divert away, preferring to push himself to the point of exhaustion on the machines but today, he keeps up pace and exits with the rest of us. I suppose the walk back to the house will be exercise enough, given that Huxley didn't return with the SUV.

The cold air leeches onto my freshly washed skin, droplets from the locker room shower still clinging to the back of my neck. My breath puffs around my face as I drag a woolen hat over my shaved head and ears, linking my arm back into Garrett's. He's tense, either from the cold or from still stewing about what Avery and Huxley are up to. It's not hard to come up with a few ideas.

We walk as briskly as our aching legs can manage. First day back at practice after the holidays is always the hardest, which is why Wyatt thought it would be a good idea to get a head start today before Coach returns tomorrow. To pass the time, I think about the warm bath and decent sized lunch I'm going to have when I get back. Soon enough, the frat house looms ahead.

White-wash walls stand out amongst the other buildings dotted along the street, standing tall and proud to belong to the Shadowed Souls. Usually, seeing it calms me. Our oasis, where we're in total control of what happens inside. Where things make sense and we are free to be ourselves.

But for some reason, my feet begin to slow. I have the strangest foreboding sense that something's off. A creeping feeling crawls up my spine. The knot in my stomach pulls tighter when I see it - the front door hanging wide open, swaying on its hinges like someone just walked through it.

I freeze. My heart kicks into overdrive, hammering in my chest. "Did anyone forget to lock up this morning?" The words come out sharp, too sharp, and I don't miss the way Wyatt's head snaps up. His eyes narrow at the door.

"Hell no," Dax growls from behind me. "We never leave it open like that."

Before I can say anything else, Wyatt is already moving, putting more speed and effort into the short run than he did all morning on the court. He bounds up the steps two at a time, and for a second, I think he's about to charge inside, ready to face whatever, or whoever, is waiting. But he stops just short of the doorway, his fists clenched so tight I swear I hear his knuckles crack.

Dax is right behind him, his jaw locked and body coiled like a spring ready to snap. I'm slower to approach, as if holding Garrett back in a slow walk will somehow slow the inevitable. The air around us is suddenly thick, the winter's bite becoming the least of our problems. My heart thunders faster, every instinct screaming that we're about to walk into a trap.

Reaching the top step, I follow Dax's eyeline to the small table just inside the door, where we usually toss our keys into a shallow dish. The only saving grace is that Huxley's keys aren't present, which I pray means they're not home, but there is a singular yellow rose placed against the wood with a tiny, scribbled card.

Welcome Home Avery.

"He knows we're back," Dax barely whispers. Wyatt's head cocks to the side, his curiosity piqued.

"When we were looking for you in the city, someone crept into the hotel room where Garrett and Avery were sleeping and left a bouquet of yellow roses," I fill Wyatt in. There's no recognition that he's heard me, his back rippling. When he speaks, it's a low growl of forewarning.

"I never told you guys this, because I didn't think it mattered," he pauses to inhale and exhale steadily. "But yellow roses were my mom's - Cathy's - favorite flower. I have my buttonhole from her funeral upstairs. It's an exact color match."

An involuntary shudder crawls the length of my spine. I didn't need confirmation that Fredrick was responsible for these spontaneous drop-ins, but having it causes the dread to surge through me like a wildfire, raging and temporarily locking me in place on the porch. I grip Garrett's arm tighter.

"He's toying with us," Garrett mutters mostly to himself, his gaze lost somewhere beyond the staircase. His jaw clenches every few seconds, like he's grinding his teeth. "Search the house."

"Are you insane?!" I yank him back when he tries to cross the threshold. "No way. I'm calling the cops, let them handle this." My phone is already out and dialing when three sets of eyes swing onto me, apparently sharing the same thought.

"What if they've got Avery up there, gagged and bound?" Dax's brows tilt, the worry in his blue gaze evident. Still typing out the number, I step into their chests and keep my voice as a low hiss.

"What if they got guns? We know they're not shy of using firearms on us, or have you all forgotten Huxley was shot last time they came for her?" A tense silence settles as I hold the cell to my ear and quickly reel off the details needed, holding Wyatt's eye contact. If anyone is on the side of not storming into a house with armed goons, it should be him. He tried to hide how much it affected him to have a gun pointed in his face last time, but I don't miss a thing. I know where to look.

"Thank you," I say and cancel the call, crossing my arms. "There's a patrol car in the area, they'll be here shortly." The fear welling inside doesn't lessen, especially as Garrett doesn't answer. He doesn't look at me either, just keeps staring at the staircase like he's already playing out the worst-case scenario in his head. Like he's about to bolt inside.

Not a single sound trickles through the house, as if the very walls are holding their breath. Fuck, if anything happens to Avery whilst we're useless standing on the porch because I demanded it...I won't know how to deal with that. For now, I hold onto the hope that no keys and no SUV mean Huxley had the good sense to keep her away.

Before I can spiral anymore, before an impending panic attack has a chance to grip me in its clutches, a deep, booming laugh rolls across the front lawn. My head snaps to the left, expecting something completely different to the swarm of football jocks scattered across our yard. There's more than ten of them, standing shoulder to shoulder, bulky and imposing. Clad in fitted T-shirts that show off their muscular physiques, most have a baseball cap turned backwards on their heads.

"The fuck do you want?" Wyatt pushes his way through us to take the front, standing at his full height. It has no effect on the men at the far end of our property. I recognize a few of them from a frat house down the road, their faces twisted with smugness.

One of them, the ringleader I presume, cups his hands around his mouth and yells, "There's the sister fucker." The air all but vanishes, all blood draining from my face. More laughter follows.

"Oh yeah, we've heard all about you. Screwing around with your sister and passing her around your friends. What a sick fuck." A meathead steps forward, toeing his shoe into the grass. I notice then that they're all wearing studded sneakers, the intent obvious. They're here to cause some damage. "Thought you'd have the good sense to stay away, glad you didn't though. I've been dreaming about this."

Multiple knuckles crack behind him, cocky grins rippling down the line. Beside me, Garrett's body is as rigid as a steel bar, and I see the moment the switch flips in him. He's ready to charge, to throw himself into this fight headfirst, like he always does. I grip his arm, holding him back just long enough for him to meet my gaze.

"Don't," I say, but it's too late. Avery and Wyatt's reputation are being dragged through the mud, and if there's something Garrett can't stand, it's bullies. His dark eyes burning with barely contained fury. I reach up and scuff his hair again, trying to bring him back to me even though it feels like there's a weight pressing down on my chest. "They just want a reaction. We have bigger issues right now."

"Oh, don't make me throw up," one of the jocks fakes a gag. "They've got gays living in that fucked up house too?!" Any hint of light in Garrett's eyes suddenly dies. And that's when I know, we're not walking away from this. Not today. Not when the panic inside churns into something more potent, something darker that takes over my mind.

Wyatt doesn't say a word. He's already moving, a slight swagger to his steps as his long legs eat up the path. Dax follows, and then Garrett and me, like we're all caught in the same gravitational pull. By the time we're on the lawn, the football guys are laughing again, their leader stepping forward with his hands raised in mock surrender.

"What's the matter?" he sneers. "Can't handle a little truth?" Placing myself in front of the guy that gagged, I lift a brow and blow him a kiss. Wyatt takes the lead, exuding confidence. I expect him to defend himself, disgusted by the notion of what they said, but that's not what tumbles from his lips.

"She's not my sister."

"You grew up with her. You knew her as a fucking child," the leader snarls, his top lip curled. "How long have you been wishing you could touch her-" It happens so fast. Wyatt's fist swings before the guy finishes his sentence, catching him square in the jaw with a sickening crack. The guy's head snaps to the side, eyes wide with shock. He stumbles back, arms flailing, but Wyatt doesn't stop. His body moves like a well-oiled machine, another punch already sailing forward. This time it lands right in the guy's gut, sending the guy sprawling to the ground.

Chaos explodes around us, fists flying in every direction, bodies colliding in a whirlwind of rage and adrenaline. I don't even have time to think. My body moves on pure instinct, recalling a time I used to fight without reason. Punishing those who didn't deserve it, but this time, they do, and I have no qualms about reacting with my fists.

One of the jocks charges straight at me, his face twisted in anger, his arms raised like he's about to tackle me to the ground. I duck just as he lunges, feeling the rush of air as his fist barely grazes my shoulder. He's bigger than me, stockier, but his size also makes him slow, predictable.

As he stumbles forward from the miss, I plant my foot and pivot, driving my elbow into his ribs with all the force I can muster. I feel the impact reverberate up my arm, the hard crack of bone meeting bone. I don't give him a chance to recover. Stepping close and planting a hand on his chest to keep him off balance, I drive my knee up into his stomach. He lets out a choked sound, doubling over, and I finish him off with a quick jab to the side of his head. He collapses, groaning, and I stand over him for a second, my chest heaving, my fists still clenched.

I look around, scanning the scene for my next target. The homophobic asshole. Bodies are strewn across the lawn, some of them groaning in pain, others knocked out cold. It's a mess of bruised faces and split lips, and we're right in the middle of it.

Garrett is breathing heavily, but his eyes are wild, fists flying faster than I can track. He's like an animal, all raw rage and unchecked aggression. Two guys come at him at once, and he doesn't even flinch. His fist snaps out, catching one of them across the face with a vicious hook. Following up with a brutal uppercut that knocks him flat, Garrett holds off so he can kick the jock who's trying to crawl away.

Behind him, Dax wades through those fighting. There's a strangely wild grin plastered across his face that doesn't look like it should belong there. A reckless type of joy shines in his blue eyes. He catches one of the jocks nearing Wyatt by the collar and throws him aside, acting as the mediator amongst the macho bullshit. Wyatt is in a world of his own, his fists smeared red with more splattered across his face. His face is twisted into a grim scowl as he takes down another guy with a brutal knee to the ribs.

For a moment, it seems like we're winning. Until we're really not. There's too many of them and not enough of us, the tide quickly turning in the jock's favor. The sounds around me blur together, the sickening thud of fists meeting flesh, the grunts of effort, the occasional pained shout.

I hear someone yell my name, but I can't tell who it is. It doesn't matter. There's no time to process anything. Another jock charges at me, this one taller and leaner, his fists raised boxing style. I lunge forward, feinting to the left before swinging a right hook that catches him across the jaw. He stumbles, but he's quick to recover. His fist flies toward me, catching my chest and then side in quick succession. An arm bands around my neck, tugging me backwards.

I hit the floor, a spike of pain explodes across my entire back. My heart pounds, adrenaline roaring through my veins as a body lands on top of me, fists sailing towards my face. In an attempt to defend myself, I bring my arms up until they're promptly tucked back down and pinned at my sides.

"Your kind disgust me," The words are hissed in my face, followed by a wad of spit coating my forehead and eyes. I writhe beneath the body pinning my hips, each blow to the head increasing the ringing in my ears. I'm dragged lower into the darkness, closer to the panic that consumes me night after night.

Hands press my shoulders into the bed of grass. A mattress puckers beneath my back. The words pummel into me as heavily as the fists, contorting, transforming.

"Let's see who wants to kiss you after this, pretty boy."

"Let me kiss you, pretty boy. Don't be shy." No, please no. Looking up, a large woman's arms hold me in place, the mattress a stark contrast to the pinch of her nails. Rolling my head to the side, I release a sob as the silky texture of my long, brunette hair glides over the pillow. I'm not that boy anymore, but I still don't know how to get out of this never-ending loop. Clutching a hand in the rough sheets, I brace myself for what comes next. How my body will betray me and give her exactly what she wants, despite the sickening twist in my gut.

"Dude!" a shout penetrates my mind. "He's getting fucking hard on me!" A new type of shame washes over my cheeks as I groan, unable to see through eyes that are now swollen shut. My mouth is numb, the coppery warmth of blood gliding down my throat. There's a round of disgusted jeers and the weight jerks off me, but it's too late for me. The terror has a hold of my mind, laboring my breathing as an attack hits before I can register it.

I'm standing now, appearing in the doorway of the ballroom. The space is filled with women of all ages in fancy ball gowns. In unison, they turn to glare at me. Gloved hands ball into fists, perfectly painted lips sneer. A walkway down the center has been left clear, my mother waiting expectantly on the podium at the far end. A sparkling champagne colored dress hugs her surgery perfected body, a usual pearl necklace hanging around her slender neck.

Stepping onto the shiny floor, my shoes echo loudly in an otherwise silent space as I make my way towards her. With each step closer, my mother's hands begin to change to a deep shade of crimson. The stain grows until I reach the raised platform, stopping just short of her wrists. Following my eyeline, she smiles wickedly and lifts a skinny index finger to paint the color across her lips.

"This is all your fault," she smirks down at me. Confusion seeps in with a feeling of unease as I look around. Pale, bare feet are poking out from behind mother's dress and catch my attention. Sidestepping, I follow the length of ankle, then leg and beyond to find Avery's blonde hair fanned around her as she lies lifelessly on the stage. Making a move to rush to her, hands grab me from behind and pull me backwards. Arms hook across my chest with impossible strength yanking me further away as my mother cackles.

"It's all your fault!" the crowd shout and jeer over and over again. I try to set my feet so I can't be moved but it doesn't work and soon I'm too far back and too surrounded to even see the podium. I reach out desperately, tears filling my eyes as I scream her name. I've failed her again, like I do every night in every scenario. I'll never be able to save Avery when I can't save myself from these visions.

The first tear spills from my eye and everyone freezes, my mother suddenly appearing before me. Her dark hair has started to fall from her flawless chignon and the bloodstain smearing her lips glistens.

"You see, Axel, you are weak. You will forever be stuck as this pathetic, little boy. You can never escape me."

A scream is torn from my throat and I jolt back to life, throwing my fists out wildly.

"Hey, hey, it's okay," a soft voice says. Small hands lightly grab my fists, then move their way up to my jaw. My head is spinning, leaving me completely disorientated. "Axel. I'm here, I've got you now." I want to believe those words but I'm still combating my mother's harsh words, or rather, the harsh words that my own brain produced. I'm fighting against myself and I'm starting to fear that's a battle I'll never win.

"Come on, Axe. Deep breaths for me." Slowly, I start to come back to myself, realizing that my chest is heaving and a cold sweat coats my entire body. I feel disgusting. Managing to force my eyes to crack open, light bursts through the darkness held within. Avery fills my vision, her face inches from mine. I push away from the hard surface I'm leaning against, falling into her arms. She hugs me as I cry, the saltiness stinging my face. I know it's bad, even before I blink up enough to see a line of ambulances along the sidewalk.

"Where-" I croak, not liking the scrape against my throat one bit. I've had some serious damage dealt onto me today.

"They're all okay. The police responded to a call and broke up the fight. Hux and I pulled in after. You'd already passed out and...um," there's hesitation before Avery exhales. "Well, Garrett is being taken up to the station. Apparently, he went ape shit on the guys who were hurting you. All three of them have been carted off with broken bones."

Not too far away, an officer slams the rear door shut and drops into the driver's seat. Garrett's silhouette moves into sight, dark blemishes marring his face. He stares out of the window and presses a cuffed hand to the glass. I attempt to reach out but pain shoots up my arm, drawing a hiss through my busted lip. Avery's face says it all, the misery shimmering in her blue eyes. That, and the fact she's kneeling in the grass with me.

I look around, taking in the scene properly at last. Wyatt and Dax are near the porch, bruised and bloodied, but standing whilst Huxley fusses over them, tugging the shiny silver blanket tighter over their shoulders and attending to the blood on their faces. The paramedics are busy loading groaning bodies into ambulances, working in haste to get on the road. A few football jocks are still scattered across the lawn awaiting medical attention, the arrogant smirks wiped clean off their faces.

"I'll take you inside when you're able to stand," Avery tells me, rubbing her hands over my arms. I remain leaning against her, despite my crushing weight against her lithe frame. I currently couldn't manage to hold myself up if I tried.

"N-no, the note," I groan. "There was a...a flower." My brows pinch with effort, a blossoming ache in my ribs making it hard to focus. Avery peels herself away from me as much as she dares, kissing my temple.

"The cops did a sweep of the house. There's no one there." I exhale loudly and wince, settling back against the wall I've been leaned against. I have no idea who moved me or what happened in the space of time I wasn't conscious for. Blue flashing lights blare to life, announcing Garrett's departure as the sirens slice through the air. My head snaps toward the street, tracking the vehicle until it disappears, wrenching out my heart along with it.

Please cooperate, Garrett. Do whatever they say to come back to me quickly.

AVERY

Wringing my hands in my lap, my eyes dart around the room. Framed diplomas and various other achievements hang on the walls, amongst photos of a very pretty Persian cat. The desk separating us from a large circular window is almost bare, every pen laying exactly parallel to the next. A singular photo frame faces in the opposite direction, sitting beside the computer monitor, slick wireless keyboard and a brass name stand.

Dean O'Sullivan. As if reading his name conjured the man himself, the door at my back opens. Clipped dress shoes enter, striding around to face Dax, Huxley, Wyatt and myself sitting guiltily in armless chairs. Counselor Lorna is beside the Dean, particularly shocked to see Wyatt's chair so close to mine. I'm not surprised - I ripped him a new one in my sessions with her, and I'm sure he's been doing the same about me for years.

Dean O'Sullivan appears strained, dark circles circling his eyes, his fingertips pressed against his temple as if to ease a headache. He's young for a Dean, and despite his deep scowl, his voice is even. "I've asked the counselor to sit in with us today so she can be best equipped for your sessions going forward." Those tired eyes linger on Wyatt and me for a moment.

Placing a brown folder down and taking the time to straighten it along the desk's edge, the Dean unbuttons his jacket to lower into his large leather chair. Lorna pulls up a stool, a notepad and pen in her hands, large glasses hanging on her pointed nose. I avoid her gaze, preferring to stare at a spot on the floor as the Dean speaks.

"So who would like to tell me why I have six members of our football team being treated for injuries, their parents screaming at me down the phone, the school board pushing for a swift punishment and our investors asking how I'm going to sweep this under the rug before the media gets a hold of the story."

Silence follows, no one daring to answer first so he continues. "Not to mention that on the second day of term, I've had to arrange transport to collect one of my students from the police station." I bravely look up, wanting to ask if Garrett is okay but the sharpness of the Dean's eyes gives me pause. He analyzes each one of us in turn. "Please, don't all speak at once."

"You know how it is," Huxley takes the lead, trying to play off the chaos we pulled up to yesterday afternoon. "The usual rivalry ahead of Midnight Madness got a little out of hand, is all." The Dean doesn't buy Huxley's smirk and shrug.

"Well your little rivalry skyrocketed when the families involved discovered this fight was led by the son of Nixon Hughes. There's talk of pressing charges."

"I didn't lead shit," Wyatt straightens in his seat. I briefly close my eyes, quickly seeing the situation plummeting south. "Riley Buckshaw stepped onto my property first, spewing vile lies. I was well within my rights to defend myself. Add in the homophobic slurs and you had a recipe for disaster. Perhaps instead of questioning us, your time would be better suited teaching your football team about the consequences of prejudice."

Wyatt's hand twitches on the rim of his seat, as if it's taking a conscious effort to remain in it. I catch sight of his long fingers, the veins popping along the back of his hand and disappearing into his hoodie sleeve. The orange hoodie I once clung to, inventing a connection to Wyatt through the soft cotton. I catch myself staring at Wyatt's hand and shoot my gaze back up, chewing on my bottom lip.

"Be that as it may," Dean O'Sullivan drawls, his sole attention on Wyatt now. "We made a deal when you requested that house for just the five of you. I could have taken on another ten to fifteen students, raising our grade standards and bringing in more external funding."

"Unless they shared a singular brain cell like your football team," Huxley mutters loud enough to be heard. He's another one in this room who hasn't slept, putting it on himself to watch the street through the windows all night. Dax warns him to not make it worse so we can leave soon. I don't want to be here either, I want to be still in bed cradling Axel's swollen face into my chest. Alas, all of our presence was mandatory.

Wyatt's bruised knuckles crack. "I've held up my part of that deal. My trust fund pays our way and Huxley funded your new gym. Dax has straight A's, Axel hasn't relapsed. I even keep Garrett on a tight leash, otherwise he'd be a regular at the police station by now. Nothing has changed."

"What about Avery?" the Dean asks, raising a single brow. Lorna pauses her writing to peek up through her glasses, gauging Wyatt's reaction.

"What about her?" the man beside me bristles, speaking as if I'm not currently sitting right there.

"Is Miss Hughes living in your residence now too? And is she aware of the rules? Whoever stays under your roof must maintain good grades and not cause any issues." That last part is emphasized to us all. The Dean leans his elbow on the arm rest and presses his fingers against his temple again, that headache returning in full swing. Wyatt continues to command control, letting the rest of us shrink into the background.

"Avery still has her dorm room place; she can choose where she stays. As for her grades, Avery is the best dancer this school has ever had the fortune to host. Whatever she decides to do in the future, Waversea will be continually noted as the school who enabled her. I would count your lucky stars she's here, rather than insinuating she's causing trouble."

I sit, stunned into silence, my eyes flicking up to Wyatt's tensed jaw. He ignores me, as usual, but his words are out there now. There's no taking back the skip of my heart or the prickling awareness that he knows me better than I realized. He's been paying attention to me.

"I see." Dean O'Sullivan steeples his fingers, his expression unreadable. "Well, I haven't found any sort of clarity thus far. I'll need time to consult with Lorna and some other senior faculty members to come up with a fair punishment for all parties involved. I'm afraid when things become so public, it's no longer in my control to bend the rules in your favor, no matter what your circumstances, Wyatt."

Wyatt's jaw clenches, but he doesn't argue, leaning back in his chair, arms crossed over his chest. I have to wonder how much they know, how much Wyatt has confided in Lorna. I, on the other hand, am still reeling at everything I've heard in the past five minutes.

Dean O'Sullivan shifts his gaze toward me, his intense eyes scrutinizing my reaction. "Miss Hughes," he says, softer now, as though he's moving from interrogation to a more personal tone. "You've been quiet so far. Is there anything you'd like to add? Or, perhaps, to clarify?"

I swallow hard. There's a knot in my chest, the room becoming impossibly small. My mind spins through every interaction, every instance that's built up to this point, everything I continue to hold inside. The blame for yesterday, the damage done to Axel, it all settles on my shoulders. I wasn't even there but it's still my fault. I made them all come back here.

In another slip of Wyatt's character, his head slowly turns to face me. No emotion pierces his green gaze but his foot shifts to press against my shaky one. I freeze, interpreting his small nod as permission to speak my mind. I'm hit with the sense of validation, of reality. This wasn't my fault at all, and since when have I sat back while other people fight my battles?

"Yes, there is something I'd like to say." I sit forward, borrowing some of Wyatt's bolster. Our sneakers remain pressed together. Both Dean O'Sullivan and Lorna lift their heads, indicating they thought we were done here. Clearing my throat, I level out my shoulders.

"I wasn't present for the fight, and had I been, perhaps things wouldn't have escalated so quickly. However," I lick my lips, "there's an underlying problem you're failing to address. Since we have a counselor present, it may be more impactful to discuss how to best support your top students rather than reprimand them for protecting me when this college has failed to do so."

"Excuse me?" Clearly, the Dean is caught off-guard. I feel Dax and Huxley tense up, rather than see it. Wyatt's shoe pushes harder against mine, encouraging me onwards.

"Wyatt and his friends have been doing everything in their power to keep me safe, given that a convicted felon has managed to approach us on campus at least twice that we know of. I'm sure you're aware of the police report we filed up-state. Rather than appeasing your investors and worrying about the students you could have taken in, maybe you should try to secure the premises for those who already attend here. Why is it we've been left to the mercy of my past and the paparazzi, without any crowd control from yourselves?"

I stare directly at Dean O'Sullivan. I may have started off somewhat tentative, but once the words started to flow, the more convinced I became that I'm right. It's really no wonder that the boys snapped, taking violence into their own hands when the opportunity presented itself. We've been fighting invisible ghosts for so long now.

There's a dangerous silence. Counselor Lorna shifts uncomfortably on her stool, pushing her glasses up her nose. "Avery," she finally says, her voice gentle, trying to deescalate the harsh rise and fall of my chest. "None of this has been mentioned to me, from any of you. If you felt unsafe, my door has always been open. We can't help if we don't know."

"But that's the point, isn't it?" I protest weakly, twisting the truth. "We were handling things just fine."

"Until yesterday," Dean O'Sullivan observes. My lids half-lower, my lips becoming pursed. Wyatt straightens now, his arms falling to his sides where his hand brushes over the back of mine.

"I believe we're done here," Wyatt's voice is sharp, tipping the power scale back into his favor. "We accept responsibility for our actions and will take whatever punishment you see fit, as long as the football team incurs the same accountability. They can't be allowed to go around campus spreading the shit they said."

My eyes flick towards his tense jaw again, wondering what was actually said yesterday. All I heard is that the jocks called out Axel for liking men. Wyatt doesn't stand immediately. Instead, he fixes his eyes on the Dean, a challenge in his gaze. For a long moment, it feels as though the air between them is crackling with unspoken tension. Dean O'Sullivan breaks the silence with a heavy sigh.

"In light of the stress you've all been under, I'm going to cover for you all this one time. Make sure no more violence happens on my campus. You're all dismissed."

We rise from our seats, the legs of the chairs scraping against the polished floor. Wyatt is the first to the door, but before I follow, I chance one last glance at the Dean. His eyes are already down, focused on opening the brown folder and spreading the paperwork in front of him. Lorna tracks me, a look in her eyes that closely resembles regret.

Out in the hallway, the strain between us still lingers like an unwelcome shadow. Wyatt's pace is relentless, his long strides quickly putting a distance between us. I quicken my steps to keep up.

"Wyatt, wait," I call after him, my voice quiet but urgent. His shoulders stiffen, and for a second, I wonder if he's going to keep walking, leave me behind like he's done a thousand times before. But this time, he stops. His brown hair has fallen out of its usual style, flicking over his forehead. His eyes are fixed on the hallway ahead, his demeanor tense as if he's seconds away from bolting.

"What?" he snaps, his voice clipped. It's a familiar tone, a defensive wall he throws up whenever I get too close. My chest tightens as I step around to the front of him, refusing to let him ignore me anymore.

I step in front of him, forcing him to face me. "Thank you," I say, my voice softer, more vulnerable than I'd like. "For what you said in there. You didn't have to do that."

For a brief moment, something flickers in his expression. Something deep and profound, as if his soul just burst to the surface before he had a chance to stop it. I falter at the vulnerability in his green eyes, a low breath escaping his parted lips. "Someone had to."

"Why?" The question slips out before I can stop it, exposing me. I don't want Wyatt to know how much he affects me with a few simple words. No matter what he does, I'm prepared to forget it all if I can get just a few words of his praise.

Wyatt's eyes darken, and for a moment, I think he might answer. Shuffling sounds behind him, Huxley and Dax lingering close. Just as quickly, Wyatt's open expression is gone. He shrugs, his jaw clenched tight. "Don't read into it, Avery." Pushing past me, the echo of Wyatt's footsteps fade down the hallway, leaving me standing there with more questions than answers. Huxley is quick to step forward, crushing me against his chest.

"Let's get you home, Swan. Axel needs you." My heart clenches, a choked breath becoming locked in my throat. Many things were said in that room, but one I banked to think about later was the mention of Axel relapsing. There's so much about my men that I'm still uncovering, still trying to understand. Keeping me close, Huxley eases us along the hallway as Dax falls into step, taking my fingers between his. I already know there's a sweet smile waiting for me before I glance up at his face.

"Dax?"

"Yes, Angel?" he replies immediately, so open and ready to bend to my every whim. I lean into his shoulder, inhaling the crispness of his sea mineral body wash.

"What's Midnight Madness?"

AVERY

Turns out, Midnight Madness is a big freaking deal. The boys gave me a very jaded description about destroying the other frat houses and proving they're unbeatable, even after I pointed out that the Shadowed Souls aren't a real fraternity. Garrett, despite his night in a cell, had the energy to be utterly offended at that.

"We buy our way in," Huxley explained, dishing up a bowl of soup for Axel. This led to an argument about who would take it up to him, with Garrett winning. He's surprisingly agile when he has bruised ribs and a lump on his forehead.

I snuck away after dinner to call Meg, who gave me a much more in-depth description. Apparently, for one night every spring semester, the fraternities and sororities on campus participate in a series of athletic events, with basketball taking center stage.

I can't say it wasn't a particularly lengthy call, as none have been since getting our cell reception back. We've text here and there but I've been trying to give her space after the revelations at the beach house. Ironically, finding out we're twins has caused a distance I've never felt from her. It'll take time, I remind myself.

Retreating into my room, I rub my tired eyes. Where the weight of exhaustion ends, and an endless knot of anxiety in my chest picks up. One day, things must get easier. Right? Heading into the bathroom, I relish some time to myself, showering without interruption. Garrett is going to care for Axel tonight, a pair of broken boys consoling each other so I can get a full night's sleep. I'm going to need it ahead of going back to the dance studio tomorrow, knowing I'll be the height of gossip again.

Once wrapped in a towel, I relieve my hair from the shower cap, allowing it to drape down my back. Stepping back into the bedroom, I notice the door is slightly ajar, a note sitting on the vanity. My heart skips a beat before I can catch it, knowing full well it's not from who I think.

Mr. XO wouldn't be able to get in the house when it's full, but that doesn't help the disappointment from sinking in. Is he nearby? Did he see what happened yesterday? It's insane that his presence doesn't scare me the way it should, as if I've rationalized which stalker I should fear and which one I've built into a protective presence. It's not like he's ever actually done anything for me, other than send the occasional note that lifts my spirits.

Instead, the note, which I suspect he wrote with his non-punching hand, is from Garrett. It lies next to my familiar pink dildo and a small, circular pill. *'Found these in Axel's bag. Enjoy some 'you' time, Peach. It won't happen often.'*

"So romantic," I mutter, rolling my eyes. Picking up the dildo in one hand and the pill in the other, I examine it between my index finger and thumb. There's nothing to suggest what exactly it is, nor that it's safe. A strange mixture of curiosity and caution swirls inside me. Garrett's always teasing, always pushing my boundaries, even when he's not in the room. But this? This feels like a dare. I bite my lip, feeling the familiar ache of temptation bloom low in my belly.

"Axel's asleep," a sudden sharp voice penetrates my room. I flinch out of my skin, accidently dropping the pill on the carpet. Wyatt has stepped inside, his voice trailing off as he looks from the pink veiny monstrosity in my hand, to the pill and back again. "I just thought...you might want to know...What is that?"

"It's a dildo," I frown, still trying to calm my hammering heart. "I know it might be bigger than what you're used to seeing-"

"Not that," Wyatt huffs. "*That.*" His gaze is fixed on the floor now, staring at the pill with a hint of panic and curiosity. His shoulders bunch. I note the moment he's about to lunge, and I beat him to it. Diving forward, I grab the small pellet before his hand has a chance to close around it. My towel tugs, threatening to come loose but Wyatt doesn't care about that. His eyes are crazed, staring at my closed fist.

"Avery don't-" he lashes out wildly. Adrenaline surges through me as I drop back onto my ass, all modesty and good sense forgotten. There is no thought process, just the fact Wyatt is ordering me not to that causes my hand to slam against my mouth, shoving the pill inside and my throat to swallow on instinct. A horrified silence hangs between us, both of our faces just as shocked as the other. Fuck, what did I just do?

Exhaling heavily, Wyatt composes himself first. He stands to a towering height, his T-shirt and gray sweatpants seeming far more imposing than casual now. Turning on his heel, I prepare myself for Wyatt to leave me with the consequences of my own stupid actions. What kind of stupid idiot takes something when she has no idea what it is, just to spite the person that's usually spiting her. Approaching the door, Wyatt braces his hand flat on the wood, and slowly pushes it closed.

"What are you doing?" I gasp, backing up to lean against the bed. Whether I'm scared of Wyatt or the prickling spreading through my chest, I'm not sure.

"Apparently, I'm babysitting," he groans, pressing his forehead against the wood. Whilst his back is to me, I push myself upright, securing my towel. My legs fail me, the tingling sensation spreading through my limbs. Dropping onto my mattress, the pink dildo I tossed aside rolls closer.

"I-I don't need you," I say, my voice completely failing me. Is it hot in here? Warmth is creeping across my skin, my cheeks flaming. Wyatt glances back over his shoulder, his eyes half-mast and completely unconvinced.

"I'm afraid you made the decision for the both of us when you decided today is a good day to get high." I zone out from his face, the colors in the room blending together. A kaleidoscope appears behind my eyes and I reach out for something solid to hold onto. It just so happens, it's a nine-inch silicone cock. Holding it up to my face, I try to make out the shape of it, blinking rapidly to bring some of my vision back. Wyatt has moved, his arms crossed as he stands at the foot of my bed.

"Are you just going to stare at it or are you going to put it away?"

"Is using it not an option?" I answer, not a single thread of thought passing between my ears. Wyatt's brows raise until he scoffs.

"Nah. You're too lazy."

"*Excuse me?*" I attempt to look shocked but I can't be sure what's happening on my face. He tilts his head.

"Why would you get yourself off when there's four men outside eagerly waiting for you to lie on your back and let them do all of the work?" My mouth goes dry, my tongue thick and heavy. He didn't include himself, and he knows full well I'm not a lie-back-and-take-it kind of girl. I jut out my chin.

"There's a self-satisfaction in doing it myself."

"Liar." Wyatt moves to the dresser and pushes himself up to sit on it, knocking aside the stack of school offer letters. He leans back against the wall, the picture of boredom other than his eyes. I focus too hard, causing his irises to pass from green to purple, brightening with lust before they ignite with fire. I feel that fire deep down, my skin too tight. Fuck, it's so hot in here. I pry my towel open.

Those eyes, alive like coals burning into Wyatt's skull, widen. I can't find it in me to care. The tingling takes over, radiating down to my core, vibrating with the need to be matched. I toss the dildo aside, burning up from the inside. Reclining on the bed, I throw my head back and search for the source of heat. My fingers don't feel like my own, passing over my nipples, rubbing over my ribs. The lower my hand travels, the tighter that coil pulls until I find it. Sliding two fingers over my clit, I gasp and push down harder. The pressure against the small bud penetrates the numb sensation rocketing through me.

I no longer exist. Only the quivering of my legs, the jerky movements of my fingers and the insatiable drive to be consumed by this blinding force.

"Feet together and let your knees fall apart." The order slices through me. Rolling my head to the side, I briefly catch the hardening in Wyatt's crotch area. Licking his lips ever-so-slowly, he regards me carefully. "If I'm going to be here, I might as well have a good view."

"No one asked you to be here," I exhale, continuing to stroke myself lazily.

"No one has asked me to leave yet either." There's a challenge hiding within his words, one he apparently doesn't have the patience to see through.

"You," I breathe, lost to the fog consuming my mind. Everything in me screams yes, but the last trace of my dignity says no. "You have to grovel." Wyatt's brows raise mockingly but I don't back down. "You've been nothing but an asshole to me. I deserve your groveling."

"Avery," Wyatt says my name like a whispered curse. I shudder. "Please, open your damn legs." I'm a slave to my own dark desires after that, unknowingly responding to his deep growl, my body deceiving me. My feet draw upwards, legs dropping aside like he asked. I'm completely exposed, bared to him, but he's also more visible to me now too.

Through glimpses of my hooded eyes, I watch as Wyatt's own hand travels south, stroking himself through his sweatpants. He watches closely, his jaw tense, and those haunting eyes are locked on me, mirroring every movement I make.

A strangled sound escapes my throat. My fingers glide in circles and my body arches involuntarily, spiraling towards an aching release building deep inside me. My breaths become quicker, each one a sharp, needy gasp. Every brush of my clit is hypersensitive, every nerve screaming for more, and yet, my hand isn't enough.

"Fuck," I pant, writhing against the bed, my thighs trembling with the effort to keep control. But control is slipping fast and I can feel the tension begging with me to snap. I'm so close, I can taste it. But there's something missing. Something that will push me over the edge.

I meet Wyatt's glazed gaze, his expression unreadable but his pupils blown wide. I know that look. I feel it right now too. Lust, hunger, and a darkness simmering just beneath the surface. I might not currently remember my own name but I suddenly know what I want. Not my thighs being rutted in the dark. I want him to look at me, to acknowledge me while I'm brought to ruin.

"Wyatt," I breathe, his name slipping from my lips before I can stop it. My voice is thick with desperation, need curling around every syllable.

He doesn't respond immediately, just holds my gaze with an intensity that makes my heart pound, steadily stroking his clothed cock up and down. Then, slowly, he slides off the dresser, his body moving with a deliberate slowness. My skin prickles with anticipation. Lowering on the end of the mattress, he doesn't touch me, but he's close enough now that I can feel the heat of him, his presence a tangible force that only fuels the fire inside me.

"What do you want?" His voice is low, a soft growl. A shiver races down my spine.

I can't think. Can't even form words. My fingers falter, stalling as I look up at him, eyes half-lidded, pleading. "I... I need—" He cocks his head, a wicked smirk playing on his lips.

"You can't even say it, can you?" A dull sense of recognition knows he's mocking me. Forever the man who will belittle and humiliate me, who gives me every reason to never talk to him again. Yet, I crave him. His efforts only push me to work harder, to walk the blurred line of his boundaries, hunting for a hold in the fence.

I swallow, the knot of tension in my chest unraveling as his gaze burns into me. "Please," I whisper, my voice breaking. Surprising me, Wyatt's hand moves to the pink dildo I discarded earlier. He picks it up, turning it in his hands as if assessing its weight. A surge of wetness rushes to the apex of my thighs, the sight of him holding it undoing my years of hard work. I can't help it, I'm weak for him.

"Is this what you want?" His voice has that dangerous edge again, like he's daring me to say no. Giving me the final chance to back out. I nod, barely able to breathe, let alone answer properly. My body is screaming for release, for anything, and I'm far past the point of modesty.

Wyatt takes his time, watching me with a predatory gleam in his eyes. Gliding the silicone over my thigh, he rises higher and higher, just to divert just before touching where I really want him. He's careful to never let his fingers brush my skin, never crossing that damn wall he's cemented between us. But I'm chipping away. Then, without warning, he presses the cool silicone against my pussy, sliding inside with agonizing slowness. My whole body tenses, every inch of me hyper aware of the sensation.

"I'm praying you don't remember this tomorrow," he says, watching the dildo disappear inch by inch. "But you have the prettiest cunt." To emphasize his strained observation, Wyatt pushes the dildo in the rest of the way, slamming it against my G-spot. "Why do you have to be so perfect?"

"Why do you have to be so annoyingly stubborn?" I groan back. He holds the toy still inside of me, so full but still not close enough. The pause is excruciating, and as I recognize the indecision cross Wyatt's face, I rotate my hips and ground down. He's not changing his mind on me now, I might just die of disappointment if he does.

"Wyatt, please," I beg, my voice barely more than a whimper. Rolling my hips again, I moan, the sound raw and needy. He still doesn't give me what I want right away, although he teases the silicone shaft by moving it back and forth, just enough to keep me on the edge, but never enough to let me fall. Finally, I reach down and clasp his wrist. "For once, can you just forget who I am and just fuck me like some dirty whore who's gagging for it? Choke me, spit on me, I don't care anymore, just do *something*."

I drop back into the pillows, a wave of dizziness passing through my head. I moved too fast, throwing myself into a delayed spin. My entire body is prickling with needles, pulled so taut I can't inhale properly. But it was worth it.

Finally, Wyatt relents, pulling the dildo out of me in one smooth motion. As soon as I feel the loss of it, it's thrusted back inside, repeatedly pounded into my pussy like he's possessed by desire. Or perhaps by the need to dominate me. Either way, I'm here for it.

I cry out, my back arching off the bed as pleasure rips through me, fast and hard, like a tidal wave bursting free. My hands grip the sheets and my mind goes blank, consumed by the colors sparking behind my eyelids, lost to the sensation of Wyatt letting loose on me. We've wanted this for so long. I feel him watching me with dark, burning eyes.

His movements become more forceful, more deliberate. Each thrust sends me spiraling deeper into the abyss, my body responding without thought, arching into him, desperate for more. The friction inside me builds, heat pooling low in my belly, coiling tighter with every stroke of the toy. And that's all before he finds the button that triggers the vibrations that suddenly ripple through me.

"*Fuuuuck*," I groan, pushing back into the mattress. It feels so, so good. More than that, it's freaking phenomenal, the release of him finally pleasuring me even if it's not with his own hands, face or cock. He's no less affected, his breath coming in sharp, controlled pants, betraying how difficult he's finding it holding himself back. I see it in the way his jaw clenches, the tension in his broad shoulders, the barely restrained need to unleash everything he's kept bottled up for so long. But still, he maintains that maddening control, refusing to give in fully.

"More, Wyatt," I moan, my voice thick with desperation. "Harder."

His lips quirk into a dark smile, but he doesn't speed up. Instead, he leans closer, his mouth just inches from my ear as he growls, "I'm not one of your puppets, Avery. You don't get to tell me what to do."

His free hand moves to my throat, fingers wrapping around it without fully applying pressure, just enough to remind me of what I asked for, what I wanted. My pulse jumps beneath his grip, the thrill of it sending a fresh wave of heat through me as I bite back a gasp.

There's something intoxicating about Wyatt holding me like this, the power dynamic balancing on a feather. It's his authority pressing down on me, exposing me in the best possible way. I yearn for it, to feel small beneath the crushing weight of him. The bully of my nightmares has become the embodiment of my darkest fantasy.

"Is this what you wanted?" Wyatt's voice is low, dangerous. His other hand pumps the pink dildo in and out of me with ruthless precision, the silicone slick with my arousal. I try to keep my composure, but my mind has already dissolved into a haze of need.

"Yes," I nod frantically, barely able to form coherent words. "Please... I'm so close..."

"Then beg for it," he commands, his grip tightening slightly around my throat, pushing me to the edge of control. Wyatt's fingers tighten just enough to make my pulse race faster, the pressure at my throat both thrilling and terrifying. His grip reminds me of the control I stole from him in the ballerina dressing room. Well, he's taking it back tenfold now. My body trembles beneath him, utterly at his mercy. "Beg for it," he repeats, his voice darker, more insistent.

"P-please," I choke out, my voice barely more than a whimper. I don't even recognize myself, the strong-willed woman I pride myself on being has officially packed her bags and moved out of my mental space. The toy inside of me slows and I instantly come back to my senses. "Please, Wyatt, I need it."

He lets out a low, satisfied growl, picking up the pace once more. Wyatt's hair is erratic, wild brown flicks shifting in time with the muscles pumping in his arm, veins coursing beneath his forearm and neck. The hold on my throat loosens to brush his thumb lightly over my lips. His touch is electric. All I can do is surrender and let myself be swept away by him.

Then, when I think I can't take anymore, he leans down, his breath hot against my ear, and murmurs, "You don't know this, but you've always belonged to me." The possessiveness is enough to send me spiraling into oblivion.

A surge of pleasure explodes through me, every muscle locking up as I come undone beneath him. My orgasm crashes over me like a wave, raw and uncontrollable. I cry out, arching off the bed, pushing myself into the thrusts that tear through me. Wyatt doesn't stop. His movements lack any trace of pity, the rhythm of the dildo matching the rapid beating of my heart. His hand at my collar bone tightens ever so slightly, keeping me grounded in the storm of pleasure ripping through my body. My legs shake, toes curling into the sheets as the release pulses through me, leaving me breathless, gasping for air.

My body finally relaxes, limp and spent but not completely satisfied. Wyatt withdraws the dildo, pausing briefly until he wins the war with himself. Ducking his head, he runs his tongue along the pink surface, tasting the white smeared mess I created. I instantly grow weak, lost in the intimacy of it all. Reaching for Wyatt's sweatpants, he swiftly perks up and jerks back out of my reach.

"I don't think so," he shakes his head, one brow raised as if *I'm* the one being ridiculous here. His sweatpants are tented, despite him moving off the bed and disappearing into the bathroom. I lie there, stunned, confused, empty. However, I don't have the good sense to move or close my legs when

Wyatt returns with a cleaned dildo that he places on the dresser.

"Why can't I have you?" I frown, quickly sinking into myself.

"You know why." Except I really, really don't.

Wyatt refuses to meet my gaze, his jaw ticking profusely. He fumbles around to find my discarded towel, promptly covering me with it and finding a spot on the wall he'd rather stare at. "Let's not pretend you weren't imagining someone else with you just then. It will never be me."

I open my mouth and then quickly shut it again. Why should I tell him he's wrong? Why should I stroke his ego? My thoughts are private, they're dark and depraved and have no business being voiced because Wyatt is pretending he's not worth my time. He's digging this grave and despite the pull of my body, the urgency with which I want his cock buried in me, I won't lie in it with him.

Running a hand down his face, Wyatt groans at himself. Tugging his phone out of his pocket, he quickly taps the screen and holds it up to his ear.

"Avery needs you." He ends the call and walks out without a second glance. Without stalling long enough to close the door. Tears prick the back of my eyes as I roll onto my side, a new side effect of whatever I took settling in. Dull hollowness sweeps through my bones, an aching void ripping into my chest. By the time the door is gently pushed open, I'm sobbing, shivering and still utterly naked beneath my towel.

"Angel, what's wrong?" Dax rushes over to me, stripping out of his clothes as he goes. In his boxers, he eases me beneath the covers and cradles me so gently, I cry harder.

"This is going to seem really weird," I mutter whilst weeping against his chest. "But you need to make love to me." Pulling me back a few inches, Dax's face is impassive, a slow smile creeping across his face. He kisses each one of my eyes, coming away with wet, salty lips and then cuddles me closer.

"I will, Little Swan. Let me hold you for a while first and once you're out of tears, I'm all yours."

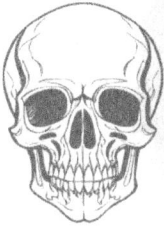

DAX

Interlinking my fingers with Avery's, we stand tall against the lingering stares. From the very moment we stepped through the door of English Lit, the whispers started. They ripple across the room, low and sharp, approaching us from every direction. To her credit, Avery doesn't falter. Not that I'd expected her to, but she did indeed cry through sex with me last night. Most would have insisted on stopping, but I found it endearing. Being able to cradle her into my chest, kiss her tears, slowly pump my hips and fill her completely. She needed grounding, and I vowed to always be her safety net.

Squeezing her hand, I lead us further inside. Even Mrs. Patrick is watching us carefully, no doubt fully aware of the fight that broke out across our lawn two days ago. Everyone knows, since there are videos and photos circulating the student messaging board from onlookers I didn't realize were present, and if there were any doubts, my face proves it. Sporting one black eye, a split lip and busted knuckles on one hand, I don't appear as in control as I like. But it's not me I'm currently concerned about.

As we make our way to the seats near the back, Avery's eyes remain fixed ahead. A couple of people glance our way, then quickly turn back to their friends, whispering behind cupped hands. I catch snippets, words like *fight* and *slut*, harsh and ugly. My stomach twists, a flash of anger heating up my chest, but I force myself to keep walking. Once seated, I attend to Avery first, removing her highlighters from her backpack whilst she opens her notebook. Handing her the purple one, her favorite, she catches my gaze and smiles discreetly.

"It will pass," I whisper, quietly reassuring. "They're jealous, is all. You've taken quite a few studs off the market." At this, a small laugh bubbles from her.

"A stud now, are you?" A familiar twinkle returns to her blue eyes. I lift a brow, tugging her chair closer so I can breathe into her ear.

"Am I not? Do you need an action replay of last night?" Avery tucks a strand of hair behind her ear, her cheeks coloring faintly as she lets out another soft laugh. The tension between her shoulders eases just a bit, and I can't help but smile, knowing I've at least chipped away at her nerves. It's these little moments, the quiet ones, that feel like victories. When the chaos outside doesn't matter, and it's just us.

The whispers continue and I feel eyes burning holes into all sides of my head. But I don't care. If anything, it makes me pull Avery closer, like we're in this impenetrable bubble where no one can reach us. She feels it too.

"Did you sleep at all?" I ask quietly, handing her the textbook I'd pulled from her bag. Her fingers brush mine as she takes it, and I catch the quick flash of shame she tries to hide. There's no reason for it. I cherish the moments where Avery falters. The times when she lets me see her in a way the others don't get to.

"Barely," she admits, her voice low. "But I'm okay. What about you?" I shrug. I'd stayed up most of the night watching her after she fell asleep, her head resting on my chest, her breath slowly evening out after the sobs. It wasn't until sunrise that I let myself drift off.

"Same."

Mrs. Patrick clears her throat at the front of the room, a signal for everyone to settle down. The murmurs still float around, although quieter now, like a persistent hum in the background. As class begins, I'm not paying much attention to the lecture. My thoughts are stuck on last night. The way Avery held onto me like I was her anchor, like without me, she'd drift further away. How she murmured she loved me, placing wet kisses over my neck and collarbone. All that mattered was the gentle shift of our bodies, seeking pleasure from the despair she was battling.

Avery scribbles notes in her notebook, occasionally underlining something in purple, her focus entirely on the words. But every now and then, her finger traces small circles on the back of my hand. A quiet gesture, just for me.

There is no chance of me focusing today. I'm sleep deprived, but also, nothing Mrs. Patrick is saying holds any interest to me. Everything regarding my grades, my scholarship, this campus, it all seems so inconsequential. Not that Wyatt would let me throw away all of my hard work, nor would I insult him by flunking out now. He's been my biggest supporter.

My attention shifts to the way the winter sun streams through the windows, casting soft shadows across the room, playing over the rows of desks, and then back to Avery. Beneath a woolen burgundy hat, her hair is loose today, falling around her in golden waves. She's opted for fur-lined boots, skinny jeans and a casual beige hoodie in which her shoulders are squared, her spine rigidly straight. She's holding it together in front of all these people, despite everything, making my chest expand with pride. She's so damn strong. She glances at me again, catching my stare, and for a second, the world outside of us ceases to exist.

Mrs. Patrick's voice pulls me back into the present. She's stepped away from her desk, walking slowly across the front of the room. Her cane clicks softly, her voice measured and calm.

"-which leads me to announce your next assignment for this semester. Up to now, we've focused on the analytic composition of works by the greats. It's time to move onto creating some of those pieces yourselves. For this topic, I will give you a subject theme and leave it up to you to decide how to present it." She stops, her eyes briefly landing on Avery and me before moving on. "The theme for this project is '*Hidden Demons*'."

The room goes quiet, the last few whispers dying out as students start to perk up, intrigued. Avery's hand tenses on mine for a split second, and I give it a gentle squeeze, reassuring her without looking away from Mrs. Patrick.

"There are several ways to approach this. Hidden demons can manifest in various forms, both literal and metaphorical," she continues, pacing slowly. "I want you to explore this in a way that feels meaningful to you, but your arguments must be supported by source material from English literature. Think about how authors grapple with inner conflict, human flaws, and societal pressures in their works."

The students around us start scribbling in their notebooks, quickly jotting down words of significance, including Avery. Mrs. Patrick uses a clicker in her hand to bring up a long list of examples on the whiteboard, using her cane to point at each one in turn.

"You might consider characters in literature who battle personal demons, like Macbeth's obsession with power or Hamlet's struggle with indecision and madness. Or perhaps you'll focus on societal demons, such as class struggles in works like Great Expectations, or racial injustice in To Kill a Mockingbird. Whatever your chosen demon is, link it back to a piece of text to demonstrate that everyone has struggled, and everyone has the possibility to prevail."

Avery's highlighter freezes mid-sentence. I raise a brow, having shared the same thought. The timing of this topic seems highly suspect, but also perfect. It will give those seated nearby a reason to delve into themselves and realize no one is perfect. We all have things to hide. I catch Mrs. Patrick's gaze and she ducks her head, continuing with her whiteboard presentation.

"I expect your pieces, whether they be essays, poems or another medium of self-expression, to be thoughtful and well-researched," Mrs. Patrick says. "Draw from the text, analyze deeply, and consider how these hidden demons affect the world around you."

Avery finally moves, highlighting the word *demons* in her notes. She doesn't look at me this time, but I know she's thinking. She's going to throw herself into this assignment, lock onto the theme and let it sit in her mind until it makes sense. It's good to have a focus outside of the turbulence happening in her life, although this time, it feels awfully personal. The bell rings soon after and we're packing up again, a rushed skip in Avery's steps.

"Hey, where are you going?" I rush through the throng of people now dividing us. Catching up to her, I link my arm through Avery's just as she's about to turn in the wrong direction.

"I'm heading to the library," she frowns as if I'm the one who's forgotten where she's supposed to be, but allows me to pull her through the packed hallway, too focused on her thoughts and oblivious to those throwing disgusted looks as we pass.

"This project is going to be brilliant actually," a wide smile spreads across Avery's face and I know I've officially lost her. "I was thinking we could look at The Picture of Dorian Gray. We can tie it into the way Wilde explores vanity and the moral consequences of living a life of hidden indulgence. Oh!"

Avery quickly pulls to a stop and I think she's realized the time. "Or how about the psychological battles in Dr. Jekyll and Mr. Hyde, where the characters' darkness comes to the surface? Wyatt has given us so much material to work with for that." Maybe not then.

"Angel, you have ballet in ten minutes." I tilt my head, hating the way her face falls. The excitement ebbs away and I wish I'd kept my mouth shut. But if Avery starts skipping dance, especially when Huxley told me about the rumors that are circulating, people might get the wrong impression. They'll start to believe their words have power and no one is going to keep my girl from her passion.

"Do I have to go?" Avery whines, her legs wooden now as I tug her along. I kiss the top of her head with a small smile.

"Yes, you do. I made Axel a promise that you'd need a muscle relaxing bath when you get back. He's going to join you." Avery groans but doesn't resist, letting me pull her through the hallway. Her steps are sluggish, but I know she'll feel better once she's there, dancing like she always does. Graceful, fluid, free.

As we reach the studio, I nudge her playfully. "It'll be fine, I'm going to stay and watch." Avery looks up at me, her lips curving into a small smile, and for a moment, the shadows in her eyes lift. She heads out back to go change while I pick a spot near the piano to sit against the mirrors. Jenna and Nikko laugh mockingly as they pass and I remain unaffected. None of the rumors or the stares matter, because they won't break us and they sure as shit won't push Avery out of doing what she loves, or loving who she wants. She's too pure for that.

AVERY

It's surprising how quickly a routine can settle. The Shadowed Souls seem to take everything in their stride, pivoting and adapting to each other's needs.

Bath time with Axel has become a daily occurrence, after Dax has accompanied me around campus each day. It isn't lost on me that he's the only one who seems to take me out in public, acting as my bodyguard and boyfriend. And it's worked. The rumors have calmed down, no one stops to pull out their phones and record us walking hand in hand anymore.

Garrett attends to Axel during the day, the pair of them taking their classes online until Axel's ribs are fully healed. Once I get home to take over, Garrett heads out with Huxley to work out and they've started stopping for food some evenings. Huxley always comes back in a mood, pissed off that Garrett has pushed him too hard in the gym and dared him to eat another few bites when he's said he's done, but I couldn't be more thankful. Without realizing it, Huxley is quickly bulking up again and he doesn't even question it when I hand him a bowl of cereal each morning.

Wyatt, as per usual, does his own thing. Sometimes he goes to work out too, other times he sulks around the house or disappears for hours, with no one knowing where he's gone. Today is a sulking day. He's currently sat at the kitchen island, rapidly tapping at the keys of his laptop with his headphones in.

The first few flakes of snow appeared in the early hours, dusting the backyard in a coat of sparkling white. I peer out of the window, watching as the frost clings to the tree branches and softens the edges of everything. Behind me, the sound of Wyatt's fingers flying across the keyboard is the only thing breaking the silence in the house. He's got that familiar furrow in his brow, the one that says he's deep in thought. Probably a similar assignment to the one I should be working on with Dax at the dining table.

I've made a decent start, coming up with loads of ideas but now I need to just pick one and roll with it. Instead, I opted for a time out to clear my mind, wanting to put some distance between those 'hidden demons' I've been thinking about.

Stretching my back, causing a few cracks to sound, I return to the mixing bowl clutched in my arm. I relish the burn, whisking the batter by hand, letting the repetitive motion ground me. The scent of vanilla fills the kitchen, warming the air.

Wyatt clears his throat suddenly, pulling me from my thoughts. I glance up to find him watching me, his headphones now resting around his neck. "What's all this in aid of?" he asks, only just realizing I'm in the room with him. Shocker, I know. We've been in the same room for a while now without any of the usual tension.

"I'm making Axel a cheesecake to lift his spirits." I smile, and Wyatt frowns harder. I ignore him, placing down the bowl to retrieve the chilled base from the refrigerator. He watches me quietly whilst pouring the mixture onto the base.

"We all got beat up, you know," he drawls and rolls his eyes. I stop pouring, sure my ears are deceiving me. Setting the bowl aside, I lean further over the kitchen island, searching for clarity.

"Are you saying you want me to bake for you? Maybe I should hold an ice pack to your bruises or rub you down in the bath?" I flutter my lashes, thoroughly enjoying the way Wyatt's eyes blow out. Oh yes, I went there. For a man who fucked me with my own vibrator, Wyatt has been acting unaffected around me for days and the only one he's fooling is himself.

Putting the cheesecake back into the refrigerator to set, I round the island. He follows my every movement, twisting himself so I can place myself between his legs. When I speak again, it's a hoarse whisper with my lips inches from his.

"It's okay to be jealous. You can admit you want me to take care of you, if you're able to swallow your damn pride." I tilt my head. Wyatt's jaw is taut, his eyes growing dark.

"How about you get on your knees and swallow it for me?" he says, then leans back as if someone has slapped him. A rush of heat floods my cheeks, the image now flashing in my mind. Wyatt is losing his grip on that iron-clad control he holds so dear, and I'm here for it. Just waiting for it to slip completely.

"What on earth did I just walk into?" Garrett asks from the front door, although his face is lit up like a Christmas tree and he's grinning from ear to ear. Huxley is just behind, shouldering both his and Garrett's gym bags.

"Nothing," Wyatt snaps his laptop shut and pushes through me in an effort to get away. I can't help the small laugh that escapes me. I'm still smiling when Huxley drops his bags by the door, shaking his head at Wyatt's dramatic exit.

"What got his panties in a twist?" Hux asks, wiping sweat from his brow. Clearly, their work out went harder for the weekend.

"I've made cheesecake, but I think he wanted muffins," I shrug, a hint of mischief still playing on my lips. Garrett smirks, giving me a playful nudge on the arm as he passes.

"Your muffin, maybe," he winks. I snort, making no comment. At this point, the only person standing in Wyatt's way is himself. I gave in a while back, realizing that we're inevitable. I just need him to catch up. Footsteps sound on the stairs and I raise a brow, wondering if Wyatt is back so soon, but Garrett rushes forward. "Woah, what are you doing out of bed?" He gently puts an arm around Axel's lower back.

"I'm bored," Axel winces, putting his arm over Garrett's shoulders. He grips the banister, lowering himself step by step with careful effort not to pull at his healing ribs. The bruising is hidden beneath an oversize white tee, but I know it's there. I frown at Axel's flimsy shorts, although I suppose it would have been too much effort to pull anything else on. Ushering the pair towards the sofa, I help to lower Axel down and fetch a blanket.

"How was the gym?" Axel asks, lowering his head back on the cushion. He's exhausted, even from such a short walk, but that comes with the territory of not sleeping well.

Huxley steps in behind him, his mood lighter than usual but he still gives me that familiar grumble when he catches Axel's eye. "Garrett says I need to up my pre-workout shakes and double my creatine to bulk up even more. He also says I'm not trying hard enough." Hux's chocolate brown eyes roll towards Garrett, who pushes his hands into his sweatpants pockets.

"Just calling it how I see it. Your body is all that keeps Avery interested, so I wouldn't let it slip if I were you." I smack Garrett's shoulder, reserving a small smile just for his eyes. I know what he's doing, goading Huxley to get back to full form. He just goes about it in such a Garrett way, I can't even be angry.

"Don't listen to him," I tell Hux. He grins, freeing his blond hair from its top knot and shaking it free. "You all know it's your dicks that keep me interested." Hux stops midway through dragging his hand through his hair, a blur of movement shifting to my left.

"Is that so?" Dax tackles me into an armchair, tickling my sides until I'm screaming for relief.

"Stop! You're hurting Axel!" I shout through fits of laughter, knowing full well Axel is on a different seat over two meters away. Dax doesn't stop. In fact, another two pairs of hands join in with Axel calling out instructions to not let me get away. My cries split through the recently silent house, re-energizing us all until they finally relent.

I lay limp on the armchair, my chest heaving and my smile infectious. Four beautiful men smile back, their eyes glinting with adoration and it's all centered on me. Despite external situations, sometimes I don't know how I got so lucky.

"We should do something together this afternoon. Play some games like we did at the beach house," I suggest once I can breathe again.

"I'm in," Axel nods, looking more relaxed than he has all week.

"I need a shower," Hux leans over the back of the armchair to kiss my temple, "then I'm all yours."

"I'll get snacks," Dax announces.

"And I'll get Wyatt," Garrett adds. I wish him luck with that one, but I should know that Garrett is rarely denied. Whether through being charming, or just annoying enough that saying no wasn't an option, he returns a short while later with Wyatt begrudgingly following.

I sit between Axel and Dax, the three of us covered with the blanket as the snow starts to fall harder beyond the window. If I ignore the macho decor, I can almost imagine we actually are back in the beach house. Huxley returns, shirtless with his hair damp. He retrieves a case of beer and a bottle of pink gin he had stashed, placing them on the coffee table beside my cheesecake. And just like that, this became a party.

"Alright, who's dealing?" Garrett takes charge, shuffling the cards with practiced ease. No one immediately steps up so I shrug.

"We could do paper, scissors, stone for it?" I sit forward, my closed fist at the ready. The others do the same, except for Garrett.

"Excuse me?" he stares at me like I've gone another head. "We could...what?"

"Paper, scissors, stone?" I repeat, my eyes flicking between the others. They're smirking but only Garrett seems to have a problem.

"You're fucking with me, right?" Garrett holds the cards closer to his chest as if I've offended them as well. "She's fucking with me." He huffs out a laugh, looking for backup and finding none.

"Just give me the cards. I'll deal," Wyatt reaches over. Garrett does what any man lacking sense would do and throws the entire deck over his shoulder, scattering the cards all over the floor. Wyatt looks to the ceiling for patience, probably wondering why he bothered coming downstairs, then crawls over to start picking them up.

"Forget it, Wyatt can deal." I sit back, feeling suddenly out of place.

"No, no," Garrett insists. "I'm afraid this is now embedded in my brain." He shifts off the armchair to kneel in front of me, his fist held out. "It's rock, paper, scissors. Repeat that back to me."

"I'm not an idiot, Garrett. I was just incredibly sheltered as a child, some of the fundamentals are missing." I roll my tongue over my teeth. These days, it's not often my past creeps up to irritate me so easily. Garrett's dark eyes shimmer with something I'm sure he thinks is understanding.

"Peach, I was neglected to the point of almost dying, but I've never heard of paper, scissors, freaking stone." I push his fist away, tutting the word *asshole*.

"Lay off dude. It's endearing," Dax pitches in. Axel is leaning his head towards mine, attempting to kiss my cheek. I put him out of his strained misery and meet him halfway, pressing my cheeks against his lips.

"Actually, I prefer it," Huxley says, leaning over. I give him an appreciative smile, and suddenly, there are four fists in front of me. Hux counts us in, as we play paper, scissors, stone like grown adults. Garrett moans that he's died a little inside, but somehow wins. When he turns back to the table, we all find that Wyatt has already dealt and is waiting for us with an impatient expression.

"If you guys have quite finished," he grumbles, grabbing himself a beer. Just like that, the tension is snapped and soon, the living room is filled with laughter and trash talk again. Garrett whines the entire time that he was dealt the wrong cards, and Wyatt surprisingly joins in without issue, his earlier annoyance fading into the background. Axel's voice rises in playful protest as, on his other side, Huxley tries to read his hand over his shoulder.

"Don't even think about it!" Axel warns, attempting to shuffle his hand away. Hux huffs in mock defeat, his lips quivering into a smile. The banter around us blends into a comforting backdrop as I steal glances at Axel, hunting for any discomfort. Beneath the blanket, his hand casually rests on my thigh. The warmth of his hand against my skin sends a shiver of anticipation through me. It's a simple touch, but it's warming to know that no matter what has transpired in the past week, he's still here with me. With us, when it could have been so easy to retreat into his own mind.

The laughter continues as the drinks start to flow, each joke and tease drawing us closer together. The cheesecake is a huge hit as well, lasting through two rounds of a game Garrett calls 'Skinny Joker.'

"I'm out," Wyatt tosses his cards aside, but the glimmer in his eyes betrays his feigned disinterest. Huxley chuckles, and I can see the camaraderie blooming around us, a flicker of what could be coming to life before me. I find myself becoming more invested, not in the cards but in the way everyone interacts.

Garrett has his way of pulling the best out of people, and soon even Wyatt is leaning back, laughing more freely. Huxley's competitive spirit flares up, and he's gloating every time he wins a round. Dax is laughing, a sound I love, and it only deepens the butterflies in my stomach. I lean into Axel slightly, our shoulders brushing, and I can't help but savor this feeling. After a week of worrying, of attending to bruised bodies and split knuckles, of facing the rumors flying around about me, this is nice. No, scratch that, this is home.

AVERY

Replying to Meg's vague message about her latest lacrosse match, I sigh and toss my phone into my backpack. I suppose I'll return to tapping my purple highlighter against the notepad balanced across my knees and staring at the paper in front of me. The white page has started to mock me, only a title staring back. *Hidden Demons.*

Considering how excited I initially was for Mrs. Patrick's assignment, I've been coming up blank with where to start, the words running through my mind without taking shape. I've tried listing a few ideas, jotting down snippets, but nothing sticks. Every time I start to settle into a train of thought, I find myself easily distracted by the basketball court once again.

The gym smells like sweat and effort, mingling with the faint scent of Axel's cologne beside me. It's all so distracting, in the best and worst ways. A stack of books from the library sit on the bench between me and Axel, since my study time coincided with the boys' practice.

Where possible, the six of us have stuck together under the guise of keeping Axel well protected, in case the new *'Inclusive Practice for Athletes Programme'* introduced by Dean O'Sullivan isn't enough to deter the jocks from harassing him again. Most probably call our dynamic unhealthy, as our closeness hasn't gone unnoticed by those always sticking their noses in our business.

The steady squeak of sneakers on polished wood sounds, punctuated by the sharp thwacks of balls hitting the floor. Coach's whistle cuts through the air in timed intervals, commanding the rhythm of the entire gym. Amongst the rest of the team and a large group of subs, the Shadowed Souls run back and forth, dribbling their ball with keen control.

Garrett jogs past, his forehead glistening with sweat under the harsh lights. He's quick to pull his hoodie off and wipe his head with it. I doubt he's noticed how damp the material of his T-shirt is, sticking to the ridges of his abdomen. Making a point of not looking too closely, I prefer to watch as he tosses the hoodie onto Axel's lap, the two exchanging a brief, affectionate look. Coach's whistle pierces the air again, louder this time, snapping Garrett back to attention. He rushes to rejoin the others, his broad shoulders rippling as he takes off toward the far end of the court.

"I thought you said you'd be able to focus here," Axel muses, not even looking my way. My chin jerks back from its resting place on my fist and I straighten to match his posture.

"I can. I was just thinking of an impactful first sentence," I purse my lips. Axel rolls his hazel eyes, a smile playing about his lips. He's practiced in hiding his pain, although it's evident in the stiffness of his spine and shoulders if you know where to look. His ribs have much improved in the last two weeks, allowing him to venture out in small doses. We all insisted he should stay in bed for longer but Axel explained there is only so long anyone can lie in bed before the nightmares they're running from start to bleed into every waking moment. Since then, we take him everywhere we're able without doing him any additional damage.

"Where was I?" I mutter to myself, dragging my gaze back to the two words double underlined at the top of the page. Surely it shouldn't be this difficult. I have enough hidden demons to write an entire book, yet I can't seem to decide which one I'd like to delve into. In some respects, I could use this exercise to face some home truths I haven't quite come to terms with. On the other hand, there are things I don't need preserved on paper.

Maybe I'm being too literal. I could just as easily write about the demons tearing up the court, putting the Subs to shame. There is definitely something hellish about the way they're distracting from what I should be doing. I chuckle to myself, wondering if I could shock the socks off of Mrs.

Patrick when Huxley nears, giving me a flirtatious wink. Thanks to his constant workouts with Garrett, Huxley is in his element today, keeping pace with Dax and Wyatt like it's second nature. His footwork is quick, cutting across the court with a burst of speed that leaves his defender stumbling.

In the same jersey and shorts as everyone else, the sheer definition of his muscle gives Hux that blond Adonis vibe I love, having snapped straight back into shape. I want nothing more than for him to stride his sweaty body over here and dominate me on the bench for all to witness. I bite my bottom lip, worried I might accidentally drool at the thought. And the best part is that he's smiling.

Dax is right there with him, his lanky form moving with a fluid grace that perfectly matches his gentle and graceful persona. Between him and Garrett, they make a mockery of those who usually occupy this bench during real games. They pass the ball with sharp, intentional movements, their silent communication honed over hours of practice.

And then, despite myself, my gaze wanders. Even before Wyatt is passed the ball, he's poised and ready, his green eyes entirely focused on the play taking place before him. There's a swagger in his steps, a confidence that draws my attention. I hate to buy into Wyatt's God-complex, but it's obvious that on this court, he is King. The rest of his team set him up to take the victory, and all the gloating that goes along with it.

Receiving the ball, he jolts into action, dribbling only three times before he leaps to make a shot. His muscles tense, his back arches, and the ball leaves his hand in a perfect arc before swishing through the net. The sound is soft but somehow deafening in its perfection. I blink, suddenly aware that I've been watching for too long again. My highlighter hangs limp between my fingers.

"How's that impactful first sentence coming?" Axel grins. I officially give up, putting my notepad aside and throwing my face into my hands. I'm overthinking it. Axel chuckles, reaching over to gently peel my hands away. "It's just an assignment, Swan. Stop beating yourself up over it." I know he's right, but I can't explain why I feel the need to throw myself into this. To embrace student life for what I thought it would be and hold on tight with both hands. Maybe it's an attempt at normality.

"I'll be fine when I decide what to write about. Can you just pick a topic for me?" I pout, gesturing to the pile of books. Titles such as '*Psychological Shadows*' and '*Literary Stereotypes*' are peeking out from underneath Garrett's now-folded hoodie. "Whatever demon of mine you choose, I will just run with that."

Axel looks at the pile thoughtfully, then gestures towards my backpack. I pass it to him, saving the effort of shifting his ribs too much. Digging around inside, Axel pulls out a piece of folded, mostly crumpled, paper and offers it to me with a knowing look. My cheeks instantly set on fire.

"You carry this letter around with you everywhere, clinging to the words that seem to bring you a sense of comfort." Axel places it on my lap when my hands don't obey. How long has he known? Opening my mouth to explain, he quickly holds up a hand to stop me, wincing at the sudden movement. "There's no judgment here, Swan. All I'm saying is, if we're talking about hidden demons, maybe you should start with what you've been hiding at the bottom of your bag."

I frown at Mr. XO's latest letter, having read it so much I know the contents by heart. The connection I've imagined into existence with the author is ridiculous, borderline psychotic. And Axel has been fully aware.

"Do the others know?" I ask beneath the sound of grunted exercise and the Coach's hollering. Axel leaves his arm balanced on the book stack so I can toy with his fingers.

"Only Garrett, he was searching for a snack whilst watching your ballet practice the other day and came across it." I puff out my cheeks, still blushing incredulously. If Garrett knows I've been hiding the letter and hasn't blabbed to anyone, it's because he's preparing to use it as leverage against me. That could mean anything from a home cooked meal to anal whilst bent over the porch railing. He's utterly unpredictable and completely desire driven like that.

"How am I supposed to use this for my assignment without the world finding out I'm utterly insane?" I gently lift Axel's hand to cradle the side of my head. His need for comfort has reflected directly onto me. His thumb strokes my hair, not once complaining if I'm causing him any discomfort.

"Forget the assignment. Do it for yourself. Write him back." I almost jolt right out of my seat.

"What?!"

"If you had the chance to meet him, what would you want to say? What do you think he deserves to know?" Axel's hazel eyes hold my gaze, undeterred and serious. He really isn't judging me for this at all. The corner of his mouth quirks up and all other worries fade away. "You said you'd run with whatever I choose."

"Fine." I agree, shoving down the tremor of excitement that sparks to life within me. "But I don't want anyone to know, not even Garrett." Axel nods in understanding. It's not that I think the others would judge me either, but this part of my life is mine. It's private, not something I want to share. I've held onto Mr. XO's words like a dirty secret, but I've never once entertained the idea of penning a letter back.

The thud of bodies colliding reverberates in my chest as Huxley and Dax's laughter bounces off the walls of the gym. The sharp whistle signals the end of practice, but I'm already in motion, packing up my belongings and lifting the stack of books on the bench beside me. My heart races with the need to get out of here before anyone starts asking questions.

"What's the rush, Peach? Practice just finished." Garrett is suddenly next to me, wiping his sweaty hair with his hoodie, his dark eyes scanning me with curiosity.

"Oh," I blink rapidly, scrambling for an excuse, the first lie that pops into my head. "I totally forgot the library is closing early today. There's an...annual inventory count happening tonight, and I need to get these books back or their numbers will be wrong." The words come out in a rush, and I flash him a quick, nervous smile. Garrett raises an eyebrow, but before I can slip away, Dax steps in front of me, his tall frame blocking my exit.

"I don't know of any inventory count," he says, narrowing his eyes, clearly not buying my excuse. Behind him, Huxley scratches his scruffy jaw, watching me like I'm about to bolt.

"Really seems like something they'd have done in the holidays," Huxley adds, his tone casual but pointed. I'm surrounded now, their attention heavy on me. The weight of the books in my arms is starting to strain my muscles, and my shoulders tremble under the pressure. Thankfully, Axel's voice breaks the tension.

"No, she's right," he interjects, pushing himself up from the bench. "It was on the online bulletin board. All books need returning before four. I'll walk her down." He moves to stand, but as soon as he shifts his weight, a sharp gasp escapes him, and he stumbles. Garrett catches him instantly, his arm wrapping protectively around Axel's waist.

"You aren't going anywhere but home to bed," Garrett declares, leaving no room for argument. He holds Axel close, the two of them slowly hobbling toward the locker room, Axel leaning on Garrett's body.

I manage a small, awkward shrug, taking advantage of the moment to edge around Dax and Huxley. "Um, so...I'm just going to run these back. I'll meet you guys at the house?" I glance between them, hoping they'll let it go. But the tension is palpable, a nervous glance exchanged between the two. I get it. No one wants me walking alone, but at some point, I have to reclaim my independence.

"I won't be long. Don't forget your girl used to have a personal self-defense trainer," I say, trying to inject some humor into the situation. Still, the books in my arms are getting heavier, and I'm starting to shake from the effort of holding them.

Dax and Huxley hesitate, their heads lowering as they share another look. They're on the verge of relenting when Wyatt suddenly cuts through the group, his growl catching me off guard.

"I'll walk you down," Wyatt says, his voice low and hard. I hadn't realized he'd been listening, but his sneakers are already changed, and his bag is slung over his shoulder. Without waiting for my response, he takes the stack of books from my arms with ease.

"Wait, no—" I start to protest, but Wyatt's already heading toward the door, his back to me.

"Come on. I don't have time to waste," he calls over his shoulder, leaving me no choice but to follow.

As we step out of the gym and onto the long road leading toward the courtyard, the cold air hits my face, biting through the thin layers of my T-shirt and sweater. I trail behind, glaring at the back of Wyatt's head, wishing for a moment of peace. What's a girl got to do to be left alone around here? The rest of the Shadowed Souls might be obsessed with keeping me safe, but Wyatt? I didn't think he cared. Yet here he is, acting like he's doing me some grand favor. He doesn't speak, nor does he look back, but I make a point of flipping him off, knowing he won't see.

We walk in silence, the rhythmic crunch of our shoes against the frosty path filling the quiet. At the end of the road, just before we reach the courtyard, Wyatt suddenly stops short. I barely stop myself from crashing into his back, stumbling to keep my balance. He turns, his expression unreadable, and deposits the books back into my arms.

"You've got an hour max before the guys come looking," he says, his voice dropping lower, more serious. "Whatever shady shit you're up to, spend your time wisely." I blink at him, surprised.

"And where are you going?" I raise a brow, quickly getting over the shock of his gesture. I'm not foolish enough to think Wyatt lied just to cover my back, but also to protect himself. We're each other's alibi's here.

"I have places to be." He adjusts his bag on his shoulder, his eyes flicking away from mine. "You keep my secret, and I'll keep yours." A small scoff works its way out of my lips, my blonde ponytail flicking to the side as I readjust the weight in my arms.

"So we're keeping secrets now?" I tilt my head, watching him closely. "Careful, Wyatt. I might even start to think you don't totally hate me anymore." It's a test and he knows it. He doesn't respond right away, his jaw clenched tight.

"Don't push your luck," he finally says, his voice colder than the air around us. But I see the flicker of something else in his eyes, something unguarded. Now I really am curious about where he's been spending his time.

Before I can press further, Wyatt turns and walks away, disappearing down the path without another word. I stand there, clutching the books to my chest, watching him leave, a swirl of emotions tightening in my stomach. I could follow him, see what he's up to. But he's right - I have an hour tops before Huxley or Dax casually pass by the library to find me. I need time to mull over Axel's request without anyone looking over my shoulder.

Dashing off towards the library, I feel lighter than I have in weeks. I'm taking back control. I'm finally facing my demons.

WYATT

Stepping out onto the front porch, I still to simply inhale. The crispness of winter expands my lungs, sharp and biting, reminding me of the coldness I'm trying to fight off. They merge into one, welcoming me into the evening. I hold on for a moment longer, listening for any signs of life within the frat house. Any hint of Garrett shuffling around for a late night snack or Huxley's irritating questions asking me what I'm doing, anything that might suggest someone knows I've left. But the house is silent, the guys either passed out in Axel's super king size bed or glued to whatever screen is holding their attention. Good. I pushed them harder at practice today for a reason.

I pull the door closed with a soft click, careful not to let it creak. The moon is my only witness as I slip down the steps, hands shoved deep into the pockets of my hoodie. I probably look sketchy as hell, slinking through the shadows like this, but I can't risk any of them knowing where I'm headed. Not yet at least.

The path leading away from the frat house crunches beneath my shoes, and I wince at the noise. I force myself to slow down, even though my heartbeat is racing ahead of me. The air nips at my exposed skin, pinching at my cheeks and ears. I tug my hood up over my hair, breathing a thick puff of cloud around me. I'm shivering before I've even made it to the end of the street, but the cold is a relief. It keeps me grounded.

I walk for about ten minutes before the streetlights fade into the distance, and I'm left in the quiet of the back streets. No one heads this far off campus at night, especially not in this weather. *Perfect.* My Uber is ready and waiting, a short ride of being asked standard questions and me responding in clipped grunts. Pulling up at my destination, the driver slips down in his seat and pulls out his phone. It's the same guy who's been picking me up for the past couple of weeks, so he knows the deal. Wait until I get back and I'll pay him for the entire day.

Standing tall, I glance around again, checking we haven't been followed. The temperature is dropping by the second but I couldn't care less. Now I'm so close, there's no slowing my long strides. I pick up the pace, feeling the familiar pull toward the one place where I don't have to explain myself or put on a front. A few more turns, and the faint glow of the building comes into view, flickering like a beacon drawing me in. I slip in through the side gate, having done this multiple times now, rounding the corner to almost flatten an aged woman with wiry, white hair.

"Careful, Wyatt!" she gasps, clutching at the cardboard box in her arms. I mutter my apology, pulling my hood down. Jules looks me over, a knowing tilt to her faint brow. "Cutting it fine tonight. I was about to lock up."

"Sorry, I couldn't settle." I take the box from her arms and walk with her towards the supply shed. Jules directs me to the shelves where there is an open space labeled 'brushes'. Slotting the box in place, I wait for her to secure the padlock, rocking on my heels with my frozen hands in my pockets. "So, is he still awake?" I ask when I can't wait any longer. Turning back to me, Jules rolls her eyes.

"Here," she offers me the huge set of keys. "I have a spare set at home. Lock up when you're done." I exhale, thankful I'm not too late. Thanking her profusely, Jules huffs a small laugh and leaves via the side gate. I push into the building's main entrance, not bothering to switch any lights on. I know the way. Two hallways later, I enter a long room alive with the distinctive sound of whining and scratching. Indoor pens sit side by side, and I pass every single one until I reach the end where the longtime residents are kept. The dogs no one's interested in, the ones too scruffy, too old, or just plain overlooked.

Unhooking the latch, I let myself in. The warm smell of hay and wet fur greets me. Baxter is in his bed, his fur a mess of brown and gray, like he's been through too many harsh winters. Too many days on the streets where there's no mercy to be found for a mutt like him. His head lifts when he sees me, those tired eyes lighting up just a little, and damn, it hits me every time.

"Hey, old boy," I whisper, crouching down next to him. There's a dull thud of his thin tail hitting the wall as Baxter shifts closer, his body pressing into my side, and I run my hand through his coarse fur. It's rough under my fingers, but there's a comfort in it.

I have to admit, when I stumbled across this place whilst jogging and losing my way a few weeks ago, the appeal of stroking some cute, fluffy puppies initially spiked my interest. I may be many things, but who can't find solace in puppies? However, it was Baxter who caught my attention. He doesn't beg and whine like the others. He's resolute that he'll die here, alone and unclaimed. Hence, we seem to have an understanding.

I sit on the cold floor of the kennel, my back against the wall, and Baxter rests his head in my lap, sighing like he's been waiting all day for this. Maybe he has. I gently stroke the scruff of his neck, my fingers threading through the tangled mess there, and finally feel the tightness in my chest ease up. Being this far from Rachel and still on the backfoot of the Shadowed Soul's new dynamic with Avery, there's not many places I feel like I belong anymore. But here, I don't need to pretend I'm okay. I can just be.

Dozing off, his tail lowers as we share warmth. I sit for a long time, as always, just running my fingers through Baxter's fur, my breath matching his slow, steady rhythm. There's peace here in the quiet, in the way this old dog's weight leans into my thigh as if he trusts me not to let him down.

I used to feel the same way when my brothers leaned on me for support, whether it was through securing us a place to live, keeping Garrett well-fed, having a mutual understanding of Huxley's rich kid problems, helping Dax through his exams or sitting by Axel during therapy. I chose each one of them for a reason, building a family around myself when I didn't have another to fall back on. The Hughes said they loved me, but I always knew it wasn't quite true. They needed me to keep up their facade. They used me in the same way I'm using Baxter to push my responsibilities aside for a while.

Baxter shifts in his sleep, his nose twitching as if chasing some dream, and I smile softly. The shadows around us inch closer, the one I cling to ever-present. It hangs over my shoulder, always just out of reach in my peripheral vision. I wonder if Ray liked dogs. I'll have to ask Rachel next time I call. That smile slowly fades, a deep sigh rattling my chest. Baxter jerks, shaking his head further into my abdomen as if he senses the shift within me.

How did it come to this? Imagining my dead father's presence whilst sneaking out at night to sit with an old mutt the world forgot about? I'm supposed to have everything. Money, status, a future laid out in front of me like a red carpet. I'm supposed to feel invincible. But lately, none of it feels right. Not the fake smiles I put on, not the endless pressure to live up to everyone's expectations. Definitely whatever is brewing between me and Avery.

I wince, thinking about her. Avery and I, whatever the hell is happening there, we're on unfamiliar ground. She's stopped pushing me away, but instead, seems to find every reason to draw me in. It won't end well, like we're both standing on a cliff's edge, waiting to see who's going to fall first. Every time I look at her, I feel this pull, this ache. And every time I look away, it's like a punch to the gut. She's got me twisted up, and I can't get untangled, no matter how hard I try. So I don't. I let it fester, like everything else.

But here, with Baxter, none of that matters. He doesn't care about the mess I'm in, the lies I tell, or the front I keep up around everyone else. He just lies there, his chest rising and falling against my leg, content to just be. It's enough for now.

Eventually, I know I've stayed longer than I should. As much as I wish I could stay here, I have to get back. If there was another attack without me present, I don't even want to think about what could happen. I give Baxter one last scratch behind the ears before standing up. He looks at me with those longing eyes of his. "I'm sorry," I frown, not fully believing that I'm apologizing to a dog. The old version of myself, who paraded around proud and cocky, wouldn't recognize the man I've become. He couldn't have known what would transpire since Cathy's death.

I lock up the pen and make my way out, my steps lighter than when I arrived. It's like Baxter soaked up all the anxiety, all the things I can't say to anyone else. All that's left is the sinking guilt that I've taken what I need and left him behind until the overwhelming weight of stress returns, and I'll come back to do it again. I can't offer him a home, no solace in whatever time he has left. I'm not here to save him. Hell, I think he's the one saving me.

Stepping back into the freezing air and pulling my hood up, I catch a glimpse of my Uber driver, still slouched in his seat, waiting. The keys jingle loudly in my pocket as I jog over, about to slide into the passenger seat when someone calls my name. A short snap that couldn't have come from Jules or anyone else I know.

I freeze, one hand on the door handle, my eyes snapping up to search the dim street. A figure steps out of the shadows, lingering under the weak glow of a streetlamp. Large and imposing, dressed all in black, his silhouette cuts a sharp contrast against the soft haze of light. From laced boots to broad shoulders, the guy looks like he was built to intimidate. But he doesn't move any closer, giving me just enough space to decide whether I want to approach or pretend I didn't hear him.

I clench my jaw, every instinct telling me to get in the car and go. But something about the way he's just standing there and watching me feels deliberate.

"I'll be right back," I mutter to the driver, closing the door with a soft thud. My breath hangs in the cold air as I step around the car, cautiously walking closer but keeping my shoulders square. "Can I help you?"

From beneath a hood of his own, the man doesn't smile, doesn't even shift. Just stares me down with calculating eyes.

His silence lingers long enough to make me shift, a twinge of trepidation running the length of my spine.

"My boss would like a word." The calmness in his voice is unsettling, too casual. Like watching and waiting for me to leave the shelter is just another part of his day. I narrow my eyes, my fingers twitching to ball into fists. It's that fight or flight response kicking in, and my knack of self-sabotage is ready to take option one.

"And who would that be?" I ask, trying to sound indifferent, but I can feel my pulse drumming in my ears. The man reaches into his jacket. I instinctively take a step back but all he pulls out is a small card, holding it between two fingers.

"Text him a time and location," the man says, his voice flat and leaving no room for negotiation. "He has a proposition you're going to want to hear."

My stomach twists. This immediately feels like the kind of thing I don't want to get mixed up in, but at the same time, I reckon I'm already mixed up in it. The way he said it, the way he's looking at me. He's all too familiar with who I am, yet I have no point of reference for him. I take the card from him, but I don't look at the typed text. Not yet.

"And if I don't?" His lips twitch, maybe the closest thing to a smile I'll get.

"You will." The guy turns and walks away, disappearing into the shadows like he was never there. I'm left standing under the streetlamp, cold seeping into my bones as I stare down at the card in my hand. All it has is a name and number on it, one that fills me with dread. *Fredrick Walters.*

For a second, I debate burning it on the spot. Maybe I could head back inside and feed it to the dogs, but something stops me. I slide the card into my pocket and head back to the car. The driver barely glances at me as I settle into the seat, my mind racing.

That guy, or rather, that goon knew exactly where to find me, what my routine is. He would have had no issue sneaking up behind me, brandishing a gun in my face or putting me in a hole six feet under. But he didn't. That can only mean Fredrick Walters wants my attention, and I'm ashamed to say he's got it.

AVERY

S itting cross legged on my bed, my hand hesitates over the notepad, the pen stuck in mid-air. How do I even finish a letter to a total stranger?

Yours, Avery.

No, that's too much.

From Avery.

No, A. Just A. I give the letter a flourish, sitting back to look over the page before me. Axel was right, this was exactly what I needed to find some closure, to be able to close the door on Mr. XO. He can continue to send letters if he feels the need to do so. Now I've written my own, I understand the appeal but I'm ready to sever the connection I've built up in my mind. It's been an evening for revelations.

Another thing I've decided is that absolutely no one can see this response, ever. It's too personal, and let's face it, absolutely freaking nuts to pour my heart to a stalker. But it also gave me clarity that the relationships I need to be focusing on are with those under this roof. No more fictional ones.

With that thought in mind, I hide the letter beneath my mattress and step into the hallway. It's long past midnight, but that didn't stop a certain someone from creeping back in. Where he's been is anyone's guess, and it doesn't really matter. He's back, I'm awake and feeling far too reckless to sleep.

The soft sound of snoring seeps from Axel's bedroom, the tv still on in Huxley's. A faint glow leaks out of the small crack in Dax's door and when I peer in, I see he's fallen asleep by lamplight, a book sprawled across his chest. No chance of him talking me out of what I'm about to do then. Moving on, I listen outside of Wyatt's room before knocking for his ears only. No response comes, so I do the opposite of what any sane person would and I let myself in.

Wyatt's cologne hits me like a blow to my senses, the entire room pulsing with his scent, his darkened energy. The curtains are drawn, his clothes tossed across the bed. Steam billows from beneath the bathroom door, my heart pounding in my chest. Raising my fist to knock again, I hesitate. What would I even say? *Oh erm, hi Wyatt, didn't realize you were totally naked, wet and what's that? Oh you're rock hard and thinking about me? Perfect.*

The sound of running water continues to filter through the thin wood, and I bite my lip, trepidation buzzing beneath my skin. I should turn around and head back to my room. But we've been playing the strange game of cat and mouse for weeks and I'm done with it. Whether I'm accepted or shunned to forever live in embarrassment, I'm getting my answer. Tonight.

Taking a deep breath, I push the door open an inch. The air is so thick with heat, I can barely see through the fog clinging to the mirror. But I can hear him. The ripple of water pouring over his body, the occasional splash as he shifts beneath it. My stomach flutters. The thought of him so close, so exposed, fills me with a hesitant burning. I haven't felt this nervous in a while, but I also haven't actively pursued someone like this before. The Shadowed Souls decided my fate with them long before I surrendered. Now the tables have turned.

I slip further inside, closing the door behind me as quietly as possible. My heart is beating so fast I swear it's going to alert him to my presence. The shower curtain is half-drawn, revealing a glimpse of his silhouette through the mist. He's facing away from me, his broad shoulders flexing as he runs his hands through his wet hair, streams of water tracing paths down his muscled back.

Taking a step closer, my feet are moving before I've fully made the decision. Being this close to him, unsuspecting and oh, so vulnerable is intoxicating. I quickly grow drunk with danger, no longer thinking at all. I pull my tank top over my head, letting it drop silently to the floor, followed quickly by my shorts. Standing there in nothing but my panties, I feel my body respond. Skin warming, pulse quickening. I take a shaky breath, forcing myself to be brave.

Answers, Avery. We need a definite yes, I want you, or no, it's never really going to happen. It's now or never. In one quick motion, I hook my fingers into my underwear and slip them off, leaving me bare. The cool air hits my skin, a stark contrast to the steam swirling around me. Slowly, I ease back the shower curtain and step inside.

He doesn't notice at first, too lost in the stream enveloping him. His head is tipped forward, water dripping from his dark hair, running in rivulets down the sharp lines of his body. I let my eyes linger on him. His back, his thick arms, the way his muscles flex with even the slightest movement, the cute indents to his incredibly toned ass. Who knew he was concealing such a gorgeous ass specimen?

I predict the exact moment he feels my stare. Straightening, he braces himself on the tile, only turning his head back. My breath catches. Green eyes go wide for a split second, surprise flashing across his face, but then his gaze darkens as it sweeps lower, taking in my body, my heaving chest.

"What are you doing?" Wyatt growls so low, it's barely audible over the pounding of water. A tiny squeak bubbles out of me, as if I didn't expect him to ask questions. In my head, Wyatt would be like every other man in the world and simply ravage me. Grappling back an inch of my self-control, I close the distance between us and press myself against his back.

"Not giving you the option to avoid me," I state calmly, although inside I'm a frazzled mess of estrogen. Wyatt's ribs flex beneath my hands, his control slipping. "You've been pretending to ignore me for weeks. I won't let you push me out anymore."

My hands travel lower to settle on his hips. At the edge of my fingertips is the deep indent that travels south. He still makes no move to turn around, using his back as a barrier between us. However, his cock tells a whole different story when I bite the bullet and take the bull by the horns. Or rather, take the shaft by the thick, veiny base.

"You want this. I want this." I breathe desperately. There's no room for shame, no point acting coy when my nipples are pressed against his back, aching for more. Wyatt has been forbidden for so long, but all bets are off now. When he stayed to fuck me with my own dildo, he opened the floodgates, given me the signs and now I won't take no for an answer. Or I will, and I'll never be able to look him in the eye again.

I stand, molded to his wet back for so long, slowly sliding my hand up and down his cock until I'm convinced he isn't going to move. Simply let it happen this way so he can claim he played no part. I squeeze his shaft tighter, an exasperated huff puffing out my cheeks.

Wyatt moves so suddenly, I squeak again as he spins and lifts me in one smooth move, slamming my back into the tiles. I'm met with his stern green eyes staring directly through me, so piercing I'm frozen in place. Legs locked around his hips, my hands on his chest. The heaviness of his breathing causes the tattooed dragon to shift beneath my fingers, the heat seeping from the ink enough to burn me. But I don't pull away. I lean in.

Wyatt's head turns just before our lips meet, my mouth clumsily brushing his cheek. A quick lash of embarrassment cracks against my confidence, despite his hardness between my center proving he wants this just as much. Water cascades over his hair and back, spraying from his shoulders. His voice is thick, raspy. A final warning he desperately wants me to hear.

"I won't be gentle."

"Good." Wyatt's eyes return to mine, hunting for any hint of uncertainty. That's all it would take to pull away from me once more, but he finds none. I've been building myself up to this all evening, to show weakness now would be a waste. Once satisfied I'm not going to back out, Wyatt reaches between us and strokes the plump head of his cock from my pussy to my clit. My breath hitches, my thighs tightening on his hips.

"I'm not going to prep you." He growls beside my ear, our cheeks touching. I arch my back, forcing my breasts against him. He draws his cock back down to my slit, teasing my opening before moving back to my clit again. A slow delicious torture. He hardens a little more each time, growing insistent against me.

"I want you to feel every raw, hard inch of me. I want you to be branded with the sting of stretching around my shaft. You won't get it twice." I weaken at the gruffness of his voice, the dirty, dangerous edge to his words.

Hitching my legs up higher and pushing my knees into my sides, Wyatt exposes me, the weight of his chest pushing mine back into the cold tile. As promised, he doesn't delay. His cock pushes inside of me and the tightness causes us both to groan. I try to shift to better accommodate him but Wyatt is statue still, his grip on my thighs bruising. The only part of him to move is the agonizingly slow tilt of his hips.

Once he's fully seated, we're both tense, groaning in time with each breath. It's affecting him just as much, but even so, the corner of his mouth quirks up in a slow, knowing smile. Wyatt doesn't say a word, simply holds me there on the edge of his torture.

"Please," I whimper, my brows knitted together. I'm so full that my thighs are quaking from the intensity of it. Wyatt's hand slips around to the small of my back, pushing me flush against him. I mewl, twisting my head away. I can't handle the size of him so deep, but there's nowhere to go. I'm at his mercy, exactly where I put myself.

"Why did you really seek me out, Avery?" he asks, his voice low, the rough edge to it sending a shiver straight down my spine. His other hand slides lower, fingers grabbing at the curve of my hip, the heat of his touch stealing my breath. I'm pinned in the lion's gaze, whining for him to take pity on me.

"I couldn't help myself," I admit breathlessly as I avoid looking into his eyes. The water beads on his skin, glistening under the bathroom light. I can't tear my gaze away from his chiseled jaw, the way his lips part slightly as his eyes drop to my mouth.

"Why?" Those haunting green eyes seek mine out, holding me captive in the same way his cock is holding me on a precipice of losing my freaking mind. My breath hitches as I search for an answer, my chest heaving against his. I'm drowning in him; his heat, his weight, his presence, every nerve ending in my body wired to the place where we're joined. His question cuts through the haze, demanding more than just the shallow truth I've been telling myself.

"Tell me why couldn't you stay the fuck away? Why is it my cock you crave so much when you have so many other options?"

"Because..." My voice trembles as I force myself to meet his eyes, that deep green gaze piercing straight through me. I don't want to give him the truth, not wanting him to have that much power over me. I came to him because he sees through every facade, every wall I've put up. Wyatt strips me bare in ways that go far beyond my body, exposing every fear, every desire I've kept hidden. He knows the version of me I keep hidden from everyone else.

Wyatt grows impatient, dragging me an inch away from the wall just to slam me back into it. The jolt of his dick so deeply inside causes my vision to waver. "Because you aren't enamored with me," I rush to say, arching further. "You don't care about me enough to make sure it doesn't hurt. You're selfish, inconsiderate and savage." I sigh, biting on my bottom lip.

"And?" Wyatt presses his hips into me impossibly further, bringing his hand up to grip my chin when I try to twist away again. My chest is heaving, my toes so curled that they've lost all feeling. Gripping his wrist, I lower Wyatt's hand and clasp it around my throat. Just like last time.

"And I want to be used," I admit in a tiny voice. Wyatt's eyes track the movement of my lips and settle on the hand on my neck. He looks crazed, barely hanging onto the last thread of his honor. It's far too late for that now. Forcing his grip to tighten, I gasp against his fingers. "We've both been used against our will for years, forced to feel what others demanded of us. At least this, we can control. If anyone can understand, it's you."

Not even a beat passes before Wyatt's lips crash down on mine. The water pours over us as he finally withdraws his cock, but only for a second. Slamming back inside, Wyatt's hips snap back and forth, fucking me with abandon. His hands explore, possessive and hungry, like he's wanted this as much as I have.

Wyatt's lips are everywhere, devouring, tasting, claiming. The weight of his body presses me deeper into the cold tile, but the heat between us is so intense that I hardly notice the chill anymore. His mouth trails from my lips down to my throat, where his hand grips tightly. The pulse of his fingers around my neck sends a ripple of pleasure straight down to where we're connected, where his cock is stretching me to the point of delicious agony.

"Is this what you wanted?" he growls, his voice vibrating against my skin, lips brushing the shell of my ear. His hips pound into me, each thrust harder, deeper than the last. "To be used? For me to destroy your concept of pleasure and construct my own? A fullness only I can give you?"

"*Fuck*, yes," I breathe, my voice cracking. "All of that, *yes*." I buckle under the weight of everything I'm feeling, his relentless cock, the way his body envelops mine, how his hands leave bruises on my skin. Every moment feels like fire, like I'm teetering on the edge of an explosion I can't control.

Wyatt pulls back slightly, just enough to look down at me, his green eyes burning with something fierce, something dangerous. His expression twists between dominance and raw need, his control fraying with each second that passes. His hand tightens around my throat, and my eyes flutter closed, surrendering completely to the way he consumes me.

"Open your eyes," he demands, his hips stilling for just a moment, leaving me quaking on the edge of losing my mind. "I want you to know exactly who holds your life in the balance right now." I obey, my eyelids heavy as I meet his gaze. His face is so close, our ragged breaths mingling between us.

His hand slips lower, wrapping around my thigh as he lifts me higher, opening me up even more. I'm helpless against him, completely pinned between the wall and his body. Each stroke sends lightning through me, building higher, faster. My throat flutters with the edge of panic, my lungs burning for air. I try to maintain Wyatt's stare but it's starting to become fuzzy around the edges.

"Tell me, Avery," Wyatt pants, his voice dark and low. "If you pass out, would you expect me to stop fucking you? Because I won't. You'll wake so sore, permanently feeling me buried inside of this tight cunt, long after I've left."

"Do it," I whisper, my body trembling, every muscle tensing as the pleasure quickly speeds towards oblivion. "I need you to destroy me, Wyatt."

The words barely leave my lips before he snaps his hips harder, faster, and I cry out, the sound swallowed by the echoing walls of the shower. There's no mercy, no hesitation. Just raw, animalistic passion, the kind that leaves me breathless and dizzy, teetering on the edge of a blackout.

His hands are bruising, one gripping my throat, the other on my waist, pulling me down onto him with each punishing thrust. His mouth crashes onto mine again, hot and desperate. There will be no hiding the chaos which we've unleashed. It's going to be marked on my skin for all to see.

"Wyatt. I'm gonna...I can't breathe-" I gasp, my nails digging into his shoulders as I hold on for dear life.

"I don't need you to breathe. I need you to cum for me. Now." Despite everything, my chest heaving for air, my limbs quickly going limp, my body responds. The tension inside me snaps, and I'm free-falling into a tidal wave of release, my entire body convulsing with the force of it. I scream his name, my voice raw and hoarse, and Wyatt follows a moment later, his grip releasing on my throat as he groans through his own climax, his body shuddering against mine. I wheeze, swallowing gulps of air. My head spins, dropping back against the tile with a crack that rings through my ears.

"I knew you'd be this fucking tight, Avery," Wyatt mutters into my ear. His head drops against the tile beside mine, his entire focus on his throbbing shaft stalling inside of me. "This fucking perfect."

It's the first compliment Wyatt has ever given me. I swallow down past the lump in my throat, berating myself not to cry right now like a little bitch. The release of emotion, the relief of finally having Wyatt in ways I didn't dare dream of, it's all too much but I manage to hold it together as he settles me back down on the floor. My legs threaten to fail me, my body slipping against Wyatt's muscled abdomen.

Ducking my head, I wash myself down and exit, quickly wrapping a towel around myself. My hair is plastered to my back and as promised, the soreness between my legs runs deep. I abandon my clothes, rushing through Wyatt's room in an effort not to overstay my welcome. This was perfect, despite the rage simmering beneath Wyatt's surface. I'm not going to wait around long enough for him to say something to ruin it. I'll face his gloating tomorrow.

Two steps from the door, a hand grips my hair. I muffle my scream whilst being wrenched back against Wyatt's chest. True terror shatters my expectations that I could screw Wyatt and escape in one piece. Lowering his mouth to my ear, I shudder at his heated breath.

"Where do you think you're going?" he growls, pushing his still-hard cock against my backside through the towel. I bite my lip, eyes widening. Wyatt uses his grip on my hair to pull me towards his bed, whipping the towel free from my body. He tosses the clothes onto the floor and peels back the covers, holding me as if I'll bolt if given the chance. I probably would. This sudden change in dynamic leaves me utterly in his control, not a place I intended to be.

Pulling me onto the mattress, Wyatt's arm winds around my middle, tugging me roughly into his body. I pant, waiting for him to push himself back inside me, to screw me into the pillows until I cry, but none of that happens. Instead, Wyatt pulls the cover over us and holds me tight, our wet and naked bodies molded together.

"Do you normally make a habit of taking what you want and running out?" Wyatt asks into the darkness. It's only then I realize how rigid I still am, my thoughts colliding like a battering ram. I'm spooning with Wyatt. How does that notion feel so much scarier than the aspect of him rearranging my organs?

"I-I didn't think you'd want me to stay." I frown, more uncomfortable now than ever. There's a rumble passed through Wyatt's chest and into my back, something akin to a small laugh.

"I reckon it's safe to say you don't have a clue what I want, Avery." Wyatt's body softens as he pulls me back to brush his nose against my nape. There's something muted about his hold now, a vulnerability that wasn't there before. As his breathing evens out, I stare into the abyss, too confused and wired to rest. This could be a trick. Maybe I'll wake to binds pinning me down and Wyatt standing over me with a hacksaw. To be fair, if there's a Ghostface mask involved, I might not be as terrified as I should be. Fuck, I really need to stop reading Dax's books.

GARRETT

The frat house is alive with a certain buzz this evening, or perhaps that's just me. I've been practically vibrating with the need to get out of here since sundown, barely able to keep my hand steady whilst attending to Avery's neck.

"Are you sure this is going to last?" she huffs from her stool at the kitchen island, keeping her head stretched to the side. I gently pat the concealer down, blending out the edges so no one would know the difference.

"It's the highest grade of tattoo covering cream, Peach. Of course it will last." Tilting her head to the other side, Avery flicks over her mass of hair and holds it out of the way.

"I've never even seen you cover your tattoos," she mutters from beneath her mane. I grin widely.

"Because I don't. What I do cover is Axel's hand necklace every time I go a bit too hard so the guys are none the wiser. Big hands and brute strength aren't always easy to control." Avery stiffens beneath my fingertips as I continue dabbing the cream into her skin.

She snuck out of Wyatt's room in his orange hoodie around midday, bruised and ashen, eyes ringed with lack of sleep. I was waiting against the wall for hours just to witness her walk of shame, and it was glorious. I've never been prouder.

Finishing with the marks on her neck, I offer to check her body for other bruises but she smacks me and jumps from the stool, rushing off to Dax's room. He offered to braid her hair like all of the other sorority girls do theirs, and now she doesn't need to explain who tried to choke her out. I did offer to take the fall like the noble gentleman I am, but she preferred to not address the issue at all.

Left with only myself for entertainment, I start to limber up, swinging my arms in wide circles and lunging across the living area. Excessively pushing Huxley to get back into shape has done wonders for my own fitness, snapping me back from my winter break slump. As soon as Axel is healed up, I'll be dragging him along too. Our Peach can only be seen with the hottest of men groveling at her perfectly pointed feet.

Speaking of hot men...

"Riot!" I spot the broodiest of us all slumping down the stairs and bound over, coming up short at his attire. It's a nice suit, the matte black slacks and tie against a pastel purple shirt. Expensive, just like the polished dress shoes upon his feet. "Dude, you can't play ball in that," I laugh incredulously. Wyatt's frown doesn't shift, his hair gelled back to perfection.

"I'm not. I have somewhere I need to be," he tries to walk on by. I step into his way.

"Um, have you forgotten it's Midnight Madness tonight? You're the team leader," I give him a rough shake. "We need you." Wyatt pries my fingers from his arms and brushes down his jacket.

"You'll manage. You've got your pretty little cheerleader to spur you on," he drawls, his no-bullshit expression weighing heavy. Squinting one eye, I continue to obstruct his way whilst pondering that for a second.

"Just to clarify, are we talking about Avery or Axel?"

"Hey, there's nothing little about me," Axel says as Huxley aids his descent down the stairs. I smile warmly at the sight of him, freshly shaven and showered. He's not even participating tonight but he's wearing sweatpants and a college sweater, the Waversea Warriors logo printed onto the sleeve. Maybe Wyatt just didn't get the memo?

I open my mouth to suggest such a thing when Wyatt shoves me aside and leaves, slamming the door behind him. Sadness wells in my eyes, a strange twinge tugging in my chest. Some of the best fun we've had has been during this event, running circles around our competitors. We've housed the trophy in a spare room for the past few years, not even giving a shit about displaying it. It's all about the bragging rights.

"Where's Wyatt running off to?" Huxley asks. I shrug.

"Fuck knows. He wasn't very chatty." Slipping into Huxley's place, I walk Axel over to the front door and help to put his sneakers on. He's probably more than capable these days, but I reckon he likes the attention. It's an excuse to maintain the physical touch he loves so much, and a reason for me to shower him with the kind of care he deserves.

What a sappy fuck I've become.

Avery and Dax appear hand in hand, her hair styled beautifully in slick braids. Without smearing her cover-up, she's managed to change into the yellow and black halter top we had ordered for this very occasion, adamant that she would be supporting our team's colors throughout the night. On her lower half, a mini skirt that will do nothing against the winter chill has been paired with woolen black leg warmers and suede ankle boots.

The five of us gather in the entrance hall and my excitement plummets into overdrive. "I seriously can't wait to kick some fucking ass!" I bounce on my heels, beating my fists through the air at some invisible foe. Avery raises a single brow.

"I thought you were just playing basketball?" God, she's cute when she's clueless. I sling my arm over her shoulder, careful not to smudge the concealer.

"The referee's for these events are student sport's representatives who mostly follow football. Last year, the guy had never stepped on a basketball court in his life and learnt the rules online the night before! It was a shitshow," I grin wider, glancing into the distance to relive the memory behind my eyes and Dax takes over.

"Basically, anything we can talk our way out of goes." He shares a sly smile with Huxley and I squeal. It makes me tingle when Captain Noble gets a little naughty. Hux shoulders the bag with all of our water bottles and hand towels in, grabbing his keys from the small dish by the door. I snigger knowingly.

"Wait, isn't Wyatt coming?" Avery pulls against my arm and looks towards the stairs.

"Don't worry, Peach, there's more than enough of us to keep you entertained." I lightly push my finger against her neck as Avery tries to shove me away. Her cheeks line with the faintest blush, causing some gooey reaction to happen inside of my gut. Maybe I'm just hungry, or maybe I find it adorable that she is still shy after what I caught her doing last night.

Holding her firmly beneath my arm, I walk us out onto the porch, keeping her lack of dignity as our dirty little secret. I'm good at keeping secrets when necessary. We pile into Huxley's SUV, Dax calling shotgun before anyone else can get a word in. I don't even bother to fight him for it, happy to sit in the back grinning, keeping my fidgeting to a minimum.

As soon as we turn out of our street, it's evident that the art geeks have put more than a little effort into decorating campus. Strings of bunting hanging from every streetlamp, banners plastered on every wall and fence, my face printed across many of them. Sure, the others are there too, but mine looks the best.

"Damn, I'm just so beautiful honestly," I comment, not meaning for that thought to leave my head. Avery and Axel laugh to the point of offensive, Avery's hand slapping down on my knee.

"I swear, if you weren't self-conscious, you'd be a stripper." A sudden tension spreads throughout the car, Avery quickly sobering with wide blue eyes. "Shit, Garrett, I didn't-"

"Fuck," I breathe. "I would have been such a good stripper!" I throw my head back on the headrest, visualizing it now. The confidence I could have had on a pole, slowly shedding my clothing to the whoops and hollers of a packed nightclub. Just when I thought my neglectful childhood couldn't take anything else from me. "It's probably for the best really. Axel would start trading his body parts for dollar bills again." A soft chuckle ripples through the back seat.

"Yeah right. Gare, you are many things but you'd be a horrible stripper." Axel rolls his head my way, looking over Avery's blonde braids. "You'd end up paying me to watch you dance. Before long, you wouldn't be able to afford clothes to wear anyway and just become a nudist."

"What an equally lovely thought," I smirk, nudging Avery. "Just twenty or so more tattoos to cover up my bland spots and that could become a reality." She scoffs, leaning into my side and keeping her hands low.

"I see enough of your dick already," she lies. Pure lies. I bet she can't even keep a straight face whilst saying it.

Our conversation is drowned out by a distant roar. The closer Hux drives to the arena, the louder the chant becomes. It seems the whole student body has come out to watch the match of the year. It's bigger and better than finals against another school, because these are students we know. People we see all the time. I get to stroll around playing I spy for wonky noses and broken jaws tomorrow. I get to vent my aggression with absolutely no repercussions.

From the direction of the field, people are spilling out into the street, decked out in our team colors. Black and yellow, baby. The football jocks are amongst them, caked in mud and blood from their own Madness game. Damn, I wish Axel hadn't talked me out of signing up. I'd have sold my soul for a chance to nut Riley Buckshaw in the balls with a shin guard on. Alas, I'll have to take the few members who've put themselves forward for our basketball game as the consolation prize.

"Look at that crowd," Dax says, wide-eyed, taking in the mass of bodies gathered outside the arena. I sit up straighter, peeking over his shoulder, my heart thumping like a bass drum. Students are waving flags, some sporting face paint, others pumping their fists to some tune I can hear faintly through the window. I roll my shoulders, hyping myself up. It's good to be on top again. We pull up to the packed parking lot, easily gliding into the space which has been reserved for us.

"You guys head on in. We'll be there in a sec," I tell the two in the front seat. They both give me a look which can only be interpreted as 'no backseat blowjobs' and I roll my eyes. If I thought I had time, I'd already be shaft-deep in Avery's throat while Axel tickled my balls. "We'll literally be right in?!" I protest. They hesitantly agree, the full force of the noise hitting us as the front doors are opened.

"I'm not kissing your dick good luck," Avery looks at me through half-mast eyelids. Why does everyone think I'm so obsessed with my cock? Taking Avery's chin in my hand, I twist her to face Axel.

"You owe this sexy beast a little something, and I want to make sure you hold up your end of the bargain before I head inside to defend your honor."

"And what bargain is that?" Avery asks, her cheeks shifting against my fingers. I release her face in favor of toying with her braids, marveling how I could use them like a leash if I wanted. Axel is looking at me as if he's trying to figure out my angle, his chiseled face catching the dim shadows of the rear seat. I smile softly, leaning forward to speak directly into Avery's ear.

"I believe you told Axel that you wouldn't tell him you love him until he's sorted his nightmares out." Avery stiffens beneath me.

"That wasn't exactly what I said."

"And guess who hasn't so much as twitched in his sleep in two weeks." I peer up into the stunning hazel eyes watching our exchange closely. Avery is looking too, and Axel shrugs guiltily. "So in my opinion, you owe him. He deserves to hear how you feel about him."

He deserves the fucking world, and I'll do whatever it takes to give it to him. Starting with the precious woman sandwiched between us. Avery breathes deeply, the air pushing through her parted lips.

"You first, Garrett." She tilts her head, her lips brushing my cheek. "Tell Axel how you feel about him." An instant bolt of panic flashing through me, which is no doubt evident on my face. The smile has slipped and I swallow hard, trying to tamper it down. I haven't repeated those words since that night on the porch swing, and I definitely haven't continually got over the fact that Axel hasn't said it back. My first instinct is to refuse baring my heart for a second time, but Avery's right. I can't keep these bold promises to Axel if they don't exist outside of my mind. I can't expect him to know how he completes me if I don't get comfortable saying it.

"I love you Axe," I whisper, meaning it from the depths of my soul. I love him, and I love the ripe little Peach shuddering beneath the weight I'm pushing onto her.

As if she's been waiting to hear me say those words, Avery snaps into action, carefully crawling onto Axel's lap. Her hands are on his face as she kisses him, hot and heavy, his fingers digging into her thighs. Soft moans fill the car, a desperate need to convey the height of emotion we all feel. Sliding closer, I add myself into the equation. Mouths and tongues all blend into one, the three of us sharing comfort and oxygen.

My hand glides over Axel's shaved head whilst the other tugs at Avery's pulling her head back. Only the thought of Wyatt's love bites lingering beneath the concealer prevents me from creating my own. It's taken Wyatt this long to come to terms with his feelings, with more than a little pushing from yours truly, I'm not going to plant mine directly on top. Let him have his small wins.

Parting and panting, the three of us remain huddled together. I'm not a soppy man, but there's no denying this feels good. It feels *right*.

"I love you too Axel," Avery leans into him, pressing a kiss to his jaw and actively not touching his tender ribs. "You're so incredibly special, you need two of us to give you the love you deserve." A choking sound escapes Axel's throat, the glisten of a single tear rolling down his cheek.

"Fucking hell you guys." Using the cuff of his sweater, he wipes his eyes and I take my cue to escape the spell his weakness puts on me. If I get sucked into consoling Axel and kissing his tears away, I'll never leave. Wrapping an arm around Avery's middle, I pop the door and drag her out too.

Time to get back to the competition. The noise descends on us, people rushing forward to shove their phones in our faces. Waiting for Axel to round the SUV, Avery leans up and presses her mouth to my ear.

"That was really sweet. Who knew you could be so vulnerable?"

"Don't expect anything to change, Peach. I'm still a jackass," I say, grinning as I give her a playful squeeze.

"I wouldn't have you any other way," she deadpans, but the smirk playing on her lips betrays her. That fluttering in my chest threatens to drag me down but luckily, Axel has made it to my side. Linking my fingers with his, I sling my arm over Avery's shoulders and walk the pair of them towards the arena. The crowd parts like the Red Sea, the volume increasing. A few slurs are thrown in, calling Avery some unsavory names but she doesn't let it affect her posture. She remains glued to my side, smiling as if she owns the fucking world. I've never been more attracted to her.

Once inside, the atmosphere turns electric. The stands are packed, the air buzzing with the sweet smell of popcorn and sweat. A giant screen above the court is already flashing our team's logo and heavy-bass music pumps through the speakers. Avery catches the attention of the cheerleaders, a few giving her a small wave. I recognize one as the redhead she used to share a dorm room with, who's apparently swapped track and field for a set of pom poms. Avery pauses before waving back hesitantly. They quickly go back to their warm-ups as if the exchange never happened.

Dax is yelling at me to head into the locker room for a pre-game pep talk with the subs we chose to join our team tonight. I wave him off until Huxley puts his fingers in his mouth and whistles sharply. It seems he's taken on the role as leader in Wyatt's absence. What a fucking let down Riot has become.

Withdrawing from Avery's hold, I catch her looking curiously towards the jocks across the court, most likely because they're glaring at me. A few are on crutches, awkwardly trying to take their seats on the opposition's side. I vaguely recognize them but without a red haze over my vision and my fists ramming into their bruised, swollen faces, it's hard to tell. Cupping Avery's jaw, I lift her onto her tiptoes to meet my direct gaze.

"Don't pay them any notice. You should be too busy cheering for me," I tease, tugging her closer for our lips to touch. She blinks once, her lashes fluttering over my cheeks.

"I will, when you earn it," she fires back, her eyes twinkling. Axel laughs under his breath, ignoring the fleeting moment where he winces. I drag Avery the last millimeter, planting a possessive kiss on her mouth. A mark of ownership.

"Challenge accepted, Peach." Setting her back on her feet, I see Axel to the bench on the sidelines to make sure he has enough space. Avery takes his side and his hand, and I promptly shove my tongue into his mouth. The crowd at his back is a cohort of screams and wolf whistles until I finally pull away, leaving him breathless.

"Give 'em hell," he smirks, cheeks pink and eyes alive. I wink before jogging across the court to my team, throwing my arms wide to soak it all in.

"It's about time," Hux folds his arms. Dax tries to mirror him but he has a harder time staying mad at me.

"I've been waiting weeks for this." Turning Huxley in the direction of the lockers, he walks with me.

"You do know everything you're doing is being caught on video," he huffs.

"Exactly!" I exclaim, unable to hide my grin. "They're talking anyway. It's about time we showed people we don't give a shit about their rumors. We're going to do our thing regardless. Feel free to join me by accosting Avery at half time." Dax catches my eye, shooting me an approving glance as he pats my shoulder.

When we get back on the court, the momentum just keeps building and building. Every pass, every shot, it's like we're moving in perfect sync. The Subs do a much better job than I anticipated, given that their only instruction was to make sure either Hux, Dax or I had the ball. I catch sight of Avery often, especially when she's up on her feet, fist pumping and bopping to the beat of the music. To be honest, she's more of a distraction than a help but I wouldn't change her being here for shit.

I end the first half with a dunk, swinging off the rim and milking it for all it's worth before dropping down and jogging back to the bench. The crowd's on their feet, Avery jumping up and down, clapping and cheering, her face lit up with pride. It strikes me like an arrow to the heart, everything clicking into place. Our girl, the center of our universe.

Whisking her into my sweaty arms, I'm promptly shoved in the face and she's torn away by Hux. I laugh, admitting defeat. Returning to stand shoulder to shoulder with Dax across the court, I ignore the groans of the jocks I've elbowed at any possible opportunity. I have no doubt Kevin Tyler sprained his ankle when I tripped him up, and then ran back over said ankle to make sure. Now, my focus is pinned on Huxley's hand.

Sitting on the bench beside Axel, he's pulled Avery into his lap, his fingers trailing especially high up her thigh and disappearing beneath her short skirt. She bites on her lip, leaving nothing to the imagination. Arching slightly against him, she inhales sharply through her nose. I can't look away. There's nothing else I want to watch, other than Avery trying to hide how quickly she's reaching her peak. I told Hux we should do our thing, and honestly, I'm impressed. I just need to figure out how I'm going to finish this game with a rock-hard boner.

WYATT

Pausing outside of the door, I exhale and ask myself for the millionth time, what the fuck am I doing? I blame Avery, of course. She caught me off guard last night, and my brain hasn't been able to switch off since. I slept better than I have in months, her soft curves pressed against my body, my cock nestled against her ass. And with a good sleep brings clarity. We can't keep going on like we are, constantly looking over our shoulders.

Pushing the door open, a small bell announces my arrival. The smell hits me first. Garlic, tomatoes, and basil hang heavily in the air, almost too rich for my senses. I was surprised by the choice of location when I received the text of where and when to meet, but it's slowly starting to make sense. This isn't an ordinary Italian restaurant. It's a front, being passed off as a quaint, family-run joint, but a dark undercurrent lingers beneath the surface.

The lighting is low, the kind that would make it hard to recognize a face across the room. The place is small, too intimate for comfort, with old wooden chairs that creak when you sit down and mismatched tablecloths that look like they've been around since the seventies. Photos of Italian landscapes hang crookedly on the walls, and the whole space feels cramped, like the walls are closing in on me.

Straightening my smart jacket, I make my way toward the back, where Fredrick Walters is seated in a corner booth, his back to the wall. I've never seen him before, but given that the rest of those seated are muscled meatheads sporting guns in their waistbands, I made an educated guess.

As it stands, the man is creepy as hell. Thin and pale, with sharp features that look like they were carved out of ice. His hair is slicked back, jet-black and too neat for someone with an unhinged glint in his eyes. He wears a similar black suit to mine, except it's cheap and scuffed. Not what I'd expect of a person who is acting as if he owns the room.

His blue gaze locks on me, like a predator sizing up its prey. His smile, slow and deliberate, only heightens my nerves. In fact, it makes my skin crawl. There's a coldness in his eyes, something devoid of humanity. Like he doesn't just deal in crime; he thrives in it. Lives in it.

Every step holds more weight than the last. My heart pounds in my chest, but I keep my face neutral, unreadable. I can't let him see how much this freaks me out. If there's one thing I know about men like Fredrick Walters, men that terrorize little girls, it's that they feed off fear.

"Wyatt," Fredrick says smoothly as I reach the table, his voice unsettlingly calm. "You're right on time." He gestures to the seat across from him with a flick of his hand. I hesitate for a second. I'm crossing a line I won't be able to uncross, but then I think about Avery, about everything she's been through at his hands, and I pull out the chair and sit.

The scent of the food makes my stomach turn, despite its mouthwatering appearance. Pasta dishes are laid out in front of Fredrick, untouched. I wonder if he even eats. Somehow, I doubt it. He's too much of a snake, too focused on power and control to enjoy anything as simple as a meal.

"Do you have an aversion to Italian food?" he asks, following my gaze. That knowing smirk doesn't leave his face for a second.

"No. I'm just surprised you've chosen to meet somewhere public. Aren't you a wanted man?" I counter back, feigning ignorance that everyone in here looks like a convict. Fredrick glances up into the far corner, apparently in thought.

"Am I? The police questioned me in relation to some recent reports. Turns out, I had an alibi for all instances," he smiles a slimy grin that tells me he either planned ahead or had one of the men lingering nearby lie for him. Something they would no doubt do again if he decides I'm not walking out of here alive. I swallow hard, my hands resting on the table to keep them from shaking.

"Why am I here?" I cut to the chase. I don't plan on staying longer than necessary. Fredrick's smile widens impossibly more.

"Straight to the point. I like that. But let's not be so hasty, hmm? We're both men of business, and business, Wyatt, takes time." Fredrick's tongue rolls across his yellow, stained teeth. Being so close to a man who would hurt a young child, an innocent one like Avery no less, makes my skin crawl, but I force myself to sit and endure it. I can't afford to lose my cool here. Not with my every move being watched by so many.

"What kind of business?" I question. Fredrick leans back and folding his hands in front of him, the picture of relaxed menace.

"We're the same you and I, Wyatt."

"I don't abuse children," I immediately shoot back. Several men nearby tense but Fredrick doesn't even falter, waving his hand dismissively. He has no qualms with his past, the personality of a madman.

"You can deny it but I'm not wrong. Excusing the affliction we share for Avery, Catherine Hughes used us both. We were pawns in her life, an existence she never stopped running from. Do you reckon she's watching down on this union?" He lifts his glass into the air, gesturing at the ceiling. That's when I know he's officially lost it, and I'm certainly not bonding with a man I loathe.

"You had a proposition for me. Let's get on with it," I press, eager to be out of my seat. Fredrick leans in slightly and I catch the faintest whiff of cologne. Sharp and metallic, like gunpowder mixed with aftershave.

"Strange," Fredrick murmurs and sits back, assessing me both closely and from afar. I straighten my shoulders, not cowering as this lowlife grins. "Nature or nurture indeed."

"Are you going to make any sense?" I can't suppress a sigh.

"Hmmm? Oh, bad habits I'm afraid. Ten years in a prison cell will do that to you." He tips his glass as if I'm supposed to cheers the notion that hurting Avery put him behind bars. I don't move, yet he smiles. Always damn smiling, like he has so much to be happy about. "I was merely commenting on the fact that you didn't know Ray, yet you're so much like him."

Cold dread rushes over me as if someone has tipped a bucket of ice over my head. What does Fredrick know of the Perelli's? And Rachel. Oh god, if he approaches Rachel-

"You should really try the wine, Wyatt. You've gone white as a sheet." His mocking laughter travels but I make no attempt to take my glass. For all I know, it's laced with poison.

"You knew Ray?" I ask through a clenched jaw. I notice the same moment Fredrick does that I've taken his bait. Hook, line and fucking sinker. His blue eyes twinkle with glee.

"Not personally. Do you know, it's marvelous how much clarity one can gain from simply sitting back? All that chasing and tracking, exhausting honestly. It's been much more fun watching Nixon squirm, constantly looking over his shoulder. Do you know he moves hotels every other day? Equally as exhausting to watch, but I enjoy his efforts."

Fredrick lifts his fork to pick at a piece of pasta, popping it into his mouth and chewing carefully. Thoughtfully. I grip the edges of my seat, not leaning into the game he's encouraging me to play. I won't ask for more answers, and the cunning side of him can't resist telling me anyway.

"I located Ray Perelli first, before any of this started. I knew you weren't mine, it's intrinsic you know. I thought tracing your origins would bring me clarity, a straight child swap perhaps. But Nixon, despite his many flaws, is too calculated for that," Fredrick sighs.

"He didn't tell anyone where he hid my second child, not even his wife at first. I know this because the housekeeper kindly offered up Cathy's journal to me after I took the liberty of removing a few of her fingers. I tore out the pages which were of interest, holding onto them for twenty years until I delivered them to your frat house for Avery's perusal. I thought it was time she learnt the truth of her origins." He grins viciously.

One more piece of pasta goes into his mouth, not a shadow of regret for maiming an innocent woman. If the odds weren't stacked against me, I'd launch across the table and stab him with his own fork. Maybe that's what it means to be Ray's son. Except for now, I'm forced to sit and endure this rambling monologue, coming to the realization that Fredrick is years ahead of us, having overseen the entire picture while we've scrambled for snippets.

I need to bring this to an end, just being in close proximity to him is toying with my boundaries. I don't want to be a man filled with hatred, harnessing rage to hurt those around me and keep them at a distance. But I'd hurt Fredrick Walters without a second thought and not care about the mark on my soul for it.

"What do you want from me?" I clench my jaw, feeling the tick beat there. Fredrick's eyes lift and widen, as if he'd forgotten I was there. All of his focus was directed at his pasta.

"Now that is a smart question," he exhales loudly. "Like I said, truly exhausting keeping tabs on you all. I made some worthy connections during my incarceration, but they have their own thirsts too. I can only keep a handle on them for so long before something slips through the cracks," Fredrick gives a few of his men a pointed look. It darkens his eyes, pressing on until the smile slowly vanishes from his face.

"Take Cathy's tragic demise for example. I'd asked for a small scare, is all. When I received the news that she'd died-" Fredrick lifts his glass by the top. He glares at it, the wine inside offending him. I watch his knuckles turn white, his arm beginning to tremble until the glass shatters, thick shards spearing his palm. He doesn't even flinch.

"Let's just say, the culprit paid in kind. Cathy was all I wanted. She's all I ever wanted." It's like watching a thriller movie, the scene before me unfolding and leaving me as merely a viewer. Without the crazed smile, Fredrick's entire face has changed. I don't know what's more unsettling, his far-off daze or his sneer and twitching eye.

A waitress appears out of the back, a young girl in a simple uniform who's stick thin with purple circles around her eyes. I can't tell if they're from lack of sleep or being punched. My stomach flips as she approaches, quietly attending to

Fredrick's hand like it's the norm. Picking out large, bloodied shards, she pats his hand with a cloth and tucks it back into her front pocket. I trace her footsteps, see the deadened look in her eyes and have to physically pin myself to my seat. She's not my problem, not who I'm here to save.

"Look," I straighten my shoulders in my jacket. "I don't give a shit about any of that. I don't care for your explanations, you'll always be a piece of shit in my eyes, but you've asked me here for a reason. Tell me or I'm gone." The smile spreads across Fredrick's face and I've made my choice. It is decidedly more horrifying. Fredrick flicks his injured hand out, spraying blood across his pasta.

"But that's exactly what I've been saying! The men keeping tabs for me are becoming restless, I can't hold them back much longer. If I don't pull them back soon, they'll take what they want and believe me when I say," Fredrick chases the eye of one of his goons watching our interaction from a few tables away, and leans closer to whisper. "We're not the only ones who see Avery's appeal."

My eyes harden. "If anyone of you touches a single hair on her head-"

"So it's time I ended this," Fredrick talks over me. "I'm going to call off this whole charade, leave you all alone. That's what you want, isn't it?" One of my brows dips while I try to anticipate his angle.

"You're stopping? It's over, just like that?" I ask, not believing it for a single second.

"Well," Fredrick grins wide, putting all of Garrett's smiles to shame. The malicious intent pouring from that tight pull of his lips will haunt me for a while to come. "Not empty handed, of course. I've come too far to walk away with nothing to show for it." My foot taps with impatience as he stalls, pushing me to the edge of my curiosity before continuing. Setting his eyes squarely on mine, Fredrick leers across the table.

"Give me the identity of my other child, and I'll leave Avery alone. Scout's honor." He uses a finger dripping with blood to draw a cross over his heart. The man was clearly never a scout. I fold my arms and sit back in my chair.

"What, so you can take your aggression out on someone else because your affair went tits up?"

"All I ever wanted was Cathy," Fredrick repeats in a lower voice, the rattling sound grating my ears. "She ruined my life by letting me fall in love with her. She promised me the world, but it was all a lie. Pregnant or not, she was never going to leave her superior life behind. She lied to me." That eye twitch is back, Fredrick's teeth grinding together. "I deserve something." I let my head roll on my shoulders, no longer filled with trepidation. He's revealed his cards, now it's time for me to play mine.

"You had something. You had Avery and guess what," I tense up, bulging my arms further against the cotton of my shirt, "you fucked it up." Fredrick nods, wiping his hand over his jaw and leaving a blood stain there.

"I've had ten years staring at the same four stone walls to reflect on my actions. I don't need you to explain what I already know, but it will be different this time. I've reformed."

"You're deluded," I bark a laugh. The goons all around stiffen and inch forward. I should probably worry more about getting out of here safely, but I haven't cared about my own mortality for a while now. I'm on a downward spiral, destined to take everyone I care about down with me. Perhaps I can still have a purpose after all. "Take me instead." Fredrick's gaze, which had been investigating his hand, slowly rises to me, his curiosity piqued.

"You?" He licks his lips. I nod.

"Like you said, we've got a lot in common. Cathy chose me to be Avery's replacement. It's all I've ever been. Why change the record now?" Fredrick smiles, then laughs and his goons take the cue to join in. Their mockery beats against me, echoing through the chasm in my chest that screams I've never been good enough. Not even now in the eyes of a psychopath. "Fine. Forget it. I'm not giving you shit," I push back from the table, the need to get out of there overwhelming.

Fredrick's face snaps into a serious expression and the laughter dies instantly. "I don't mean to insult you, Wyatt, but taking you wouldn't affect Nixon. I doubt he'd even notice." I inhale deeply, hating how well Fredrick knows our family dynamic. Or lack of. "I know you don't believe me, but I really have reformed. I lost my mind when Cathy left me and spent the next ten years taking every drug I could get my hands on. It's not an excuse and Avery paid that price. I regret it, and I have a chance to do it again. To be better."

"Whilst hurting Nixon in the process," I add. Fredrick chuckles to himself, tilting his head side to side.

"It's an added bonus."

I jut out my chin, nostrils flaring. "I thought you kept tabs on us. Surely you've figured out who she is by now." I catch my mistake too late, revealing that I do in fact know who Avery's twin is. Fredrick rises himself to stand, marking the white tablecloth with red handprints in the process.

"I don't have the resources you do. I spent what little I had, resorting in paying these men in promises and threats. Once I have what I want, they're going to publicly rip Nixon limb from limb. But if I make them wait much longer, they're growing to storm your little frat house and take Avery for themselves. The choice really is yours."

I stall, thrown into this stand-off of wills. Fredrick is a patient man, he's waited over ten years for this. Long enough to twist his story into a narrative where he isn't the bad guy. He truly believes Cathy did this to him, that he played no part in Avery's suffering. Striding around to my side of the table, Fredrick places his bloodied hand onto my shoulder, not a hint of pain in his smirking expression.

"I'm growing old, Wyatt. I just want the chance at retribution, so I can do it right. I just want what's owed to me."

"Money or revenge?" I ask, wanting nothing more than to shove him out of my space. The blood seeping into my jacket will be a bitch to dry clean.

"To be a real dad. Free from the bullshit Cathy put me through. Give me the name." I don't buy it, so I keep my jaw clamped shut. He only steps closer, the rank stench of his breath washing over my face. "Make this easy on all of us. I'm going to find out eventually." Fredrick's eye starts to twitch again, his crazed and deranged sides merging. He straightens my tie, taking every opportunity to get directly into my personal space. "Please save Avery from any more suffering. Give me the name."

The laughter that wants to brew doesn't come out. He's pleading with me to save Avery when he's the one who's always causing her to be in danger.

Instead, I just stand there, ignoring the cold sweat dripping down my back. I could call Fredrick's bluff and potentially put Avery at the mercy of the men sitting behind me. A dozen of them easily, more than my brothers and I could take on. These aren't small-minded jocks. These are practiced gun men, most likely rapists too. Or I force Meg to face a horror she can't outrun. Either way, I have to risk one of their lives and neither will forgive me for it.

It's up to me. It's my decision, and I choose Avery.

AVERY

I sink into the couch, my body melting into the cushions as the faint sound of music hums in the distance. The sports rally is still in full swing but I volunteered to bring Axel home early. He wasn't the only one starting to zone out, the boys tearing across the court seeming to suck the energy from the crowd's cheering. Despite the call of joining Axel in bed, I thought I'd steal myself some time to wind down.

Twirling the spoon in my hand, I lick off the last bit of ice cream and lean my head back, eyes half-closed. The air smells like vanilla, the scent emanating from the candle I lit to accompany my unhealthy late night snack. A rare moment of peace I've created for myself.

Tonight's sports event is something I've never experienced before. The hustle and bustle, the noise, the sheer amount of people. And for once, I didn't shy away or look for the nearest escape. I thrived in it, cheering on my men. Pride doesn't even come close to how I felt watching them dominate the court, with Axel huddled into my side for warmth and comfort.

However, now it's time for calm. I'm fully peopled out. A small sense of fulfillment tugs at my chest as I scroll through my phone, aimlessly flicking through some of the photos I took. Most are blurred, action shots, the flood lights smearing across mine and Axel's selfie smiles. I've been getting better at remembering to capture odd moments.

Heading further back into my camera roll, I find the random images I've collected over the weeks. Garrett enjoying an overly large hot dog more than anyone should, Dax reading quietly in the bath. There's a picture of Huxley that I took from the upstairs window while he was working out in the yard, and another of Axel enjoying a face mask with cucumber over his eyes. I giggle at that one.

I stop on a photo of Wyatt. It's not one I took, but that I stole from Garrett's phone. The image fills my screen of Wyatt from a few years ago, mid-laugh, his green eyes wild and alive. He seems so happy. I can't help but stare at it longer than I should, tracing the outline of his face with my gaze. Despite the dam we've broken through, he still doesn't smile for me like that. No, all I get are dark looks that promise death by cock and asphyxiation apparently.

I shake the thought away, setting my phone down as I stretch, feeling that wonderful ache in my muscles. The ache of dancing on the sidelines and throwing my arms in the air every time Huxley flashed his abs at me. We weren't haunted by the whispers on campus or the pressure of keeping it all together. We could just be ourselves, laughing and playful.

Settling in to watch the candle flicker, I find a smile working its way onto my face. Just me and the quiet hum of the world outside. The moment feels fragile, like glass that could shatter with the smallest touch. And then, of course, it does.

My phone buzzes on the cushion beside me, the screen lighting up with a text from an unknown number. Not what I expected. I left Meg six voicemails yesterday, wanting to check in. I get the distinct impression she's avoiding me, but I want to arrange a meet-up soon. My heart aches without her. Lifting the device, I swipe to unlock it casually, the words barely registering.

Avery. I thought you should know your debt has been paid and I'm relenting. You're a lucky girl. Wyatt sure cares for you. All the best, Dad.

Signed with an emoji of a rose.

I blink a few times, rereading the sentences in different orders until I shoot upright. My spoon clambers to the ground but I'm on my feet, my hand trembling around the phone. Not even Nixon calls himself 'Dad'. My legs are suddenly moving, propelling me up the stairs two at a time. That delicious burn I felt from dancing quickly becomes a burden, slowing me as I skid down the hallway and let myself straight into Wyatt's room.

He's in there, freshly showered and hunched over his desk in deep thought, pen in hand. A scowl is cemented into his features, shadows clinging to his eyes. He opted out of the sport's event, but he sure as shit hasn't slept either. Upon seeing me, Wyatt bursts out of his seat, putting himself between me and the desk.

"Haven't you heard of knocking?" he asks, his voice missing its usual sharpness. It was more of a whine. I don't care for his fatigue as I storm forward.

"What the fuck is this?" My heart thunders in my chest, adrenaline flooding my veins as I shove my phone in Wyatt's face, my hand trembling. My rational side is screaming to take a breath, slow down and gather all the facts, but the betrayal surging through me is louder.

Wyatt squints, quickly absorbing the words before his posture sags. For a split second, he just stands there, looking utterly defeated.

"Ahh fuck," he mutters beneath his breath, rubbing a hand over his face. Ahh fuck is right. I can't hold back the rage rising inside me.

"What have you done?" I demand, refusing to let him look away from the phone. The evidence is in black and white, and I dare him to try to talk his way out of it. Wyatt exhales, turning away from me as if he can avoid this confrontation by sheer force of will.

"It's not what you think."

"Not what I think?" My voice cracks, and I hate how weak I sound. I don't feel weak. I feel like a bomb ready to detonate. Wyatt presses the heels of his hands against his eyes, as if he can block out reality for just a moment longer. When he finally speaks, his voice is low, controlled, but there's a tremor beneath it, like he's struggling for the words.

"I took care of it. I handled it so you wouldn't have to."

I stare at him, disbelief and fury warring inside me. "Took care of what? Don't mess me around on this. What the hell did you do?" He turns back to me then, his green eyes locking onto mine with that dangerous intensity I know too well. Gone is the moment of vulnerability, the shame he was wallowing in.

"I did what I had to. I wasn't going to let him have a hold over you anymore. I wasn't going to let him keep using you as leverage. So I made a deal." I feel the ground shifting beneath me, like the world I've been standing on isn't as solid as I thought.

"What kind of deal? With whom?" I ask, but I already know the answer. I'm holding it in my hand, I just don't want to believe it. Wyatt's jaw tightens, and just when I think he's going to keep stonewalling me, he drops his gaze to the floor, his voice barely above a whisper.

"Fredrick Walters." The name hits me like a slap to the face. I take a step back, the full weight of it crashing down on me.

"You went to him? Wyatt, are you out of your freaking mind?" Wyatt flinches at the accusation, but there's no denial.

"I didn't have a choice."

"There is always a choice!" My voice rises, echoing off the walls of his room. "You went behind my back and made decisions on my behalf! And for what? To play the hero? Is this your big redemption?!" I'm shouting and I don't care. The others will know soon enough when I ask them to help dig a six foot hole with me in the yard.

Wyatt's face hardens, his eyes flashing with a dangerous light. "This isn't about being a hero. This is about protecting you from your father. From the shit he's done to you." My eyes blur with angry tears.

"And since when have you actually given a shit?" I toss my phone onto the bed to free up my hands, promptly shoving them into Wyatt's chest. I don't even know what he's done, what he's sacrificed and I'm already angry about it. This was my fight. "Tell me what you did."

"I..." Wyatt's voice cracks with raw emotion. He looks awful, haunted. "I gave him Meg."

The entire world around me goes silent. My arms fall to my sides, immobilizing my entire body. Wyatt is still talking but no sounds reach me. *I gave him Meg.* The admission swirls around me, bouncing off the walls of my mind, but I can't make sense of them. My chest tightens, each breath suddenly harder to take, my vision narrowing as though the room is closing in on me.

"Meg?" I repeat, but the word feels distant. My body moves without permission, stumbling forward, searching for something solid to hold on to. Gripping the edge of Wyatt's desk, I struggle to remain upright. I'm going to be sick.

Through the stinging behind my eyes, a collection of letters cover the desk. Wyatt snaps into action, rushing to push aside whatever he was hunched over when I entered. A vague recognition toys with my numbed senses and I slam my hand down before he can snatch it away.

"What the fuck..." my voice is raspy, wheezing out of me. The writing, the cursive. I know this writing style. Some of the words stick out, a lengthy apology begging for forgiveness, but nothing is as apparent as the signature at the bottom. XO. "Wyatt?"

The panic I was already struggling against claws harder at my throat, relentless to steal my voice. My skin feels too tight, my lungs too small. I can't breathe. I back up to the wall, my legs giving out. He's right there, alarmed green eyes inches from my face. Kneeling in front of me, his hands are everywhere, looking for a way to help when that's the exact opposite they're doing. "Don't touch me," I squirm away. "I don't know you. I don't...I don't know you," I repeat over and over.

"Avery, listen to me. I didn't want you to find out like this. I never wanted you to find out." His voice cracks, full of guilt and desperation, but it only makes it worse. The edges of my vision blur as I try to suck in air, each breath more shallow than the last. My throat constricts, and I claw at my chest, trying to make room for air, but nothing helps. He realizes what's happening at the same time I do.

"Fucking hell. Breathe with me." Wyatt's voice is more insistent now, his hands finally gripping my shoulders, grounding me just enough to focus on him. "Breathe, Avery. Just breathe." He presses his forehead to mine, his warmth seeping into my skin. He's close, too close, but I'm not sure if I can push him away.

"I did it for you," Wyatt whispers, his breath mingling with mine as he holds me there, not letting go. "I did it to keep you safe."

I barely hear him over the rush of blood pounding in my ears, the rapid fire of my heart slamming against my ribcage. I draw my knees up to my chest and bury my face in my hands, squeezing my eyes shut, willing this to be a nightmare I wake up from. I want to scream at him, hit him, do something, anything, but my body won't cooperate. I'm stuck in this loop, spiraling into a void that keeps dragging me down. My head spins, a sickening vertigo pulling me deeper into the panic that takes over, blanketing me in the only way I know how to protect myself.

He traded my life for Meg's. He *gave* her to Fredrick.

AVERY

I come to, my head lulling forward on something cushioned. Someone is fussing around me, gently stroking the hair back from my face. Wyatt has shed his hoodie and covered me with it, my body still on the floor but with his pillow beneath my face. It takes a few attempts to push myself up to lean back on the wall and accept the glass of water Wyatt holds to my lips. I drink, despite the slices of pain lacing my throat. I vaguely wonder if I've been screaming.

Taking the glass away, Wyatt slumps against the wall too, exhaling loudly. He's exhausted, and luckily for him, I don't have the energy to start yelling at him again just yet. The offensive letter has slipped to the floor and slid beneath his desk. I can't stand to look at it, the weight of what it means causing the bile to resurface.

"It's been you this entire time," I say numbly. Wyatt doesn't move. Somewhere between the utter betrayal and unfathomable knowledge that my twin might be in danger, a small bout of harsh laughter stirs within. "All these years, all the times I clung onto those letters. You truly are a callous bastard, Wyatt. This is by far your best trick yet."

"You think I'd spend so long and put so much effort into a trick?" Wyatt asks hollowly, his body tense beside mine. It wouldn't take more than a twitch to close the gap between our arms, so I shuffle the opposite way.

"You locked me in a cupboard covered in whiskey. What else am I supposed to think?" I glare at him, still not trusting my limbs enough to attempt punching him in the face. Sunken, haunted green eyes slowly ascend to mine, a look of pure misery dragging his mouth into a frown. He's really planning on keeping up this charade. "So, what? You're, like, in love with me or something?"

Wyatt reels back, his face suddenly contorted.

"In love with you?" he echoes back like the idea alone tastes bitter in his mouth. There he is. That venomous tone has returned, that barrier Wyatt hides behind resurrected with steel. Reaching out, Wyatt grips my T-shirt in his fist. I welcome the cruel tug of the fabric with my chin raised.

"Love is a word for fluttery feelings and sweet gestures. It's for warmth and intimacy. I'm not in love with you, Avery."

He suddenly lunges at me and I shriek, crashing to the floor. Wyatt mounts me, knocking aside my arms in my feeble attempts to smack him. I close my eyes, resigning to a blow that doesn't come. Instead, he grabs my face in his large, warm hands, bending so I can feel the heat of his breath.

"I'm fucking *obsessed* with you. It's harsh and bitter, this need to have you completely at my mercy." His eyes are blown, wilder than I've ever seen. I tremble as Wyatt's gaze lowers to my lips, his soul bared for me to witness. "I can't love you, because that would involve doing something noble like setting you free. No. I want to possess you, control you until you can't breathe without me. If I had my way, I'd bend and break you until you're as hollow as I am. Until I can finally believe I'm worthy of even a piece of you."

All thoughts and words fail me. I stare up at him, panting and strained. It's easier to believe it's all lies, I can protect myself better that way. But there's no denying the truth laid bare in Wyatt's expression. It's as breathtaking as it is horrifying. He leans closer, the tension coiled beneath his muscles barely restrained.

"Do you have any idea what it's like to look at you every day, for my heart to try and carve itself free of my chest just to get closer to you? Every goddamn day I watch you from a distance, denying this hideous desire inside of me that wants to destroy your happiness because your smiles aren't meant for me." Wyatt's jaw clenches, his grip tightening just enough to make my skin burn where his hands press.

I shouldn't buy into this fantasy. The fall out will be worse, but I can't stop the words from leaving my mouth.

"Why did you have to deny it?" My voice cracks, and I hate how small it sounds. "We could have-" I stop, swallowing hard. "It could have been so different." Wyatt laughs, bitter and raw, releasing me just enough to let his fingers trace down to my throat.

"Different?" Wyatt's voice drops, dark and deadly. "Aren't you listening? I'm broken. The kind of broken you should run from, not try to fix." His thumb brushes the pulse in my neck, and I shudder. "The day you appeared in my life, so frail and scared, I instantly understood that nothing would surpass the territorial need I felt to pull you into my arms and protect you from harm. Then they announced you were to be my sister, and the entire world came crashing down. I could never have you, never tell you what I felt staring into your big, beautiful eyes. So guess what?"

"What?" I whisper, pressing my hands against Wyatt's chest just for something to hold onto. I'm spiraling into his green eyes, into the rush of memories assaulting me.

"I left. I became the harm I so wanted to protect you from. I'm your villain now, the asshole who can't stand being near you, but I can't keep away either. It's killing me."

I lie beneath Wyatt, every word hitting harder than any punch. My brain struggles with the torrent of emotions flowing through me, but mostly because there's a twisted sort of understanding. Nothing between me and Wyatt has ever been simple. We're toxic, damaged. We create the driving wedge that keeps us apart simply because we were never supposed to be together.

Wyatt is whispering now, working through his own torment. "No matter how I try to push you away, you keep coming back. Why can't you just stay away? Why can't you let me be?" Wyatt's hands are still on me, warm and firm, the weight of his body pressing me down. I can feel every inch of him, feel the tremble in his grip as if he's fighting against his own need to let go and obliterate the fragile line he's drawn between us.

"I never wanted this," I whisper, the words a sweet lie on my lips as I push against the memory of the Wyatt I thought I knew. Pushing the boundaries of my asshole stepbrother is one thing, accepting he's been the stalker I've spent my life clinging to is something else entirely. "I never wanted any of this."

Wyatt's gaze softens for the briefest second before hardening again, his fingers twitching around my throat just enough to remind me that he's still in control.

"Neither did I, Avery." He leans closer, his cheek pressing against mine. "But we don't always get what we want, do we?"

His breath ghosts across my skin, and for a moment, all I can hear is the thunderous beating of my heart. There's no air between us, just the unbearable weight of everything left unsaid. Every unspoken desire, every forbidden glance, every moment we let slip through our fingers.

I want to scream, to tell him how unfair it is for him to do this, how cruel it is that he's waited so long to confess this vicious truth. But nothing comes out. I'm trapped beneath the weight of what I've always felt but was too scared to admit. He presses a kiss to my forehead, and I gasp, the sensation both tender and suffocating.

"It could never have been different," he whispers. "You'll always have been my weakness."

A shiver rolls down my spine. His rejection shouldn't be a reason for me to brush my lips across his cheek, but I can't bring myself to fight him. Not when my traitorous body is betraying me, not when part of me wants to believe there's still something left to salvage, some piece of us that isn't irreversibly splintered. But Wyatt's right. He's always been right.

Wyatt starts to pull away, and instinct takes over before I can stop it. With a raw, burning need I didn't realize had been building, I crash my lips against his. The world tilts as our mouths collide. A fierce, desperate longing extends from the column of my throat to my strangled gasp as I extend to be closer to him. To stop him from withdrawing from me, physically and emotionally. Wyatt's breath hitches, but then he's kissing me back with the same crazed intensity, his hands slipping from my throat to tangle roughly in my hair.

It's not sweet or tender. It's a cyclone, swirling with hatred, blazing hot in the chaos we create. His teeth graze my bottom lip, and I let out an unhinged sound, lost in the whirlwind of everything that is Wyatt. His rage, his obsession. We plummet into an undeniable passion that's been buried for far too long. I grasp at his shoulders, pulling him closer, needing more, even though I know this will burn us both.

Wyatt devours my mouth like he's been starving for this, his fingers pressing bruises into my skin as if he's afraid I'll slip away. But I can't. I'm tethered to him, bound by the poisonous, broken thing that we've become.

His lips leave mine only to trail down my jaw, his breath ragged against my neck. I arch beneath him, every nerve ignited. For a fleeting moment, it feels like we could burn the world down together, like we could drown in this madness and somehow come out alive on the other side. But even in the heat of it, I know it's temporary. This fire will consume us both.

Suddenly, Wyatt jerks back, ripping himself away from me as if he's been scalded. He stumbles off, gasping for breath, his green eyes wide and wild, as though he's just woken from a nightmare.

"Don't." His voice cracks, and when his eyes meet mine, they're hollow, haunted by whatever darkness is clawing at him from the inside. "Don't try to save me, Avery. I'm not worth it."

I sit up, dazed, my heart pounding in my chest, still feeling the phantom of his lips on mine. Wyatt is pacing now, raking his hands through his brown hair, his face twisted with anguish. The anger surges through me like wildfire. Before I can stop myself, I'm on my feet, my hand swinging out and connecting with his face. The slap rings out in the room. His head whips to the side and remains there, reeling with shock that has his chest heaving. I steel myself, my body trembling with fury.

"No." I state coldly. My jaw is set, my shoulders squared. "I won't let you drown yourself in some noble version of self-loathing, and you don't get to make the decisions anymore. You've had too much power over me for too long."

His face remains turned away, his cheek red where I struck him, but his jaw is clenched, a muscle twitching as he struggles to keep his composure. Slowly, he straightens up, his back stiffening as he faces me again, the storm brewing behind those wild green eyes.

"I'm no good for you, Avery." His voice is low, broken, like he's tearing himself apart just to speak. "I'll ruin you." A bitter laugh escapes me before I can stop it.

"You already have." At Wyatt's small wince, I turn my back on him, unable to bear it anymore. We continue to balance on his line between hate and something just as dangerous, and I'm losing resolve. Losing sight of what really matters. "Contact Fredrick, tell him the deal's off. I would die before I let any harm come to Meg."

"I had a hunch you'd say that," Wyatt mutters, moving towards his desk. I ignore him, gripping the footboard of his bed to get a grapple on my heart.

How have I gained and lost so much in just a single conversation? Wyatt's truth has rippled through me like an atom bomb, shattering what I thought I knew of Mr. XO. He was never a stranger. He was right here under my nose, unaware of how his words have served me through the years. Maybe, deep down, I had a feeling. Maybe that's why I could never fully discount him.

My cheeks flame as I think of the letter sitting beneath my mattress, of what Wyatt would think if he ever saw it. I still can't bridge that gap. How the words I wrote for that man is the same one who has handed my twin a death sentence. I should be yelling and screaming, punching and kicking at the injustice of it all. But there's still time. I can fix this. I can still save them both.

Coming up behind me, Wyatt's body presses against my back. I welcome his warmth, reminding myself of how I slept last night, cradled in his arms. Wyatt finally gave in, I just need him to do it again. Leaning back, I rest my head on his shoulder, staring up at the ceiling. We remain like that for so long, content to listen to each other's breathing, that I flinch softly when he speaks.

"It's a good thing I'll never allow myself to love you. It'll give me clarity." My brows pinch together, mouth parting.

"What are you-?"

Before I can finish, Wyatt's hand snakes around my waist, pulling me in close. His lips brush against the sensitive skin just beneath my ear. "Your safety has always come first," he whispers, his voice low. "Above all others."

I barely register the press of his lips before a sharp scratch pierces the side of my neck. A jolt of panic floods my system, but Wyatt's arm tightens around my waist, trapping my arms at my side.

"What the hell," my words slur as a cold rush of fluid spreads through my veins, whatever he's injected me with seeping into my bloodstream. My knees buckle, but Wyatt holds me up, his grip firm as I gasp, struggling to breathe. "Fu..fuck...you, Wyatt," I choke out, my vision blurring, the room spinning around me. My hands claw weakly at his arm, but there's no strength left in them.

"Shh," Wyatt soothes, his breath warm and tingling against my skin. Everything fades into a cold, numbing darkness as for the second time tonight, I slump against him, his grip the only thing keeping me from hitting the floor. The last thing I hear before everything goes black is the sound of his voice. Soft, regretful, and final.

"It was always going to end this way, Avery. I was always going to make sure you hated me because that's the only way I know how to keep you safe."

THE LETTER SHE WROTE

Mr. XO,

This is the first and last letter I will ever write to you.

I've sat down to write this so many times, my hand and my heart have gone numb. It's impossible to find the words, when the ones you've delivered to me hold so much power. In fact, I've turned to your letters for guidance, picking out the pieces that turned my burning curiosity about you into something darker. Something I shouldn't have felt, but convinced myself I did anyway.

You already know so much about me, but you can't be aware of the thoughts I'd become stuck on. How your letters came into my life when I needed them most, how your kind intentions alone helped me find the strength to carry on. Confident women aren't born, they're forged by those who impact their lives, for better or for worse. I've found my own tribe to bolster and protect me now, and as always, you will remain just out of reach.

I've read and reread your words on nights when sleep wouldn't come, held onto them like a promise that somewhere out there, someone saw me for who I really was. You saw the parts of me I tried to hide from the world, the broken, fragile parts that I was too scared to show. Yet you don't judge or criticize. Instead, you speak of me in such high regard, detailing how I've saved you from the all-consuming darkness, when the exact opposite is true.

It's me who's been drowning. Me, who's lost her way too many times to count. Me, who needed saving just as much. You have been my comfort, my escape from a reality that felt too heavy. I clung to your words, to the hope they offered. You believed in me, even from afar, and that belief carried me through some of the hardest days, because someone, somewhere, thought I was worth saving.

So this letter is a thank you, as well as a goodbye.

I can't keep living in this in-between space, waiting for something that might never happen. I can't keep putting my life on hold, waiting for you to step out of the shadows. I can't keep pretending that you are the man I've conjured up in my mind. I deserve to live fully, to experience life and love without this constant ache of longing for someone who was never really a part of my world. I deserve something real, and that's not you.

Thank you for seeing me when I couldn't see myself, for offering your love, even if it was from a distance. You gave me the strength to believe I was worth more than the pain I was feeling. You saved me in ways you'll never truly understand, and for that, I'll forever be grateful. Now, I need to let you go.

I need to move forward, to find happiness in the present, with men who have offered their hearts and souls to me without restraint. Who aren't afraid to step into the light and show me exactly who they are. You taught me that I am worth loving, worth saving, and I truly hope you manage to find that same solace too one day. You can continue to write me letters if you wish, but I will no longer read them.

With all my gratitude, but no longer yours.
A.

SPECIAL THANKS

Who guessed Mr. XO's identity ahead of the reveal?
If you did, well done for picking up on the tiny easter eggs I've
been planting. If you didn't, surprise! You're not alone and a
Mr. XO support group can be found in my reader's group. I'll
supply to the coffee, you bring the heart ache.

Thank you for reading Bound by Obsession. Your support
means everything to me. I really hope you've enjoyed it and,
if you have, please kindly leave a review on Amazon and
Goodreads.

I would like to give a special thanks to:

The Authors who support and boost me on a daily basis.
Kat Elley PA for the edits.
Victoria and Bianca for being incredible Alphas.
My street team for sharing and getting involved prior to release.
The PA teams who hosted blog tours on my behalf.
Kristina and Ella for being my betas, support system, and mostly importantly, my friends.

And of course, you!

Plain and simple, I wouldn't be here without my incredible readers! Thank you for diving into the worlds I create, for sharing in these stories, and for becoming true friends along the way. I'm endlessly grateful to get to know you, to see your beautiful shelves, and to build connections with so many talented and inspiring souls. You make this journey worthwhile.

WHAT'S NEXT?

Ready for the final book of the series? Haunted by Secrets is a live pre-order and I promise, it will be worth the wait. Wyatt needs to peak the hill of his redemption arc and absail down the other side, Avery needs to decide if she can find it in herself to forgive, the Shadowed Souls need to lock Avery down once and for all, and a sacrifice needs to be made (author's cackle ensues).

Follow this link to make sure book three hits your eReader without delay.
Haunted by Secrets
Shadowed Souls Book Three
www.books2read.com/hauntedbyshadows

ABOUT THE AUTHOR

If you're a new reader to Maddison – welcome to the Mole's Burrow!!

Maddison is a married mum of two, and a serial daydreamer. As a huge fan of all romance tropes herself, it was time to pen the stories which consume her mind most hours of the day.

As a child, Maddison was a jet setter and has lived all over the world, only to return to the south east of England, where she is now happily settled. With a double award in applied arts and art history, Maddison is a creative with a dark passion for feisty females and spicy stories.

Join my Newsletter via my website:

www.authormaddisoncole.com

Facebook – **Author Maddison Cole**
www.facebook.com/Maddison.Cole.314

Facebook readers group - **Cole's Reading Moles**
www.facebook.com/groups/colesreadingmoles

Instagram and TikTok - **@authormaddisoncole**

OTHER WORKS

If you'd like to keep reading from Maddison's backlist, please check out...

Shadowed Souls Series – (set in Waversea)
RH Dark Academy Stepbrother Romance

Forged by Shadows
Bound by Obsession
Haunted by Secrets (preorder)

Billionaire Brothers RH (set in Waversea) – Standalone

Beautiful Delusions

I Love Candy
Dark Humor RH - Completed Series

Findin' Candy (novella)
Crushin' Candy
Smashin' Candy
Friggin' Candy

All My Pretty Psychos
Paranormal RH with ghosts and demons - Completed Series

Queen of Crazy
Kings of Madness
Hoax: The Untold Story (novella)
Reign of Chaos

Bound by Fate
Fated Mates RH Shifter – Standalone

Moon Bound

A Deadly Sin
MMA Fighter BSDM RH - Standalone

A Night of Pleasure and Wrath

A Wonderlust Adventure
A Twisted Menage Retellling

Descend into Madness
Embrace the Mayhem

Billionaire Badboys
Con Artist/Billioanire RH Romance – To Be Completed

Wreckin' Amethyst

The War at Waversea
Basketball College MFM Menage - Completed

Perfectly Powerless
Handsomely Heartless
Beautifully Boundless

Co-Writes

Teacher/Student Age Gap M/F Romance
Life Lessons - with Emma Luna

Printed in Great Britain
by Amazon

53455930R00304